PRETENDING
TO BE
His

EVERLY SUMMERS

Contents

Dear Reader

Thank you for picking up my debut novel and allowing me to join your bookshelf!
Writing a book and letting it out into the wild world of readers?
It's not exactly a walk in the park, but here we are! This dream has been brewing for a long time—let's say it's been brewing for a few decades. And to anyone reading this who's ever dreamed of writing, go for it. Dust off that laptop (or typewriter if you're vintage like me), type up that story and give the world a peek.
And to you, the wonderful reader holding this book right now—thank you for diving into the first of what I hope will be many swoon-worthy, feels-inducing romances.

Special Note:

For those who like their romance with a hint of spice but prefer things on the subtle side, here's your handy list of chapters to skip or approach with caution:
Chapters 27, 28, 38, 39, plus a little extra heat in 42 and 43.
Now, go enjoy the romance—and thank you again for making this dream a reality!

Prologue – Violet

Eight months ago...

"So, THE CALL WENT well this time, huh?" Max says, lounging on his sofa while I've already thrown myself onto his bed, taking my anger out on his throw pillows and perfectly made covers with their hospital corners and all.

What man makes his bed every morning, so it looks like a five-star hotel?

Max, that's who.

"Great. Peachy. Same as usual." I grab one of Max's ridiculous pillows and scream into it, knowing he's likely groaning about my lip gloss smearing across it. He can wash it. My problems are deeper than his need to toss some Oxi in with his next wash.

No one needs this many pillows on their bed anyway, but Max makes his meager studio apartment look straight out of Home & Garden. I wouldn't call it minimalist because of the pillows, but his style is very simple, making his studio look more prominent than its 400 square feet of cozy.

"Feel better?" his voice is low, sounds muffled by the pillow I'm currently suffocating myself with.

"Nope," I say, emphasizing the pop of the 'p' as I yank the pillow off my face and stare at the ceiling. Max crawls into the bed, his massive frame settling next to me before sliding an arm under my shoulders.

I'm tired, I'm cranky, and then I had to endure the weekly torture known as the Saturday call from my mother. It's the same drill every time: she pretends to care about how I am, but really, she's just waiting for me to crumble, to admit I'm a failure, and to tell her she was right all along—that my dreams of being an author and working at a publishing company will get me nowhere in life.

"How's the book coming along?" Her opening line during our chats. Every. Single. Time.

It's not. I haven't touched it in days, weeks... okay, months.

"Great," I lie, oozing fake enthusiasm.

"Have you gotten a promotion at work yet?" Again, keeping herself right on point with the usual.

No, because Margaret hogs all the credit while I fetch her lavender lattes.

"Yes! Mr. Hartley told me I should be a senior editor by the end of the month." It should concern me how easily I can lie to my mom, but let's be honest: she created this monster.

"And everything with Jake is going well?"

Jake is my boyfriend. We've been dating for almost a year, and hopefully, things will move to the next level soon. He's a senior editor at the same publishing company where I work, and his team has been working longer than usual hours, which means I have seen him less, but that's what tonight is for—we're going to celebrate.

Part of me wonders if he's going to propose. It has been a while, and we've even talked about marriage and our future together over the past few months. Perhaps his distance is a sign he's finally getting ready to pop the question.

"Yes, perfect. We're going to dinner tonight." I say to my mom, and that's the truth for once.

I can do that sometimes with her.

From there, the conversation spirals out of control. My mother hits her usual notes, reminding me she and Dad are disappointed I haven't reached my goals. I'm 28, for Pete's sake. I have time to thrive. She acts like my ovaries are shriveled and dead and I'll be some old spinster recalling the good ole days on my porch in minutes. I'm more worried about the fact that I can't recall the last time I had an orgasm...especially since I have a boyfriend.

By the time I hang up, I feel raw, like I've been flayed open and sprinkled with salt. Every conversation with her leaves me feeling like I've run a marathon barefoot on broken glass and now it's time to break out the tweezers and slowly pluck each piece of my soul that she shattered and hopefully put something together that resembles human. What do they call super glue that puts you back together?

Therapy, probably.

I remove the pillow from my face, staring at the ceiling, trying to shake off the call from earlier this morning. "Why do I let her get to me?" I mutter to myself.

Max pops his head up from the mound of pillows he's on. "At least you survived the call."

"Barely," I groan. "She's got this way of making me feel like a complete failure, even when I'm lying through my teeth about how great everything is."

He sighs into my hair, which, by the way, is a ratted mess from me practically pulling it out by the root—not just today, but this week in general. If it keeps going like this, I may need to invest in a wig.

My mom's call of the week was the perfect way to round out a week that couldn't get worse... but I'm so wrong because it will and it does.

Max chuckles softly. "You know, one day you'll look back on this and laugh."

"Doubt it," I grumble, turning my head to look at him. "Do you think if I faked my death, my mom would stop calling?"

He snorts. "Not a chance. She'd probably haunt you from beyond the grave."

I roll my eyes. "Ugh, you're right. She's like a determined telemarketer who never gives up. Except instead of trying to sell me something, she's just selling me disappointment."

Max squeezes me gently. "You know you're amazing, right? And that she's just... well, your mom."

I snort. "Yeah, yeah. So, what's on the agenda for tonight?"

He grins. "How about a bad movie marathon? I've got a new playlist of movies to stream that are just begging to be mocked."

I grin back. "If only. Remember what tonight is?"

Max reaches over to his meticulously organized list on Netflix, purposely hovering over Pride & Prejudice and wiggling his eyebrows at me. Groaning, there is a part of me that would much rather stay here on the couch watching that, but tonight my luck might finally take a turn for the better. Jake's given off the signals that something big is happening, and I have to go to dinner and find out.

I compose myself—or rather, Max composes me. Quite literally. He picked out my outfit, brushed my hair like I was a toddler, and even helped me with my makeup. Too much? Maybe for any other guy, but this is Max.

Max, who quickly became my work bestie.

Partner in crime.

Hater of all people named Margaret. Okay, there's only one Margaret we actually hate and no offense to the others out there.

I'm sure all other Margaret's would be horrified at how this woman does their name such a disservice. Not only is she my boss, but she's also the bane of my existence. Wicked wench of the west. A thorn in my side.

Every day, I fetch her the same lavender oat-something latte from the same coffee shop. They see me in line and already start it before I reach the register. Is that pathetic? Probably, but I'm not going to dwell on it.

Yet, every time I show up—early, mind you—with a smile on my face and bring it into her office, I get a mumbling growl and then get told yet again that the order is wrong.

How is it wrong? It's the same drink I get every single day. And just like every day, she sits there and mouths the words of the order to me like I'm hard of hearing and tells me to remember it next time.

One time, she wrote it on a neon Post-It note in capital letters, line by line, detailing how to repeat the order to the barista. I did just that, looking ridiculous. It was still "not right" when I gave it to her.

Perhaps she doesn't know her actual drink order.

Do I say that to her?

Of course not.

Her latte is tattooed on my brain at this point. Hard to forget, and the smell of lavender is now forever ruined thanks to that witch. Thanks to her I had to remove all lavender-scented lotions and hair products from my house -- the smell creates a violent physical reaction that resembles a very unattractive gagging fit.

But her coffee fits are the least of my concerns each day. While I don't look forward to them, things could be worse. Instead, it's when she comes to my little desk outside her massive, glorious office to drop off a manuscript to edit.

I'd like to consider myself a person with a good work ethic.

Tell me to be there on time. I am.

Tell me to do a task that's a little below me and insulting. Whatever, I'll do it. I have bills, so let's be real.

Maybe that makes me a pushover and not a hard worker. At this point, the lines are rather blurry.

Regardless, I spend all week editing my heart out, reading the world's most boring manuscript about some nature informative crap I hope doesn't burn itself into my mind. Hartley & Co. Publishing does various genres, but Margaret typically edits the non-fiction—it's utter torture for someone with a creative brain.

Mental and emotional torture.

Aside from the fact that I've picked up some witty facts and random bits of information on just about any topic you'd expect to see in the non-fiction section at the library, it's not my jam. There's no passion in it for me. Still, I do the job, of editing the manuscript by hand because that's how I edit best. Does that mean I have to then turn around and go back into the system and edit it electronically? Yes, but that's fine. I get the satisfaction of pulling out my favorite red pen, watching the gel ink swipe across the page as I adjust sentences, and make notes in the column, and my brain hums to life.

One day, someone will edit my manuscript just like this. It will be handed to them as a big juicy stack of papers for them to dive into, and hopefully, it is not boring swill like what's before me now. Likely they will not be old school and just open to a never-ending scroll fest of a manuscript, but the effect is still the same.

I almost want to make sure my novel is as pleasant to read and edit as possible so the poor schmuck that edits it doesn't secretly hate me for life like I do all of these authors.

Do people want to hear about the mating habits of the passer domesticus, which, by the way, is the House Sparrow? Yeah, facts like that are now embedded in me for good, and what will that do to further my career? Help me write a novel? Not much.

It comes in handy when conversations run dry and I can break that awkward silence with a random fact, but other times I come off like a crazy person, and I can't say I blame them. No one should know these facts.

After spending the week editing said manuscript on the mating habits of the House Sparrow—which I Googled just to see an image of it—it's as boring as the book makes it seem. I turn it over to Margaret by noon on Friday. She wanted it by three, so I pat myself on the back for finishing it early and sent up a thank you to the coffee gods who got me through it.

"No, this won't do," Margaret says, shaking her head as she looks at her computer screen. Her bleached blonde curls bounce like balloons as she taps a hot pink painted fingernail against her mouth. "It needs something..."

Care to elaborate on that?

I sit, hands clasped in my lap, nails nipping into my skin, waiting for her pea-sized brain to come up with something, only for her to look from the screen to me with a pouty lip.

I know what the pouty lip means...

"Violet, if you want to get anywhere in this company, you must do better. Some of these lines are just dull," she says as if one can make the mating habits of birds a thriller. I mean I could, but it would move from a non-fiction resource to a fiction entertainment where two birds are star-crossed lovers on a three chili pepper scene.

Doubt the author wants it to take that angle.

But I let her continue, "I'm afraid you will need to work on this over the weekend, and I want it back Monday when you bring the right latte to me that morning."

And there it is.

Now it's Saturday, and my eyes officially bleeding from working on the manuscript, changing sentences out, and trying to make the mating habits of the House Sparrow read like a literary god wrote it and not some professor who, I must say, has a fascination with this one species of bird a bit too much.

So here I am, standing in front of Max's full-length mirror, looking like I have my life together. Max fusses over me, making sure every hair is in place, and every bit of makeup is flawless. He steps back and nods approvingly. "There. Now you look like you're ready to take on the world—or at least Jake at dinner."

I smirk. "Thanks, Max. I don't know what I'd do without you."

"Probably show up to work looking like a disaster and let Margaret eat you alive," he replies with a grin.

"True," I say, rolling my eyes. "I can't wait to fetch her latte again tomorrow. Maybe I'll throw in a side of arsenic."

Max laughs. "Tempting, but prison orange is not your color."

I sigh dramatically. "Fine, I'll settle for spitting in it."

"Atta girl," Max says, giving me a playful shove. "Now go out there and show off how hot I made you."

I take a deep breath, feeling more confident with every passing second. "Alright, I'm off to face the dragon."

Max gives me a thumbs-up. "Slay, girl, slay."

"You look lovely," Jake says when I open the door, giving me an appreciative once-over. I'm wearing a tight-fitted black dress for our special dinner. Truly, I didn't even know I owned this gem, but Max found it stuffed in the back of my closet.

"So do you..." I reply looking him over. He's wearing a suit, but with a casually open jacket and a blue dress shirt buttoned up, hands in his pockets.

Is Jake a good-looking man? Most definitely. I can't wait to show up at my folks' house for the holidays with this hottie and announce our engagement, so that's one less thing for them to lecture me on. Maybe my mother will finally stop talking about my ovaries.

I get it; they're getting old.

Everything seems normal. Jake even pulls out my chair and scoots me into his reserved table.

See? Perfect gentleman.

I'm looking around the restaurant. It's one of those romantic hotspots for proposals—literally, it was listed as a top place to propose in Manhattan. My heart is practically drumming its wedding bells as I take in the space.

The twinkling fairy lights above us, candle lights—okay, faux flames, but the thought is there—the dim lighting, the velvet chairs, the tables for two that are all romantic and cozy. When I look around the room, it's all happy couples either deep in conversation or just holding hands. I sigh, soaking it all in. Tonight is my night, and I couldn't think of a better place to find out I'm the future Mrs. Jake Thomas.

Okay, I could think of a better place, but Jake is not the romance writer here. I am. Have I pictured this moment more times than a rational adult woman should admit?

Absolutely.

Did I picture it in a restaurant already listed as a top place to propose, making it rather cliché? No, but like I said, I'm a romance writer. Jake is, well, a man.

After our champagne is poured and the waiter places it in the golden ice bucket next to us, Jake reaches across the table with his large hands, and I place mine in his. This is it. This is the moment. My moment.

"Violet..." His husky voice is like a caress up my spine, and butterflies are fighting for control of who gets to make my stomach tumble more.

I can feel it, my heart racing, my skin going hot and cold and clammy simultaneously. The world around me is a puffy cloud of hearts, pinks, purples, and gooey love. I swear I can see Cupid flying in the haze, blessing the words he's going to ask me, his arrow of eternal love locked and loaded and ready to fire.

"You know I care about you, babe..."

Okay, not words I would expect a proposal to start with, but maybe he's nervous. You'd think an editor could come up with a better starting line at least.

Blinking away the thoughts and silently cursing Max for putting on fake lashes that make my eyelids heavy, I smile at Jake. That chiseled jaw, those eyes. Doesn't matter he fumbled some words.

"And you know I love you, Jake," I say, trying to reset the tone by helping him with word choices. I'm oddly getting flashbacks of this very moment when Elle was dumped in Legally Blonde but I try to ignore how similar it all is or the fact I can recall scenes from that movie so .

He smiles, that same devilish smile that got us together in the first place. I wish it was a romantic story, but it's far from it. We were at a work party, got drunk, and had sex. I wish I could say it was like in the romance books I read—mind-blowing orgasms, multiple at that—but it was sloppy and floppy (him, not me). Things went from that one night to being coworkers with benefits to a relationship. Yeah, Hallmark or Lifetime won't make a movie out of that anytime soon. Sadly. That's almost real life; maybe they should stop giving us all false hope.

But I'm still going to get my guaranteed HEA. Which is romance writers speak for happily ever after.

"That means a lot, it does," his hands tighten their grip on mine. "But I just don't think we'll work out anymore, babe."

Did he just combine a compliment with a breakup and then toss in a 'babe'?

I look at our hands still joined, then the bucket next to us, which is sweating more than I am, holding the ice and open champagne.

"I'm confused..." I mutter, trying to tug my hand back, but he has a vice grip on it.

Sighing, he looks at me. "I think we just won't work. I know you want to be a writer someday, but you don't even work on your book. You aren't serious about your career, and if I'm going to be serious with someone, I need someone serious about themselves. You don't even wear makeup to work half the time."

Because it's gross and heavy, and is he saying I need it?

Just when I think my night can't get worse—because not only am I being dumped when I'm supposed to be getting proposed to—but I'm also getting a déjà vu moment like I'm on a call with my mom.

Did she talk to him? Because a lot of his words are eerily like something she'd say.

You're not good enough, Violet.

If you were going to be an author, you would have finished a book by now, Violet.

You aren't going anywhere in life, Violet.

You are a failure, Violet.

And, now, you need makeup when you go out, Violet.

"Luckily," his voice picks up a beat, and I'm not sure how you can break up with someone while still holding their hands and use the word 'luckily' like that is the appropriate way to round out the conversation. "I've found someone who can do that, and I want you to be happy for me, babe. Be happy for us."

I'm being dumped, insulted, and now I'm being told there's someone else and I should revel in my boyfriend's—no, sorry, ex-boyfriend's—happiness?

I don't even know how to categorize this conversation.

So, I blink.

Then I blink again.

I'm positive I'm in the middle of a stroke.

"Violet?" Jake squeezes my hand, and I snap out of my blink fest.

"I'm sorry, so you're breaking up with me and telling me you met someone?"

He lets go of my hands, and thank God for that. Leaning back in his chair, he drapes his arm over the backrest casually, like this is an everyday casual conversation. "I've been seeing her for a few months, but I think you'll be happy for us both because we are happy together. She's everything I've ever wanted, and you will be happy to see her so happy with me."

Sure, if you both are in hell, dancing in the pits of fire with the devil...

"So you have been cheating on me?"

I mean, that's what he's saying, right?

I've never experienced a conversation like this in my life. A cacophony of emotions and oddities—going from being dumped to insulted to being cheated on, but then being told to be happy for him and even congratulate him. I'm not losing my mind. This is utter madness.

"I wouldn't call it cheating. We weren't working, Violet, so I found someone else."

I'm positive that's somewhere in the definition of cheating.

He goes on. "But you're going to love her."

Are we serious right now?

"And why would I love her, Jake?" I'm not sure why I'm asking, but this circus is already way overboard, so I might as well go along with the ride that is my life.

Jake smiles. "Lisa. Your best friend." He leans forward, resting his arms on the table, and it groans as if it, too, has had enough of this conversation. "See? I'm making your best friend happy. I'm happy. We all should be happy."

Being the mature adult I am, I push out from my chair, stunned, speechless for probably the first time in my life. I grab my clutch and then pick up the bottle of champagne. This baby is coming home with me on the subway. It's New York—no one looks twice at that, even if I cry in the corner, mascara and fake lashes a mess while gulping a champagne bottle. With my free hand, I take the bucket of ice and pour it slowly into his crotch.

Like I said, mature.

Violet

I WAS BORN TO write romance. No, quite literally. No one names their child Violet Hart, giving them essentially the only name that would work for a romance author's pen name, right? It's the chef's kiss as far as pen names go.

Sadly, that wasn't my parent's intention at all — instead, that's akin to their worst nightmare.

In the grand and prestigious Hart family, sweet little Violet was expected to follow in their footsteps. My parents, Richard and Victoria, had dreams of her attending college and then law school, just like all the other successful members of their esteemed family. My mother adored the name Violet for some reason, though she couldn't quite recall how she came up with it. Maybe it was because of her favorite flower or a color that reminded her of my father's proposal... but no, I suppose that's just my romantic imagination at work.

Truth be told, the name just appeared one day, 29 years ago, and here I am now with an arguably perfect name for someone destined to write romance novels - yet not a single published manuscript to my name. Nothing but half-finished drafts mocking me were saved to my cloud.

Yes, I admit it - I am an aspiring author, currently working on multiple romance novels while residing in the bustling city of Manhattan. And as cliché as it may sound, I am also most definitely single. Because let's face it, what successful romance author has time for a perfectly well-rounded and healthy relationship?

Oh, wait... all of them do.

Maybe that's why my book remains unfinished. In fact, if you read my acknowledgments page, you would find no mention of a supportive and inspiring boyfriend or loving husband. No one to thank for helping me pour every gooey ounce of love into my writing.

No, I am single and constantly reminded by my mother that I am "getting too old" for a man without baggage - conveniently ignoring the baggage I carry myself. Not that 29 is old... but as I near 30, my prospects don't seem promising.

My last serious relationship left no room for romantic inspiration. Still, I *thought* I loved him.

For a woman wrapped up in the world of romance, reading more romance novels than is healthy for an adult likely, I don't think I've experienced genuine love. The sparks, that feeling of passion, or maybe all those romance novels I read have tainted what is and isn't when it comes to love.

That's a rabbit hole I don't intend to go exploring any time soon. Denial is a lot more comforting.

This is what led me here, sitting in a bar on a Friday night, without a date and definitely not looking for one. No romance comes from meeting anyone in a bar. I'm waiting for Max, who was supposed to be here 20 minutes ago, but texted that he would be late and told me to get a drink and relax. I didn't want to hog a table for myself or look like that woman in the bar drinking alone and all wallow-in-self-pity sorts, so I perched myself at the bar, people-watching and drinking my martini and feeling incredibly out of place.

The Velvet Clover is not where I'd usually go for a drink.

It's high-class and yet charming, located in the heart of Manhattan. While it is known for its selection of craft cocktails, including the signature martini I'm enjoying at this very moment, the place is too sophisticated. Books line the shelves—odd for a bar, not a library—but I get the vibe. Dim lighting, everything composed and elegant. Meanwhile, I'm here in a pencil skirt and my old NYU sweatshirt because I forgot my jacket. It's late October in New York, and fall isn't exactly forgiving.

But there is an undeniable magic in the air as fall descends upon New York City. As if the city itself has donned its finest, most romantic attire just to show off. The crispness of the air works tirelessly to sweep away the lingering smog, revealing a clear blue sky above. And amidst it all, the leaves begin their transformation from tired greens to vibrant russets and gold yellows, painting the parks in a dazzling display of color.

Strolling through Central Park on a brisk autumn day, with a steaming latte warming your hands and the touch of a loved one's hand in yours? It's a feeling that cannot be bought or replicated.

Fall in New York City is simply bursting with inspiration, begging to be captured and immortalized. Yet, even surrounded by such beauty and charm, I find myself stuck in a writing slump. It's as if the season itself is aware of my creative constipation and taunts me mercilessly. "Look at all this brilliance," I hear it say. "Too bad you can't seem to string two coherent sentences together!"

When I left work, the wind nipped at me so hard it might as well have left teeth marks on my skin. And what was my armor against the elements? My trusty NYU sweatshirt, of course. It's always in my car, looking as faded as a movie star's career after a scandal. This thing has seen better days, especially since it was my uniform during that dark month post-breakup when I wore it exclusively, cried myself to sleep, and was a complete mess.

Picture this: showers were a rare luxury, my hair was a rat's nest, and I was convinced I was destined to be a spinster. Well, if you ask my mother, I already am one. But come on, this is Manhattan. You're not a spinster at 30. Here, 30 is the new 20, and 40 is the new 30. That's what all the magazines say, so who am I to argue? I'm rolling with it, armed with my battle-worn sweatshirt and a dash of what little confidence I have left.

Of course, with my naturally wavy hair now officially windblown and resembling a bird's nest rather than anything tame, I pulled it up into a messy bun and touched up my makeup. No way was I walking into a swanky bar looking like a complete trainwreck. This place demands a semblance of class, and the patrons here? They're the ones who boss around assistants like me, not the other way around. These people don't worry about scraping by paycheck to paycheck.

No, this bar is a playground for the moneyed and the polished, where they chat, sip overpriced drinks, and mingle with their equally well-heeled peers.

I'd never choose this place myself, but Max has been dying to come here. Max, who can dress and act the part of someone with class — even if he's a low-hanging fruit assistant like me.

Glorified   coffee   fetcher,   copy   maker,   and   occasional do-all-the-work-while-boss-gets-the-credit doer. I help edit transcripts for Margaret, a lead editor, and a royal stick-up-her-ass type, but she gets all the glory while sitting on phone calls planning her next dinner party or family function or whatever socialites like her do.

She's a walking New York City cliché. Pretty, tall, blonde, always in the latest fashion while I'm stuck a few seasons behind, thanks to my meager salary. She lives off her trust fund and works just enough to appear ambitious until she can catch herself a hot man to carry her the rest of the way.

Talk about life goals.

Margaret is insufferable yet younger, prettier, and richer than me. And I'm the one fetching her lavender oat milk lattes twice a day so she can "keep up with the workload." *Insert an eye roll here, please.*

The only workload she keeps up with is deciding what color to paint her nails, and yes, she has an entire rack of nail polish in her office. Meanwhile, I endure endless paper cuts, leaving work with red ink smears permanently tattooed into my skin. I've given up bothering to try and wash it out.

I'm barely scraping by, struggling to keep my studio in Manhattan. So why I'm spending my hard-earned dollars at a bar that sells martinis at highway robbery prices is beyond me.

But Max insisted, and I caved.

After a day like today, a buzz from overpriced alcohol doesn't sound like the worst idea, even if that means my grocery budget is just reduced to ramen and apples for the next week.

My phone buzzes on the counter, and I see Max's face appear. I can feel a wash of panic and outrage course right through me. If he's canceling on me, leaving me here to look pathetic and stood up, I might actually hurt him.

"Noooooo, you aren't bailing on me. I'm already sitting here with a drink." I hiss into the phone.

"Babe, not bailing, just stuck in traffic, and my Uber can only go so fast."

Thank god.

Max is my best friend and has been since I started working at Hartley, which was about four years ago. Yes, four years working your ass off and still a glorified espresso-getter. We don't need to go down that road, though. Just knowing my mother would tell you so is enough to make me cringe. Max is also an assistant, and after I struggled to finish last-minute edits on a manuscript that Margaret couldn't be bothered with, I practically pulled every strand of my hair. Max came up to my desk, insisting I go out because he knew I'd sit there fuming at home, likely reading a romance novel or worse, re-reading one that I had already read a few times just to get swept away in the blooming passions of someone else.

Live vicariously and all that.

I'm almost positive those thoughts lead you to become an actual spinster, but again, we're avoiding those rabbit holes tonight.

"Did you hear?" Max had to work late since his senior editor actually edited transcripts and needed him to stick around to make copies, but he had promised to meet me here.

"Hear what?" I watch the green grapes in my martini swirl around the glass, the liquor a tinge of green and flavored like an apple, and I have never had an apple martini before. To be honest I never had been a martini type of woman, but when I saw the prices, their signature apple martini was the cheapest option here, so I went with that. Plus, it's cute that they use grapes instead of olives. Though, are you supposed to eat the olives anyway? Drink rules never quite answer that question.

"Next weekend, Hartley is hosting a publication party, one of the books they published launched and went viral, so we're celebrating. The author, editors, news, investors, the whole team…"

Jake...that's who he was trying not to mention and let it trail off.

Jake, my ex, a senior editor at my work. He thought way too much of himself, and he just wasn't that attractive. Okay, that's a lie. He is attractive, but he's an arrogant self-centered ass that dumped me like I was a discarded cup of coffee. Worse, he and my now ex-best-friend are this disgusting happy couple, all in love, engaged, and everyone coos over Jake and him being so lucky to have found such a gorgeous, smart woman.

Hello. I'm right here.

Lisa might be gorgeous. She's one of those women who fit in well in Manhattan since she looks like she just stepped off the catwalk, and we were best friends since college, crossing paths when I was studying English Literature (what else does an aspiring author get a degree in?) while she was studying marketing, but being in college was about all we had in common outside of our love for going to clubs, having a few drinks and dancing. Once we had to be adults with jobs, it all changed.

Her family is rich. Mine is far from it.

She's gorgeous, I suppose I'm more average.

She's flawless, I'm a mess.

She's got no moral compass, I do.

She also screwed my boyfriend, so now she's a cheating whore. I suppose the friendship would have never lasted, especially after the whole sleeping with my boyfriend part, but still, it stung a lot worse to find out the way I did.

"Jake will be there....with Lisa." I mutter the words in between a generous swig of my martini.

"And are you going to be okay with that? Can you...keep it cool?"

Okay, so the last time I was at a public event where Jake and Lisa were, I may have lost it.

In my defense, it was barely a month after the breakup. The wounds? Oh, they were still raw, like freshly opened cuts that you'd be stupid to poke. And yet, there I was at a company event, only to find them there too—wrapped up in each other like two love-struck idiots, full-on PDA, in coordinated outfits. Honestly, gag me.

As if that wasn't enough, they might as well have announced their engagement with the way they were smiling at each other. Lisa, of course, caught my eye. She knew. She absolutely knew it would hurt. The way she glanced at me, smug as hell, like she'd won some grand prize? Ugh.

So, yeah, I got a little too drunk. Sue me. And maybe I caused a bit of a scene—a big, embarrassing scene, to be specific. Right in front of my boss, because if you're going to implode publicly, you might as well do it spectacularly, right? Go out swinging.

"Okay, so maybe I had too much to drink," I say, still feeling defensive as I recount the whole fiasco over the phone. "But I stand by what I said. The world deserved to know how terrible he was in bed. Like, truly awful. I'm the only ex in that room who could confirm it. And let's be real, Lisa wasn't about to confess that the dick she's getting now is...well, subpar."

I hear a cough next to me, someone clearly trying to stifle a laugh, but I ignore it and keep going. I'm on a roll.

"That man wouldn't know how to give an orgasm if it bit him in the ass. His idea of foreplay? The most boring, vanilla dirty talk you can imagine. And going down on a woman? Forget it. Never happened. And when I tried to reciprocate?" I pause, raising an eyebrow though no one can see me. "He literally pushed me away. Who does that? I mean, look at these lips," I gesture dramatically, even though I'm on the phone, pointing at my own mouth like it's a sales pitch. "What man wouldn't want these hot lips wrapped around him?"

Another cough, this time more of a choke, catches my attention. Out of the corner of my eye, I catch sight of a guy in a dark suit standing nearby, clearly overhearing my conversation. I roll my eyes but keep going.

"Some women need a little revving up, you know? And let's just say he was the poster child for a two-pump chump." I hear a muffled snort from my uninvited audience, but I'm too far gone to care. "It's fine. It won't happen again. I have some class, you know. I can totally handle another event with them flaunting their 'undying love,' or whatever," I add, making air quotes that no one can see. "But I stand by what I said: worst. sex. of. my. life. I've had better orgasms with a vibrator than whatever that man's 'inadequates' were offering."

Another cough, this one louder, and I glance at the guy next to me, who's failing miserably at pretending not to eavesdrop. I ignore him and refocus on the phone.

There's silence on the other end of the line, then Max's telltale sigh.

"Okay," he says, voice dripping with judgment. "How much have you had to drink?"

"Oh my god, I'm still on my first martini, you jackass," Lie. This was my second, and I'm working quickly to earn my third.

"Okay, well I should be there in 15 if traffic moves. Please don't get absolutely wasted at a bar while I'm not there to keep you from, well, being you."

"I don't need a babysitter. I will see you when you get here.. Oh god."

"What?"

Because life loves to mess with me, Jake and Lisa walk in, hand in hand, with two other couples. Of course. You've got to be kidding me. Do they have an AirTag on me or something? Honestly, it's like they're tracking my every move because lately, they've been popping up everywhere I go.

Seeing them at work is one thing—Jake's one of my bosses, after all—but at the random bar Max and I picked for a Friday night out? C'mon. This place isn't even close to the office, and Max always picks spots far enough away to avoid any potential run-ins. And yet, here we are, me looking like a hot mess while they stroll in like they own the place. It's like I'm a sitting duck in the middle of a social viper's nest. Is that even a thing? Well, it is now.

"Jake and Lisa are here," I whisper, even though they're all the way across the bar. It's loud enough that I could probably shout and they wouldn't hear me, but the last thing I need is to be that girl, causing yet another public spectacle.

"Can you leave without them seeing you? We can head somewhere else." Max asks me.

I'm already on high alert, mentally mapping out the bar like some secret agent plotting a stealthy exit. Only, it looks like the universe is out to get me. My options are limited. There's an emergency exit with a massive red sign that practically screams, "Press me, I dare you!" But it's not like I can bolt out the door in heels, setting off alarms like a crazy person. I mean, running through the back alley barefoot?

Not happening. I love my feet too much for that.

So, the front door it is. Of course, that just so happens to be conveniently located right next to their table, surrounded by all their impossibly pretty friends. Why does life have to be this cruel? Can't a girl just enjoy a night out after a week at a mediocre job, wallow in some well-deserved self-pity about her lack of career progression, and do it all in peace?

Is that too much to ask?

Yeah, you're asking too much Violet.

"I want to crawl into the deepest, darkest hole and never come out... but of course, they took the booth right by the damn door." As if the universe wasn't cruel enough, they didn't even have the decency to sit with their backs to me. Nope, Jake and Lisa are front and center, with a full view of the bar like they're holding court, ready to lock eyes on their prey. And guess who that prey is tonight? Me.

"Okay, I'll be there soon," Max says, sounding like my lifeline. "Just promise me you won't do anything stupid."

I snort, rolling my eyes at his faith in me. "Define stupid. I don't think we're on the same page here, Max." I even throw in some air quotes for my own amusement, even though he can't see them.

"You know exactly what I mean."

"Yeah, yeah, I'll see you when you get here," I mutter before hanging up. Max knows me far too well. If he doesn't show up soon, there's a very real chance I'll do something spectacularly stupid. I mean, after the debacle at the work party, it's basically guaranteed.

I glance down at my martini. One more of these and 'stupid' is pretty much inevitable. Babysitter status: required.

With a dramatic sigh that earns a raised eyebrow from the bartender, I motion for another drink. Then, in a frantic attempt to pull myself together, I yank off my NYU sweatshirt and shove it onto my lap. My eyes dart to the door again—yep, they're still there, looking like they stepped off the pages of some glossy magazine. Meanwhile, I look like I've been shipwrecked on a deserted island, surviving solely on coffee and questionable life choices.

I pull my hair out of its messy bun, fingers working frantically to tame the wild waves that are determined to betray me. Of all the things to inherit from my mother, it had to be this unruly, dark brown mane. Each curl feels like a rebellious reminder of her, like she's haunting me with every strand. Thanks, Mom.

There's no way I'm going to sit here looking like a wreck while they parade around like a power couple straight out of a fashion ad. Sure, I'm not cover model material right now, but I refuse to look like the chaotic storm brewing inside my mind. I'm better than that. Or at least, I'm trying to be.

I don't even have the luxury of a proper emergency kit. No compact, no extra makeup in my clutch because, well, that's not who I am. I'm practical. I've got hand sanitizer, lotion, a dab of lip gloss, and my wallet. The essentials. So, I've got to make do with what I've got and pray for a miracle.

I catch my reflection in the bar's mirror and wince. Okay, not a total disaster, but definitely not my finest hour. Still, if I'm going down tonight, I'm going down with some dignity. I smooth my hair one last time, exhale slowly, and prepare myself for whatever fresh hell the universe has in store for me.

"What does one consider vanilla dirty talk? I didn't know dirty talk could be vanilla." The smooth, rich voice comes from a man who has obviously been eavesdropping on my conversation. Welcome to New York, where privacy is a myth. You're constantly crammed in with people, and everyone listens to whatever you say or do, even if they aren't part of the conversation.

I turn, ready to snap, but the words catch in my throat when I see him.

Leaning casually against the bar, like he owns the place, is the most gorgeous man I've ever laid eyes on. Want the definition of tall, dark and handsome? He's right in front of me — and then some. I'm sitting, but he's towering over me, his dark brown hair with a hint of a curl, a jawline that could cut glass, and those piercing blue eyes that look straight into your soul. He's wearing a perfectly tailored suit that screams designer, and there's a Rolex gleaming on his wrist. Did this guy just drop out of a GQ magazine or something? There's no way he's real. I'm half-tempted to poke him just to make sure he's not an illusion from the wacky martini I'm drinking.

Compose yourself, Violet.

I tap my finger on my lips, trying really hard not to make eye contact with those mesmerizing blue eyes even though I want to stare at them some more, catalog them and possibly use them for one of my characters.

Without thinking, I just let whatever is at the tip of my tongue slide right on out.

"Well, I dunno. Not creative. Not fun. Not accurate half the time? I mean, use your words." This is why I need a babysitter. I hate when Max is right. I'm about to make myself look like an idiot in front of the most beautiful man my eyes have had the pleasure of seeing in person.

Mr. Gorgeous looks down at me, a freaking giant of a man, and smirks. "Uh huh. And what words does one using vanilla dirty talk not use?"

Oh my god, am I really having this conversation right now, in a bar, with a ridiculously hot stranger?

Apparently I am, thanks to two martinis down and a third placed in front of me.

Liquid courage is a real thing, and I've got it in spades tonight.

"Cock, dick, pussy..." Yup, those words tumbled out before I had a chance to reel myself in and I won't lie when I say the hand I used to smack over my mouth hurt a bit. "Oh my god, sorry," but he looks more entertained than the horrified I'm feeling all up inside right now. I could blame it on the liquor, but I've never been one to self-filter. Alcohol only makes it worse it seems.

His lips curl into a smile, and this time there's no polite cough to cover up the shock as he takes a sip of the scotch set in front of him by the bartender who gives me a look — clearly overhearing those three words I just said. "Fair enough," is all he says and I turn back to my drink, assuming our bizarre little exchange is over now that he's got his drink. But no, he doesn't leave.

"So, did you really get up in front of your work and announce how your ex was a bad lay?"

Holy hell, how much of my sad life did this man overhear?

"It's rude to listen in on a person's phone calls," I say, taking a sip of my drink and trying very hard not to flush. Too late. Can I blame it on the liquor?

"It's hard to ignore a conversation when someone is yelling into their phone right next to you," he leans in, his eyes twinkling with amusement. I didn't realize eyes could twinkle, but yes, they are indeed twinkling.

"Okay, well despite your rude eavesdropping, I'm pretty sure we don't need to have this conversation."

"I'm just curious why you'd be so upset if your boyfriend left you—"

"Cheated on me," I bite out, not really caring about holding back even though I'm in a very weird, very unexpected conversation with Mr. Gorgeous.

"Oh, ouch, that stings."

I whirl on my bar stool to face him fully. "Thanks?"

He smiles with one of those wicked smirks that only hot men can pull off, and he's definitely in that category. I tell my hormones to chill because he's not just out of my league, he's in another galaxy. He's all fly-first-class, probably has his own driver, buys custom suits kind of man.

Why does he look familiar? Maybe he just has one of those faces. You know, the sea of beautiful men in Manhattan with three-piece suits and perfectly tousled hair? Those men. Yeah, he's probably one of those.

I look over at their table and realize the only way I can keep from getting noticed is to turn more toward the man who is making this conversation incredibly awkward. Putting my hand up to shield my side profile, I keep myself facing the hot stranger. He'll leave soon anyway, right?

"Is that him?" he nods in the direction of the couple behind me.

"How much of my conversation did you listen to?"

"Almost all. Quite entertaining. Riveting, really."

I can feel my cheeks heat. Hot and an arrogant ass. Great.

Also, is that a slight Italian accent to his voice? My insides are liquifying, so I'm going to go with a yes. So he's gorgeous and Italian, which would explain that beautiful olive skin. Pull out my list of the perfect man in the looks department and now he's got them all checked off.

"Okay, well don't you have some board meeting to get to? People to fire? Children to make cry?"

The smile he gives me makes my stomach flutter. It's half smirk, half amusement.

"What did he do to you, aside from the awful sex? I have to know. The info was just getting interesting before you hung up." He scoots closer so that someone can dip in to his right and order a drink, making our arms brush against one another and I can't help but notice the goosebumps taking over my skin.

Rolling my eyes, I sneak a peek back at the happy couple that makes me want to gag and then back to the hot stranger who is awfully interested in my personal life. Apparently I'm a living soap opera for Mr. Gorgeous, and knowing what he overheard, can't really blame him for finding himself invested.

"Are you always this nosy?"

He grins, that smirk widening. "Only when the story's this good."

"Fine, why not," I say, taking a long sip of my drink for some liquid courage. "My ex, Jake," I nod my head toward their pretentious group, "left me a while ago. But instead of just breaking things off like a normal person, he and my best friend—well, ex-best friend now for obvious reasons—were sleeping together for four months behind my back. But wait, it gets better. Instead of coming clean, he told me I wasn't serious about my career and needed to wear more makeup in public. Apparently, I wasn't pretty enough, didn't fit the lifestyle he wanted, and my career goals didn't align with his. Basically, he gave me a laundry list of flaws to make any girl feel all warm and fuzzy inside. Then, he finishes it all off telling me I should be happy for him, mind you he's dumping me in the same breath, that he found someone who is all of those things and surprise, it's my best friend. She's the blonde over there hanging onto him like a designer handbag. So I'm supposed to be thrilled they found each other in their eyes. I apparently did him a favor showing him everything he didn't want in a girlfriend so he could find what he did. Really, I'm a saint."

Saying it out loud makes it even worse. I wasn't good enough, so my friend steps in to show me how it's done. Yep, I'm a real catch now.

Don't worry about me meeting a man with baggage, Mom, I've got plenty of my own.

The hot stranger gives me a pity smile, making this situation more unbearable.

"So, yeah, anyway..." I turn more toward my drink, trying to hide from Jake and Lisa's line of sight.

He smiles and leans in. "If you want to make him regret picking her over you, which I'll say looks like a downgrade, just flirt with a hot guy here at the bar. There are plenty of options."

"You offering?" I ask, raising an eyebrow.

"No."

"Such a gentleman," I spit out, taking another sip of my drink. He just smiles.

"Good luck," Mr. Gorgeous says before walking away.

Do not look at him or watch him walk away, Violet.

I do.

Dammit.

He rejoins a group waiting for him at a table in the corner, taking his seat and unbuttoning his jacket, eyes locking with mine while he lifts his glass as if he's toasting my endeavor...or downfall.

Whatever asshole.

Max finally enters the bar, and I'm relieved, but he's already too late for me to have not embarrassed myself. Just as he and I lock eyes and he starts my way, he's stopped by a group he knows, and to my utter delight, he's instantly recognized by Jake, who then whispers something to Lisa and they both look around until they lock eyes with me.

Perfect. Just perfect.

Alex

I DON'T DO BARS. They're not my scene. Why pay for an overpriced scotch when my favorite one is sitting at home, waiting for me along with my comfortable leather sofa? Everything better is at home. Including my sweats.

Sure, I look damn good in this suit, but I can't relax in it, and after this week, I need to unwind by sitting at home, drinking alone, and calling it a day. I'm almost positive those are the first words of someone teetering on the edge between casual drinker and full-blown alcoholic, but I'll table that self-reflection for now.

Either way, I don't want to be here. Nothing screams "welcome to hell" like a Manhattan bar. Stale cigar smoke mixed with a gag-worthy cacophony of colognes and dull conversations. I don't need to converse. I do it all damn day. I want to get away from people, and yet, here I am, doing the opposite of what I need to unwind after a long week.

From the moment she strode into the dimly lit bar, I couldn't take my eyes off her. The way she confidently walked in wearing an NYU sweatshirt paired with a skirt and high heels was hard to ignore. Most women who entered this establishment did so with a purposefully chosen outfit that screamed "look at me," but not her.

She didn't play that game, and it instantly drew me to her. I was tired of the standard, cookie-cutter women New York had to offer - all dressed alike, looking alike, and acting alike — they're vanilla and I'm a man that needs flavor.

It has become a mundane dating pool, and I refused to swim in it any longer. But there was something different about her, something refreshing and intriguing, and for the first time in a long time, I wanted to get to know her.

Not that I'm here to find a date or a one-night stand. Neither is my style, especially at this bar. I'm here on business, promising a few associates drinks while they pitch ideas I'll kindly ignore. Yet, I found myself at the bar after she sat down, looking to get another drink despite having an untouched one at my table.

I had no intentions of speaking with her, just wanted to watch. She was a unique creature, gulping down her first martini without any ladylike pretense. Her messy hair was poorly tamed, her NYU sweatshirt faded from years of wear. Nothing about her was composed like the perfectly made-up dolls surrounding her. Yet, I wasn't the only man watching her. Quite a few did, and I could see why.

She was gorgeous.

Not the usual stunning hotness that parades around Manhattan. No, this woman was naturally beautiful, wearing minimal makeup—a rarity in this crowd. Her petite figure perched on the barstool made it irresistible not to approach. I wanted to see what was behind that hot mess exterior before someone else did. I am a curious man after all.

Taking the spot next to her, I asked the bartender for another drink, despite my table full of waiting men. It was rude to listen in to her call, but she wasn't exactly keeping her voice down. It took all my self-control not to burst into laughter when she not-so-shyly talked about her lack of good orgasms. What made me stay was when she used the word *vanilla*.

Don't ask me why, but that's how I describe half the people in Manhattan. Okay, more like 99.9% of them. When she said it, I wanted to hear more. And when she revealed she got wildly drunk at a work party to announce her ex's inadequacies? Damn. That hooked me. So, despite my intentions, words slipped out of my mouth and I spoke to her.

I had to know *what vanilla was to her*, and nearly choked at her honesty. Was this woman real? No one had ever spoken to me so blatantly, and it made me more interested in her.

When she shrugged off the old sweatshirt and let her hair down, I honestly considered walking over to her ex and kicking him in the balls. This woman wasn't just gorgeous; she was the type you'd lose yourself in. Those expressive green eyes and chestnut hair, her sleeveless cream blouse, and pencil skirt left little to wonder about her figure, which was all sorts of perfect.

I'm a man, I look, and I don't apologize for it.

I wanted to learn more, ask her more, which was odd for me. I give zero shits about anyone. I don't even know my own assistant's middle name, and she's been with me for nine years. I still mess up her last name. I don't need personal connections clouding my thoughts. I have enough on my plate. I know, woe is me, but I was utterly fascinated by this woman, and I had no idea why.

Probably because she was the polar opposite of anything I'd ever seen, a classic beauty and witty.

She was far from vanilla. No, she was a rich, decadent tiramisu, each layer of complexity more intriguing than the last. A sweetness that was genuine, but with a bold, spirited kick that shocked you just when you thought she couldn't surprise you again. And just when you thought you'd figured her out—usually, I could read a person in five minutes or less—she'd surprise you with another unexpected facet. Damn me to hell because I wanted to learn more.

Groaning, I saw my business associates waving me over. I didn't want to leave this woman, and I knew I'd probably never see her again. But the experience was eye-opening, to say the least.

Strolling over to my table, I kept an eye on her. The men beside me droned on about their wives, mistresses, and headaches—again, all reasons I avoided serious relationships. I'm a rare beast in Manhattan: I have no intention of cheating on my partner. Maybe that's why I was more intrigued to hear it happened to her, especially when I looked at her ex—did she say his name was Jason? Ken Doll Douche sounded more appropriate. He was insane for leaving that gem for Barbie sitting next to him. She was pretty but not gorgeous. No, she was as vanilla as it gets. She blended right into the crowd of other women who looked just like her, and I didn't need to hear her speak to know her personality was as bland as day-old toast.

I maintained a good balance between my work life and completely avoiding a personal life. I didn't need drama, and half the women here wanted you for your money and then cheated on you anyway—or their men cheated on them. I'm not about that. Been there, done that, never again. If I ever fell into a relationship, it would be when hell froze over and the sun decided to take a detour close to Earth. Maybe then I'd entertain it before I died. Until then, no thanks.

I'm not the troubled CEO cliche either. I'm no playboy, I don't have deep underlying issues that leave me dark and mysterious. Compared to most of my associates, I'm an enigma. I don't do the casual hook up thing either. We all know it leads down routes you were purposely trying to avoid by being casual. No, I'm perfectly fine on my own, working on building my empire and worrying about the wife and picket fence another day.

And yet, here I am with my eyes unable to deviate anywhere but her. My hand drums nervously on my thigh, like my entire body is itching to get up and go talk to her again. An obvious draw, pulling at me, gnawing at me, but I ignore it. I'm not in the right space to entertain the idea of dating anyone, so instead I'll sit here, torturing myself and watching her.

Clearly, she was nervous, constantly biting her lower lip—a tell of hers I wondered if she even knew she had. She was freaking adorable, and the fact I thought that bothered me, and didn't, at the same time.

"Alex, what do you think?" Eddie, a business associate — and my cousin — I loathed every minute of being around, turned to me, pulling my gaze from my mystery beauty at the bar. Eddie was here to talk about a new opportunity he wanted my company to invest in, which meant it was a bottomless pit I'd never profit from. But I heard him out because he was, unfortunately, part of the family.

We were Bennettis. Despite what the news liked to throw out there, we were not the mafia. Okay, some of my family is, but my parents and our entire side were clean, now at least. I stayed out of the other family business for good reason—I enjoyed staying out of prison. I had no intention of going there.

I'm not going to deny that my family name gave me a lot of connections and opened too many doors that would never open for others, but I rarely used it. My business was too successful on its own, and despite what the gossip columns said, I built it myself.

My trust fund still sits untouched in my bank account, growing and blossoming with interest. I love money that just makes more money without me lifting a finger. Bennetti Innovations Group was my prized baby. I raised her, taught her well, and while now I have a board of directors dictating my life, including my personal one, it's better than relying on family money, which, myself and the FBI both know, is not legal.

No one was going to come after my business with a warrant, unlike many family companies in the past. Nope, I was a man who made himself, and I was damn proud of it.

Now I sat here, sipping my scotch and listening to Eddie drone on about something with mining. You've got to be kidding me, Eddie. *Jesus Christ.*

Rolling my eyes, I watched my little doe at the bar. Her green eyes flickered nervously around the room, and then I realized why. The Ken Doll Douche and Barbie noticed her, both giving sneers that made them some of the ugliest Manhattanites I'd ever seen, and they were getting ready to approach her.

Saving a damsel in distress isn't my style, and yet, I wanted to go over there and save this damsel who caught me off guard in the whopping five minutes I'd been around her. I did, after all, tell her to flirt with a hot guy and then walked away. I walked away because the scent of jasmine wafting off her mixed with that fiery personality chipped away at my rather calm and collected self. That and her having no problem saying the word "cock" to a complete stranger.

God, that was hot.

Again, far from vanilla.

I had this urge to peel back every layer and find out what else was in there. That primal male thing came about all too quickly, making me want to jump up and help, even though I basically told her she was on her own.

What can I say, I'm a walking contradiction tonight.

"Eddie, it's a dumb fucking idea. I'm not doing it," was all I said to shut him down before I stood, buttoned my jacket, and excused myself. I strolled slowly, watching the ridiculous couple approach her. Despite her nerves on the phone with her friend, she composed herself well. Perhaps that third martini she was no longer gingerly sipping but gulping helped a bit.

Ken looked her up and down, smirking like he truly thought he got the better option with Barbie on his arm. These two were laying it on thick, hand in hand, leaning into each other, and pecking each other's cheeks.

Wow, classy assholes.

I neared just enough to listen in to yet another conversation I shouldn't, but hey, I'm a curious man.

"Oh gosh, I just told Jake how sad it was to see you sitting here alone, and we had to come up and talk to you so it didn't look like you were by yourself. Care to join us?" Barbie pouted her lips, giving my mystery woman a once-over. I leaned against the wall just out of sight but close enough to listen, arms crossed and doing my best to appear casual. "I'd hate for you to sit here alone."

Something told me she relished the idea of her "friend" sitting there alone.

"Oh Lisa, I'm not alone," she laughed. Okay, so Barbie's real name was Lisa. I preferred Barbie. "My...boyfriend is coming to meet me. He just got held up at work." Maybe the friend she was on the phone with earlier was this supposed boyfriend. But the way she crossed her legs tightly and straightened her back for confidence told me no boyfriend was coming.

Ken and Barbie scanned the room for this so-called boyfriend, and the smile on Barbie's face was nothing short of evil.

Fuck it.

Without thinking, I stepped forward, wrapping my arm around her waist. She let out a surprised gasp, but I tugged her close, her back flush against my front as I leaned down and kissed her neck.

Damn, that jasmine scent was intoxicating.

"There you are, baby," I said loud enough for Ken and Barbie to hear. "Sorry I'm late. Traffic."

For a moment, she squinted up at me, those green eyes catching the light, and something inside me cracked a bit.

Who has eyes like those? Not just green, but green with flecks of amber and blue, a swirl of trouble all mixed in. She smiled, realizing her role to play. "Oh, it's no problem at all. I was just catching up with some old friends."

Friends? I suppose that was an easier way to introduce what those two were. I looked up at them, smiling. Before Ken could open his mouth, I spun her stool to face me, threading my hands through the silkiest mess of hair I'd ever felt, pulling her mouth to mine. At first, she stalled, but then she wrapped her hands around my neck and kissed me back.

Damn, she was not vanilla in that department either. The twitch it gave my dick when her legs opened and I stepped between them to tug her close was immediate. When my lips touched hers, it was like a spark ignited. My entire body tingled and spread like a wildfire. Her lips were soft and perfect moving against mine with a rhythm that felt gentle and yet urgent. My tongue swept across her perfectly soft and plump lips until she opened her mouth, and I basically devoured her right in front of them like the starving man I am.

The gentle way she nipped at my lips and gripped the back of my neck made me reluctant to stop kissing her. No, I wanted those lips on me for the rest of the night. At this point, I might have forgotten what I was even doing. She tasted like a martini and sin, for sure, but also sweet, like honey, and that jasmine scent was pulling me in even closer. I deepened the kiss, relishing the slight moan that escaped her mouth. My heart pounded in my chest each time her tongue tangled with mine, and I lost myself in the feel of exploring her lips, my hands roaming over the small of her back, anchoring her to me.

What was I doing this for again?

In those seconds—minutes, hours, fuck if I know how much time passed—I am lost. I'm not thinking about how I was supposed to be entertaining business associates and preventing my cousin from losing yet another business I'd have to bail him out of. I wasn't even thinking about the board meeting that pissed me off this morning.

I'd never felt so consumed by a woman's lips that the world completely faded away, until now.

If there was such a thing as a drug that came off a woman's lips, it had to be hers. Magic lip gloss or something because I was addicted and didn't know if my greedy ass would pull away or just consume her for myself right here in this bar.

Finally coming back to my senses, or at least the few that remained, we pulled away from each other. She looked at me with wide eyes and panting as heavily as I was, but I leaned in, pretending to nip at her ear. "Play along," I whispered before turning her back around to face Ken and Barbie. I wrapped my arm around her waist, leaving my hand against her stomach to trace idle circles against her waist, enjoying how Ken watched closely.

Oh he is jealous? Weird.

"I didn't realize you were dating someone," Barbie says and I don't need to know this woman to know I hate her.

Then Ken Doll's eyes widened—yup, he recognized me. Good.

"Oh, you're Alexander Bennetti," he stammered. I felt my mystery woman stiffen under my grip, so I took my other hand and slowly trailed it up and down her arm, pulling her closer to me.

Yeah, I'm Alexander fucking Bennetti.

Everyone knows who I am in Manhattan, and apparently, this woman who just gave me the wildest ride of her lips hadn't recognized me. Until now of course. Interesting.

"That I am," I said, giving them my best *I-don't-give-a-damn-who-you-are look* and kissed her on the neck, barely glancing at them and giving her all of my attention. I'd gladly put down a million right now if she turned and kissed me again, but her gaze was locked on the couple that looked like they were torn out of a wedding catalog—sickeningly in love and making you want to vomit. "And you would be...?"

Barbie's eyes widened as the realization hit her, and it was like her entire image, makeup, and Chanel combo fell apart. God, I love catching people off guard. No one expects to run into me in places like this; hell, I prefer not to, but for once, I was happy to be here.

"Violet, why didn't you mention you were dating Alexander—I mean, Mr. Bennetti?" So, my mystery woman's name was Violet.

Not shocked.

She definitely pulled off the name. Actually, she could be named anything and still pull it off.

"Well, since you slept with my boyfriend for a few months, I figured we weren't really onto that part where we chat about our sex lives." God, she was so incredibly unfiltered I wanted to laugh, but I settled with a smirk.

Barbie's perfectly manicured eyebrows shot up in surprise as she looked between Violet and me. Her judgment evident in the way her eyes narrowed. She couldn't fathom how a woman like Violet could possibly be with someone like me, and it was starting to grate on my nerves.

"I like to keep my personal life private," I said to Barbie, keeping Violet close with my arm around her. "But I've decided that I don't want to hide our relationship any longer. Right, babe?" I looked down at her, those green eyes almost promising me death. God, that was the hottest look a woman had ever given me, especially now that she knew who I was and did it anyway.

Bennetti's get looks, but not like that. We get awe or fear, but no one has dared look at me with the promise of injury. I'm not in the family business, but still, my name is known. Even if she didn't know the family history, and she might not since I kept myself as separated as possible in New York—the smallest fucking state ever—no one had the balls to look at me, Alexander Bennetti, like that.

I'm not full of myself. Just facts.

Barbie cleared her throat and redirected the conversation, trying to save face. "Will you be joining us at the company party next weekend for Hartley?" Ah, so she worked for a publisher. There is only one Hartley in Manhattan, and that's the CEO of Hartley & Co Publishing.

I gently ran my fingers along Violet's neck, planting another kiss and not really giving a damn that they were watching. In fact, this could work to my advantage if some photos were taken of her in my arms and leaked to the press. Always thinking miles ahead, and this woman wrapped up in my arm was about to be a Christmas present. "Oh, wouldn't miss it for the world. I've been meaning to catch up with Hartley anyway. He owes me a few favors."

Violet's eyes widened just a fraction, processing the unexpected turn of events without giving it away two the couple of the year in front of her. Finally, her body relaxed into mine slightly, as if understanding how to play the game. "Yes, we're looking forward to it," she said, her voice not missing a step.

Barbie's expression was priceless, a mix of disbelief and frustration. Ken, on the other hand, seemed more uncomfortable by the second. "Well, it's been...interesting seeing you, Violet," Barbie said, trying to muster some dignity. Hate to break it to her, but she won't find it in whatever cesspool she crawled from.

Another man approached us, the one I had seen Violet watching for a while when he entered. Boyfriend? I hoped not, or this was about to get really awkward. He looked at Barbie and Ken, then Violet, then at me with my arm wrapped around her.

"Max, you remember Alexander, my boyfriend?" Violet says with a smile. I hadn't been someone's anything for a while, and not going to lie, it made part of my chilled interior warm just a bit.

Max didn't even flinch. He smiled, extending his hand to shake mine. "Of course, great to see you again."

I liked him already. Quick thinking and saved his friend some face. You don't find many genuine people around here anymore.

"Well, don't want to keep you. We have a group waiting for us to discuss our wedding," Barbie threw out the barb, and I couldn't help myself.

"Oh? Pick the venue yet?" I asked, not really caring, but it was one of those comments you threw out to act interested.

"The Gardens," she smiled at Violet, and I felt there was a back story there.

Buy The Gardens and cancel their reservation. Done.

"I sure hope we get invited. I love a good wedding," I smirked with the kind of face that meant there was no option but to invite us. No one in New York doesn't invite a Bennetti, or we just show up because we technically don't need invites anywhere. We have tables reserved at any restaurant; there's never a wait. It's like the sea parts. I'm not tooting my horn. It's the family name and fear.

Honestly, I wouldn't mind, for once, not being recognized, but I gave up on that decades ago.

Barbie's face tightened, realizing the unspoken rule. "Of...of course," she choked out, nodding before spinning back to her party. Ken lingered for a minute, looking us over—my arms practically wrapped around the woman with that jasmine scent I couldn't get enough of. When they finally went back to their table, I whirled her bar stool around to face me.

"See, flirt with a hot guy."

"You said you weren't volunteering," she snapped back, completely ignoring the other guy's nervous glance between us. Judging by the way his eyes widened, he knew exactly who I was.

I shrugged, playing it off like I had all the time in the world. "Changed my mind. See, baby, I have the luxury of doing that. When you're me, you don't operate with limitations."

Alright, I sounded like a tool, but there was something about the way she didn't flinch, didn't immediately fall at my feet because of my name. It was like a switch flipped, and now, I wanted—no, *needed*—to see if I could make her look at me like I was worth chasing. Like I was the one she should want.

"Oh god," her friend, Max, chimed in. "You're...uh... *him*. The tenth hottest bachelor in New York *him*?"

Gay, then. Definitely not her boyfriend, based on his immaculate but understated outfit—a crisp blue shirt, perfectly tailored dress pants, and a jacket that showed he knew how to dress. Classy, but not over-the-top. I respected that.

"Indeed," I said, not tearing my gaze away from Violet. Her green eyes were locked onto mine, studying me like she was trying to figure out my game, only I had no idea what my game plan was either. But there was a growing part of me that wanted to find out. I could already feel ideas beginning to take shape in my head, the kind that would make this whole encounter... more interesting.

"So, Violet," I said slowly, savoring the taste of her name. *Violet.* "are you always this feisty, or is it just my charm?"

She rolled her eyes, but I didn't miss the slight tug at the corner of her mouth. Almost a smile. Almost.

"You wish," she shot back. "And I'm pretty sure your 'charm' has nothing to do with it."

I smirked, leaning in just enough to make it clear I wasn't backing down. "That's where you're wrong. But I'm invested in this now."

She arched an eyebrow, challenging me without a word. "Invested how?"

I leaned back, casually, as if the answer was obvious. "Didn't I just offer to be your boyfriend at your work party?" My voice was steady, unwavering. I always kept my word—she just didn't know yet how far I was willing to go. "Now I'm curious. I want to know more about what I've invested in. I mean, you can't just be a magnet for drama. There's got to be more to know."

A laugh slipped from her lips, light and musical. I felt it, like a spark, a pull that I couldn't quite explain. Addictive, that sound. "Oh, I've got layers," she teased, her eyes gleaming. "But I'm not sure you're ready for all of them."

I found myself leaning in just a fraction closer, unable to resist. "I'm a fast learner," I countered, my voice low. "Show me."

Her gaze softened for a moment. "Maybe we can test that..."

Victory. I signaled the bartender, a slow grin spreading across my face. "Another round for us, please."

As we waited for the drinks, I couldn't help but feel the thrill of it all. I hadn't come here expecting much—just a couple of drinks before retreating to my penthouse, business as usual. But Violet... she was something else. Someone else. More interesting than any deal or investment I'd ever made, and I found myself wanting to see what was beneath those layers she hinted at.

She downed her drink faster than I expected, a silent but clear message that she was ready to leave, her exit probably prompted by the watchful eyes of Barbie and Ken from across the bar. They were practically devouring us with their stares, and I could tell she was done with the show — hopefully not done with me though.

"Well, thanks for...whatever this was," she said, standing abruptly. Her body brushed against mine as I stood with her, the contact electric. My hand instinctively found the small of her back, guiding her closer, holding her there for just a moment longer. Her body was a masterpiece—none of that frail, breakable frame you see on most New York women. No, she had curves, real curves, and I couldn't stop my mind from racing at the feel of her against me.

"What? No goodbye kiss Violet?" I drawled, letting her name roll off my tongue, slow and deliberate. "*Violet.*" Not to tease, though it had that effect. No, I said it because it felt natural, like her name was meant to be spoken by me *and only me*.

She stared at me, her eyes widening, clearly mortified. But I didn't let her go. Not yet.

"They're still watching," I murmured, leaning in just enough to make sure my words were for her ears only. "Won't it look strange if you leave your billionaire boyfriend here without a goodbye kiss?"

What was I doing? Dropping the "billionaire" card like some arrogant prick? That wasn't me. I never had to flaunt what I had. But something about her—about Violet—made me desperate, grasping at anything to hold her attention.

Maybe it was because I wasn't used to a woman who wasn't immediately impressed. Maybe it was because she wasn't supposed to be. But here I was, clinging to every second, trying to buy more time with her.

Her lips parted, and for a split second, I wondered if she'd kiss me. If I'd feel her mouth on mine and if it would be as maddening as I thought it would.

"Nothing about this is not weird," she muttered. But I didn't wait for her to make the move—I pulled her in and kissed her anyway. And damn, she didn't fight it. Not even close. Instead, she practically melted into me, her hands sliding up to tangle in my hair. Normally, someone messing with my hair in public would drive me up the wall, but with her? She could do whatever she wanted.

Mess up my hair? Go for it.

Smear her lipstick all over me? Absolutely.

Kidnap me for a weekend getaway? I'll pack a bag.

Ask me to buy her a house in the Hamptons? *Stop it,* man.

The kiss was too easy. Too natural. Like we'd done it a thousand times before, even though this was our first. It didn't have that awkward, stumbling quality most unexpected kisses do—it just fit. And hell, if I didn't want to keep going, tasting and exploring every inch of her mouth like I was mapping out new territory.

When she finally broke away, I couldn't help but follow her lips for just a second, resisting the urge to pull her right back in. She licked her lips, slow and deliberate, like she was savoring every last taste of me. And damn, I was already considering going in for round two — I guess technically three and I was not opposed to round four, five or twelve.

"Better?" she asked, her voice laced with amusement.

Better? The woman had no idea.

"Well, goodnight, fake boyfriend," she added, a teasing smile on her lips. "Thanks for saving me, though now you've left me in the awkward position of explaining why you won't be at the event next week."

I hummed, my mind already racing with possibilities. Oh, I'd be at that event, all right. But now wasn't the time to let her in on that little detail.

I glanced over at Max, who was staring at us like he'd just witnessed an alien invasion. "Have a good night," I said, giving them both a nod, though my attention was already back on Violet.

As she walked away, I finally allowed myself a full view of her retreating figure. And yeah—just as I'd suspected—she had a great ass. My suspicions had been spot on, and I wasn't sure if that made things better or infinitely worse. Either way, this thing with her? It wasn't even close to over.

I slipped my phone from the inner pocket of my jacket and called Holmes, my family's head of security. He picked up on the second ring, his voice groggy and unamused.

"You're calling me late on a Friday night. Do you ever sleep?"

I glanced at my watch, rolling my eyes at his dramatics. "It's not even ten, Holmes."

My gaze drifted across the bar to Max, who was holding the door open for Violet as she tugged her NYU sweatshirt back on, trying to shield herself from the chill outside. There she was, looking both adorable and utterly frustrating. Adorable because of the way that oversized sweatshirt swallowed her up. Frustrating because I couldn't stop thinking about her—and it was driving me insane that she had that effect on me when I didn't even know her for more than an hour.

"Anyway," I continued, "not to interrupt your thrilling Friday night, but I need you to find everything you can about a woman for me."

A raspy chuckle echoed through the phone, loud enough to cut through the bar's noise. "A woman? Really? What's her name?"

"First name's Violet," I said, watching as she disappeared through the door. "She works at Hartley & Co., a publisher in Manhattan. I don't have much more than that, but you're resourceful. You'll figure it out." I leaned back against the bar, my mind already spinning with the possibilities.

"Let me guess," Holmes said, his tone thick with amusement, "is this a one-night stand you need dirt on to, what, get rid of?"

One-night stand? Not even close.

Violet's the kind of woman who pulls you in so deep, you'd willingly lose yourself for a weekend just to savor every inch of her. The thought of her in my bed, tangled in sheets, definitely didn't involve anything remotely vanilla or one night.

I shook my head, trying to clear the image from my mind. "No, not like that." My voice betrayed me, the lie coming out awkward and unconvincing. *What the hell is wrong with me?* "It's... a potential business associate," I added, though even I didn't believe the words as they left my mouth.

"Uh-huh." The skepticism in Holmes's voice was thick, but he didn't press. He knew better than to question too much—especially when I was like this. Holmes was a pain in the ass sometimes, but he was the best at what he did. He could hack, erase records, find leverage—basically anything I needed to keep my hands clean while my family reveled in dirtier dealings.

"How soon do you need it?" His question came with the same undercurrent of irritation that he always made a point of shoving at me.

"Tonight. By midnight," I said. "Bring it to my place."

Holmes sighed, but before he could get another word in, I added, "Oh, and one more thing. I want you to find out everything you can about The Gardens. It's not for sale, but I'm looking to change that. Find something to... encourage the owner to sell."

"You want to tell me why?" he asked.

"Do I pay you to ask questions?" I shot back. "See you in a few."

Tonight had taken an unexpected turn, and I had a gut feeling things were only going to get more interesting from here.

Violet

I woke up early, a faint throbbing in my head, courtesy of three green martinis. Or was it four? Not quite a hangover, thank God, but enough to have me groaning as I rolled out of bed, rubbing my temples.

Shuffling into the bathroom and splashing cold water on my face, I hope to wake up from what felt like a wild dream. The memories of last night flickered through my mind like a montage from a rom-com with a twist. One minute, I'm pouring my heart out to Max, deep in my "woe-is-me" mode, and the next? I'm swapping stories—and a whole lot more—with a complete stranger who just happens to be one of the wealthiest and eligible men in Manhattan.

And then there's the fact I kissed him. Twice.

I stared at my reflection, blinking as if that would somehow erase the memory.

Nope. Still there.

I kissed Alexander Bennetti. You can't blame a girl for wondering if she downed too many drinks and hallucinated the entire thing.

But oh, those kisses. His lips on mine? Wow. Just... wow.

Even now, my lips tingled at the thought. I had practically floated home, spilling every juicy detail to Max, who had been just as floored as I was. I mean, how does someone like me—who can't even get my boss's lavender oat milk latte order right—end up kissing the Alexander Bennetti?

This morning, though, I tried to convince myself it had all been a bizarre dream. Because seriously, what kind of fairy tale universe am I living in where that actually happened? Had I known who he was, martinis or not, there's no way I would've said half the things I said last night. Nope. I would've been the awkward girl sitting there with wide eyes and a nervous smile, incapable of forming a coherent sentence and gaping like a fish.

But instead, I let every single word flow out like I had no filter. *Did I really say all that to him?* I cringed at the thought. There's no undoing that, no convenient memory eraser to save me from my own mouth. The worst part? I'm *sure* it wasn't the martinis talking.

Wasn't he dating a supermodel? They always are, aren't they? Guys like him—the rich, hot, walk-in-a-room-and-everyone-stares kind of guys—usually have a goddess on their arm. It's like some unwritten rule.

Definitely not an assistant who barely keeps the lights on, juggling between paying rent and praying my power doesn't get cut off.

With a heavy sigh, I resigned myself to the inevitable truth—last night was a one-time, fluke encounter that would never happen again.

It's Saturday morning, which means my usual weekend routine has kicked in, yanking me right back into reality.

I started tidying up the chaos that was my apartment—because, let's be honest, my life was basically one big mess in motion. Stripped the sheets, lugged myself down five flights of stairs with a laundry basket that probably weighed more than I did, rushed back up, and dove straight into tackling the disaster zone of dishes and clothes scattered everywhere.

I wanted to write. Truly, I did. But who was I kidding? My creative spark had packed its bags and gone on a long, very inconvenient vacation. All the authors I knew had these beautifully organized, color-coded outlines for their books, while I was here, proudly waving my pantster flag.

Outlining? Nope.

It's supposed to just flow, right?

Well, here's the thing—when that flow slows to a trickle, or worse, careens off into the wilderness with no map, you're left stranded. And I'm not talking about a cute little "whoops, I'll figure it out" stuck. No. I was "lost at sea on a sinking ship with no life raft" stuck. One of my novels was practically Titanic at this point, and, needless to say, no new words were being typed today.

So, I redirected all that pent-up frustration into scrubbing the mountain of dishes that had been glaring at me from the sink all week. There's something oddly therapeutic about cleaning up last week's disasters, like each swipe of the sponge was washing away a layer of stress. As I scrubbed, I gave myself five minutes. Just five glorious minutes to replay last night in my mind.

Alexander Bennetti and that kiss. *Dear God, that man doesn't just kiss—he creates masterpieces with his mouth.* A full-on performance that made my knees buckle and my heart race like I didn't even know was possible. And don't even get me started on what he did with his tongue. Pure. Talent.

Whoever gets to experience that on the regular? She's one lucky woman.

Occasionally I glanced at my laptop sitting on my desk, and a spark flickered. Maybe—just maybe—the absurdity of last night would be the thing to get me writing again. If nothing else, it definitely made for one hell of a story.

My Saturday morning started like clockwork—with my mother's *delightful* weekend call at precisely ten a.m. The kind of call that, in our family, is less about catching up and more about reminding me why my dreams are apparently a one-way ticket to Disappointment-ville.

Because obviously, going to college and wanting to be a writer? That's the stuff of family legends—the kind they bring up at every holiday gathering, just to keep me grounded.

What they always manage to forget—conveniently, of course—is that they only paid for my first year of college. Yet in their magical version of events, that single year somehow covers the cost of an *entire* four-year education. Like, what? Basic math apparently isn't part of their parental skill set.

But hey, details, right?

So, I hang up the phone, feeling that familiar twinge of inadequacy settle in my chest. "Yep, I'm totally my parents' greatest disappointment. Love you too, Mom," I mutter to the empty apartment, because obviously, it's not enough to hear it once—I've got to replay the scene for dramatic effect.

And don't even get me started on how they've been holding that "investment" over my head for the last eight years. According to them, I should have a shelf full of bestsellers by now. Never mind the fact that I haven't even submitted my first manuscript yet. Nope, in their eyes, I'm wasting my entire education.

Gotta love the unwavering support of family.

Shoving my mom's motivational guilt trip to the back of my mind, I turned to my desk, which looked like a tornado of papers had blown through. And there it was—my laptop, staring me down like the enemy I'd been avoiding all week. If laptops can taunt, mine would. I think it does. If only I knew that was a feature that came standard with PCs I would have opted for a Mac.

With a dramatic sigh, I surrendered and flipped it open. What greeted me? Three romance novels in various stages of disaster, each one a bigger mess than the last. Plot holes everywhere, characters half-formed and wandering aimlessly through stories that didn't know where they were going. It was like trying to put together a jigsaw puzzle where none of the pieces fit.

The spark? Long gone. Probably snuffed out by the spectacularly tragic ending of my last relationship—a crash-and-burn event so epic, I'm honestly shocked I still believe in love at all. Let alone lust.

Enter Max, who had his own, very Max solution to my writer's block: "Watch porn," he said, as if that would somehow magically unlock the inspiration I needed for steamy scenes. I mean, I already read romance novels like it's my job, but sure, why not throw porn into the mix? When in doubt, research, right?

I caved. Strictly for professional purposes, of course. I watched, took notes like the dedicated nerd I am—carefully jotting down what worked and steering clear of anything too kinky that didn't fit my characters' vibe. Did I feel like an awkward weirdo? Absolutely.

Max found the whole situation hilarious. He gave me that look, the one that said, *You're such a prude*, while I shot him a glance that screamed, *And you're a total deviant*.

But you know what? The man had a point. How was I supposed to write hot, toe-curling love scenes when my own love life was... well, the Sahara Desert of romantic prospects? And not the picturesque kind with camels and oases. No, I'm talking full-blown wasteland, all sand, no water, no hope in sight.

That's when it hit me—a sharp realization of just how bleak things had gotten. Yep, I had reached that level of single where even research involved adult entertainment.

Romance author life wasn't quite as glamorous as I'd imagined.

After my mom's *delightful* guilt trip, I texted Max. He was already on his way over with our usual lattes—none of that oat milk or lavender nonsense—and since it was officially PSL season, he knew better than to show up without one.

Seriously, no pumpkin spice, no entry.

Max was my lifesaver, especially after the weekly parental pep talks that made me question all my life choices. Every Saturday, hungover or not, he'd swing by, watch me half-heartedly clean, and then force me to vent about my latest chapter of "why do my parents hate everything I do?"

When the knock finally came, I didn't bother looking up from my desk. "Max, you have a key! Just come in!" I called, shuffling the mess of papers around like tidying up my desk would somehow fix the disaster that was my life.

Sure, Violet, clean your desk and—*boom*—instant bestselling author.

Another knock.

Growling, I go to swing open the door.

"Max, if you lost your key again, I swear I'm not paying for another lock change. I'm not about to have some random perv wandering in because you can't keep track of your stuff—"

I froze mid-rant. It wasn't Max at the door.

Nope. It was *him*.

Alexander. The guy from last night. The rich, devastatingly handsome guy. The guy whose kiss had basically short-circuited my brain and left me questioning my entire existence.

And there he was, standing at my door in a freaking three-piece suit. On a Saturday. Looking even better than last night, if that were even possible. No, scratch that—he looked sexier. Because apparently, the universe decided that this man needed to defy all logic and reason.

Meanwhile, I was standing there like a deer caught in headlights, probably with my mouth hanging open. I kept waiting for a camera crew to jump out and yell, "Gotcha!" Surely this couldn't be real life. I mean, did I stumble into some hidden prank show? Because this level of hotness at my front door on a Saturday morning didn't happen to regular people like me.

"Violet," he said, his voice smoother than I remembered, and yep, there went my brain—completely fried, again.

Violet

"Is THIS A PRANK?" I finally managed to get out, pushing past him to check the hallway for hidden cameras. There had to be some mistake. Maybe I was still asleep, and this was some weird dream.

A smirk tugged at his lips as he leaned casually against the doorframe. "I don't usually come down to this part of town just to prank people—especially not on a Saturday morning."

He gave me a once-over, and that's when it hit me: I was standing in front of Manhattan's most eligible hottie wearing nothing but my workout booty shorts (which, according to Max, left *very little* to the imagination) and a tank top that was just as unforgiving. I had planned to work out later, okay? Cleaning and working out required minimal wardrobe changes, and I wasn't about to haul more laundry down those five flights of stairs.

Still, standing there under his gaze, I suddenly felt... exposed. Which was ridiculous because this was *my* apartment, *my* Saturday, and he was the one crashing the party. But with him standing there, all polished and proper, I couldn't help but feel a little underdressed for what was quickly turning into a very unexpected visitor.

"What are you doing here?" I blurted, though my brain was clearly preoccupied with how insanely well his suit fit. Those broad shoulders, the way his biceps filled out the sleeves—it was like he just rolled out of bed looking effortlessly perfect. Must be one of those secret rich-man genes the government won't admit exists.

"I came to talk about your problem," he replied, casually leaning there like he wasn't currently turning my world upside down.

"My problem?" I echoed, trying to muster some of that effortless confidence he seemed to ooze.

Spoiler alert: I failed.

"Can I come in?" he asked, though it didn't really sound like a question. More like an expectation. "I'd rather not talk business on the porch where everyone can eavesdrop."

Without much of a choice, I opened the door and let him in. He stepped inside, his gaze sweeping over my small, cozy (okay, cluttered) apartment. I could practically see him cataloging the second-hand furniture, the haphazard room divider separating my "bedroom" from the rest of the space, and the kitchen sink still overflowing with dishes because I didn't finish scrubbing them all. Some just have to "soak" for a day or so. Meanwhile, I was sure his place was all sleek lines, shiny black surfaces, and spotless countertops—probably with some gilded gold accents just because, you know, rich people.

"Uh, have a seat," I said, scrambling to pick up the pile of clothes I'd dumped on the couch earlier. My second-hand floral couch that most people would call hideous, but I adored it. There's just something about tacky furniture that gives me life.

He sat down, looking completely at ease as he crossed one leg over the other, while I perched awkwardly on the armrest, unsure where to place myself in my own apartment. My place was small, barely enough room for a tiny table, my sofa, and a bookshelf on the verge of collapse from all my books.

"What kind of business do you think we need to discuss?" My voice came out a little higher than usual, and I fidgeted, crossing my arms, then my legs, only to switch back to my arms again. Sitting still wasn't an option near those eyes. It felt like he was sucking all the air out of the room, leaving me both hot and cold at the same time. How was that even possible?

He raised an eyebrow, clearly amused. "You don't have to hover. Sit here." He patted the cushion next to him.

"I'm not a dog. I know how to sit," I growled defeating the point I just tried to make. *Why did I growl?*

"Didn't mean to imply you were," he said, his smirk deepening, sending an annoying mix of frustration and something *else* crawling through me.

Why did he have to be so annoyingly attractive, and why did I feel like I was the one out of place in *my own home*?

"Fine," I grumbled, sliding off the armrest and onto the actual sofa, making sure to keep a good amount of space between us. But of course, he scooted closer, because personal boundaries? Apparently not his thing.

And, *dear God*, did he know how good he smelled? Like sandalwood mixed with something spicy, as if he'd just stepped out of a commercial for "Irresistible Man" or "Heartthrob in a Bottle." Meanwhile, I was sitting there in my workout shorts and a tank top, looking like I'd just wrestled my laundry pile. Unfair? Absolutely. He smelled like a forested paradise with a dash of danger, and I was basically in full-blown comfy mode.

"What's this about?" I asked, trying to sound calm, though internally, I was still recovering from just the smell of him.

Instead of answering, his eyes drifted to my overstuffed bookshelf, and he stood, walking toward it. His finger trailed along the dusty wood like he was examining my entire life's clutter, making me flush with embarrassment. Of course, I'd forgotten to dust. Lie. I don't dust. Dust adds character. He pulled out a book—old, worn, and barely hanging on by its spine—and quirked a brow as he held it up.

Pride & Prejudice.

I'm more than aware I'm a walking cliché.

I jumped up, snatching the book from his hand, and quickly tossed it onto my desk, feeling like I'd just exposed my secret soul. "So, you read... a lot," he said, his gaze still scanning the titles on my shelf. "Romance?"

"I believe I embarrassed myself enough last night. Let's not dig deeper, okay?" I muttered, feeling the heat rise in my cheeks.

He chuckled, that infuriatingly charming smile spreading across his face. "Well, if you want to be a romance author, I suppose reading is a good place to start."

Okay, now I was suspicious. How did he know so much about me? Had he been stalking my Facebook profile or something? I can't even recall the last time I posted there, but he knew a lot more about me than I knew about him so we weren't playing fair right now.

My patience was wearing thin, and the laundry timer went off, reminding me I had actual, mundane things to handle. "Look, I need to go swap out my laundry in the basement. I don't really have time for... whatever this is. And I'm sure you have somewhere else to be besides admiring my book collection."

He didn't blink. "Where's the laundry room?"

I stared at him, utterly confused. "I'm sorry, what?"

"The laundry room," he repeated, slower this time, like I was the one not following along. "Where is it?"

"Five floors down... in the basement?" I answered, unsure why that was suddenly relevant.

Without missing a beat, he pulled out his phone. "Antonio, go to the basement and move Miss Hart's linens from the washer to the dryer. Yes, I did just say that." He tucked his phone away like he hadn't just casually assigned someone to do my laundry.

My jaw dropped. "Did you really just... send someone to do my laundry? What if my lingerie was in there?"

His gaze locked onto mine, a wicked gleam in his eyes as he looked me up and down. "I'm not sure your idea of lingerie and mine are quite the same."

I had no words. *None.*

This man was the literal embodiment of arrogance, yet somehow he wasn't coming off as the douchebag he should've been. He spoke with such confidence, a sprinkle of condescension, and yet there was no malice in it—just pure, infuriating charm. And damn it if that wasn't unreasonably sexy or I was just that desperate that a hot guy could insult me while I swooned over it.

Regaining a scrap of composure, I sat back down on the couch, eying him warily. "Can I offer you some coffee?" That's what you do for fancy guests, right? I wasn't entirely sure of the protocol when a billionaire randomly shows up at your apartment.

He declined, but I grabbed a cup for myself anyway, seriously debating whether a splash of something stronger should be added. I made my way back to the couch, sinking down as it squeaked under my weight. I clutched the cup in both hands like a lifeline because, honestly, it was starting to feel like one.

I also wasn't above throwing it at him if things got weirder.

Billionaire hottie or not, this was officially entering strange territory.

Just as Alexander was about to speak, Max barreled into my apartment. "Hey, did you know there are a few guys in suits just—" He froze when he spotted Alexander sitting on my couch and me, curled up in the corner clutching my cup of coffee and wishing it was more liquid courage. His eyes darted between us before he finally asked, "Oh... I suppose those are yours?" He directed the question to Alexander, who only gave a small nod.

Max gave an awkward chuckle and gestured toward the door. "Tell you what, I'm just gonna head back down the hall and... catch up with you later." He thumbed over his shoulder as if waiting for my approval to escape, but I gave him a wide-eyed *do not leave me alone with him* look.

Max and I lived in the same building. In fact, he's the one who found my studio for me after we met at work. I was apartment-hopping like a vagabond, and when he mentioned this place—decent rent, no roaches planning to overthrow the tenants—I jumped on the chance. Max and I had developed a great routine: commutes or walks to work together, late-night vent sessions about the pathetic state of my life, and now, apparently, his grand disappearing act when things got too awkward.

"You really don't have to leave," I said, my voice a little higher than usual as I tried to save face.

Alexander turned his attention to Max, flashing a smile that wasn't so much a suggestion as it was an order. "He does. We need a minute."

Max nodded furiously and made his exit, slipping out of the room like he thought Alexander might morph into a bear and maul him.

Coward.

With a sigh, I pulled my knees to my chest and took a sip of coffee, the warm cup doing very little to ease my tension. "Okay, enough with the mystery. You have someone doing my laundry downstairs, and you've thoroughly judged my taste in books. Let's get to the point so I can tell you no."

Alexander's piercing blue eyes locked onto mine, and for a second, I swear I forgot how to breathe. "Last night was..." he trailed off, his jaw tightening, clearly debating how to phrase whatever it was he came here to say. "I believe I can help you with your little situation, and you can help me with one of my own. I am, after all, invested in you now." There's a flicker where I do recall him saying something about that last night.

I raised an eyebrow. "Oh, really? And how's that?"

He leaned back, casually draping one arm over the couch, but there was tension in his posture. "I have a proposition for you," he said, his voice smooth but his jaw clenched. "Actually, more of an arrangement I guess."

I blinked, then blinked again, sure I hadn't heard him right. "I'm sorry, an *arrangement*?"

He nodded. "You mentioned you needed a date for your company party last night since I labeled myself as your boyfriend. I need a date for certain events as well, mostly to appease my board and investors, and then tackle all of the holiday invites I get around this time of year. It will make my board happy to see me arrive consistently with the same woman and not different ones."

I snorted, unable to help myself. "Too many 'billionaire playboy' headlines to clean up?"

He smiled faintly, brushing the accusation off with a wave of his hand. "I pride myself on not being a cliché, thank you very much. But no, it's more that my board needs to see me looking stable. Showing up solo to every function has become an issue, bringing different dates makes me a playboy. Apparently, it also makes me a target for every gold digger within a hundred-mile radius, and I don't have time to vet a new date for every dinner invite tossed in my assistant's inbox."

"Oh, I feel so flattered," I muttered sarcastically before taking another sip of coffee. "So, what exactly are you asking me to do?"

He paused, rubbing his thumb along his bottom lip as if deep in thought. I tried not to notice how distracting that was.

"You need a date for your work event so you don't show up single in front of...sorry, can't remember their names. I need a woman who doesn't come with drama for a meeting with a few of my big investors and my date to all of the holiday events coming up. Here's my offer: we agree to this exchange. You'll be my date when I need you, and I'll be yours. Since your *friends* think we are in a relationship, we can keep up that facade at your work party, and when you come as my date, I'll do the same so they quit hassling me about my single status."

I stared at him, processing his words. Well, trying to at least, but I'm positive I only blinked.

"One thing, Violet. In public, you need to play the part," Alexander said, his voice firm. "I'm under a lot of scrutiny—cameras, gossip columns, the works. They love to dig into my family, especially the side I've distanced myself from."

The mafia side, he means. I might've Googled him on my Uber ride home last night, and let's just say, paired with that sexy Italian accent, the rumors about his family being tangled up in the mafia? Yeah, I'd bet good money they're true.

"So, this has to look real."

"And your idea of real is...?" I raised an eyebrow, trying to ignore the way my stomach flipped.

He shrugged, completely nonchalant, as if fake dating were a totally normal thing to suggest. "The usual couple stuff. Kissing, holding hands, doting on each other—whatever it takes to sell it. I don't want anyone questioning the arrangement. People at your work will refer to me as your boyfriend, so we need to keep up appearances for both our sakes."

I crossed my arms, staring at him like he had two heads. "And then what? We high-five after the holidays and move on with our lives?"

His fingers drummed against his leg, like he was already orchestrating this plan in his head. "Possibly. I haven't thought that far ahead. I'm too busy to start dating random women, and I don't have the energy to look for something serious. But there's chemistry here," he said, his gaze locking onto mine in that way that made my heart stutter. "Obviously, last night proved that. It'll make this whole thing easier."

I blinked. *Chemistry?* I mean, yes, there was kissing, but did he really think we could just fake-date like this was normal? "Okay, hold up," I said, holding up a hand. "If—and that's a very big if—I agree to this, we need to clarify some things."

"You don't want a relationship," I began, crossing my arms tighter, "but you want me to play your girlfriend. You want us to kiss, hold hands in public, and then what? Do you just call me up whenever you need me to appear as your 'girlfriend' on demand?"

His jaw clenched again, and for a second, it looked like he was holding something back. "It's been a long time since I've dated, let alone been in a relationship," he said, his voice quieter but still steady. "The media has a way of invading every inch of my personal life. It's a necessary evil. If we go to your work party, and someone calls you my girlfriend, the world will take that and run with it. I could sneeze near an apple, and tomorrow the headlines would be 'Alexander Bennetti allergic to honeycrisps.' It doesn't matter what the truth is *really* as long as I make it what I need it to be to save me some sanity."

I opened my mouth to respond, but he wasn't done.

"You're helping me. I'm helping you. I need to please my investors, get through the holidays without endless questions about my relationship status, and appear to be dating someone seriously. You're beautiful, smart, and—" his lips quirked up in a half-smile, "—unfiltered in a way that should be annoying but is actually kind of entertaining. We'll have a good time, and clearly," he added, with a smirk that made my pulse race, "we have no problem kissing in public."

Oh, great. Now my heart decided to skip some beats, and I had to bite back the urge to smile like a lovesick fool. "Okay..."

This was surreal. Like I'd stepped straight into one of the romance novels stacked on my bookshelf, except this was real life.

"Can I ask one question?" I blurted out, watching as Alexander stood, buttoned his jacket, and casually checked his phone like this whole conversation was just another item on his to-do list.

"Go ahead," he replied, his fingers still tapping away, not even glancing up.

"Why me?" The words spilled out before I could stop them. "I mean, you could pick anyone—an heiress, a model, someone with actual class. I don't even own clothes that would fit in at the kind of events you go to."

He didn't even flinch. "I'll get you a new wardrobe. That's not really the issue here. Can't have a girl of mine underdressed."

I blinked. *A girl of mine?* Seriously?

"Great," I muttered. "So, I get to be dressed up like your personal doll?"

That got his attention. His head snapped up, and before I could process what was happening, he was in front of me, towering over me so fast I barely had time to yelp. His hands braced on either side of me, his face so close I could feel the warmth of his breath. I tried to breathe through my mouth, anything to avoid inhaling his scent that was already making my brain fuzzy.

Focus, Violet. Focus.

"I don't want a doll," he said, his voice low and firm, making my pulse quicken for reasons I refused to analyze right now. "If I wanted one, trust me, I'd have plenty of options. I'm buying you clothes so you fit in at my events. I hate it more than you do, but society has expectations, and I'm on camera. A lot." His tone almost defeated acknowledging this as a reality, so I decided to not press on with it.

Swallowing hard, my heart racing as I tried to keep my voice steady. "But... why me?"

He pulled back, adjusting his tie and smoothing his sleeves like he hadn't just knocked the air out of my lungs. "Because, Violet, you're not vanilla."

Oh. Well, that cleared it up. *Only not at all.*

"How long do I have to decide?" I asked, desperately trying to regain some semblance of control over this situation, which was spiraling faster than I could keep up with.

"I'd prefer an answer now," he said, glancing at his watch like this was just another timed transaction. "My schedule's packed, and the first dinner party is Tuesday. Not much time between now and then and if you agree I have to get an NDA over here for you to sign."

I crossed my arms, refusing to let him steamroll me. "You'll get my answer this afternoon."

He sighed, clearly not used to waiting for anything. Then he pulled his phone from his jacket and handed it to me. "Add your number. I'll send you mine. Hopefully, you'll accept my offer. You get a wardrobe, a date at your beck and call, free meals, and a chance to save face in front of Barbie and Ken."

Offer. Not relationship. Not date. Just... *offer.*

I nodded, but my mind was already spinning as I walked him to the door in some kind of autopilot mode. Before I could even blink, he was gone, leaving me standing in the doorway, wondering what alternate world I woke up in this morning.

That kiss last night? It clearly hadn't affected him the way it had scrambled my brain. For him, this was just an opportunity, a neat solution to a social problem. All business. And here I was, caught between feeling like a transaction and wondering if that kiss—at least for me—had meant something more than just a convenient arrangement.

Before I could even start processing the madness of the morning, Max slipped back into the studio, his eyes wide, his mouth forming the words *Oh my God* in slow motion, like he couldn't believe what he'd just witnessed.

I slumped back into the sofa. "You have no idea," I muttered, staring at the door where Alexander Bennetti had just walked out of my life... or more accurately, walked right into it, leaving me with a whole new set of questions and no idea what to do next.

All I knew for sure was that I'd rambled my way into this mess, kissed a billionaire hottie, and now had about 40 minutes before my linens were dry, courtesy of some guy named Antonio.

Alex

I HAD A PLAN when I showed up at her apartment—well, I *had* one. But the second she opened that door, every meticulously crafted idea I had vanished into thin air.

Why?

No fucking clue.

Violet Hart was beautiful, smart, daring—everything this world severely lacked. And the moment I saw her standing there, hair in a messy bun, wearing shorts that I sincerely hope she reserves for inside the apartment, my mind did something it never does: it blanked.

Completely.

For the first time in my life, I found myself nervous.

Me.

Nervous.

I don't get nervous—I make people nervous. It's what I do.

But when Violet opened the door, expecting someone else, her wide green eyes staring up at me like I was the last person she expected to see, I felt rattled while her expression was adorable.

I have no idea what the hell is going on in my head anymore.

Holmes showed up at my penthouse last night, just before midnight. He was on time, of course—he knew better than to be late—but his disdain was practically radiating off him. He slapped a file against my chest, muttering a few choice words under his breath before storming back to the elevator.

The man is barely human during his prime hours of noon to three, and outside that window, you're rolling the dice on what kind of beast you'll get.

I spent the rest of the night reading through the file he brought me. Took a quick nap—because apparently, I run on zero sleep and a lethal amount of caffeine—and reviewed the plan I had. Now, I knew everything about Violet Hart. Everything that could be found on paper or online, but there were so many more facets to her I wanted to know.

It's eerie how fast Holmes can dig up information, but that's why he's on my payroll. He works for both the family business and mine, finding intel that private investigators who enjoy keeping their licenses can't touch. Asking him to gather intel on Violet was probably the cleanest thing he did all week. So really, I was doing him a favor. In some twisted way, I'm a saint.

Violet had an *outrageous* amount of student loan debt. Honestly, it baffled me, considering her parents. Richard and Victoria Hart were well-known, highly respected human rights attorneys out in California—the kind of people who probably spent weekends planting trees or fighting for endangered wildlife. I couldn't see them surviving a day in Manhattan. Sure, they weren't partners in some high-end law firm, but they made good money. Respectable money. And yet, they only paid for one year of Violet's college tuition. After that, she was on her own.

She didn't just stop at a Bachelor's either. She powered through and got a Master's, and now here she was, working as an assistant at Hartley & Co. Publishing.

Through Holmes—who could probably tell me the exact time she brushes her teeth—I found out she wanted to be an author. A romance writer, of all things. Why did that make me find her even more interesting?

Working for a publisher made sense, but what didn't was the fact that after four years, she was still an assistant. *Four years.* Her salary was pathetic, especially for Manhattan. She was barely scraping by. Her studio apartment was in one of the shadier parts of town—not the worst I've seen, but I knew the rent in that area. I owned property two blocks down. With her salary, combined with student loans, it was a wonder she wasn't living on ramen noodles alone.

But her place? It was *her*. The thrift store furniture, the quirky decor—it was all so Violet. Eccentric, a little messy, and unapologetically her. She didn't care what anyone thought, and it wasn't like she was embarrassed by it. I liked that.

The fact that she had no clue who I was last night? *That* was what hooked me. Most women in Manhattan see me and immediately start making their move. They don't care about me; they care about what I can offer—money, status, or a scandalous headline.

But Violet? She talked to me like I was just some random guy at a bar. She didn't see the gossip column subject or the man rumored to have mafia ties. She saw *me*. And I wasn't used to that.

So, here I was, working a plan. It's a shitty truth, but I can't just pursue someone like a normal guy. Not with my reputation. Every woman I show interest in has to be checked out. It's not just about protecting my name—it's about security.

But for Violet? I'd intended to go to her place and ask her out. Simple. Direct. A normal date.

Then I chickened out.

I'm Alexander Bennetti. I don't chase women. They chase me.

God, I'm an insufferable prick.

But that didn't change the fact that, for once, I was thrown off balance. When she opened the door, looking at me like I didn't belong in her world, every plan I had flew out the window. I knew she had that company party coming up, and that was supposed to be my way in. I was going to offer to be her date, make up for the awkward situation I put her in at the ba and then I'd ask her out—properly. Like a man interested in a woman who has a pair of balls.

It was a solid plan, right?

Help her out, then casually suggest we keep seeing each other. Because the truth is, from the moment I met her, I've been drawn to her. There's this pull toward her that scares the hell out of me. The more I learn about her, the more I want to be around her, and I'm not used to wanting anyone like this. It's confusing, infuriating, and—damn it—irresistible.

And don't even get me started on that kiss. Standing in her doorway, it took every ounce of willpower not to kiss her again.

I sit in board meetings during hostile takeovers, facing some of the most powerful men in the country without breaking a sweat. I don't get intimidated. And yet, here I am, unraveling over a petite woman with green eyes and messy brown hair.

Why? Because she's everything this world lacks. And because, for the first time, I feel like I could lose control because there is something about this woman that draws me into the deep end.

So, instead of following through with my carefully crafted plan, I did the one thing I never do: I threw caution to the wind. Offered her an arrangement instead. Because for some reason, I couldn't risk just asking her out. I needed a way to be near her without the pressure of her saying no or, worse, walking away after one date. An arrangement meant I could stay close to her. It gave me a way in without putting everything on the line, and gave me a chance to date her without us labeling it that way.

Besides, she was the one that had floated it out there when she dismissed me last night as her "fake boyfriend," and apparently, I'm sticking with that route for now.

I offered to take her to the company party, sure. But let's be real—it was a pathetic excuse just to be near her, to learn more about her, and maybe—just maybe—figure out why she smells like jasmine.

Perfume? Lotion? Shampoo? I needed to know.

It's not like me to obsess over details like this. Women don't normally take up this much space in my mind. My Saturday mornings usually follow a rigid routine—run, weights, business meetings. Order. Structure. But Violet? She's thrown me into chaos.

And now I'm stuck waiting for her answer, which is maddening. Why the hell did I even tell her she had time to think about it? This woman has me bending over backward, and I don't bend for anyone. I like control, but here I am, losing sleep and thinking about *her*. She'll accept. She *has* to accept. Right?

I tried to stick to my routine today—tried to act like it was any other Saturday. But today? I woke up, showered, and changed suits *five times*. Five. Because I couldn't decide if the blue tie would be better than the gray one.

Pathetic.

I even told myself, on the drive over, that she wasn't *that* pretty. That it was the bar lighting playing tricks on me. You know, how dim lighting and alcohol can make anyone look like a ten. But in the bright light of day? Without a drop of makeup on her face? She was heartbreakingly beautiful. Natural. Real.

Women I've dated before? They're all beautiful, sure, but it's Daddy's money and a lot of artificial fillers to do the dirty work.

Once the makeup comes off, they're someone else entirely and despite the facade, there's nothing remotely interesting inside their shell. But Violet? She's the kind of beauty that makes the sun look like it's bending over backward just to touch her skin and worse I almost feel jealous the sun gets to touch that skin.

This woman is going to be the end of me if this is how I keep thinking.

So, after blurting out the offer to take her to the company party in exchange for her going with me to my events, it hit me—I can't date this woman in a normal sense.

She's out of my league, plain and simple.

My investors need to see me with someone consistent, and Violet isn't a typical socialite that will try to use this to gain social status. So, she will come with me to my dinner, I will help her save face in front of her work, and then maybe after that we could see where things go while we continue this arrangement. I didn't want to lead her on telling her that we could see where it would go, but we've established I have no backbone around this woman.

That kiss last night already proved I had no control around her. She could do whatever she wanted, and I'd let her. And after my last relationship imploded, I'm not in any position to get lost in someone. No matter how much I *want* to.

So, the exchange made sense and as for what the hell I will do after the holidays when I don't have endless excuses to take her out? No fucking clue, but I bought myself time to grow a pair while still having a chance to be near her.

More importantly, she'll be herself around me. I'll get to know the actual Violet, not some version of herself she might create for my benefit.

I was itching to figure out who Violet Hart really was. The real her, without the facade. And maybe, just maybe, she'd get to know me too—something I hadn't let anyone do in a long time. There was a small, pathetic part of me that hoped she felt the same pull I did that night at the bar. But admitting that to anyone? Not a chance. I'm not the kind of guy who spills his emotions.

Am I really this desperate? Setting up a whole arrangement just to see her again?

The thought twisted in my head, making me cringe. At least I hadn't stooped so low as to offer to pay off her student loans as part of this deal. That would've been crossing into some twisted, modern-day prostitution.

I pinched the bridge of my nose, letting out a low growl. Antonio, my driver—and now, thanks to this morning, the laundry-fetcher—was already giving me a side-eye as he opened the door to my SUV.

"Don't fucking say it," I snapped.

He smirked into the rearview mirror, pulling away from the curb outside her apartment. My Escalade stuck out like a sore thumb in this part of town. The only reason it wasn't messed with was because the locals knew who it belonged to, who *I* belonged to. They knew about my uncle, my cousin, and they wouldn't dare touch it.

While in the SUV, I shot off a quick text to my attorney, telling him I needed an NDA—along with a few extra clauses this time. No questions were asked, just a quick confirmation that a courier would deliver the documents to her place, ready for when she agreed to my absurd plan.

I loosened my tie, sinking back into the leather seat, watching as the city transformed outside the window. The shift from rundown buildings and graffiti-covered walls to pristine brownstones with green lawns, and then to the sleek, cold glass towers and concrete span of downtown, was almost disorienting. New York was a strange beast. You could cross one street and go from living in a nightmare to a life of luxury. Nowhere else was quite like it.

And now? I'd somehow managed to bring Violet into this twisted reality of mine, where nothing is what it seems, and everything comes with a price tag. But if it meant I could get to know her—*the real her*—then I'd pay it. Because right now, the only thing I was sure of was that Violet Hart had me hooked.

Violet

"OH MY GOD, VIOLET! This is literally the start of an epic romance novel! You meet a billionaire in a bar, fall for him, happily-ever-after follows. Isn't this, like, the meet-cute in every romance novel ever?" Max was full-on, head-in-the-clouds gushing.

Meanwhile, I sat there stunned, my brain still catching up. Sure, I loved escaping into the world of my characters, where crazy things like this happened on a regular basis, but this? This was real life, and I wasn't so sure I was ready to embrace it.

I cringed at the overused cliché, but he wasn't exactly wrong. Billionaire meet-cutes sell. I know this because if you look at my second bookshelf, it's loaded with billionaire romances, contract romances—basically every trope in the book.

And now? Now I'm living it. I'm that girl, only I'm freaking out instead of coolly handling it like the women in those books. They all seem to effortlessly navigate these situations, usually with the help of rich friends or a solid support system, playing pretend and then—bam—falling madly in love.

And what am I?

An aspiring novelist with no actual novel—not even a messy first draft. I'm living paycheck to paycheck just for the privilege of calling Manhattan home. Who needs food or decent clothes when you can walk to work, right? In New York, that's a luxury in itself. If I lived any farther out, I'd be blowing my whole paycheck on cabs and Ubers. So basically, you're either broke, sort of broke, or filthy rich. There's no in-between. Judging by the sad state of my fridge—two apples, a yogurt, and some half-and-half for my coffee—I'm pretty solidly in the broke category.

I don't think I get that happily ever after in this set up. I'm not Cinderella, and this is the real world. Men like him end up married to some trophy wife, which I'm not even close to being. Clearly he had a temporary need, and I was the one to fill it.

"So, are you going to do this? I mean you get new clothes out of it, and since it's him they are going to be very expensive ones," Max said, plopping onto the couch like this was the most normal thing ever. His fresh latte in hand while mine sat cold and abandoned after Alex's little visit.

"Honestly? No idea." I rubbed my temples, feeling one hell of a tension headache blossoming.

Because seriously—what do you do when your life feels like a romance novel, and the plot just threw you off a cliff with no parachute?

I had a notepad in front of me, doing my usual pros and cons list while Max groaned.

"He said we have to look together for his events and obviously my work party since Jake and Lisa think he's my boyfriend, but that could get messy. You know me. I don't exactly think with my brain...and those lips..." My pen hovered over the pro column, then the con. Which would I put kissing him under? He makes me want to melt, and his kissing abilities should be a crime, but also would it make me get attached faster? I can be that pathetic. I write it in the "Not Sure" column in between the two. I'm totally for embracing the gray area when necessary. "Well there will be no post-date sex, that's for sure."

Max shot me a look, his frown so exaggerated it looked like I'd just told him his favorite TV show got canceled.

"He's hot, Vi. Like, down and dirty hot. As his girlfriend for these events and fancy dinners, you might need to help him, you know, relieve some stress."

I glared, shaking my head. "No. Sex." I wrote it down again, underlined it, and then immediately crossed it out. Did he expect sex? Our first real conversation was about orgasms and vanilla dirty talk, after all.

Oh God, what if he thought I was the kind of girl who'd just jump into bed with him because of that conversation?

Panic bubbled up as my stomach did an ungraceful flip. I suddenly realized how I must've come across at that bar—two martinis deep, talking about cocks and dirty talk like I was some expert. This is why I shouldn't be allowed out unsupervised. Two drinks and I'm practically handing out life lessons on bedroom language to strangers.

"He probably picked me because I came off as easy," I groaned, sinking lower into the couch.

Max rolled his eyes, stretching out lazily on the couch, his latte in hand. "You're overthinking. But, fair warning, you will have to kiss him. And if those lips ever touched mine, I think I'd die."

Yeah, me too. Because, honestly, it's all I'd thought about for the past 24 hours.

I shook off the thought. "Okay, so give me some reasons not to do this." My pen tapping on the list and lets just say the cons column needed more love.

Max's nose wiggled—a quirk I've grown to love, signaling his brain was hard at work. "Well," he began, "you could end up not wanting it to end after the holidays, then you will be that pathetic girl clawing at him to not leave her. Of course in the pro column you could add the fact that you get to make Jake think he lost the hottest thing on earth—which, by the way, he did. Annnddd...one of the hottest men in Manhattan scooped you up. It's a win."

Then Max leaned in, a devilish smile on his face. "Plus, let's be real, you're not exactly overflowing with romantic action, so why not ditch the purple friend for the real thing even if its temporary?"

I hated that he knew me so well.

"Yes, but see here?" I point to the "no sex" underlined. "There will be no benefits."

Okay, maybe this will work out. I go on these dates, then I can always look back and say I went out to dinner, wined and dined, and had a billionaire pretend to be the doting boyfriend. Not every woman gets to put that in her brag book for her 20's — so I suppose that's a plus and with my 20's a few months from their expiration, I needed something good to write down for this decade.

He says he doesn't want the drama of a relationship, but relationships still require work — even fake ones. Sure, he's buying me clothes, but Jake and Lisa are going to grill him to death at the party, possibly grill me Monday when I'm at work. I can't go unprepared.

"I need to get to know him better to do this."

"What? Why?"

"Because you know Jake will ask questions on Monday. He's not going to believe I snagged someone like Alex," which makes me frown. Am I really that down on myself? I mean I can attract a good looking man, right? Maybe not Alex level, but still. Close-ish, maybe, okay sort of.

I glanced at the clock. It was already five.

"Crap," I mutter, grabbing my phone. "I should probably tell him I'm doing it."

I stop. Well, I guess I'm doing this then if that was my first thought when I looked at the time. I really hope I don't regret this.

Looking down, I noticed a text from an unknown number waiting for me. My phone had been on silent. Of course.

> Unknown: I'm going to assume from your silence that you're not rejecting my offer and taking it?

My fingers hovered over the screen. Should I really do this? Am I actually doing this? I'm not desperate for a man, but let's be real—a man like him wouldn't go for a girl like me under normal circumstances.

We ran into each other, we're both in a bind, and it just… works out and it's not even dating. We will get what we need from one another socially, and remove the awkwardness of this being a new relationship.

When will I—no, when does anyone—ever get that kind of opportunity?

> Violet: I think so, but is there anyway we could possibly meet up? Jake and Lisa will never believe you and I are dating, and I need at least some info so that when they grill me Monday, let alone Friday at the party, they have no reason to believe we aren't dating and if I can't convince them, I'm not sure how we are supposed to convince anyone else.

> Alex: I suppose. Though no prep needed for my dinner. They don't care enough to ask.

> Violet: Can't wait for that then. When could we meet?

> Alex: What are you doing this evening? Come over and we can chat.

> Violet: Okay, seven work?

> Alex: See you then.

I rushed to the bathroom to shower and change. Forget about that workout I never got to today—I'd gotten enough cardio from running around my apartment in a frenzy just trying to decide what to wear. Even after a shower and a full shampoo, I still looked like a mess.

No, I am a *mess*.

Still wrapped in a towel, I sulked out of the bathroom. "Max, this is stupid. I should call this off. Cancel. Something." I waved my hands dramatically before collapsing onto my bed, which I knew Max had made while I was in the shower. The man hated unmade beds with a passion, and I left them unmade so he could do the one chore I loathed. Win-win in my book.

My hair was still twisted in the towel, and I sighed as I loosened it, brushing through the tangles. My hair was pretty much the metaphor for my life right now—soaked, tangled, and a complete disaster.

I could hear Max mumble something, followed by the scrape of my desk chair before he plopped down beside me.

"I can't do this. I don't belong in his world. I don't even know how to be the kind of woman he'd date going to fancy dinner parties. How would this work? I don't even own clothes that would allow me into those fancier restaurants." My hairbrush caught on a knot, and I cursed under my breath.

Max, ever the fixer, held up a hand for me to stop fussing. He untangled the knot and sat me up, gently brushing my hair for me. "Didn't he say he'd buy you clothes?"

"Yeah, but clothes don't change the fact that I don't fit in," I said, glancing around my tiny apartment. "You saw him, Max. He was wearing a custom three-piece suit, sitting on my thrift-store couch. He doesn't get it—he doesn't know what it's like to live paycheck to paycheck. What am I even going to talk to these people about? They'll go on about their yachts and courtside seats, and I'll be over here talking about how I walk six blocks to work in running shoes and change into heels in the lobby."

"Okay, maybe don't start with that..." Max said, finishing the brushing and dragging me back to the bathroom. He blow-dried my hair, and once it settled into loose waves, he gripped my shoulders, his eyes serious. "Look, you're overthinking this. You are just using him for the party to save face, he's using you to keep up his image. If you don't like how things are going, quit after Friday's party at work. But you definitely can't go to the work party solo—not with Jake and Lisa likely telling everyone you're dating Alexander Bennetti already."

I groaned. He had a point.

Fine. I must at least go to the work party, make my appearance, and make Jake and Lisa eat their words. After that? I could call it off if I didn't like it.

At least, that was the plan.

I let Max do his thing—which meant picking out an outfit and basically playing my personal stylist for the evening. No makeup, though. I hated makeup. It was bad enough that I had to wear it to work ever since Margaret not-so-kindly suggested I "try harder" with my appearance, but I wasn't about to show up at Alexander's place with the intent of impressing. This wasn't a date. I wasn't the type of woman he'd go for anyway. I was just a convenient solution to his problem, and he was one to mine, so the man would have to deal with soaking me up without all the pretties put on for him.

I'd seen enough of the gossip pages to know the kind of woman Alexander actually dated. Tall, blonde, and model-thin. The complete opposite of me. The only asset I had that came close to fitting his type was the one Max was currently wrestling into a bra.

After some back-and-forth, I finally settled on skinny jeans, much to Max's dismay. He kept tossing a sweater dress at me like it was a life-saving raft, hoping I'd grab hold. "You're impossible," he huffed, throwing his hands up in the air dramatically. Max, the master of over-the-top gestures, was in full form tonight.

"You'll thank me later," he grumbled, scooping up the discarded outfit options and hanging them back in my closet like the perfectionist he was. Again, why pick anything up when you know he will?

"Want me to walk you to the subway?"

"I think I'll take an Uber." I slipped on my shoes, checking the time. "I don't know how far the walk is from the subway to his place, and I don't want to risk being late."

Max smirked, raising an eyebrow. "Or staying overnight?"

I shot him a look. "It's not that kind of arrangement."

He raised his hands in surrender, but that mischievous grin stayed firmly planted on his face. "Sure, sure. But if it were..."

"Hopeless," I muttered, grabbing my bag and rushing out the door.

Alex

SHE WAS TEN MINUTES late.

Normally, lateness irks me—time is money, after all. But the second I opened the door and saw her standing there, all my rational thoughts vanished. The cold, calculated part of me? Gone. It wilted like a rose left out in the scorching sun.

Damn. She really was beautiful.

She wore skinny jeans that clung to every inch of her curves, leaving very little to the imagination. A cream sweater hung off one shoulder, teasingly exposing the strap of her bra, and her hair—*that hair*—was loose, wavy, thick, and way too tempting. I'd tangled my hands in it when I kissed her at the bar, feeling its softness slide through my fingers. The thought of doing it again—while doing other things—sent a wave of heat surging through me.

Get it together.

I close million-dollar deals without batting an eye, and here I was, getting thrown off by this woman's presence. Completely unraveled by just a glance.

"Thanks for coming," I said, managing to keep my tone steady. I should've pointed out that she was late—it's what I normally do. I hate having my time wasted. But looking at her now, with those bright green eyes, I couldn't find a shred of irritation.

Odd.

No one else had ever disarmed me like this. No one. Except her, apparently.

"So," I said, closing the door behind her, "you want to get to know me enough to satisfy Ken and Barbie?"

She glanced up briefly, then back to the floor. "Their names are Jake and Lisa," she muttered.

I shrugged. "Ken and Barbie works better." It did. I had a few other names for them too, if she was open to suggestions.

She nodded, but her eyes stayed glued to the floor, as if it was suddenly the most fascinating thing in the room. Endearing, for sure, but that wouldn't fly for long. If she was going to pull this off—if she was going to be my *girlfriend*—she couldn't act like a nervous little doe.

So, I stepped closer, tilting her chin with two fingers, making sure her eyes met mine. Her skin, soft and warm under my touch, did something to me—a punch to the gut, but in a way that left me wanting to be hit again.

"You need to look at me without flinching," I said, my voice low and deliberate. "No one's going to believe you're mine if you act scared."

Mine. God, I liked the sound of that more than I should.

Her lips tightened into a line, a spark of defiance flickering in those green eyes. She pulled back slightly, just enough to make a statement. "I'm not afraid of you."

"Uh huh," I smirked, gesturing for her to follow me inside.

She hesitated just a few steps in, her eyes widening. "Wow."

She stood frozen at the entrance, staring wide-eyed at the floor-to-ceiling windows that framed the entire New York skyline. The view I'd stopped noticing long ago, something I passed by a dozen times a day without a second thought, but watching her take it all in? The awe in her expression, the way her eyes practically sparkled as she absorbed it—it hit me in a way I wasn't prepared for. Suddenly, I felt like the world's most ungrateful bastard.

I'd told people I bought this penthouse for the view, the best in the city. And yet, standing here with her, seeing it through her eyes, I realized I'd never truly appreciated it until now.

I cleared my throat and gave her a quick tour, keeping it brief as if walking her through my multimillion-dollar home was no big deal, but made sure to not come off like some entitled prick. Kitchen, dining room, living room, library—done.

As we made our way down the hallway, I pointed out the guest bedrooms—three of them—and then, for reasons that made no sense to me, I found myself offering them to her. "If you ever need a place to stay, or if we have a late event, you can use one of these rooms," I said casually, like that was a completely normal thing for me to say, which it isn't.

The truth? If she stayed here, I wouldn't want her in a guest room. The thought of her in my bed popped into my head, and I shoved it aside just as quickly.

Get it together, Bennetti.

Shaking off the non-PG thoughts, I continued the tour, leading her to the office, the master suite, and finally, the library. And that's where she stopped dead in her tracks.

She didn't move. Her eyes widened, locking onto the towering bookshelves that stretched two floors high, each one lined with more books than anyone could possibly read in a lifetime. Ladders and staircases wound around the shelves, offering access to every title. Most people were impressed with the view or the state-of-the-art kitchen, but *this*—a library—was what had her captivated.

Her face lit up like she'd stumbled across some kind of hidden treasure. She looked up, her gaze trailing the shelves like she was seeing a piece of herself in every book. The awe in her eyes was so genuine, so pure, that it hit me harder than I expected.

She was mesmerized by a room filled with books, and that said more about her than I'd realized.

She wasn't vanilla. Not even close.

Clearing my throat, I forced myself to look away from her and led us back to the dining room. I pulled out one of the cream-colored chairs, trying to shake off whatever unwanted feelings were floating in my head. Once she sat down, I poured us both a glass of wine, sliding one her way. My hands were steady, but internally? Not as much.

"So, what do you need to know?" I asked, keeping my tone casual, hoping she'd take the wine and not read into the gesture. This wasn't a date—just a simple conversation. *Right?*

I was half-tempted to offer her dinner, but that would make this too... *date-like*. And the last thing I needed was to blur the lines between us any further than they already were — for now at least.

She set her bag on the table, pulling out the signed NDA I'd had a courier deliver earlier. The NDA was non-negotiable in my world. Whether it was one date or a hundred, it was a necessity. I hated making her sign it, but I'd been burned before, and the ashes from that were still falling all around me. I couldn't risk it again.

"What's that?" I nodded toward a piece of paper that had slipped out of her bag along with the NDA.

Her eyes widened slightly. "Oh, that? Nothing." She quickly tried to tuck it back into her bag, but I was faster. Reaching across the table, I placed a finger on the edge of the paper and slid it toward me, ignoring her protests.

The second I saw what it was, a grin tugged at my lips, no matter how hard I tried to contain it.

"A list of terms for accepting my offer?" I raised an eyebrow, but as I scanned the page, I realized it wasn't a list of terms at all. It was a pros and cons list—complete with some rather amusing entries.

And there, nestled among her careful notes, I spotted it. Kissing me. Mentioned more than once, bouncing between the pros, cons, and even a "maybe" column. *Impressive.*

I couldn't help the smile that spread across my face. The situation was absurd, and yet here she was, listing out the pros and cons of *me*.

"Didn't realize I required a whole list of considerations," I said, glancing up at her with a playful smirk. "Though I have to say, I'm curious which side of the list I end up on."

Her cheeks flushed slightly, but there was that defiant spark in her eyes that I was starting to like more than I should. "Don't get too cocky," she said, but there was a hint of a smile threatening to break free.

I leaned back in my chair, watching her, feeling that familiar conflict stirring inside me. She had this way of getting under my skin—like she belonged there, even though I knew there's no reasonable reason she should. The lines between what this was supposed to be and what I *wanted* it to be were already blurring not even a few hours in, and I wasn't sure if that was a good thing or a very, very bad one.

"Ugh, can we not?" She groaned, dropping her head onto her sweater-covered arm in a move that was both irresistible and completely disarming.

"'Hot as sin,'" I read aloud from the pro column, biting back a laugh.

"That was all Max," she replied quickly, her cheeks turning a shade almost as red as the wine in her glass. But there was a playful smile on her lips as she took a sip, not nearly as embarrassed as she wanted me to think.

Then I came across another line that made me pause, a grin tugging at the corners of my mouth. "I'm an 'alpha male controlling type'... and that's listed under the pro column?"

Her teeth sank into her bottom lip, her gaze flickering away. "I forgot about that one."

I raised an eyebrow, intrigued. "What gives you that impression about me?"

She glanced around my penthouse, as if the space itself held all the answers. "You take control of every situation. You had no problem kissing some random woman in a bar — for all you knew I could have kneed you in the balls or broke out the pepper spray. I mean I am in your house, discussing a fake dating arrangement you want to control the narrative about you. For starters..."

Leaning back in my chair, I scanned the list again, holding it up between us. "Interesting analysis. Especially coming from an aspiring author and not a psychologist."

She shrugged, clearly growing more comfortable with each sip of wine. "I read a lot more romance than one probably should."

I glanced back at the paper and couldn't resist reciting another line. "'Won't have to worry about stupid pet names.'"

Her eyes narrowed in mock seriousness. "I'm not going to be anyone's 'Pookie.'"

I couldn't help it—I laughed, a deep, genuine sound I didn't realize I'd been holding back. "Trust me, I couldn't call you that even if I tried."

Her list was ridiculous, yet it had me more entertained than I'd been in a long time. I kept reading through it, but I could feel her eyes on me, tracking every reaction I had to her notes. By now, she was halfway through her glass, the tension of earlier forgotten, and honestly? We were having a lot of fun. More fun than I expected for what started as just an arrangement.

I liked Violet. Probably more than I should, considering how little I actually knew her. Sure, Holmes had dug up the usual background information—things you'd typically learn over the course of a few dates—but that wasn't what drew me in.

There was something about *her*, something real. She didn't see me as some walking solution to her financial issues, even though it was clear she had them. She met my gaze without flinching, challenged me in ways that kept me on my toes, and didn't try to pretend she was anyone other than herself. Even down to her ridiculous pros and cons list, with an entire gray-area column just to decide whether she should take up my offer.

Were there other women like her? Maybe. But something told me the more I got to know Violet Hart, the more I was going to like her—and that could make it complicated or make things great. Jury is still out.

I refilled her wine glass, then mine, and we sat for a moment, both leaning back as we sipped in a silence that was surprisingly comfortable. I wasn't in a suit today—a rarity. Slacks and a button-up shirt felt more appropriate at home. I spent enough time in suits, suffocating through ten-hour meetings six days a week. At least here, with her, I could relax.

"'Can't have sex with him,'" I said, reading the next line from her list as casually as if I were discussing the weather. The line had caught me off guard, though. More interestingly, it was in her middle-ground category, that gray area where she seemed to be debating with herself.

She choked on her wine—almost spitting it out—but managed to hold it together.

"Well," she said, her voice a little strained, "I hope you didn't get that impression from the bar about me..." She bit her bottom lip nervously, that tell of hers again. And, damn, it was an attractive one—one that made me think all kinds of inappropriate things about those lips.

Somewhere in the back of my mind, alarm bells should've been going off. *This is supposed to be an arrangement,* they should've warned. But if they were, I wasn't listening.

"I didn't get that impression," I replied, though the thought had definitely crossed my mind. I'm a man, after all.

"These are just dates," she continued, twisting her wine glass between her fingers. "I'm not expecting anything beyond that. No... invites up for coffee or nightcaps afterward."

I should've felt relieved. But for some reason, hearing her say there'd be nothing beyond the dates—nothing beyond the act we were putting on—didn't sit well with me. It should've, but it didn't, because right now it's obvious I've put myself in a corner. Skipping my plan of just asking her out on a date sort of eliminates half of the benefits of *actual* dating.

Her bottom lip was back between her teeth, and I had to shift in my seat, reminding myself—*and my body*—that now was definitely not the time to think what was stirring up in my mind right now. The way her fingers absentmindedly trailed up and down the stem of her wine glass wasn't helping either. Did she have any idea how incredibly seductive the simplest things she did were?

Probably not. The innocence in her actions told me she had no clue just how maddeningly attractive she was. How she could drive me crazy without even trying—and I barely knew her.

And that was the problem. I *wanted* to know her. It wasn't just her beauty, though God knows that was a factor. She was sharp—really sharp.

She was also two years into prepping for law school before she switched majors, which explained why her student loans were sky-high.

And now? She was stuck as a glorified assistant for Hartley. A woman like her, running for someone else's coffee? That didn't sit right with me. No woman of mine—whether she was mine for two dates or a hundred—was going to be fetching lattes. She deserved to have coffee brought to *her*. A bit overboard to think, but the thought was there all the same.

"Maybe we should put that in writing," she said, breaking through my thoughts.

I blinked. "Put what in writing?"

She gave me a sly smile, one that made my pulse quicken. "The no-sex thing."

No sex. Yeah, right. "Oh no, I don't think we need to be that official," I said smoothly, lying through my teeth even though the truth was crystal clear. Ever since our lips had collided in that bar, it was all I could think about. And now, with her sitting here, so close, in my penthouse, I couldn't stop the vivid images flashing through my mind—picking her up, laying her across this table, and showing her just how far from vanilla I really was — not tonight, but eventually.

Still, there was no way I was putting that agreement on paper. I never signed an agreement I couldn't keep, and knowing Violet for less than 24 hours? There was no way I could hold up my end of a *no-sex rule* if the opportunity presented itself.

I'm a man of my word after all.

"So, we're still on for Friday?" she asked, her voice light but with a hint of nerves beneath it.

I nodded. "Yeah, but first, we've got Tuesday. Dinner with a few of my colleagues. They're all married, and their wives will be there, so you'll be my date." That was one of the reasons this idea worked. A fancy, quadruple-date situation with investors who all expected me to look more "settled." Apparently, in their eyes, a stable relationship was proof I was trustworthy enough to handle millions. Go figure.

I watched the color drain from her face, her fingers tightening around the stem of her wine glass. "I'm not really used to fancy business dinners."

"You don't need to be," I said, my voice softening in a way I don't normally do. "Really you show up, make small talk, and there is barely five minutes of actual business. Just be yourself. Maybe leave out some of the info you shared at the bar though..." I really couldn't help myself.

She crossed her legs, shifting in her seat, and tossed her long, wavy hair over her shoulder. The movement exposed the smooth skin of her collarbone and shoulder, and I couldn't help but stare for a second longer than I should have. Her skin was so fair, dusted with faint freckles that made her all the more captivating. She barely wore any makeup, but she didn't need it. She was flawless. It'd be a crime to cover her up.

Most women I knew wouldn't dream of stepping outside without layers of makeup, but Violet? She could walk out with nothing on her face and still turn heads. And all I could think was how *Ken*—that asshole from the bar—must've been the one to break her self-confidence. Those fleeting bits here and then you see of her doubting herself because of that idiot's thoughts. If only she knew the way people looked at her—the way I couldn't stop looking at her.

"So," she said, breaking the silence, "we should probably talk about the backstory of this little relationship." She glanced up at me, her expression more focused now. "You know, how we met, how long we've been dating, any details we can figure out so people buy it. And I guess we'll figure out how to end it when the time comes." She frowned slightly at that last part, and I hated it. I knew exactly why, too.

I leaned back, smirking just enough to ease the tension. "Just make sure you tell Ken and Barbie you dumped me when it's over." I hoped it would give her some leverage, a way to keep the upper hand.

But in the back of my mind, something about that "when it's over" stuck with me. And I wasn't sure I liked where it was heading.

"Okay... how did we meet?" she asked, her brow furrowed as if she was actually trying to work out the logistics of this fake relationship.

"At the bar?" I shrugged. "I mean, it's true."

"And so cringe-worthy." She waved a hand up and down, gesturing at me like I was some untouchable god. "You think anyone's going to believe that a man like you would pick up someone like me at a bar?"

Did she really not know how gorgeous she was?

The way her face fell after she said that told me everything. *No, she really doesn't.*

I would've hit on her in a heartbeat, because I did just that. The fact that Ken and Barbie offered up a convenient excuse to get closer and see where things could go was icing on the cake. It wasn't even about saving her from embarrassment with her ex—it was about getting to know her, this intriguing woman who fascinated me in a way I couldn't quite explain.

But none of that was anything I could say aloud since this plan was already in motion. *Yeah, keep it cool, jackass.*

"So, how *did* we meet?" I ask.

She thought for a second. "Your gym?"

"Have one at home."

"Your favorite coffee shop?"

"My assistant handles that, and I don't even know where it is."

"The park?"

"I don't do nature."

She sighed, rolling her eyes. "Okay, fine. Bar it is. But can we leave out the part about exactly how we came together in that bar?"

"Sure," I said, amused. That wasn't exactly the story I wanted to tell either. It was a story that belonged to us only, and I liked that.

"Next... how long have we been dating?"

"A month," I answered without missing a beat, my attention drifting to an email on my phone.

She gave me a look. "Wow, you had that ready to go."

I glanced up and smiled cautiously. "I may have been telling my board I was in a relationship for a month, so... no wiggle room there." I flashed a grin—a rare, boyish smile that wasn't really my thing. And yet here I was, smiling for *her*. A woman I met in a bar, pretended to be her boyfriend for a night, and now, here we were planning a fake relationship to get through my corporate dinner and her company party. It was... surreal.

What was even more surprising? She didn't seem fazed by who I was at all. Her confidence only wavered when it came to her worth, but she wasn't nervous about being around me for who I was — and I wanted to know why.

Most women either feared me because of my family name or wanted me *because* of it. Violet? She didn't care about any of that. She wasn't here for the Bennetti name or the money. She was just... *her*, and somehow that unnerved me in the best way possible.

"Okay, and the reason no one has seen us together for a whole month?" Violet asked, her brows furrowing as she tried to piece together the story.

I leaned back, considering. "I'm followed constantly. People are always trying to snap photos of me. It'll be easy enough to say we've kept things quiet to avoid the press. No one will question that. Trust me."

She nodded slowly, absorbing the information. "Are we serious? In this relationship, I mean."

I sighed, running a hand through my hair. "I don't know. Are people serious after a month?"

She winced slightly. "Yeah... I'm not exactly the best judge of relationship timelines."

I let out a dry chuckle. "Same here. Hence, this whole situation."

"So, at this dinner... they'll already know about me?" Her voice had a mix of nerves and curiosity.

I paused. This was where things got tricky. "Well, like I said, my board had... concerns. Ridiculous ones, but they exist. So yeah, they'll already know you as the woman I've been dating for a month. You'll be expected at any future functions, too. And the same goes for your work party. Oh, and my younger brother will be there Tuesday since he's the COO of my company, but he will be the only one that knows the truth."

She blinked, processing. "Okay, that works... I guess."

I glanced back at my phone, typing out an email, but truthfully? I wasn't paying attention to a single word on the screen. Those green eyes of hers were making it hard to think straight, let alone concentrate. I was going to need to master the art of avoiding eye contact if I wanted to keep my self-control intact.

"Anything else?" I asked, pretending to be focused on the email while trying not to stare at her like a fool.

She shook her head. "I suppose not. What time is this dinner on Tuesday?"

"Seven," I replied, finally looking up. My gaze roamed over her, lingering just long enough for my thoughts to stray before I snapped back to reality. "I'll make sure a dress is sent to you before then. Do you know your size?"

Her cheeks flushed slightly. "Uh, I've never been officially fitted for a dress. But I think I have an old bridesmaid dress in my closet. I can check the size and text it to you."

"Perfect," I said, standing up. I offered her my hand, helping her to her feet. It was late, and I didn't want her to leave... but I also didn't want her to stay. The longer she lingered, the more my self-control slipped, and I wasn't ready to deal with what that meant.

"So, I guess I'll see you Tuesday night then, Alexander." Her voice was soft, her lips curving into a small smile as she turned to head to the door.

When she stood, I instinctively joined her, my hands finding her arms and pulling her flush against me. Her breath hitched slightly as I leaned closer, my voice low. "Alex," I whispered, correcting her.

"Right, Alex," she repeated with a teasing smirk. "Figured an alpha male like you would prefer Xander." The corner of my mouth twitched, almost laughing.

"Sorry," she added, her voice a little rushed and those cheeks practically crimson, "I read too many romance novels. The whole 'alpha male' persona is one of the hottest sellers, and you'd fit right in, with all the, uh, other... things you have going on." Her eyes trailed down my body, not touching me but leaving a trail of heat in their wake.

Hell, she was cute. *Too cute.*

"I've always been called Alex by family and friends," I said, feeling my voice soften, despite myself. "And now you. My girlfriend. If anyone hears you call me Alexander, they'll never believe we're together."

"Fair enough," she murmured, her hand drifting up to smooth my dress shirt. Her fingers lingered, tracing the fabric as they slid lower, and I swore, something as simple as that made me harder than the damn granite table in the dining room.

"I'll see you Tuesday, Alex," she said, her lips curving into a smile that made it hard to think straight.

I nearly grabbed her again, wanting nothing more than to kiss her—*really* kiss her—but I knew that was a terrible idea. Instead, I forced myself to place a gentle kiss on her cheek, lingering just long enough to make her pulse quicken. Then I stepped back, walking her to the door.

"One of my drivers is downstairs," I said as I opened it. "He'll take you home."

Her mouth opened, probably to protest, but I wasn't about to let her leave in a cab or some random rideshare. Not from my house. That's when it hit me. "From now on, you'll have a driver. As my girlfriend, it's expected."

"Even if we've only been dating a month?"

She had a point. No one in my past relationships had ever gotten that kind of treatment — including my ex-fiance. But for Violet—who wasn't even really my girlfriend—she was going to get it all.

"Even if it's *only* been a month."

She nodded, accepting it without further argument, and walked toward the elevator.

"Night," she called over her shoulder, giving a little wave as the doors shut.

I leaned against the cool metal surface of the door, smacking my head lightly against it. *Is there a way to see her before Tuesday?*

Talking with her tonight—about the stupidest things, no less—was more fun than I'd had in years. The idea of waiting 72 hours to see her again just didn't sit right with me.

And then it hit me. *She needs a dress and some clothes...*

Violet

I WAS JUST SETTLING in to attempt working on my novel. By that, I mean sitting in front of the screen, reading the last few sentences I'd written, and then dropping my forehead onto the keyboard, silently willing something—*anything*—to magically type itself out.

Writer's block.

A very real, very unfair force.

You can have a million ideas buzzing around in your head, but the second you sit down to spin them into a story the world might actually want to read, your mind decides to blank. The cursor on the screen blinks at you, mocking, taunting, while your ideas hover just out of reach. It's like trying to grab smoke.

I stared at the screen, hoping—*begging*—for inspiration to strike, but nothing came. Just more frustration. The harder I tried, the more the words slipped away.

Defeated, I leaned back in my chair, wallowing in that too familiar sense of failure that hits me every time I try to write.

And then—ping—my phone lit up with a notification.

Thank God. A distraction. Honestly, at this point, I welcomed it because clearly, this novel wasn't happening today.

> Alex: Hey, I was thinking—you need dresses for Tuesday and Friday. What if I took you shopping today?

My heart skipped a beat. He wants to take me shopping? I had just assumed a dress would show up with one of those *"Wear this"* notes. Nothing too personal.

> Violet: Sure, if you want, of course. I know you're busy.

Alex: Not today. And I told you I'd handle clothes for my events. Can you be ready in an hour? I'll set up an appointment with a private shopper.

Violet: Sure, see you then.

The moment the text conversation ended, I called Max. He was at the gym, but this was too important to wait.

"Oh my God, it's like Pretty Woman!" I can only hope there are not a ton of people around this man at the gymn right now as he says it.

"I'm not a hooker, Max!"

"I know, I know," he said with a dramatic sigh. "I meant the shopping, obviously. I can only imagine the designers you're about to try on. Do you realize the dresses he buys are more expensive than our rent?"

I groaned. "Not helping my nerves here..."

"Right, sorry. Okay, focus. Wear the navy pencil skirt with the light blue blouse and a sweater. It's classy enough for wherever he's taking you to shop without looking like you tried too hard."

I let out a breath. "What would I do without you?"

"Walk around horribly dressed and ruin my reputation as your best friend," he quipped, and I could practically hear him shuddering on the other end.

Rolling my eyes, I hung up, grinning. Max always knew how to make me feel better, even when I felt like I was about to dive headfirst into something completely out of my league.

And let's be honest—shopping with Alex Bennetti definitely felt like new, uncharted territory.

I walked out of my apartment, fully expecting to hail a cab, when I spotted a sleek black Lexus parked out front. Leaning against it was a man in an expensive suit, looking like he was straight out of a James Bond movie -- dark sunglasses and all. The moment he saw me, he straightened up, nodding in my direction. Definitely not the same driver Alex had sent to take me home last night.

"Good morning, Miss Hart," he greeted me in a deep, professional voice.

This was New York. You trust no one. Especially not in Manhattan. People here could charm you with a smile and stab you in the back before you even blinked. Snakes in suits, every last one of them.

I gave him a once-over, my instincts on high alert. Tattoos crawled up his knuckles, barely peeking out from his pristine white collar, and his sheer size was... intimidating, to say the least. This guy was massive—like he could bench press a car and not break a sweat. I wasn't tall by any means, but he towered over me in both height and width. If he wanted, he could probably crunch me into a ball and toss me like a child's toy.

"And you would be...?" I asked, crossing my arms in an attempt to look unimpressed.

Intimidation wasn't exactly my forte—I was no Margaret Thatcher—but I gave it my best shot.

Before he could answer, the passenger door swung open, and Alex stepped out. There he is, in a perfectly tailored three-piece suit, hair styled just right, and those ridiculously blue eyes locking onto me... it was unfair.

No one should be that good-looking. I wanted to file a complaint with the genetic lottery because clearly, there was a conspiracy going on here. It's like all the attractive genes had been hoarded by people like him—and whatever secret skincare routine half the women in Manhattan were using to pass for 25, but really they're 50. Where do I sign up for that?

"Antonio is my driver," Alex said smoothly, interrupting my internal rant. Something about the way he said it made me think Antonio did more than just drive. Bodyguard, perhaps? "I thought it'd be better if I picked you up, make sure we weren't late."

He gestured for me to get into the car with a gentlemanly sweep of his arm, and I slid inside, feeling a little too aware of how perfect everything seemed around him. He closed the door behind me with a soft click, and as Antonio walked around to the driver's side.

There was no way a man that size could possibly be comfortable in the driver's seat of a Lexus, but somehow, he made it work. Because apparently, in Alex Bennetti's world, everything just... worked.

Alex slid in next to me, settling into the seat without a word. As Antonio pulled away from the curb, I couldn't help but wonder if Alex was regretting offering to take me shopping himself. It's not like he had to. But here we were, and I couldn't shake the nerves that came with the idea of stepping into some fancy couture shop. Whether it was his money or not, I had zero idea what I was supposed to buy, and shopping alone in a place like that? No, thank you. Oddly enough, despite only knowing him for 48 hours, I felt more comfortable with Alex there.

For most of the drive, he was glued to his phone, his fingers tapping away like he was conducting some major corporate deal from the back seat. He might very well be. I'm not really sure how these CEO types work, but I assume they work at all hours and never heard of a day off. Out of nowhere, he leaned forward, grabbing something from Antonio and not saying a word, he handed me a coffee cup and a bag, his eyes fixed on his phone.

Inside the bag? A blueberry muffin. I blinked, surprised.

"Oh, thank you," I said, but all I got in return was a small, distracted hum. Not exactly the same guy from last night, but I brushed it off, turning my attention to the window.

Manhattan never stopped. Not even on a Sunday. The streets were still packed, traffic as chaotic as ever, and while you saw more tourists out, there were always people in business attire, heading off to who knows what. As much as Alex was preoccupied with his phone, I could tell he'd probably rather be in the office right now.

"So... how does this whole private shopping thing work?" I finally broke the silence, mostly because the sound of me trying to discreetly devour the world's best blueberry muffin was getting awkward. Seriously, where did he find this thing? It was perfectly sugared on top, fluffy as a cloud, and so delicious I had to stop myself from moaning like an idiot. I mean, I'd started the day with a sad little banana. Payday was still a few days away, which meant my meals had consisted of apples, bananas, and protein shakes. I know the cliché is that Manhattan women survive on minimal carbs, but me? I needed bread, frosting, and whatever magical carbs were in this muffin to live.

Alex finally clicked his phone shut, tucking it into his pocket before turning to face me. "I'm assuming you don't have experience with it?" His tone was teasing, those eyes scanning me as if he already knew the answer.

I glanced down at my outfit and shrugged, waving a hand over myself. "I think we both know the word couture has never come near my wardrobe."

He smiled, his gaze trailing over me in a way that made me acutely aware of every detail of my outfit. I had tried—really tried—to dress up for this. My nicest pair of black strappy heels? Check. Because, of course, that's what fancy women wear to private shopping boutiques, right? Max had picked out my outfit, and I trusted him to make sure I looked polished. But standing next to Alex, wrapped in his expensive, custom-tailored suit, I felt like a kid playing dress-up.

I mean, my go-to for clothes is Bloomingdale's, but only during their sales. I've never stepped foot into a high-end boutique that wasn't attached to a department store. And Target? Well, we have a bit of a bestie relationship. It's where I've mastered the art of looking cute without actually spending half my paycheck.

Margaret, in all her condescending glory, never missed a chance to point out when my wardrobe looked Target-like, but then I would gently counter with how surprised I was to hear she knew what Target carried. Hey, you can't say its from the store without going in, so she was a closet Target shopper and didn't want to admit it.

When the car pulled to a stop, I looked up at a towering building made of glass and intricate stonework, the kind of place that screamed, money lives here. The doorman was already holding the lobby doors open, and before I could even reach for the handle, Antonio was out of the car, opening my door with a practiced ease and holding out his large hand to help me out. I was instantly grateful because, let's be honest, my heels were not exactly sidewalk-friendly.

Standing next to him this close, even in my heels, Antonio was a giant. If he was a bodyguard—and let's be real, he had to be—there wasn't a person crazy enough to try messing with him. This man could snap bones like toothpicks. Yet, somehow, his kind smile and gentle eyes didn't match the mountain of muscle he carried.

I decided then and there that he was just a giant teddy bear in disguise. A teddy bear that, apparently, carried a gun tucked neatly under his perfectly pressed suit jacket.

Teddy bears carry guns, right? Sure, why not.

Alex slid out from the car and placed his hand on the small of my back, nudging me forward. The doorman nodded, like they were old friends, and Alex led us to a set of gold elevator doors.

Suddenly, nerves hit. Hard. I didn't belong in places like *this*.

Sure, my family was full of lawyers, but if we were on the class ladder of Manhattan, we'd be hanging onto the bottom rungs for dear life. My parents weren't exactly broke, but they weren't rolling in millions either. Both human rights attorneys, they spent more time fighting for others than padding their own bank accounts. Ironic for a family that enjoyed putting their child down, but spent their lives lifting others up.

Their emotional support crumbled when I changed my major from pre-law one year into undergrad and dropped that bombshell over Christmas dinner. Yeah, that went over well. Mom cried. Dad cursed and threatened to cut me off if I didn't return to pre-law. But I stuck to my guns, declaring that I'd be a famous author someday. I'd work for a publisher while I write novels. They should've thanked me, honestly. By switching careers, I saved them a ton of money in law school tuition. Not that they saw it that way.

No, in true supportive parent fashion, they called it a stupid dream. Told me if I wanted to survive, I'd have to do it without their financial help. And so, I did. I paid for the rest of school myself, and I'd be paying off those student loans until I was dead and buried.

I couldn't help but wonder how much Alex knew about me. He knew I wanted to be a writer, knew where I worked, knew my phone number and address. I mean, how embarrassing is that? He gets to dig through my dirty laundry for a deal he proposed, and I'm left in the dark about him.

Seems fair, right?

The elevator kept dinging, and with each chime, my nerves kicked up a notch. Forty-five floors? Seriously?

I glanced at Alex, who was, of course, glued to his phone, oblivious to my rising panic. "What floor is this appointment on?" I asked, trying to keep my voice steady.

Without looking up, he answered, "33rd," while still typing away like the machine he was.

Great. Only 24 floors of anxiety to go.

My palms were clammy, and I kept shaking them, hoping a little air might magically dry them out. It didn't help. The walls felt like they were inching closer, boxing me in with each ding of another floor passed.

I hated places like this. They screamed classy, and I screamed... not.

I couldn't shake the feeling that I didn't belong. Maybe it was the whole posh atmosphere reminding me of my parents and their constant disappointment. Or maybe it was just the overwhelming pretentiousness oozing from every corner. Either way, I felt like I was in way over my head.

By the time we hit the 30th floor, I couldn't hold it in anymore. I turned to him, words spilling out faster than I could stop them. "Look, it's not that I'm not grateful, because I really am, but I don't know if I'm the right girl for this whole dating experiment of yours. I mean, I don't even know what couture is. I've never bought shoes that cost more than $200... okay, let's be real—$50. Which is probably what you spend on hair products—no offense, because your hair looks amazing—but still."

Alex sighed, finally putting his phone away, crossing his arms as he leaned against the elevator wall, clearly settling in for my rant.

"I don't belong here. People who come to these places? They're rich. Like you. They look like you. Not me. And they'll treat me like crap. I've seen the movies, I know how this goes—the rich people look down on the commoners. And guess what? I'm a commoner. If this were medieval times, I'd be the bar wench, not the princess. Hell, I see it at my own job, and I work with book nerds! They dress all nice, and my two-year-old shoes stick out like a sore thumb."

I noticed the slight smirk tugging at the corner of his mouth, and that's when I saw them—dimples. Great. As if he needed to be more attractive.

"They'll treat you just fine. Trust me," he said infuriatingly calm.

I shook my head. "You don't know that. You've never been... like me. They always talk down to you, or give you that look. I really can't handle going into a place where I'll be judged and dressed up like a charity project."

Before I could ramble any further, Alex pushed off the wall, closing the distance between us just as the elevator dinged at the 31st floor. His body was suddenly right in front of mine, pinning me in place as I backed up into the wall, his fingers gripped my chin, forcing me to look at him.

"People like that?" His voice was low, dangerous and somehow velvet smooth. "They don't work anywhere I go. You may be wearing last year's, or two years ago's fashion, but do you know what anyone in there will actually be talking about?"

I opened my mouth to argue, but his grip tightened, keeping my eyes locked on his, and my heart fluttered traitorously.

Focus, Violet.

"You. They'll be talking about you," he said in a voice that felt like a warm minky blanket swaddling me. "You're gorgeous. No, look at me." His fingers tilted my chin up, his blue eyes burning into mine like he meant every word. "No woman in there will even come close to comparing to you. And when you walk in with me? Every single one of them will be jealous and kiss your ass like you're the Queen of fucking England."

I swallowed, my brain short-circuiting for a second, while I tried to wrap my head around his words. For a moment, I almost believed him. *Almost.*

I nodded, and Alex pulled back giving me some much-needed breathing room. I swear the elevator has shrunk by at least a foot.

"Can I, I don't know, pay you back for the outfits?" I blurted out. "I mean, you buying me clothes feels... like a lot. What exactly are you getting out of this deal? I'm getting expensive clothes, a boost at work, and you as my arm candy. My boss might actually notice me for once."

Alex's jaw tightened, a low growl rumbling from his throat. He glanced at his phone, clearly ready to respond to the endless pings I heard go off in those few minutes he spoke to me, but instead, he looked right at me. "Trust me, I'm getting plenty."

I blinked. "Like what?"

The elevator dinged open to the 33rd floor, and Alex stepped out, holding the door for me. I'm pretty sure I heard him mutter, "Thank fuck," under his breath while he took his exit..

I followed him. "Are you not a morning person or something?"

His jaw clenched tighter, his expression unreadable. This was not the relaxed, charming Alex I'd met at the bar.

"No offense," I continued, wiggling my finger at him, "but this version of Alex? Not my favorite. I much preferred the one who stuck his tongue down my throat less than 48 hours ago."

That got him.

His eyes darkened, lips twitching into a half-smile, but I couldn't tell if he was fighting the urge to laugh or bite back a retort, and before he could do either we were interrupted.

A woman glided up to us, flawless in a black dress and heels that looked painful just by glancing at them. Her long black hair was sleek, but the amount of makeup on her face was... a lot. Like, does her face feel heavy with all that? It has to.

"Mr. Bennetti, we're so thrilled to have you here today," she cooed, clasping her hands together like she was greeting the owner. Wait, did he own this place? "Is this her?" Her eyes widened while she looked me over, as if she'd found a hidden gem. "Oh, aren't you just gorgeous!" She beamed, not even glancing at my clearly out-of-place outfit. "Come, come! We have the VIP suite ready for you."

VIP suite? For shopping? Really?

As we moved forward, I caught sight of the sign above the entrance: Elite Couture.

Wow, that's some elite creativity right there. But I bit my tongue as the woman—Kirsty, she introduced herself—clicked her way ahead of us with surprising speed for someone wearing five-inch heels.

I followed Kirsty, noticing that the shop wasn't laid out like a typical store. There were racks, sure, but they were tucked away, clearly for the sales associates to use and not the shoppers, while the walls were lined with doors. Doors that, I assumed, led to these suites for personal shopping. Fancy.

As we passed by a few women, I braced myself for the usual judgmental stares, but nope. No bitchy glances my way. Instead, they were all fixated on the man walking next to me. Alex, with his hand on my back, completely oblivious to the whispers and ogling. Yeah, I get it, ladies. He's drool-worthy. I bet they were all trying to figure out how the hell a girl like me ended up with a guy like him.

If only they knew...

Kirsty led us to a suite in the back corner. On the way, I noticed some doors labeled "Shopping Suite" while others were marked "VIP." So, apparently, even personal shopping has tiers? Good to know.

"Here we are!" Kirsty chirped, opening the door. The VIP shopping suite was like something straight out of a movie—plush velvet couches arranged in a circle around a small pedestal, surrounded by floor-to-ceiling mirrors. Racks of gowns were already lined up along the walls, and an entire table was dedicated to shoes, their lids popped off and boxes propped up. And then there was... lingerie. A whole table of it.

I shot a glance at Alex, ready to ask if he was seriously planning on picking out my underwear for these events too. But, of course, he was already sitting down, eyes glued to his phone, completely unbothered by the table full of lace and silk.

Typical.

"Alright, Mr. Bennetti made it clear he wants nothing but the best for you," Kirsty chirped, her voice brimming with more enthusiasm than I prefer this early in the day. "We'll need to pick out two evening gowns, shoes, and of course, matching lingerie. Plus, a few outfits for dining and day-to-day wear. So, where do you want to start?"

I stood there, still absorbing the room, feeling like I'd stumbled into some kind of Cinderella dream sequence. Did I just time travel into a fairy tale?

Pinching my arm to make sure this wasn't some elaborate hallucination, I winced at the little sting. Nope, definitely real.

"Uh... you choose," I stammered, totally overwhelmed by the sheer volume of it all.

How many outfits was Alex buying me? And lingerie? How was that part of the deal? Sure my cotton boy short undies weren't screaming high-end fashion, but I'm not flashing my little lady at any of these events, and if Alex thinks he's going to see me out of anything that covers my body, he's mistaken. I'm not making that kind of deal here.

"Okay, we'll start with these," she chirped. "See what works, what doesn't, and then we'll move on to matching shoes. Oh, and I went ahead and added a new set of un-derwear and a bra. They'll work better with the gowns." Her perfectly manicured red nail pointed to a lacy black thong and a strapless bra that looked more decorative than functional—barely enough fabric to cover, well, anything.

With a wave and the click of her heels, I was left alone to change. Fantastic.

I peeled off my clothes, stuffing my underwear and bra into my purse, and reluctantly picked up the lace thong and bra. People actually wear these? To my surprise, the material was soft and oddly comfortable. I wasn't exactly a thong girl—team boy shorts all the way. Sexy without venturing into granny panty territory.

Thongs? Way too personal. Yet, this one didn't feel as awkward as it looked. Maybe rich people had some kind of magic fabric specifically designed to make things riding up your ass feel luxurious.

Once I got the underwear situated, I grabbed the first dress. A sleek black evening gown with sheer, sparkly fabric on top. It had two thin straps and crisscrossed at the back, hugging every curve like the fabric was overpriced human-grade clingwrap.

Taking one more second to tuck my boobs in, even though they still felt at high risk for a slip, I stepped out for the big reveal.

Kirsty cooed the second she saw me, practically swooning like a proud mamma. Mean-while, Alex—who hadn't looked up from his phone once—gave a nod of approval. Not that I needed his opinion, but still. It was his money, so that was technically what he was here for. Not to, you know, watch me try on clothes.

Right?

I tried on a few more dresses, rejecting the ones that just weren't me—no matter how trendy they were. Some things I just refused to wear. Kirsty, on the other hand, was relentless, bringing in wave after wave of new outfits.

At this point, the bra had been swapped for some sort of corset top—strapless, of course—that somehow made my breasts look like they were defying gravity. And hon-estly? It was impressive.

But after a few more gowns, I was starving, thirsty, and losing steam fast. A headache was threatening to burst out from behind my temples, no doubt from all the undressing, redressing, and trying to figure out how to breathe in a corset. To be honest, I didn't realize corsets were still a thing. I was wrong there.

Why did I ever like playing dress-up as a kid? As an adult, this was full-on torture. If someone wanted to extract top-secret information from me, all they'd have to do is shove me in a dressing room and make me try on outfits for a few hours.

Forget waterboarding. Try endless outfits made by Chanel and Prada. I'd crack in minutes.

"I'll have the team bring in some drinks and snacks," Kirsty said before disappearing again. "We've still got a lot for you to try on."

I barely contained a groan. More? Please, no.

None of these clothes had price tags. Odd, but I guess when you're swimming in money, you don't need them. You just buy and trust that whatever astronomical number they throw at you is right.

Must be nice.

I tried to soak it all in, telling myself this was a once-in-a-lifetime experience. But after what felt like the tenth dress, I was losing patience. I'd paraded at least a dozen outfits in front of Alex, and all I got was a nod while he stayed glued to his phone.

It was starting to feel like I was putting on a show for the furniture and Kirsty and he was only here to help circulate oxygen.

Alex

I DIDN'T HAVE THAT much work to do. Most of my emails were handled last night, but I needed a distraction. A serious one.

Because while Violet is beautiful, I don't think she realizes just how unreasonably sexy her body is. Those curves, those hips, that ass... It's criminal. And the fact that she's in that dressing room trying on lingerie—lingerie I specifically requested—has me two seconds away from losing my mind.

When I added the lingerie to the list, it wasn't supposed to be for me. It was about making sure that any woman of mine wore the finest, from her heels to her... well, everything. And yet, here I am, sitting in this overly cushy chair, blood boiling, thinking about her in every single piece. My mind running wild, picturing her wearing each and every one of those scraps of lace that were laid out on the table. No man can see a lingerie buffet and keep his mind out of the gutter.

Damn, maybe they are for me.

No, stop. They're for her. Not me. Definitely not for me. I had to remind myself that multiple times because every part of me wanted to see her step out in those delicate pieces and nothing else. Wanted to watch her, wanted her to know how absolutely breathtaking she is.

And then there's the real problem—I want her. More than I've wanted anyone in a long time. Kissing her in that bar? It lit something in me I thought had burned out. I hadn't felt this pull, this hunger for a woman, in... hell, I don't even know how long. Sure, I'd scratch the itch when necessary, but it's been months. I'm not one of those guys who has a constant rotation of one-night stands to get by.

Work, the gym, that's been enough for me.

But her lips—that taste. It's like they're haunting me. I've kissed her twice, and now she's in my head, in my dreams, and during a few very private moments in the shower with nothing more than my hand and a lot of dirty thoughts I'd probably feel guilty about if I had a normal person's moral compass.

This deal we made? The one where we pretend for the cameras and our mutual benefit? I was seriously considering calling it off this morning because something about her was getting under my skin. Something that told me the more time I spent with her, the deeper I'd fall. And I wasn't ready for that.

This morning, in that elevator, I was two seconds away from losing all self-control. From kissing her and showing her exactly how sexy she is. Every thread of restraint I had was used up.

And now? My tank is completely empty.

Keep your shit together.

My new mantra that I'd repeat between heavy inhales and exhales or whatever that meditation bullshit does.

I knew the second she walked into that bar, I should've stayed away. And yet, I couldn't. No woman who catches my attention that quickly, who makes me claim her in public where I could be easily photographed, is someone to mess with. Not with my reputation.

I was half-joking with her about not needing to put the no-sex clause in writing, but the truth? Part of me knew that if I let myself get close—if I gave in—I'd be so deep inside her, so lost in the feel of her, that I wouldn't come up for air. She's the kind of woman who wouldn't just be a one-night stand or a fling. No, she's the type who pulls you under and never lets you back up. The kind that wraps around you until you're drowning in her.

And the worst part? I wanted to drown.

That realization was grating on every nerve I had. I barely knew her, only 48 hours, and already I could tell that Violet wasn't someone I could just sleep with and walk away from. She'd bury herself under my skin, drop me into a bottomless pit of emotions I didn't have time for. Emotions I hadn't let surface in years.

But here I am, craving her in a way that's both intoxicating and terrifying.

After going through her file, a thousand questions kept nagging at me. Not just the basics—her favorite color or her coffee order—but the deeper things. Why was she estranged from her family? Why had she given up on law school? Each question was a distraction. A way to keep myself from thinking about things I shouldn't. Things I couldn't afford to let myself imagine.

Crossing that line would ruin everything. It'd either destroy this agreement we have or it'd push me into a place I'm not ready to go—somewhere vulnerable, somewhere dangerously close to a relationship. And I've been there before. I know the scars it leaves behind. I won't go down that road again unless I'm damn sure. Like there's going to be a neon sign flashing in front of me, telling me that Violet is the one.

But for now? Denial is easier.

I stick to my phone, trying to focus on work, ignoring the pull she has over me. My thumbs tap out a meeting schedule, my mind doing its best to keep up. Then I hear it. The soft click of the dressing room door opening.

Violet steps out.

And I know I'm screwed.

"Question for you, Alex." Her voice came from behind me, but I didn't turn around, trying to keep my focus on the email in front of me, and not the fact she might not be dressed completely behind me.

"Mmmhmmm?" I mumbled, hoping my distraction would work. No such luck.

"Are these really the types of things you want your girlfriend wearing in public?"

Groaning, I finally gave in and turned—and immediately regretted it. She stood there in an evening dress that clung to her like it was painted on, hitting mid-thigh, with heels so high they had to be illegal. The straps on that dress were doing absolutely nothing to keep the material in place, not that it mattered. The damn thing hugged every curve of her body tighter than saran wrap.

I swallowed hard, my throat suddenly dry. Every nerve in my body lit up, and I had to force myself to stay composed. This was not the kind of thing I wanted Violet wearing anywhere.

"Absolutely not," I growled, my jaw clenched.

Unless it's in my penthouse, then yeah—every fucking day.

Her ass in that dress? It was criminal. The way the fabric stretched over her hips, her legs, and those curves... I could practically hear myself internally combust. What was I paying these people to do? Dress her like a walking fantasy?

"Yeah, didn't think so," she muttered, glancing down at herself. "I feel a little too on display."

Very on display.

Even her breasts were damn near spilling out of that thing, and I couldn't handle the visual any longer. It was torture.

"Okay, so this zipper..." She gestured to the back of the dress. "It's got a weird catch, and Kirsty's off somewhere gathering more clothes, but can you help me with it?"

Before I could respond, she'd already disappeared into the dressing room. I stuffed my phone in my pocket, mentally cursing everything in the universe for the situation I was walking into, but followed her anyway.

She stood facing the mirror, her back to me, hair pulled to one side, revealing a zipper that ran from the top of the dress all the way down to... hell. I took a deep breath, closing my eyes for a second to regain some control, because a zipper like that? It was made for being undone—slowly.

Every metallic clink a tease, like a countdown to something much more dangerous.

Great, this private shopping session apparently comes with a complimentary side of blue balls.

Do I tip Kirsty for that?

"The corset she put me in makes it impossible to move," Violet grumbled, and I could tell she was already flustered she had to ask me for help. "I can't even reach the zipper without risking a rib. How do women actually wear these things?"

I gritted my teeth, imagining her in something lacy, tight, and likely black. Pair that with the word "corset" and my mind was spinning in all the wrong directions. Fucking hell.

I took a long breath, trying to rein in my thoughts and hold my body in check. The last thing I needed was to walk around with a semi after unzipping her dress in a high-end boutique.

Stepping forward, I grabbed the zipper at the top, pulling it down slowly—too damn slowly—because the idea of what lay beneath was making me lose my grip on reality. As the dress peeled open, my suspicions were confirmed.

A black lace corset hugged her waist, stopping just below her ribs, revealing smooth, flawless skin. And then there it was: a barely-there black lace thong.

Jesus Christ.

"That's fine. I can take it from here." Her voice snapped me back, but I wasn't letting go just yet. I tugged her toward me on pure instinct, the scent of jasmine dousing me in a wave of temptation. That scent was fast becoming my kryptonite. Why does jasmine smell this damn good?

"Uh, what are you doing?" Her voice was shaky, her eyes wide as she stared at me through the mirror. Those freckled cheeks flushed under the dressing room lights, her green eyes looking back at me, startled but curious.

I tightened my grip on her waist, my hands sinking into her soft skin. Every curve molded against me perfectly, her body a perfect fit with mine. "This," I said, my voice rough, "is definitely not something I want you wearing in public. Ever."

She laughed, pulling away before I could lose the last shred of my self-control, the dress slipping down to the floor as she turned.

And I watched her, thinking about how dangerous it was to be this close to the one thing I shouldn't want—and yet couldn't resist.

Jesus, what is she doing to me? Standing there in nothing but heels, a black thong, and a corset, she's practically handing me material for a permanent wet dream.

"Holy shit, cover yourself," I blurted, grabbing a robe from a nearby hanger and shoving it toward her like it was some kind of shield.

"It's just skin. And it's covered," she replied casually, sliding the robe on as if she hadn't just made my self-control evaporate into thin air.

"Your ass isn't," I bit out, the image of her bare skin now permanently burned into my mind. Great, that's staying there. No chance I'm getting that out of my head anytime soon. And now I know what I'll be thinking about in the shower tonight.

She only shrugged like it was no big deal. "I'm not really the type that gets embarrassed about stuff like that. Be happy I'm wearing these at all. I'd rather wear no panties."

I pinched the bridge of my nose, praying for patience. Don't picture it. Don't picture it. Too late. That image was going to haunt me forever.

A woman who speaks her mind, doesn't care about modesty, and has an actual brain?

Seriously, karma gods, what's the catch here? I must have done something right in a past life, or maybe I'm about to be struck down by lightning for every sin I've ever committed, because there's no way I'm supposed to be handed this level of temptation on a silver platter.

"Oh!" She spun around to face me, her hand pressing against my chest, sending a shock straight through me. Her touch burned like she'd branded my skin. And now, my attention was glued to her breasts, perfectly framed by the corset, and my mind was already imagining tearing it off with my teeth. Is it getting hotter in here? Or is it just me?

"I wanted to thank you," she said, her voice sweet, oblivious to the storm raging in my head. "This is really thoughtful. You were right—no one here treated me weird at all. I don't know how much all this costs, but I appreciate it. I know it's all for appearances, but still. I wish I could pay you back."

She was being genuine, and I was being anything but a gentleman. My jaw clenched, trying to keep my voice steady when all I wanted to do was tear that robe back off her. "You don't owe me anything," I managed to say, shaking my head because forming actual words suddenly felt impossible.

I tried not to look down, tried to focus anywhere but the creamy, perfect skin peeking out from the lace. My hands balled into fists, fighting the urge to grab her, to pull that robe off, to claim every inch of her.

But I couldn't. Not if I wanted to keep this deal intact.

"Alex?" Her voice was soft, and I felt her finger tapping lightly against my chest, trying to get me to respond. I kept my eyes closed, focusing on the internal breathing technique my assistant swore by. Breathe in, hold... How many seconds was it again? Whatever it was, it wasn't working because all I could think about was how close she was, the heat radiating from her body, and the way her skin had felt under my hands.

Yeah, breathing wasn't cutting it.

My phone pinged, and for once, I was grateful for the interruption. I opened my eyes, only to find her standing even closer, those green eyes locked on me with an expression I couldn't—didn't want to—decipher. Too dangerous.

"It's nothing at all," I muttered, trying to regain control, though my voice sounded strained even to my own ears. "Like you said, appearances." I took a step back, pulling my phone from my jacket pocket, using it as a shield between us.

Focus, Alex.

"Call. Gotta take it," I blurted, my words sharp, trying to escape whatever spell that vixen was wielding right now.

What the hell was wrong with me?

I practically fled the dressing room, not just gritting my teeth, but struggling to hide the painful, throbbing erection she had caused. Every instinct in me wanted to march back in there, grab her, and forget every damn rule I had set for myself. But that would ruin everything, and I wasn't about to let that happen. Not yet at least.

Though, with her... I wasn't sure how long I could hold out.

Violet

I WAS EXHAUSTED.

Turns out, shopping for hours on end is not my idea of a good time, and today only cemented that fact. Mentally, physically—I was done. Sure, the dress for Tuesday fit perfectly, but the one for Friday? That would be delivered to Alex's penthouse in a day or two. Apparently, I couldn't escape the couture train just yet.

Kirsty had insisted I leave in a cozy sweater dress with leggings and boots she picked out for me. I looked like I'd just stepped out of a fall fashion catalog—hell, I'm pretty sure this outfit was in one of them.

Attendants hustled out with a few of the bags, but most of the clothes were being sent straight to Alex's place because obviously, my shoebox-sized studio wasn't equipped to handle a mini fashion warehouse. Honestly, I wasn't sure how many outfits Alex ended up buying for me, but when Kirsty said it would all be delivered, I had a sneaking suspicion this was more than the "few" outfits we initially discussed.

"You look like you had a good time, Miss Hart," Antonio said, flashing a kind smile before almost swallowing it when Alex brushed past us and slid into the car without a word.

I smiled back at Antonio and climbed into the backseat, sliding across the cool leather as if I were trying to avoid waking a sleeping beast. That beast being Alex, of course. The man had been in full brooding mode for the last hour, and I wasn't about to poke that bear.

I was tired, possibly hangry despite the little snacks I'd been offered. But I wasn't about to complain—after all, a ridiculous amount of money had just been spent on me for clothes, shoes, and lingerie so gorgeous that I didn't even want to think about how much it all cost. I owed it to myself—and Alex—to not act like a brat when I'd just experienced the shopping spree of a lifetime.

But as we pulled away, something clicked. I wasn't headed back to my apartment. I turned to Alex, narrowing my eyes as I realized we were heading in the direction of his penthouse.

"Wait, why am I going to your place?" I turned from the window, trying to ignore the bustling streets and focus on why we weren't heading back to my apartment. Alex, still gazing out the opposite window, didn't move a muscle.

"I figured we could go back and talk about a few things. I've already had my chef prepare dinner. I'd cook, but I'm a little tired tonight."

"You're tired?" I shot him a look, unable to help the huff that escaped me. Seriously? He'd spent the entire time sitting, scrolling through his phone, occasionally snacking or sipping on something. If anything he had a thumb cramp and he'd get over it. "You didn't have to try on everything in that store—or change your bra and stuff your breasts into a million different ones all day."

From the front seat, I heard Antonio stifle a laugh. Great, at least someone found this amusing.

"I don't think my boobs or ass have ever been squeezed in and out of so many versions of 'fancy underwear' in my life."

Alex blinked, turning his gaze toward me. For a second, I thought I might have gotten a rise out of him. But nope, he kept quiet, though I caught the subtle curve of a smile he tried to hide behind his jacket's cuff.

Then, he leaned in. "Well, lucky for you," he murmured, his breath warm against my neck, "I have a large hot tub where you can soak your gorgeous tits and perfect ass."

Oh. My. God.

My entire body went rigid as I replayed the words in my head. That wasn't just a casual observation—it was downright sinful. My cheeks flamed instantly, and I fumbled for a comeback, but all I managed was, "I might just take you up on that."

Smooth.

Alex leaned back, clearly pleased with himself. The way he'd said it? It wasn't matter-of-fact. It was deliberate. Emphasized. And now I was sitting there, flushed head to toe, feeling the ghost of his words sending shivers up my spine and making my toes tingle.

Yup. I blushed. And I hated that he knew exactly what he was doing.

He nodded, clearly satisfied with himself, and turned back to stare out the window. The rest of the ride was filled with silence. Every time I thought of something to say, I'd glance over at him and change my mind. Even Mr. Hottest Bachelor CEO could get cranky.

Surprisingly, I found his temper sort of... endearing. Sure, he was all cool and collected on the outside, but clearly, things bothered him too. And knowing that just made him feel more human.

Back at his penthouse, he barely said two words to me. Instead, he disappeared into one of the guest rooms and returned a minute later, casually tossing a swimsuit and towel in my direction.

"What's this?" I frowned, holding up the swimsuit. "I'm not wearing some random woman's suit she left behind." I slinked past him, heading for the guest bedroom, already annoyed. "Besides," I tossed over my shoulder, "I prefer hot tubs naked."

Why the hell did I say that? Maybe it was the way he referred to my "gorgeous tits" and "perfect ass" earlier. No, scratch that—it was definitely how he said it. But still.

I tossed the swimsuit right back at him before stepping into the guest room, rolling my eyes. Who knows how many women he's brought here, leaving swimsuits behind like some kind of bachelor collection. Gross.

Before I could get far, the door banged open, and Alex stood there, looking thoroughly unimpressed. He tossed the swimsuit back at me, puffing out a frustrated breath. "First of all, I don't have random anything here. No women come to my penthouse. Ever."

For some reason, that made me feel better, even though a part of me still wasn't sure. "Second, this is yours. I had Kirsty add it to your purchases."

Well, that shut me up.

He left without waiting for my reply, and I reluctantly changed. Even if it was mine, I still wasn't wearing the damn thing. He'll just have to deal with the fact that I do indeed prefer hot tubs naked.

I wrapped myself in a towel, already daydreaming about sinking into the hot water and letting the jets work their magic on my sore muscles. Between my body screaming for that kind of comfort and my stomach growling for food, I wasn't sure which I needed more. But judging by Alex's mood, asking when I'd actually be fed probably wasn't the best idea.

He's probably used to women who survive on salads and air, but me? I need real food. Carbs. Protein. The works.

Clutching my phone in hand, I stepped out of the guest room, the towel wrapped tight around me. Alex had vanished, so I padded barefoot into the living room, clutching the towel tight around me. I wasn't sure if his private chef was still lurking somewhere, and I wasn't about to risk giving anyone a free show.

A sound from down the hall caught my attention, and there he was—Alex, dressed in jogging pants, a hoodie, and running shoes. The sight of him in something other than his usual three-piece suit almost had me doing a double take. He gave me a once-over, eyes skimming my towel-wrapped body with an expression I couldn't quite read. Was that... annoyance?

He groaned, walked over to the sliding doors that led to the terrace, and waved me off like he was too busy to deal with me. "Around the corner to the right is the tub," he said, backing away. "I'm going for a run. I'll be back in time for dinner."

Well, don't roll out the red carpet for me or anything, I thought. But instead of adding some of my usual snark, I bit my tongue.

I slinked out to the terrace, realizing only then that I was in a Manhattan high-rise, visible to the world—or at least that's how it felt. Luckily, the hot tub was tucked behind a gazebo draped in ivy, offering some privacy. Still, the thought lingered—how many women had been here before?

Ugh. Let's not go there.

With a sigh, I let the towel drop and dipped my toes into the water. It was scalding. Perfect. Just how I liked it—hot enough to boil lobsters. A remote sat on a table beside the tub, and of course, none of the buttons were labeled. I pressed one, and the string lights above flickered on, casting a soft, cozy glow. Another button cranked up the jets, and soon bubbles were swirling around me like I'd entered my own little spa heaven.

I leaned back, sinking into the warmth. Even with the chill of Manhattan fall creeping around me, I was perfectly cocooned in heat. The city skyline twinkled in the distance through the small windows in the gazebo and I relaxed, soaking it all in.

And then... my phone rang.

Because of course, it would.

Groaning, I glanced over and saw Max's face lighting up my phone screen. He'd been texting me all day, but between being pulled in and out of clothes, I hadn't had the time—or energy—to respond. Honestly, I wished he'd been shopping with me. At least I would've gotten feedback that wasn't just grunts or sighs.

"So, let me see!" Max's voice chirped through the video call, his face filling the screen.

I glanced around the hot tub. "Uh, I'm in a hot tub right now. Some of the clothes are coming home with me tonight, but most will stay here. No room at my place for all this."

He raised a brow. "Are you naked in the hot tub?"

"Do you really have to ask?"

Max grinned, then his eyes went wide, practically popping out of his head. "Oh my God, is he in there with you?"

I snorted. "Would I be video-calling you if that man's body was sharing this hot tub with me? Naked?"

"A boy can dream for his bestie." He winked before leaning closer to the screen. "So, what's he like now that you've spent some time with him?"

That question had me pausing. Had we spent time together really? Sure, we'd been in the same place all day, but he wasn't *there*. He'd spent most of the day on his phone—texting, emailing, doing whatever men in expensive suits do. The majority of our communication had been grunts, sighs, and the occasional nod. Riveting stuff.

I get it—this is an arrangement. We're not supposed to be bonding or anything. But, come on, I'm human. A little conversation wouldn't kill him, right? Maybe a bit of small talk, a compliment here and there, just something to remind me I exist. When I first met him, he had this way of making me feel like the sexiest woman in the room, like I was the only one who mattered. His touch, his gaze, everything screamed you're irresistible.

Now? Now, he's distant. Like, we're sitting here, I'm literally naked in his hot tub, and the man might as well be in another time zone. Okay, sure, he invited me for dinner, but the naked part wasn't exactly his idea. Although, he did mention my "gorgeous tits and perfect ass" when offering up the hot tub.

So, yeah, mixed signals much?

Maybe this whole arrangement is a bad idea. I know myself, and after a few dates, my heart's going to get involved. It's inevitable because, at the end of the day, I'm a girl looking for true love -- and refuse to admit it might live in books and movies.

And I highly doubt Alex finds me as attractive as he claims. I'm just convenient for him. But if I'm already feeling hurt when he barely talks to me this early into our plan, how the hell am I supposed to handle it when we start kissing, holding hands, and doing all those things that make my hopelessly romantic heart leap? I'll be a goner.

"Violet..." Max drags out my name. "What's going on in that head of yours? You're way too quiet."

It wasn't unusual for Max and me to sit on a video call in comfortable silence, scrolling our phones or just doing life. Sometimes we'd eat, clean, or just chill with no need to fill the air. It was our version of hanging out when we couldn't do it in person. But he knows me too well, and my silence tonight wasn't peaceful.

I shrugged, picking at the bubbles floating on the hot tub's surface. "I don't know. It's just... weird, right? He bought me expensive dresses, and matching lingerie, and now I'm going to be his date. His fake girlfriend." I blew a handful of bubbles into the cool night air.

Max squealed, his voice reaching a higher pitch than normal. "Oh my God, you are Julia Roberts in Pretty Woman!"

"I'm not a hooker, Max!" I shot back, rolling my eyes. How many times do I need to remind him of that very important fact? Apparently twice in 48 hours.

"For that man, I would be." He gave me a dramatic look, eyes wide. "Just do the whole no-kissing thing and keep it classy."

I sighed. "We have to kiss in public, remember?"

"Right, the whole charade thing," he said, leaning back and fanning himself. "Well, I still say you should totally Pretty Woman it."

I laughed, shaking my head. Max and I had seen every rom-com and romance film out there. Even though he wasn't a big fan, he watched them for me. He claimed they were too cheesy, but I thrived on them. Books, movies—it didn't matter. I craved love stories with a wild, unrealistic passion that would probably never exist in my real life.

Max, on the other hand, was much more grounded. And despite what people might assume, considering he was gay, Max didn't fit the typical rom-com sidekick mold. He was attractive, alpha, and didn't flaunt it. He just... was.

Though I had thought about using him to make Jake jealous at one point, it never worked out. Jake knew Max wasn't into women. Everyone knew. So instead, Max became my stand-in date, and I became his buffer for family events, where his relatives still pretended they didn't know the truth. We made it work—him being my shield, me being his beard.

But now? Now I was something... I didn't even know what for Alex. A rich, moody man with enough money to make my head spin and enough attitude to drive me insane.

"I don't know, Max. I think this was a bad idea," I sighed, sinking lower into the bubbles. "I'm already annoyed that he barely talked to me today, even though we spent all day together. I'm not built for this kind of 'arrangement.' I have emotions, feelings—you know, normal human stuff. He's probably used to women who are confident, sexy, and don't care if he blows them off because they'll just move on to the next guy."

Max was lounging on his bed, fluffing one of his dozen pillows. "You know how those CEO types are. Closed off and notorious for brooding. Maybe it'll take some time to coax him out of that shell."

"That's exactly the problem. I can't coax him out. We're not actually dating, remember? He's not going to open up to his fake girlfriend. If anything, he'll close off even more." I paused, rubbing my forehead. "And let's be real, Max—I'm not his type. I'm not a supermodel. I'm not rich. I don't even have $100 to my name. I'm just... me."

"Vi—" Max started, his face softening.

I cut him off, frustration bubbling over the brim of the pot that is my life right now. "What? It's true. He reeled me in, and we both know I'm going to get hurt. I've got way too many feelings spinning around up here." I tapped my temple for emphasis as if Max needed the reminder.

He opened his mouth to say something, but then I heard footsteps—heavy ones—coming from around the terrace.

"Gotta go," I said quickly, hanging up before Max could protest.

My heart raced as I clicked off the call, turning toward the sound. What now?

Alex appeared from around the corner, his hands tucked into his hoodie pockets, looking strangely... normal. I'd half expected him to hit the gym in a tailored Armani suit or something equally ridiculous. But here he was, just a guy in joggers and a hoodie.

Please tell me he didn't hear any of that conversation with Max. My lack of self-confidence was already doing a number on me, and I didn't need him privy to my spiraling thoughts.

"Enjoying the tub?" he asked, his voice casual. Coast is clear—he didn't overhear.

I forced a smile. "Yeah, but I was just about to get out. Don't wanna turn into a prune or anything. I'll meet you inside in a minute."

He nodded but hesitated like he was about to say something more. His mouth opened, but then he seemed to think better of it. "Dinner's ready. Once you're dressed, I'll see you in the dining room?"

"Uh, yeah. Sure. Totally." My voice was breezy, though I wasn't sure I was fooling either of us.

There was an awkward pause before he finally turned and walked away. I released a breath I didn't realize I was holding. Maybe I'd pull an Alex at dinner—brooding, distant, and silent.

Seemed to work for him.

I waited until I heard the sliding door click shut, then slowly pulled myself out of the water, grabbing the towel and wrapping it tightly around me. The chilly air hit my skin like ice, but the hot tub had done its job—my body was blissfully numb. I darted inside, keeping my eyes on the floor as I hurried to the guest room to change.

Back into the sweater dress. The one that felt ridiculously soft, like cashmere, and way more expensive than anything I'd ever buy. The kind of outfit people spend hundreds—if not thousands—on just to look "casually chic." To be fair, it did feel amazing, but still... so extra.

Alex was nowhere in sight when I came inside. He was probably off showering after his run. Fine by me—some time alone was exactly what I needed to regain my composure before dinner.

My hair was a frizzy, wet mess thanks to the hot tub, and the messy bun I'd attempted to keep it from getting soaked had failed miserably. I found an unused brush and comb in the bathroom drawer, still with the tags on like they'd been bought in bulk and promptly forgotten. Great. Just great. Sighing, I tried to tame the wild waves with my fingers, but it was hopeless. This situation was calling for conditioner and some serious anti-frizz serum. Giving up, I twisted it back into a slightly less chaotic bun and called it good enough.

All I had to do was get through this dinner. Simple. Maybe I could even manage to have an actual conversation, and get to know Alex a little better. Then I could go home, have some space, and breathe. I wouldn't have to see him again until Tuesday's dinner. And even then, all I had to do was smile and play the part of the picture-perfect "long-term" girlfriend for a few hours. After that, I could take a breather until the company party.

And if this awkward limbo we're stuck in continues? Well, then I'll just call the whole thing off.

Easy enough, right?

I hoped so.

Alex

I DON'T EAVESDROP.

Except... this is the second time I've found myself listening in on Violet's conversation. With the same person. So, the evidence is against me right now.

Not my usual style, though. Timing. That's what it's all about. At the bar, I didn't plan on overhearing her phone call. I was just waiting for my drink, and what she said caught my attention. Could've happened to anyone, right?

But now, in my own damn house, I didn't realize she was on the phone again until I rounded the corner. Should I have turned back the second I heard her voice? Yeah, probably.

Did I?

No.

Instead, my feet moved me in the opposite direction of the hot tub, retreating around the corner, but I couldn't stop myself from listening. Her voice wasn't its usual bright, peppy self—the one that seemed to make the air lighter. No, this was different. Tired. Defeated, even. Maybe from the long day of shopping, but... there was more to it.

It wasn't just exhaustion. Something was weighing on her, and I felt that familiar tug of conflict. Should I go in, pretend I didn't hear anything, and let her be? Or should I stay just a second longer, listening for something I wasn't entirely sure I wanted to know?

"That's the issue, Max. I can't do this. We're not actually dating. You don't open up for a fake girlfriend. If anything, you close off more. Trust me, I'm not his type. I'm not a sexy supermodel. I'm not rich. We both know I don't even have $100 to my name."

Her words hit me like a punch to the gut. Is that really what she thinks?

I know I come off like a cocky bastard sometimes, using my name and reputation to remind people who they're dealing with. But I've never judged a woman by her bank account—or how closely she resembles a model. That's what people do to me, and I hate it.

Yeah, I was distant today. But it wasn't because I didn't want her around. Hell, it was the opposite. Keeping my distance felt necessary. For her comfort—or maybe mine. The more I'm around Violet, the more I want her. And that sends all kinds of warnings through me that I'm not used to.

Panic. Worry.

Two emotions I don't normally experience, yet here they are.

"I'm not the girl for this gig. I have emotions, Max. Feelings. You know, I'm normal."

Hearing her say that messes with me. The fact that my distance hurt her more than I realized. I thought ignoring my attraction was the safest play—just pretend she wasn't there. In hindsight, I get how acting like she didn't exist could make her feel unwanted. But if I told her the truth, told her how I was drawn to her the second I saw her, would she stay?

No. That's the kind of thing crazy people say.

I need to figure out where the hell the balance is. Somewhere between confessing that I walked up to her because she's the sexiest woman I've ever seen and pretending this whole thing is strictly platonic so I don't scare her away.

I don't know where to draw the line, and the one friend I'd ask for advice would laugh until he pissed himself. My brother? Even worse. Instead of being a normal guy and asking her out, I've set up this elaborate "fake dating" arrangement. Only it's not really fake for me, and I'm the only one aware of that little detail.

As I round the corner, I make sure my footsteps are loud enough for her to hear me coming. The last thing I need is for her to catch me sneaking up. By the time I approach, I hear her say goodbye to Max and lean back like she's been relaxing for hours. I'm trying hard not to think about the fact that she's naked under all those bubbles.

My dream girl. In my hot tub. Naked.

She leans back, completely at ease, and I catch myself feeling jealous of the damn bubbles touching her skin. Who gets jealous of bubbles?

You, you pathetic ass.

This whole thing is awkward as hell. Does she know I overheard her? Or is she oblivious? And I'm over here pretending I didn't just hear her confess her doubts about this situation. My voice comes out a little too tight when I tell her dinner is ready. Carlo, my chef, made everything earlier and left it in the oven to stay warm. The plan was simple: eat dinner, have Antonio drive her home, and then I'd shower and call it a night.

But now? Now I don't know what the hell I'm doing.

She nods, saying she'll join me for dinner, and I bolt. I head inside and straight to the bathroom, ripping off my clothes to shower and try to collect my thoughts.

All I can hear is her voice in my head. *I'm going to get hurt in this. You know I will.*

Yeah, Violet. I'm starting to think I'm going to get hurt too — the only thing is, I'm okay with me getting her if I can be with her...

That fact should scare me, but it doesn't.

I run a hand down my face, letting the scalding water pummel me, trying to drown out the chaos in my head. I don't want to hurt her, but my track record for relationships is... well, it's shit. The one time I let things get serious, I got burned. Badly. And since then? No thanks. No vulnerability, no mess, no heartbreak. I figured if I kept things with Violet in this neat little box, an arrangement with clear boundaries, it'd be safe—for both of us.

But was it really?

I grab the body wash and my loofah—yeah, I use a loofah, and any man who doesn't is a savage—and scrub away the tension that's been clinging to me for months. It's not just today; it's everything. It's her.

Hearing about her ex brought back memories I'd buried. I know all too well what it feels like to be cheated on, to open yourself up, thinking you're safe, only for everything to collapse in on you. I've been through that storm, and the scars are still there.

Unintentionally, the shower takes longer than planned, as I stand under the water, trying to sort out where the hell I go from here. Maybe I should just come clean—tell her I'm interested. But now? Now, I'm past creeper status. What kind of man investigates a woman, takes her shopping, makes her sign an NDA, and then says, "By the way, do you mind dating me for real? Could you maybe spend every waking minute with me this week because right now that's all I want?"

Yeah, I'm sure that'd go over well.

No, I've dug myself too deep. I need to tread carefully. There's got to be a way to keep this as a friendly arrangement without being a complete asshole. How is she ever going to develop feelings for me if I act like the same prick who storms into board meetings and makes grown men sweat? No one loves me there—and I prefer it that way.

But with her? I need a different approach.

It's time to change tactics.

Violet

I HAD BEEN STARVING, but the chef must have read my mind and prepared a light salad, which I practically inhaled while waiting for Alex to finish in the shower. Who knew clothes shopping could be an Olympic-level sport? It should be. My body aches like I spent hours at the gym, my mind is a foggy mess, and the hot tub only made me more exhausted. Half of me wants to curl up and head home, but the other half remains glued to this penthouse, hoping for more time to talk to Alex.

Not going to lie, when I changed in the guest room, the bed looked ridiculously inviting. That mattress? Pure heaven compared to the sagging, spring-filled disaster I have back home. It took every ounce of strength not to face-plant into the plush comforter and pass out.

Now, I'm tapping my foot, trying to distract myself by taking in his penthouse—because this place is insane. One of those open-floor concepts with ceilings high enough to make you dizzy. The dining room, if you can call it that, feels more like an extension of the living space. There are no real walls dividing it, just a large wooden table sitting on a luxurious rug, almost as if it's claiming its corner of the universe.

And then there's the living room—a step-down half-moon of leather couches and armchairs, facing a massive TV hanging above the fireplace. I mean, this place is... elegant. But it's the mantle that catches my eye. Real pictures. Most guys I've known never have family photos out, let alone prominently displayed, so I find myself padding over to take a closer look, stealing glances down the hall to make sure he's not on his way back yet.

The first thing I notice is the kids—nieces and nephews, maybe? Olive-skinned, all impossibly adorable. They look related, that family resemblance you can't miss, though Alex seems to be the only one with those piercing blue eyes. There's a picture of him with an older woman, probably his mom, and a couple who have "parents" written all over them.

But then I spot the family portrait. My jaw almost hits the floor.

There are so many people. How big is his family? I count at least fifty... no, maybe closer to a hundred smiling faces, all crammed together in one shot. It's like looking at a holiday card on steroids. And they look... happy. Really, genuinely happy.

I can't help but wonder what it'd be like to be part of that—to sit at a dinner with that many people, to be caught in that whirl of voices, laughter, and inside jokes. I bet it's loud, chaotic, but... warm. Familiar. Something I've never had. My family? We're more like strangers who share the same DNA. I've met my mom's parents maybe twice. My dad's side? I wouldn't recognize them if they walked past me on the street. Aunts, uncles, cousins—they're just names on a holiday card if I even get one. I don't know half of them, let alone their kids.

For a second, I feel a strange pull toward this picture-perfect family life. It's foreign, but it's something I didn't realize I'd missed until now.

I look back at the family photo. Big, vibrant, smiling faces—old and young—all gathered together. It's like they radiate warmth through the frame. My parents, on the other hand, only had pictures of their humanitarian work. If I was in a photo, it was because they dragged me along on a trip, and those pictures? They were meant for magazines or to impress their colleagues during fancy dinner parties. Never something just for us -- pictures taken for the sake of making a memory.

What was there to remember, anyway? I was more of an accessory than a daughter. Something to brag about when I fit their expectations. Since I no longer fit that storyline, it was like I'd been erased from their lives.

But this family in the photo? They're smiling because they want to remember this moment. It's not for show. It's not for some shallow conversation at a party. *It's... real.*

I sigh, feeling a strange tug in my chest, and turn to head back to the table—only to slam right into him, or should I say his very bare smooth skin.

"Holy crap!" I yelp, stumbling back.

And then, wow. Hello, abs.

My eyes involuntarily roam over his bare chest, soaking in every inch of the sculpted muscles. He's... ripped. Not just casually fit, but like "belongs in a cologne ad" kind of fit. There's not a square inch of his body that isn't hard muscle. Oh, and tattoos. Mr. All-Business has tattoos? That's a surprise. And not the small, subtle kind either, but before I can study them too closely, his voice cuts through the daze.

"Not polite to stare," he says, snapping his fingers as if to bring me back to reality.

My eyes flick up, meeting his amused gaze. Heat flushes through me, embarrassment hitting harder than a train. Of course, I was staring. How could I not?

"Well, you listen in on conversations, I stare. We both have our flaws," I quip, brushing past him toward the kitchen where the smell of food is practically singing to my wailing stomach. Alex follows close behind, and I can feel his presence more than I prefer. As if my body is connected to it and knows just how close he is to me without having to look.

The chef had set everything out on the kitchen island, with some dishes still warming in the oven. I glance back as Alex pulls a t-shirt over his chest. My inner self groans because, let's be honest, the view was spectacular. But the realist in me knows I wouldn't be able to form a coherent thought with that much man on display. Still, the gray t-shirt isn't helping my focus—if anything, it's worse. His toned biceps and forearms are fully on show now, the fabric doing nothing to hide the muscle there.

In the books I devour, they always go on about men with amazing bodies, chiseled muscles, and defined arms. Seeing it in person? That's a whole new level of drool-worthy. And now, I have a real-life visual to pair with every book I read. How unfair is that?

He pulls down some dishes, dips to open the wine fridge built into the kitchen island, and asks, "Red okay? Carlo made lasagna, and the red pairs better."

"Uh, sure. I'm not picky," I say, even though I totally am. But after the man just spent a small fortune on clothes for me, I'm not about to start being difficult.

He pops up from the fridge with a bottle in hand, grabs two wine glasses from a display, and gestures for me to follow him.

I sit at the table as he uncorks the wine, pours a glass for each of us, then disappears back into the kitchen. I can hear the sounds of him moving around—the oven door opening, plates clinking, silverware being set out. The domesticity of it all feels strangely intimate.

I pick up my wine glass, staring at the deep red liquid. I'm not usually a red wine kind of girl, but I take a small sip anyway, hoping to get any potential cringe out of the way before he comes back. To my surprise, it's actually good. Smooth, without the usual bite and bitterness I've tasted before.

Then again, I can't afford the kind of wine he probably keeps in that fridge. Max and I are more "under $20 a bottle" kind of wine drinkers, and even that's pushing it. White wine is easier to drink when it's cheap, but anything below five bucks? You're drinking vinegar at that point.

"How is it?" Alex's voice pulls me from my thoughts, and I jump a little. He quirks a brow as he places a plate in front of me with a perfect square of lasagna and a piece of garlic bread that smells like heaven.

"Good," I reply, lifting the wine glass. "I don't think I've ever had red wine this good before." And I'm not even lying. I take another sip. Okay, maybe a fourth sip.

He sits down next to me, unfolding his linen napkin and placing it on his lap, all smooth and sophisticated. Then, with precise movements, he cuts his lasagna into perfect little squares. Knife and fork, like he's at a five-star restaurant.

Meanwhile, I glance at my plate and try not to feel out of place. None of my napkins at home are reusable—just good ol' paper ones. Also, I've never in my life used a knife to cut lasagna. It's usually a "stab with a fork and hope it breaks apart" kind of situation.

But, determined not to look like a total amateur, I copy him, cutting my lasagna with slow, deliberate movements, pretending I know what I'm doing. Classy, right? Totally convincing.

"So, what exactly is this dinner on Tuesday?" I ask, breaking the silence. "You mentioned investors, but it sounds like it's more than just a casual thing."

He shrugs, cutting another perfect piece of lasagna. "It's a dinner with a few of my largest investors, all married. It's important, in a way. I've told them I'm dating to ease their concerns, but now they need to meet you. You can understand why."

I nod, though I'm not sure I do. Why would his board care if he's dating or not? Seems ridiculous. Alex strikes me as someone married to his job—how would a girlfriend impact that? But I guess there's a logic in billionaire land that doesn't quite compute in my world.

"Well," I say with a smirk, "at least this will be a good trial run for the company party on Friday. Although, you looked convincing enough at the bar."

I glance at him, watching for a reaction, but his expression stays neutral. I might've meant it as a joke, but I'm not sure if he took it that way. Either way, I keep cutting my lasagna, hoping the tension loosens up.

We really did sell that whole fake relationship. When he touched me, I didn't flinch or pull away. Instead, I leaned into him like it was second nature. The way he played his part, with that confident charm and ease, had me wondering if he'd missed his calling as an actor. Or maybe, just maybe, we had that natural chemistry I always read about. You know, the kind where two people just click, like they were meant to be.

God, I really need to quit comparing my life to fiction.

Still, today's version of Alex was nothing like the one from the bar or even yesterday. He felt distant like he was holding something back. I couldn't help but hope the real Alex would make a reappearance by the end of the night. But a tiny voice inside me whispered, *What if the real Alex is the one I saw today? And the guy at the bar was the act?*

No. Stop overthinking.

If he's an ass, he's an ass. We have an arrangement, nothing more.

Besides, I had a goal for tonight. I needed to get to know him. After all, we were pretending to have been dating for a month, keeping it all hush-hush. But now that the lie was out, we needed to know each other well enough to sell this to everyone else. And one thing I already knew? He could get moody.

Finally done slicing through my lasagna like I had something to prove, I admired the gooey layers of noodles, cheese, and meat before taking a bite. The moment it hit my tongue, I'm positive I moaned. Holy crap. This was good. Like, straight-out-of-Italy good. Not that I've ever been to Italy, but if I had, I imagine this is what it would taste like. Every bite was a piece of cheesy heaven.

How Italian was Alex, exactly? His name and family reputation screamed it, but the blue eyes and his first name didn't quite fit the stereotype. Then again, I wasn't sure how deep his family roots went, and I didn't think it was the right time to ask. Instead, I focused on my lasagna, savoring each bite like it was my last meal while wracking my brain for a way to start a conversation. Anything to break the quiet that was settling in between us.

Come on, Violet. You write dialogue for a living. Surely, you can handle a simple dinner conversation, right?

Wrong.

It was like my brain was locked in a weird fog. I kept chewing, pulling apart the garlic bread, and hoping something would pop into my head. But nope, nothing. Seriously? I'm usually the queen of chatter. And now, when I need my endless supply of rambling thoughts, I've got nothing.

I blame the cheese. And the butter. And the ridiculous amount of herbs.

Also, half my brain was still stuck on the tattoos I'd seen earlier. What were they? Did he get them during some rebellious phase in his twenties? I couldn't even picture him as anything but polished and professional. Even now, sitting across from me in joggers and a t-shirt, he had this aura of class and control that was hard to shake.

We ate in silence. Now and then, it seemed like he might say something, but he just sipped his wine instead. Finally, I couldn't take it anymore. I'd be the one to crack the wall of silence.

"So, you have a private chef. Do you ever cook?"

"Are you asking if I can cook?" he shot back, one brow quirked.

Well, this might be harder than I thought. I swirled my wine in my glass, trying to figure out how to navigate this, but before I could respond, he added, 'I have Carlo because I'm rarely home in time to make anything worth eating. But, yeah, I can cook."

I was just about to ask him more, but he continued. "My nonna insisted I learn. She said no grown man should be helpless in the kitchen, so she taught me when I was young. But with work, I don't get much time to do it myself these days."

"Nonna?" I asked, perking up at the word.

His lips curved into a small smirk, and for the first time tonight, I saw a glimpse of the guy from the bar. The one who had reeled me in with charm and confidence and all the other goodness that came in that package of his.

"My grandmother," he said, shrugging.

"Is Nonna Italian? Or is that just what you call her?"

"Both. It's what most Italians call their grandmothers, but she insists we call her Nonna, even though most of us were born in America. My papa was the last one born in Italy. The rest of us are from here. My mother isn't Sicilian, though. She's Colombian, which my Nonna hated at first, but she's come around now that my mama speaks fluent Italian and acts more Italian than half the family."

The way he talks about his family accepting someone not Sicilian sends an odd flutter of hope through me. Which is ridiculous because, hello, this isn't real. There's no future here.

"And yet, you have a slight accent," I blurt, then blush when his eyes lock onto mine. "I mean, sometimes I hear it, but not always."

A slow, teasing smile spreads across his face as he leans forward. "You have a thing for guys with accents?"

No. Yes. Who doesn't?

"I have a slight one, yeah. I still speak Italian fluently. My grandmother won't let me forget it. She talks half in Italian and half in English—most of my family does, actually. So if you don't know Italian, good luck keeping up. They'll switch mid-sentence without warning."

I prop my chin in my hand, watching him. "Say something."

He raises a brow, a glint in his eyes. "In Italian, you mean?"

I clear my throat, suddenly feeling like I'm in way over my head. "Yes."

With deliberate slowness, he wipes his mouth, sets his napkin aside, and leans in. His voice is low and smooth, like velvet wrapped in honey as he says, *"Sei la donna più bella che io abbia mai visto."*

Okay, wow. I'm positive my ovaries just somersaulted. Is it hot in here? It feels hot.

He leans back, that infuriating smile still playing on his lips as he takes a sip of wine, blue eyes locked on me like he knows exactly what he's doing. I don't know what he said, but I sure as hell know how my body felt about it.

"What..." My throat is dry, words impossible to form because—yeah, that just turned me on more than I'd like to admit. "What does that mean?"

His smile widens, clearly amused. "Guess you'll have to learn Italian to figure that out."

I grab my wine hoping a sip of it will prevent me from combusting on the spot. He's enjoying this way too much, and I'm a second away from melting into a puddle right here at the table.

"Did you eat enough, Bella?" His voice had that subtle accent again, and I tried not to think about the way it rolled off his tongue. No need to remind my body of things it wants but can't have right now.

I nodded, deciding that was safer than speaking. When he stood, reaching for our plates, I grabbed what was left and followed him to the kitchen. We cleaned up together, then I followed him to the living room as he carried our glasses and the bottle of wine.

The place was surprisingly warm. Wooden beams, brick walls, and soft leather couches. It wasn't what I expected, not for a guy like him. No cold, sharp lines or concrete floors. Instead, it felt...comfortable.

I sat down, sinking into the couch, while he settled close but not too close.

"Alright," I said, breaking the silence. "We met at a bar, been dating for a month. Are we in love?" I was half-serious. We needed to get our story straight.

"Do people usually fall in love in a month?" He shot back.

I shrugged. "Do people usually buy fancy dresses and lingerie for someone they're not actually dating?"

His eyes flicked to mine. "They do if she's mine."

Well, that was something to chew on.

I swirled my wine, eyeing him over the rim of the glass. "Alright, let's start easy. What's your favorite movie?"

Leaning back, he gave me a smirk. "Favorite movie? That's tough. I haven't had much time for movies lately. Too busy with business."

I rolled my eyes. "Let me guess, the last movie you watched was some business documentary?"

"Close. It was a TED Talk on disruptive innovation."

"Wow," I exaggerated my voice. "You really know how to live on the wild side."

He ignored my jab, taking a slow sip of his wine. "Your favorite?"

"Oh, that's easy. Pride & Prejudice, the 2005 version with Keira Knightley. I watch it all the time." Yeah, I'm that girl.

His brow lifted in amusement. "Should've guessed."

"Alright, books then. Surely you have a favorite book?"

He shrugged. "Well, I just finished Good to Great by Jim Collins. It's a solid read."

I groaned. "Of course you did. You're really consistent, aren't you? All work and no play makes Alex a dull boy."

A rare, genuine laugh escaped him. "I prefer the terms focused and driven."

"If you say so," I said, leaning back on the couch. "My favorite book, which will shock you, is *Pride & Prejudice*. I read it every year."

He smirked. "Starting to see a pattern here. Any other favorites?"

I tapped my finger on my leg, pretending to think even though this list was tattooed on my soul. "Let's see... The Notebook, Titanic, and Notting Hill."

"I'm definitely sensing a theme."

"And I'm sensing you need more romance in your life. It's not all about business, Alex."

He leaned in, eyes twinkling with mischief. "Are you offering to tutor me?"

I rolled my eyes but smiled. "Tell you what, if you watch Pride & Prejudice with me, I will."

He chuckled. "Sure, let me pencil that in between board meetings and conference calls."

"You're impossible."

We spent the next two hours trying to find common ground, our conversation meandering through random topics. I was practically on a mission to find at least one thing we shared. I mean, how else do we explain our "budding relationship" if we have nothing in common? We don't exactly walk in the same social circles—or even the same planet.

The more we talked, the more I felt a little defeated. He really was all business, and I... well, I was all romance.

"Do couples have to like everything the other person does?" he asked suddenly, breaking my thoughts.

I frowned. "No, but they need some common ground, right? Otherwise, what's there to connect on?"

"And what exactly did you and, what was his name—Jason? Jake? Whatever—connect on?"

I chewed on my lip, mulling it over. It was something I'd revisited a hundred times. "Honestly? I don't think we ever truly connected on anything. Which might explain why my best friend giving him a blowjob seemed more appealing than staying faithful."

Alex nearly spit out his wine, choking on a laugh. "Wait, did you not... give him one?"

I raised a brow. "That feels a bit personal, don't you think?"

"Says the woman who just brought up blowjobs."

"Fair point." I shrugged. "No, I enjoy giving them, actually. It's fun—there's a certain power in knowing you're the one driving him crazy. I liked the control, the way it made me feel in charge of his pleasure. But Jake... well, he wasn't into it. He made slurping a noodle more enjoyable."

"Okay, okay, I got it." Alex topped off his wine, trying to mask his laughter as he took a long sip.

I realized I might've said too much. There it was—the infamous overshare. Liquor was like a key to the vault of inappropriate truths in my head, and once it was cracked open, things just spilled out. This was why I avoided getting fully drunk. When tipsy, I had a thin filter, but when inebriated? The filter was obliterated, gone without a trace.

"We really didn't have anything in common," I continued, trying to steer the conversation back. "But that's not the only reason it didn't work. I mean, relationships need both physical and emotional connection. And Jake didn't meet the mark in either category."

"I think we've more than established that," Alex smiled, clearly referencing the infamous bar conversation.

Oh, right. That. Everyone already knew about Jake's... shortcomings, including Alex. Normally, I'd blush, but at this point, after that impromptu office speech, I was beyond mortification.

Everyone knew Jake couldn't satisfy.

I sighed, swirling the wine in my glass again. "So yeah, common ground might not be everything, but it's definitely something. Otherwise, you're just... drifting." I tilt my head, realizing that I never bothered to look it up when I had Google him. "How old are you, anyway?"

"Thirty-six," he says, smirking. "Funny how we've gotten this far without asking that. Though I hate to break it to you, I already know how old you are. It's part of that whole background check thing."

I twirl a loose strand of hair around my finger, a nervous habit I can't seem to shake. "Don't think that's a big age gap?"

Why am I even nervous? It's not like seven years is a dealbreaker. Still, there's something about him—maybe it's the situation, or maybe it's the fact that I'm sitting next to this insanely intimidating, ridiculously hot man.

No, scratch that—it's *definitely* the man.

I try to keep my cool, to not be the girl who swoons just because his eyes are this insane shade of turquoise, like the kind of ocean you see in travel magazines. They're unnervingly clear, like you could lose yourself just staring at them.

He laughs, and hopefully, it's not because I was practically studying his eyes. "A whole seven years, huh? Yeah, we're practically from different generations at this point." He finishes off his wine, setting the glass down and leaning back into the couch, mirroring my position. His arm props against the backrest, casual and relaxed, yet somehow commanding all the attention in the room.

"So," I say, narrowing my eyes playfully. "Why are you 36 and still a bachelor? You've got the penthouse, the success, and, well... you're hot."

He chuckles, grabbing my glass and setting it next to his. "I don't think any of those things automatically qualify someone for a steady relationship."

"They help," I tease, shrugging, but he just laughs, the sound deep and smooth.

Then he leans in, his eyes focused. "What about you? You're an assistant to a senior editor, right? How come you aren't an editor yourself? You've got the degree and a pretty clear penchant for words."

"Did you just say 'penchant'?" I'm rather amused at the word choice.

He shrugs. "I use fancy English when necessary."

I can't help but imagine him speaking only in Italian. My knees would probably give out if he did that right now, but I'm pretty sure melting into a puddle on his ridiculously expensive sofa wouldn't be the best move.

"So, Violet, why are you still an assistant after four years?"

Because you're a pushover.

Because you let people take credit for your work.

Because, apparently, you can't even order a lavender latte correctly.

"Just haven't had an opportunity for promotion, I guess," I say, trying to sound nonchalant. But really, that's just a shiny cover-up for the truth I'm not ready to face. The truth that's a little too bitter to examine this year. Or this century.

Denial? Yeah, it's my best friend at this point.

Alex shifts slightly, no longer angled toward me. He crosses his arms, leaning back against the sofa. He nods toward the pictures on the mantle. "What about your parents?"

Cue the uncomfortable squirm. "Don't you already know all about them from your little background check?" I try to quip, hoping my humor can steer us away from this topic. My parents are not exactly a subject that screams 'fun and lighthearted,' and from what I've seen of Alex, he's way too attached to the whole idea of family. My situation would just sound... sad.

It was late. Past midnight already. A guy like Alex? He probably gets up at the crack of dawn, running on some impossibly rigid schedule. I straighten myself, sitting up on the couch. "I should probably get going."

He nods, already reaching for his phone. "I'll get Antonio to take you home." His fingers are flying across the screen, but before I can think, I grab his arm. My hand wraps around his forearm, and for a split second, I'm hyper-aware of how solid and warm his skin feels under my fingers. It's the first time I've really touched him—aside from that accidental smack into his chest earlier, which hardly counts since that was more of a collision.

"That's not necessary. I can just call an Uber or something," I say, already moving toward my phone in the foyer.

Before I can even make it halfway there, his strong arm sweeps me back, spinning me around until my back is flush against the wall. Alex is all up in my space, his chest pressed to mine. My heart is in full-on meltdown mode. This man. Total alpha male, and it's turning my brain to mush.

For a moment, he says nothing. His hand is still gripping my arm, his body radiating heat like a sidewalk in July. The intensity of it makes my pulse race or stop. I'm not really sure I'm even breathing right now.

"I don't trust rideshares," he says, voice low and unwavering. "I have drivers for a reason."

I swallow the rock lodged in my throat. "Yeah, but...it's late."

His eyes close for a brief second, like he's trying to gather himself. When he opens them again, his jaw is set. "I'll drive you."

"What? No, I didn't mean for you to drive me."

But he's already pushing off the wall, walking toward the foyer. He grabs his wallet, and keys, and slips on his shoes. Before I can protest further, he bends down, scoops up my shoes, and hands them to me.

"Not up for discussion," and the way he says it makes me wonder if anyone ever tells the man no.

I try one last time. "Seriously, it's fine if I get a ride."

That's when he snaps. In a flash, his fingers are on my chin, tilting my head up so I'm forced to look at him. His touch is firm but surprisingly gentle. "You get a ride home from me or one of my drivers. Not a stranger. I already told you that part of this includes having a driver."

Okay, I'm not winning this battle. So, I nod.

We step into the elevator, descending into the parking garage, and walk past a lineup of incredibly pricey cars. "Which one is yours?" I ask, eyeing each one like I'm playing a guessing game.

There's a black Mercedes, a Porsche 911 Turbo convertible, a Tesla, and then... an Aston Martin. All black, naturally. Seriously, does no one own a car in a fun color anymore?

"All of them," he says casually, like we're talking about a collection of sneakers and not cars that cost more than my entire apartment's rent for the next five years. Who am I kidding? Probably more like ten.

"We're taking this one," he nods toward the Aston Martin, and I have to fight the urge to squeal. I've always wanted to peek inside one of these without looking like a creep through someone's car window.

He opens the door for me. I freeze for a second, not because it's so unexpected, but because I'm realizing just how low the bar was set with Jake. He never opened doors. Not for the car, not for restaurants, not even at the office. He always bulldozed through and expected me to follow.

But this? This little gesture feels...nice. Chivalry, who knew?

I slide into the passenger seat, and the car is as luxurious inside as it is on the outside. The leather is a deep, rich brown, and I almost expect Alex to put on a pair of fancy driving gloves and turn on some jazz from the '20s. Instead, he gets in, starts the engine, and waits for me to buckle up before pulling out of the garage.

The ride is quiet. Too quiet. Every time I glance at him, he's gripping the steering wheel tightly with one hand, the other resting awkwardly on the center console like he doesn't know what to do with it.

I try not to overthink it, but it's hard not to feel like I'm intruding somehow like my presence is an inconvenience. Maybe he's annoyed he had to drive me home instead of calling his driver?

Yeah. I probably should've let him call Antonio. At least that guy is guaranteed to smile at me.

Alex

HONESTLY, I NEVER INTENDED to have Antonio drive her tonight. I'd given him the night off, and while I knew he'd answer even after midnight, I wanted her to push back a little. Call it a test—one that was lame at best—but I wanted to see if she had that spark, that fire.

Tired as I was, there was no chance in hell I'd let her take a cab or, worse, an Uber with some random stranger. Not at this hour, not alone in the middle of the night.

I don't care how upscale this area of Manhattan is—the world is full of people you can't trust, especially with someone like her. My woman wasn't getting into any stranger's car.

Wait. My woman...

Yeah, I'll need to unpack that later.

But the fact that I felt so possessive after barely a day together was gnawing at me, unsettling every nerve like I was a live wire. The steering wheel under my hands was the only thing grounding me, keeping me from spiraling into the thoughts rattling around my head. The lights of Manhattan flashed by, but this tension wouldn't shake. Every muscle in my body was coiled tight, and no reason for it.

Except there was a reason, wasn't there?

I could feel her eyes on me, watching, studying, then turning away. She wants to say something—probably has wanted to all night—but I'm grateful she hasn't pressed. She practically had to drag every word out of me tonight. I've never driven a woman home before. Usually, I'd send them off in a cab, their time in my life brief and transactional.

Not Violet, though.

She's the first woman to set foot in my penthouse ever, and the first to sit in one of my cars. And why did she have to look so damn good doing it? Even now, staring out the window, she's beautiful. There's a quiet elegance about her, something that makes me want to reach over and hold her hand. Like maybe, if I could just do that, everything would fall into place.

My hand rests on the center console, but all I want to do is bridge the gap between us. Pick up her hand, and feel the warmth of her skin against mine. See what it's like to sit in comfortable silence with someone, without the pressure of filling the void with words. Just the connection—her presence, her warmth, maybe that's all I need.

But that's what couples do. I can't act on that impulse, even if being alone with her is its own brand of torture.

The entire time we talked on the couch, I found myself enjoying it more than I should. Normally, I'd be counting the minutes until I could politely end the evening, send her on her way, and never call again. But with Violet? I wanted more.

And something told me I'd get greedy and always want more where she was concerned.

She dodged the conversation about her parents, and that gnawed at me. Why did it bother me so much? Was it the way her green eyes darkened at the mere mention of them? Or the way she traced the edge of my family photo, like a kid staring longingly into a pet store window, dreaming of a puppy they could never have?

There's something there—something she's not saying—and I'm not sure why it matters to me. But I know one thing for certain: I'll find out.

There was pain behind those green eyes whenever the topic of family came up, and for reasons I couldn't quite explain, I felt the urge to take that pain away.

Tonight wasn't the time to push, though. I couldn't expect her to lay it all out when I was still keeping my own demons locked up tight. I'd be a hypocrite to want her to open up while I kept my guard up like Fort Knox.

When I pulled up in front of her building, I parked by the curb, turning off the engine. She stilled, eyes wide with surprise like she hadn't expected me to walk her to the door. Did she think I was the kind of guy to just drop her off and drive away?

Considering the asshole she used to date, maybe she did. Apparently, none of these guys had mothers like mine. If I ever dared drop a woman at the curb, my mother would disown me—after making sure I lost a few body parts.

I stepped out, walked around to her side, and opened the door. She hesitated as I reached down to take her hand, helping her out of the car. For a second, we stood there, close, and all I could think about was kissing her. My body hummed with the need to grab her, tilt her head back, and press my mouth to hers.

Her lips. Those soft, perfect lips that had molded to mine so effortlessly at the bar.

I wasn't a kissing man. When I slept with women, kissing wasn't part of the equation. It had never meant anything to me—until her. With her, all I could think about was kissing her again.

But I held back, swallowing the urge as I offered my hand instead. She gave me a confused look. "What?"

I shrugged, taking her hand firmly before she could overthink it. "Might as well get used to this—holding hands in public and all that."

It was a lie, an excuse. The truth was, her hand in mine felt perfect. Small, warm, like it was made to fit there. I squeezed her fingers a little tighter as we walked toward the building.

And then I took in her apartment building. No doorman. No security. This place was practically begging for a break-in.

Every protective instinct in my body went into overdrive. Some primal, territorial part of me wanted to scoop her up, toss her over my shoulder, and take her back to my penthouse where she'd be safe. Where I could keep her close, where no one could get to her.

A single woman in New York, living in a building with no security, no doorman, and no protection at night? It's one thing during the day, but at night, anyone could walk right in. My jaw tightened, and I bit back the flood of words threatening to spill out of my mouth.

I'll say something when this becomes more serious.

When, not if.

I've been around her for less than 48 hours, and already I'm contemplating dragging her to live with me just to keep her safe. I need to get a grip on reality. That line I was trying to define in the shower? Still blurred, still nonexistent.

We take the stairs because her building's elevator is broken—something I remembered from when I visited before. I silently thanked my cardio routine, because the last thing I need is to be winded by the time we reached her floor. As we approach her door, she lets go of my hand, and the absence of her warmth is immediate. Once she has her door open, she pauses, turning to face me.

"Thank you for today," she says, her voice soft, and there's a hint of nervousness as she rocks back on her heels. It's oddly adorable. For someone so confident, these little flashes of vulnerability make her feel real—remind me that she's not just some tough woman I met in a bar, but someone with feelings. Someone I need to make sure I don't take for granted.

Swallowing, I step closer, brushing a kiss on her cheek. My lips linger longer than necessary, but I can't help it. Her skin is soft, her scent clinging to me, and I know I won't sleep tonight without this one last inhale of her.

"Of course," I murmur, pulling back just enough to see the faint blush coloring her cheeks. "Talk tomorrow?"

She nods, that small, shy smile lighting up her face, and for a moment, all I want is to kiss her properly. But I step back instead, letting the moment sit between us.

"Goodnight, Violet."

She nods, and I take a step back, watching her close the door. I don't move, not until I hear the reassuring click of the lock. Only then do I turn and walk down the hallway, the dim light casting shadows that do nothing to ease my mood. This place is a disaster waiting to happen. I make a mental note to call the owner, and demand he installs proper lighting by tomorrow—or hell, maybe I'll just buy the damn building myself and fix everything.

It's not until I'm back in my car, the engine growling to life, that it really hits me.

I want more. I want to hold her, touch her, kiss her, and spend every waking moment with her. That possessive urge is already clawing at me, barely contained, and we've only just started. So what happens by the end of this week? Or a few weeks from now?

I thought I could keep this casual, convince her it was all just for show while secretly getting to know her, but there was nothing fake about what I was feeling. The overwhelming need to be near her, to be consumed by her, wasn't supposed to hit this hard, this fast. But here I am, barely holding it together, and this was only the beginning.

This half-cocked idea of mine—to pretend to date her as a solution to my problems—might be the smartest or dumbest move I've ever made. Because now, the lines between what's real and what's pretend are starting to blur, and I don't think I'll be able to keep them separate for much longer.

Alex

MONDAY PASSED IN A haze. I'd spent the entire day resisting the urge to call or text Violet, fighting every instinct that screamed at me to reach out. It's not the need to talk to her that's got me twisted inside—it's the fact I've purposely prevented myself from giving in. Now, I'm sitting in a board meeting, my mood dark, my temper on edge, patience long gone.

Today was supposed to be my day off from her. I convinced myself that giving her space was the right move, that if I bombarded her too soon, she'd start questioning what this thing between us really was. Hell, I don't even know if I can explain it myself.

But now? I've been sitting in this damn meeting for two hours, and I couldn't tell you what was discussed. Board members have talked, I've nodded, rolled my eyes when appropriate, maybe even blinked a few times for good measure, but not a single word has sunk in.

That's what meeting notes are for, right? Penelope, my assistant, has already kicked me under the table twice, giving me those "get your head in the game" eyes. I shot her a sarcastic smile, but the truth is, I'm barely here.

The company's doing fine—hell, we're thriving—but the board's constant push for me to "stabilize" my image is grating on my last nerve. A single CEO makes investors nervous. Really? As if being unmarried somehow affects my ability to run a multi-billion-dollar business.

It's bad enough I get the grandbaby lecture from my mother and grandmother every time I see them. Now I've got a boardroom full of people concerned about my marital status. The only ones who don't chime in are my younger brothers, Dominic and Enrico, but they're no better. They just sit there, smirking like little shits at my misery like it's the best show they've ever watched.

Honestly, when I think about the married CEOs I know, their lives are absolute shit shows. They're the ones with the messy affairs, juggling a socialite wife and one, maybe two, mistresses. Yet somehow, they're seen as a more stable investment than me, the guy who actually has his head on straight? It's laughable.

I get it—tabloids love to paint me as some untamable playboy. But let's be real, just because a man is single and dates doesn't mean he's out of control. Do I fuck every woman I take out? No. It's been months since I've touched anyone, and the only taste I've craved lately is the one I got from a certain green-eyed bombshell.

Her eyes, that mossy green that seems to see right through me, are all I can think about while I sit here, pretending to give a shit about projections I already reviewed. These meetings are nothing more than an excuse for the board to gossip, vent, throw out half-baked suggestions, and let me sit through hours of nonsense. I'll catch up on the meeting notes in 20 minutes tops, but for now, I'm stuck.

"Alex." Robert's voice cuts through the noise. He's one of the oldest members of the board, not by age, but by how long he's been here, and honestly, he's about as subtle as a brick to the face. "You've been seeing that woman for a while now, right?"

And here it is. The topic I've been waiting for, yet dreading.

Do I want to talk about it? Not really. But I knew it was coming. Last month, I told the board I was dating someone, more out of necessity than desire to share. It's like following up on an action item in a meeting—don't forget to schedule that call, and oh, find yourself a steady relationship.

The truth is, now that I have someone—sort of—I don't want to talk about her. Not with them, not with anyone. I don't want the world to pick her apart or have a piece of her. She's mine.

Which is insane, I know. The whole point of this arrangement was to show everyone I could be serious, that I wasn't some bachelor playing the field. But now, this primal, possessive urge has crept in, and it's got me reassessing everything. Where the hell is this coming from?

She was supposed to be part of the plan, a solution to my image problem. And now, I'm sitting here wanting to keep her all to myself, like the world doesn't deserve to know her. It's the kind of possessiveness that doesn't make sense, not when I barely know her, but damn if it doesn't feel real.

"Yes. Her name is Violet."

"That's a pretty name," Dillan, the resident idiot of the board, chimes in with a smirk. "She must be quite the looker to keep your interest."

His tone is worse than nails on a chalkboard. Like I'm the kind of guy who's swayed by just a pretty face. It's ironic because in Manhattan, women are all about the exterior. What's inside? Usually hollow. But Violet? She's the exception. She's beautiful, sure, but there's more.

Something beneath the surface that's rare in this city, and I'm a greedy bastard who wants it all to himself.

I shoot Dillan a look that makes it clear he's treading on thin ice. He catches on, clears his throat, and awkwardly turns back to the rest of the group. My brother Dominic, sitting next to him, barely suppresses a laugh, covering it with a not-so-subtle cough. Idiot.

Both Dominic and Enrico know about the arrangement with Violet—the fake dating situation I cooked up to keep the investors happy. For the last month, I've been telling anyone who'd listen that I've been seeing someone, but until now, I had no one to show for it. Tomorrow, that changes when Violet joins me at the investor dinner. The perfect display of my "serious relationship" for the board. My brothers have been in on the game the whole time, playing along with the story like the smartasses they are.

Dominic, our COO, is the people guy. Employees like him, and trust him. Enrico, my CTO, handles the tech side of things better than I ever could. I might own a tech company, but I dove into it because it made money. The secret to my success? Hire the best people to bring your vision to life. I'm the one with the vision, the ability to assess acquisitions, and the numbers. My brothers are the only two people I trust completely in this company.

But right now? Both of them are grinning like they've just seen me toss my dignity to the wolves.

Tomorrow night is supposed to be a win, but I'm already dreading it. Not because I don't want to impress the investors—I've done that countless times—but because I hate the idea of parading Violet in front of these people. I don't want to share her. Not with them, not with anyone. The possessiveness that's been gnawing at me since the day I met her feels irrational, but I can't shake it.

This was supposed to be simple. But now, I'm realizing just how complicated it's getting because I underestimated how I'd feel about her.

Yeah, I'm "dating" the most beautiful woman I've ever met. She's polished, perfect—nothing about her is bought with daddy's money like the socialites I'm used to. Violet is an all-natural smokeshow, the kind of woman who turns heads without even trying. The hottest, smartest woman I've ever encountered, and this world will tear her apart bit by bit if I'm not careful.

This is why people in my world don't marry for love. They marry for business alliances, and contracts. They have kids to secure heirs and meet expectations. They don't marry outside their social class because the women are like rabid dogs, waiting to tear each other apart, and the men? They're all chasing asses on the side. It's a game, one I've refused to play for years. I tried once, and it blew up in my face.

My goal is for Violet to get to know me, and things continue.

There's plenty to love about me, sure, but there's also plenty to hate. I'm not the easiest person to deal with, and most of my demons come from the same dark place—bitterness. I was already pissed at myself for showing her even a sliver of that nastiness on Sunday. She didn't deserve it. Hell, it wasn't even directed at her. I was just stuck in my head, my own worst enemy.

And she deserves more than that. More than me. But as I said, I'm selfish.

Alex

> Alex: Ready for tonight?

> Violet: Yes, you bought me a very inappropriate evening gown that I can't wait to wear for this.

> Alex: How inappropriate?

> Violet: If you didn't want me to buy these things, you should've paid more attention while we were shopping.

> Alex: Okay, just tell me how much cleavage will be on display.

> Violet: A tasteful amount.

> Alex: Did it come with a turtleneck? It's cold out there, you know.

WE TEXT THROUGHOUT THE day. It's becoming a habit—one I didn't plan on, but now, I can't seem to stop.

Last night, I sent her a goodnight text. It felt like I'd be missing out if I didn't speak to her, even for one day. Like some lovesick teenager, I watched those three little dots bounce on my screen, waiting for her response. When she finally texted me back, I went to bed with a smile on my face.

This morning, I took a risk and sent her a "good morning" text. Half of me was testing the waters, seeing if I'd crossed some invisible line. But she responded right away. And from there, it became a steady back-and-forth—light, easy and addictive.

Now, as the hours slip by, I'm counting down the minutes until I see her again. And I can't remember the last time I felt like this. That electric anticipation for someone, like they're all you can think about, and every second without them feels like a waste. It's... foreign.

I've dated women, sure, but none have ever had me checking my phone every five minutes or replaying their words in my head. And certainly not leaving me this excited to just... see them. It's like she's embedded herself into my thoughts without even trying.

And, damn, I'm not sure if I like it or if it terrifies me. Probably both.

In my last relationship, we barely texted. I could leave for a five-day business trip and not hear a word, and the worst part? I didn't even care. I understand why now, but back then, it never crossed my mind to be bothered. Never once did I find myself in the position I'm in now—waiting for my phone to ping, lunging for it the moment it does, even in the middle of meetings, just to see if it's Violet.

Feelings? Yeah, there are a lot of them, and they've come out of nowhere, ambushing me when I least expected it. I haven't even been on a real date with her, and I'm already obsessed. It's why tonight is messing with me so much. I'm not the romantic type, and I sure as hell don't believe in love at first sight.

But after seeing her at the bar that night, I knew I was in trouble. Talking to her? That just made it worse. She's unlike anyone I've ever met, and every time I try convincing myself that the more I get to know her, the less intrigued I'll be, I realize just how wrong I am.

So wrong that I'm already planning how I can see her again on Wednesday and Thursday.

Going the whole day yesterday without seeing her? It physically hurt and I don't plan to do that again.

Four days. I've known her for four days. What the hell is wrong with me?

And tonight? It's that dress. That damn fucking dress she's wearing.

I'm lost in my thoughts, spiraling, trying to figure out where the hell I go from here when she steps out of the guest bathroom. And just like that, everything else fades. She's ready for the dinner with my investors, and I'm stunned into silence. Normally, these dinners are my version of hell. I hate schmoozing people who've already made more money off me than they know what to do with and yet they expect me to kiss their ass. It's a backward world for sure.

My personality and personal life shouldn't matter to their bottom line, but thanks to pressure from my board and a few investors acting like my relationship status affects the health of their stock portfolios, here I am. Dressed up, fake smiles locked and loaded, and with Violet on my arm.

The problem? I have no idea what's going through her mind.

Does she feel even a fraction of what I'm feeling? She's certainly not showing it. Our texts have been casual, nothing too deep, and I haven't touched her since that night at the bar—even though every time I'm near her, I want to. It's killing me because, to her, this may be an arrangement with an expiration date. After the holidays, we go our separate ways. No transitions. No real future. It's like I've been friend-zoned, but worse.

And the only person I have to blame is myself. I set the terms. I practically told her this was temporary, a deal with an end date. Because I was desperate to have her in any way possible.

But now, seeing her in that damn dress? I can't tell if I'm heating or cooling off. My body is at war with itself.

"Are you sure this is okay? I feel a little overdressed. Then again, I don't do five-star restaurant meals like your people."

My people?

I try to ignore the sting of that. But then I catch sight of her dress—the same black one she picked out at the store, the one that's now hugging every single curve, making me groan inwardly. It dips low in the back, just above that perfect curve at the small of her spine, while the front wraps elegantly around her neck. She looks like pure temptation.

"It's exactly what my *people* wear to dinner." Okay, so I didn't forget her comment.

But why does it bother me that she's bothered by the fact that I'm rich?

I'm the 10th hottest bachelor in New York, for Christ's sake. Women flock to me. Except none of them compare to her, because she's not just a woman—she's a goddess, and maybe that's what's eating at me. The women I usually deal with? They want the money, the status. It's transactional. They know who I am, and how much I'm worth, and they're drawn to it.

Violet, though? She sees it as a flaw.

And somehow, that makes me like her even more.

I'm in my head too much at this point. I just need to get through this dinner. Work was hell today, my latest acquisition is turning into a bidding war I refuse to lose, and now I've got to fake my way through a meal with three men I can't stand. Fun fact: they're all married and cheat on their wives, but somehow my relationship status affects their investment decisions next quarter. Hypocrites, the lot of them.

Antonio drops us at the restaurant, and I tell him to stay close along with the promise of a to-go meal when we return. I don't plan on us being here long—just enough to make an appearance, appease the vultures, and get the hell out. Socializing isn't exactly my strong suit, but tonight it's worse. I don't want to share her.

Why the hell did I choose a woman I genuinely like? The thought of the men I do business with ogling her makes my blood boil.

We walk hand in hand into the restaurant, the hostess recognizing me immediately and motioning for us to follow. Violet shoots me a questioning look, but I just shrug. This is one of our usual spots for business dinners—upscale, Manhattan sleek, with a rotating menu and guest chefs that show up once a month. Great food, excellent wine, and no frills. Perfect for closing deals or schmoozing up morons you do business with.

Yet, as I guide her with a hand at the small of her back, it's like touching fire. Her skin is warm and smooth, and suddenly my mind is miles away from this dinner, spinning off into places it shouldn't go—especially when I'm here for work. But hell, if it isn't getting harder to think straight when she's this close. My mind is thinking about anything but work appropriate things right now when I look down, watching that fabric stretch across every inch of her perfect body.

"Ah, Alexander!" Jonathan Russo, the most obnoxious, pretentious prick I know—and my biggest investor—stands as soon as he spots us, announcing our arrival like we're royalty. All eyes turn our way, and though I force a smile, I'm grinding my teeth so hard I might chip one. "Come sit, sit! And who's this lovely lady?" His gaze slides to Violet, but I can barely focus on the asshole. I feel Violet glance at me briefly before she clears her throat and extends her hand with confidence.

"I'm Violet Hart, Alex's girlfriend," she says smoothly.

I freeze for a second. It sounds so damn perfect—natural like she's been playing the part for years.

Before Jonathan can make some snide comment, my brother Dom, who's here solo, stands up with a grin. "Violet! So good to see you again." Always the charmer, he walks over and kisses her cheek. And just like that, Violet slips into the role effortlessly, as if she's been in on this from the start.

"Nice to see you too, Dominic," she replies, the picture of ease.

I don't miss the look Dom shoots me over her shoulder. The barely concealed wink along with his smile. He even mouths *"damn"* before sitting back down. Yeah, damn is right. Violet is stunning, and she's outclassing every woman in the room without even trying. More importantly, she doesn't even know it.

Jonathan, momentarily thrown off by Dom, shifts his attention back to Violet, sizing her up with a slick smile—the same smile that snagged him a wife and two mistresses. He's doing that sleazy thing he does where he checks out women right in front of Samantha, his perfectly oblivious wife. "Well, Alexander, I heard from Russell that you were seeing someone, but I had no idea you had a girlfriend."

"I sure do," I reply, signaling for the waiter. Tonight's not a wine kind of night. I need whiskey.

Jonathan's still watching me, clearly waiting for more, but I keep my face neutral. He takes the hint and proceeds with introductions. "This is David Blake, head of finance, and his wife, Isabella. Over here we have Michael Herring from our real estate group, and his lovely wife, Evelyn."

Lovely Evelyn. I cringe internally because I know damn well that Jonathan's been sleeping with her behind Michael's back, and he's shameless enough to sit here and call her "lovely" to her face while Michael remains clueless.

All I care about right now is getting through this dinner and keeping Jonathan's leering eyes off Violet.

People in my circle are exactly why I can't share a woman I actually care about. It doesn't matter how special she is—someone will always want her. It's like business to these men, and a woman like Violet? She's a prize they'll all try to get their hands on. While I tell myself she's not the straying type, I don't really know her, just like she doesn't fully know me.

I'm supposed to be showing her off tonight. She's here for me. But as Jonathan rambles on, his wife and the other women engaging with Violet, my stomach twists into knots. Maybe she's too perfect, too stunning for this room. Every man at this table, because I know them all too well, is already thinking about how they'd fuck her.

Hell, I'm thinking about it too—but I'd like to believe my thoughts aren't as sleazy as theirs.

In our world, marriages are often little more than business deals. But when my so-called business partners—the ones with wives, no less—are eyeing my date like she's on the auction block, it drags back memories I've worked hard to bury. With my ex, I wasn't this possessive. I took her to dinners with Jonathan and his band of morons, and I wasn't as bothered when they looked at her. But the way Jonathan looks at Violet makes my blood boil.

She's not really your girlfriend.

That single thought hits hard. We don't have a real bond outside of our makeshift arrangement. Sure, it's not like we called this "fake dating," but it's not set in stone either. To her, there's no deeper connection, no future beyond the holidays. Meanwhile, I'm over here feeling possessive, like I need to stake my claim before one of these jackasses swoops in. I've never felt this strong of a pull to someone—a need to protect them, keep them away from the vultures circling us.

I sip my whiskey, placing my order with the server, barely listening as Jonathan drones on about his latest venture. He's buttering me up, angling to ask for money tomorrow.

That's why I'm here, right? But I swear to god, if he ogles Violet's chest one more time, I might tell him to shove his business deal somewhere the light doesn't reach.

My eyes keep drifting back to her. The way she smiles, how the light dusts her freckles across her nose and cheeks, the way she occasionally glances at me with those green eyes, making my chest tight. I offer her a smile, or at least the best version of one I can muster, even though my insides are a tangled mess.

This was a bad idea. I can feel my mood souring with every tick of the clock.

Without thinking, I rest my hand on her thigh, my thumb tracing slow circles over the fabric of her dress. That small connection is the only thing keeping me from grabbing her, pulling her out of this place, and taking her home.

"I hear you and Stone are battling over another bid," Jonathan says, his voice smooth but full of the usual underhanded curiosity.

I nod, not giving him anything he can use. It's not a battle—it's a strategy, but I'm not about to hand him that. The guy has his nose so far up every CEO's ass in Manhattan that he'd run to Julian Stone the second we left here. "May the best man win," I reply, my tone indifferent, eyes still locked on Violet despite the conversation circling business.

Every smile she sends their way makes my skin itch. Each laugh at a joke that's not mine tightens the knot in my stomach. And the wandering eyes—the way these men look at her—has my control fraying fast.

My hand is still resting on her thigh, but instead of comfort, my hand is numb. The touch that was grounding me just moments ago now only makes the pit in my stomach grow.

She's not really mine. I had the chance to tell her I wanted more, that I wanted to date her for real, but I didn't. And now, each minute that passes makes backtracking feel impossible.

Besides, her ex has left her with enough baggage, would she even entertain the idea?

I glance at my phone, needing a distraction, needing anything to stop me from losing my shit in front of these people. "Sorry, I need to take this," I lie, pushing back from the table knowing I can find some business associate's call to return once I'm out. I can't sit here any longer. Leaving her alone with them is the last thing I want to do, but if I don't get some air, I might very well snap.

I pace outside the restaurant, phone glued to my ear, but my mind isn't on the call. My eyes keep drifting toward the entrance, and before I know it, 40 minutes have passed. I glance at my watch and curse under my breath. I left Violet in there, in the middle of that table full of sharks. She's going to be pissed, and I'm already spiraling. Ending the call abruptly, I head back inside, determined to grab her and get the hell out of there—only to run straight into Dominic, who's clearly been looking for me.

"What the fuck are you doing?" he snaps, his expression tight.

"I had a call," I wave my phone at him like that explains everything.

"Bullshit. You didn't have to take it," he says, poking me hard in the chest with his finger. "The whole point of this dinner was to show Jonathan and his crew that you're solid. And what do you do? You leave Violet in there, alone." He lets out a breath, shaking his head. "By the way, that woman? She's putting on one hell of a show. Talking it up with the wives like it's no big deal."

I try to push past him, but his hand grips my suit jacket, holding me in place.

"What's going on with you?" His tone softens, but he's still not letting me off the hook.

"Nothing," I say, even though my clenched jaw tells a different story.

"Uh-huh."

I let out a frustrated breath. "I like her, okay? Too much."

"And that's a problem because...?"

I shrug, the tension knotting in my shoulders. "She agreed to this arrangement. To her, that's all it is, but I don't want it to end there. And she assumes it will."

Dominic raises an eyebrow. "Have you told her that?"

I shake my head, feeling like an idiot, but my brother has a laundry list of things to use against me -- this is another drop in a very large pond.

"Well, you've kinda created your own problem then, haven't you?" He crosses his arms, giving me that older brother look even though I'm the oldest. "If you like her enough to lose your shit over this, you should probably mention it. And don't tell me you're having Natalia flashbacks, especially with Jonathan in there." My teeth grind together at the mention of my ex, and I know Dom sees the tension ripple through me.

He's right. Natalia's exactly why I'm stuck in my head, even though Violet is nothing like her.

"You think leaving the woman you're interested in alone with that group is gonna make you feel better?" He leans in. "I see how you look at her. Get out of your damn head and don't fuck this up."

With that, he shoves me back toward the restaurant.

Violet

I KNEW ALEX HAD a hot-and-cold streak, but tonight was something else entirely. Yesterday, we didn't talk much, and it was fine. Today? We talked almost all day. It didn't bother me that he was quiet on Monday; we weren't in some whirlwind romance. We were here to fake-date when needed — not actually be a couple. And I'm definitely not some clingy woman who needs to be in constant contact.

But here's the thing. Every time my phone pinged with a message from him, my pulse did a jig like I was some giddy teenager with a massive crush. It's ridiculous.

So when I arrived at his place to change into one of the dresses he bought me and found him already home — early, in fact — I expected things to be fine.

Except, he was...off. He stormed into the apartment, fully dressed and ready, but when his eyes landed on me, there was this fire in them. Lust, pure and unfiltered. For a split second, I thought maybe we wouldn't even make it to the dinner, that he might just tear the dress off and forget the night altogether.

Then, as if someone flipped a switch, his expression changed. His throat bobbed as he swallowed hard, muttering that I looked "good" — nothing more, nothing less — and we headed out the door.

I asked him about his day, trying to engage, but he answered in clipped one-word replies. After the third attempt, I gave up. What was the point? The tension radiating off him was enough to make the air thick, his jaw so tight I swear he could've crushed walnuts with it. His fists clenched and unclenched like he was barely holding himself together. I couldn't tell if he was mad at me or if something else had happened. Was it work? Or did I say something wrong in our texts today?

Whatever it was, Alexander Bennetti had mastered the brooding billionaire look.

The entire ride to the restaurant was suffocating in awkward silence. Alex didn't say a word, and when he told Antonio to stay close because we wouldn't be long, I almost asked why but thought better of it. Whatever storm he was brewing, I was just going to ride it out.

Then we got to the table full of his investors, and instead of introducing me, he just...sat. Like, full-on, stone-cold silence. He might as well have been made of stone. And then there I am introducing myself to strangers without a single word slipping out of his mouth.

The whole point of this was for me to help him with this supposedly important dinner, and now I'm left to carry the show? Fine. I can play the role. Even though I'm so out of my element it's taking all my energy to keep my dinner from making a reappearance.

Everyone at the table was nice enough, but I felt wildly out of place. When they asked about what I do, they seemed genuinely impressed that I was trying to write my novel. But the wives? Oh, they were not the typical trophy wives I expected.

Isabella? She's a premier interior designer who's tried to redo Alex's penthouse a few times — and been refused every time. Evelyn? A corporate lawyer who now runs charities. My father would probably love her more than he loves me. And then there's Samantha, a renowned chef and restaurant owner.

So, yeah, not what I pictured. At all.

Alex had kept telling me I wasn't *"vanilla,"* that I was different from the women he usually met in these circles, but now I'm sitting here wondering...what exactly does he mean by that? Because these women are accomplished, beautiful, and, yes, they have that typical New York polished look, but still. My preconceived notions were way off. I expected trophy wives cloaked in designer fashion purchased by their husbands and brain power that required a hand crank to get it going.

So, what makes me not "vanilla"? What's his definition of that anyway? Right now, I feel entirely outclassed in looks and career. Not to mention, I'm not in the same social stratosphere as these people, and it's showing.

Is that the whole point? Did Alex want a date who wasn't from his world to make him look like the guy who doesn't care about class? Like some sort of PR stunt to boost his image, and make him seem more relatable?

I feel like a prop, and it doesn't sit well. I'm no one's prop.

Alex was chiming in just enough to pass as engaged, barely, but he wasn't starting any conversations. Just answering when spoken to, all distant and cold. Meanwhile, Samantha, seated next to me, was being the sweetest thing, suggesting what I should order since half the dishes on the menu looked foreign to me. Of course, I was way too embarrassed to admit I had no idea what most of them were.

Everything about this evening felt...off. His hand rested on my thigh, which was probably the most intimate thing he's done since we met, but then, as if on cue, he pulled his phone from his pocket and excused himself to take a call. And just like that, he was gone. He left me alone at the table with his investors, making small talk and nodding politely for almost forty minutes.

I kept sneaking glances at the door, silently begging for him to come back. His brother, Dominic, kept throwing apologetic looks my way from across the table, so I knew something was off if his brother was giving me pity eyes. Eventually, Dominic stood, presumably to go find him and drag him back to his damn dinner -- or at least I sure hoped.

I tried to tune back into the conversation, but my mind was too full trying to decode the evening's turn.

"So you work for Hartley? He's a good man," David, one of the other men at the table, said as dessert was served. "Looking to become a publisher one day or stick with writing?"

Oh, great. Alex misses the entire dinner, and now we're on dessert and discussing my career.

"Well, while I do enjoy publishing, I'm just working there to understand the behind-the-scenes stuff," I explained, trying not to overthink how I came off to these incredibly accomplished people. "You know, how editors choose manuscripts, what gets published, and why. But my dream is to write full-time one day. I've got a few stories I'm working on, but none are quite finished yet."

Samantha perked up, her hand gripping my arm. "Ooh, what genre?"

I felt my cheeks heat. Why did I always get embarrassed when I had to admit I was writing romance? I mean, sure, people usually assume it's all about the steamy scenes—which, okay, it is sometimes—but romance is so much more. It's the passion, the emotional rollercoaster, the raw love, and yes, the spicy bits too. I remembered when my mom once asked if I was still writing those "porn books," and I nearly rolled my eyes into another dimension. She'd never understand. I mean, yeah, I love Pride & Prejudice as much as the next hopeless romantic, but let's be real—these days readers need a little more... reality in their romance. And no one's waiting for an arranged marriage to some rich Mr. Darcy at seventeen.

Though, sometimes... I think of Alex as my own Mr. Darcy. Broody, emotionally unavailable, and ridiculously attractive.

"Romance novels," I finally admitted, bracing for judgment.

Samantha's face lit up. "Oh my gosh, I love those! I can't wait to read yours when it's published. If you ever need a beta reader, I'd be honored!"

I smiled, genuinely touched by her excitement and thankful I didn't get a wince like I get from some. "I'd love that."

Just as the dessert plates are set down in front of everyone. Alex appears, tucking his phone back into his suit jacket with the urgency of a man on a mission. "Sorry, but we have to leave," he says, not even glancing in my direction. "I have some business to handle, need to get back to the office."

No help with my chair tonight. No acknowledgment of the evening. Just... nothing.

I wipe my mouth, biting back my irritation, and scoot myself out from the table. Apparently, his investors catching a glimpse of me was enough; the rest of the evening? Not his problem.

"It was a pleasure meeting all of you," I say, offering an apologetic smile to the group. I have no idea if these people are close to him or just business contacts, but if he's going to be an ass, I'm not about to add fuel to the fire. Dominic gives me a small nod, and I can tell he's staying behind to smooth things over, so I turn to follow the jerk with zero social skills.

As I step outside into the biting cold, I spot Alex standing there waiting for Antonio to pull the car around. My teeth are practically chattering from the chill or perhaps the mood, and he doesn't even offer me a glance.

"Why didn't you bring a jacket?" he snaps, his tone sharp and laced with frustration.

That's it. I'm done. I cross my arms, feeling my pulse thrum as anger hits in full force. I'm not cold anymore. Nope, I'm now raging like a fire and ready to burn.

"Why are you such a prick?" I fire at him.

That got his attention. He finally looks at me, blinking in surprise like he didn't expect me to bite back. Well, surprise, this gal has teeth and isn't afraid to nip.

Instead of staring at the lineup of cars, waiting for Antonio to pull up, Alex's gaze snaps to me, sharp and unyielding. "Excuse me?"

I square my shoulders, heart pounding, but I don't back down. "You not only made me introduce myself to a bunch of strangers but then left me alone to carry the entire conversation while you ignored me. Then, you swoop back in to tell me we're leaving like I'm just an afterthought. I've never been so embarrassed in my life. I thought we were supposed to be dating for this important dinner with your investors, but in there, I might as well have been your secretary."

He snorts, already pulling out his phone like this conversation isn't even worth his full attention.

Fury bubbles up, hot and relentless. If people think Pompei was bad, wait until they see Violet in full-out rage. "Is that why you picked me? Because you think I'm easy to slum it with? That my standards are lower and I'll just take whatever scraps you throw my way? Or is that part of the image you needed to spruce up? Date some girl with low standards and not at your level so you get a pat on the back for taking on a charity case?"

His blue eyes dart up from his screen, narrowing at me, lips pressed into a thin, hard line. Oh, he's pissed now. But you know what? I'm not sorry. I feel like a stand-in, a doll dressed up for the show, and it's infuriating.

"You know what?" I say, my voice was cold and sharp. "I'll get my own ride. Thanks for the lovely evening," I add with a hefty dose of sarcasm, turning on my heel, and pulling my phone from my clutch to order an Uber while I head down to the corner.

"Violet!" His voice is sharp, but I keep walking, my focus on the screen and the ping showing where my ride will pick me up. Then, I feel a strong hand grip my elbow, spinning me around to face him.

"No," I say firmly, yanking my arm free. "Leave me alone. Antonio is waiting. You go. I'll get my own ride."

"Violet, please. Let's just go home," his voice is softer now, almost pleading, but I'm too far into my fit fest to let up.

I whip around, glaring at him. "In case you forgot, I don't live with you! This isn't even my dress, or my earrings, or my underwear. You dressed me up like some doll, paraded me around to entertain them, and then left me in the dust. I didn't sign up for this."

He nods at a few people walking by, trying to keep it cool, but I see the tension in his shoulders, the way his jaw clenches as he tries to pull himself together. I don't care. Not right now.

"Violet, c'mon," he steps closer again, his hand reaching out to grab me. "I'm not letting you take a ride home alone. I have a car and a driver for a reason."

"I'm not your real girlfriend, Alex. I'm just here pretending, playing along with whatever game you're running to save face. And you know what? Even if I was your girlfriend, you don't get to tell me what to do. Now leave me the hell alone."

I shove him back and, for the first time tonight, he doesn't follow as I walk the rest of the way to my pick up spot.

Violet

WHEN I REACH MY apartment, there he is—leaning against the door like a scene out of a movie, arms crossed, looking unfairly perfect in that suit of his. The second he sees me, he straightens up, like he's been waiting to speak to me for hours when it's probably been twenty minutes. Regardless he's on edge. Good. Now let me push him off the damn thing.

I'm not in the mood for whatever he has to say. I hold up my hand before he can speak, fumbling in my purse for my keys.

"Not tonight, Alex. I've had enough. I have an early day tomorrow, and honestly, I'm not in the mood. You ignored me plenty tonight—now it's my turn to return the favor."

I'm exhausted and emotionally frayed. The last thing I need is a midnight heart-to-heart when all I want is to curl up with my feelings, maybe cry a little, and prepare for the train wreck that is tomorrow: another latte run, dealing with Margaret, and pretending my life isn't a hot mess.

Tears are like a weird reset button. Either they cleanse your soul or make you feel worse. Right now, I'm leaning toward the latter.

"Violet, we have to talk eventually."

"Says who? I'll see you Friday. Actually, scratch that. I don't need you there. I've mastered the art of looking alone and embarrassed all on my own. Tonight was great practice for that, so thanks for the warm-up."

Okay, maybe I'm being a little dramatic, but he deserves it after the way tonight went down. I unlock my door, ready to slam it in his face, but of course, his hand shoots out and holds it open like it's nothing.

"Suit yourself, come on in, Your Highness," I say, sarcastic as ever, not bothering to look back as I walk inside. "But I'm not talking to you."

I hear the door shut behind him, and now I'm determined to make this as uncomfortable as humanly possible. If he wants to stay, fine. But that doesn't mean I have to talk.

I toss my keys and purse onto the desk with a satisfying clatter and kick off my heels, feeling the day—and my patience—peel away. Stripping down to nothing but a black lace thong and bra, I head for the bathroom without a second glance at Alex.

"You know, stripping for me isn't going to make me talk," he calls out behind me, his tone teasing.

"Perfect," I snap back, slamming the bathroom door shut. "Because I wasn't planning to talk to you—or do anything else for that matter."

I aggressively squeeze toothpaste onto my toothbrush, the sound of it more satisfying than it should be, but I have to take out my aggression somewhere and the toothpaste tube is my victim. Looking down, I realize I'm practically naked. Great. Just what I need for a face-off with him. I settled for a pair of shorts and a shirt I tossed on the floor earlier this morning when I darted off for work.

Opening the door, I'm met with the sight of Alex—suit jacket off, dress shirt hanging open, revealing an infuriatingly perfect chest. Like, sculpted-by-the-gods perfect.

"What the hell are you doing?" I demand, trying to keep my eyes from doing a full scan of his body.

"I'm staying until we talk," he says casually like he's suggesting we grab a cup of coffee. "So, we can either talk now, or we'll talk in the morning after we've slept."

"Go to bed?" I repeat, stunned.

"Yes, you know—sleep."

I look around my tiny studio apartment, waving my arms dramatically. "You're telling me you'd give up your luxurious palace to sleep here?" My studio is smaller than his walk-in closet for crying out loud. "Look, you don't have to prove anything to me, Alex. No one's here to see you pretend to date some lowly, wannabe editor's assistant. Just go home."

Stalking toward me, shirt still hanging open, Alex stops just inches away. His hand grips my hip, pulling me closer as he leans down, his breath hot against my ear. "Violet, I'd sleep in a tent on the street until we talk," he whispers before pulling back and casually stripping off his shirt.

Great. Now I definitely need that award for self-control. It's wildly unfair of him to use that body against me. Yes, I did walk out here in nothing but a thong, but this—this is a new level of temptation.

Ignoring the way my pulse races, I yank back the covers on my bed, shooting silent curses at Max, who clearly had a field day making the damn thing earlier. He's added even more throw pillows just to mess with me, I'm sure of it. Huffing, I toss them aside and climb into bed, punching my pillow with unnecessary force. Sleep is going to be impossible, but I'm proving a point.

The sound of his belt unbuckling snaps me out of my pillow-punching rage. I sit up, eyes wide. "If you think we're about to have sex, you're definitely misreading the signals."

I refuse to look at him—because what if he's naked? But, of course, my eyes betray me. I glance over just in time to see him unzip his pants and push them down, leaving him in nothing but boxer briefs. My hand flies up to cover my eyes.

I cannot look. Absolutely will not—but I do because I'm weak.

"What are you doing?" I grit out, keeping my hand firmly in place only my fingers happen to crack open offering me a glimpse.

"I told you, I'm going to sleep," he says like it's the most obvious thing in the world. "And I don't sleep in clothes."

I growl, flopping back down and turning my back to him just as the bed dips. His weight settles into the mattress, and I hear the sheets rustle. "Apologies," I mutter sarcastically. "They're not 10,000 thread count or made of silk. We stick strictly to Target specials here."

He chuckles, the sound rumbling through the small space. "Do they even make 10,000 thread count?"

I ignore him, staring at the wall.

What the hell happened tonight?

I get mood swings. Hell, if there's a crown for flying off the handle and regretting it later, I'd be wearing it. But Alex? This man is something else. One minute he's ice-cold, the next he's burning hot, and there's no warning, no logic to it—especially at an important dinner where he needed me. Why was I even there?

If this arrangement means I'll be treated like crap by a moody bear every time we're out, then absolutely not. And if I'm just some pawn to prove he's "dating outside his circle," only for him to treat me like garbage? Nope. I'll happily bow out now and deal with being the girl Alex Bennetti, New York's hottest bachelor, dumped at my company's party on Friday.

I don't even bother saying anything. I sigh, turning back to my bed and slipping under the covers, ready to end this day. But before I can settle in, the covers lift, and I release a loud squeak when Alex slides in right behind me, his body flush against mine.

I sit up and glare at him. "What the hell are you doing?"

"Apologizing," he says simply, wrapping his arm around me and pulling me back down, pressing my body flush against his. Every solid muscle of his body is now in contact with mine, and when he slides his muscular thigh between my legs, I silently tell the heat pooling in my core to cool down.

"I don't want an apology," I mutter, trying to wiggle away, but it's like he's a human vice grip. No chance.

I can feel his breath on my neck as his head settles into the pillow beside me. "I'm sorry for earlier, Violet. I acted like an ass at dinner. That wasn't my intention when I invited you, and it sure as hell wasn't my plan when we got there." He sighs, his arm tightening around me. "I know we don't know each other well, and normally I don't care if I piss someone off, but tonight...I felt awful. I don't regret much in life, but tonight, I do. And I'm really sorry."

"Glad it's off your chest. Hope that helps you sleep better," I grumble, trying to squirm again, only for him to pull me even closer, leaving no room for escape.

"I wouldn't do that," he growls, his voice low, and I freeze, suddenly aware of just how intimately pressed we are, and more importantly what my rear just kept rubbing up against. "You want to hear why I was in a bad mood? It might not change anything, but at least you'll know."

"If I let you explain, will you get out of my bed?"

He chuckles softly. "No. You're surprisingly comfortable, and this mattress isn't bad either."

I groan, adjusting my head on the pillow, trying not to acknowledge how ridiculously good it feels having him curled around me like this. Despite my frustration, I feel an unsettling sense of peace. Like maybe we fit together just a little too well, and that thought leaves me conflicted.

And yet, here I am, not pushing him away. Great.

He's quiet for a beat, then he starts. "I don't typically do relationships. I'm not the guy who sleeps around either like I told you, but I didn't explain why. I became CEO when I was 27, which is young, but I built my business from the ground up. I didn't touch a cent of my family's money, and as I'm sure you know from the gossip columns, their money isn't exactly... legal. I couldn't erase my last name or where I come from. Changing it would've broken my mother's heart, but I made a decision—I'd build something that was all mine. Legitimate. That meant a lot of time spent working, not dating or focusing on relationships."

He pauses, his breath warm against the back of my neck. "My family's Sicilian. Most men in my family are married by their late twenties or early thirties. Big families—it's practically a cultural requirement. My mother still calls me every Sunday, asking when she's getting her first grandchild. My father? He wants boys for the family name, of course." I can hear the strain in his voice when he mentions them. "But I was 31 and still not dating. Every woman I met..."

"Vanilla?" I interrupt because the way he uses that word has always fascinated me.

He chuckles softly, a low rumble against my back. "Yeah, vanilla. They were all the same. Polished, perfect, all after the same thing—money, status, a name. I didn't care for it. Relationships didn't seem worth the trouble."

He takes a deep breath and continues, his voice low and steady. "I started feeling pressure from everyone—my family, my board. They were all worried I was going to turn into some playboy billionaire stereotype. And sure, 31 isn't old, especially in New York, but the longer you go without settling down, the more people assume that's exactly who you are. So, I started dating. Her name was Natalia. She was a family friend and connected to some of my business associates. At first, things were... good. She was one of those polished, New York women, but I convinced myself it could work. We dated for over a year."

I shift uncomfortably, not exactly wanting to hear about his past love life, especially one that lasted over a year. But I stay quiet, listening anyway.

"My mother kept pushing me to propose, and I thought... why not? We got along. She was pretty. On paper, it made sense. I convinced myself I loved her, or maybe I wanted to love her because I refused to marry someone I didn't love and it was time for the next steps. Marriage, family, the whole thing."

He pauses, and I can feel the tension as his forearm muscles contract. "But I ignored that nagging feeling that something wasn't right with her or our relationship in general. Then, one day, a reporter showed up at my office. I thought he wanted a comment on a merger or some business deal. Instead, he handed me photos of Natalia. With a dozen different men. Some of the people I thought were my friends. Worse, she was giving them information about my company, insider information that could very well get me in trouble and possibly tank what I worked so hard to build."

He lets out a low, bitter laugh that sends a shiver down my spine. "One of those men was Jonathan—who you met tonight."

Of course. Jonathan. The sleazy investor from dinner who couldn't stop ogling me.

"I know the way people in our circle operate. Affairs, mistresses, lies... it's like a given. But I'm not like that. My father, for all his flaws, was always faithful to my mother. I didn't want to be like the men I work with, the ones who parade their wives around while sleeping with someone else on the side. That's not me. So, when I saw those pictures, Natalia wearing her engagement ring in every single one... I lost it."

His voice turns darker, rougher. "I paid off the reporter not to run the story. Then, I bought the media company he worked for, just to make sure no one else could publish it. Over the next year, I bought nine media companies to cover my tracks. After I broke things off with Natalia, I sold them all and made a nice profit, but I spent millions to save face."

I can't help it—I snort at his attempt to make it sound like a win. "That's why I never heard anything about it. No articles, no gossip." I state.

"Yeah. I made sure of that."

I finally wiggle away and get up, propping myself on my elbow so I can look at him. His jaw is tight, and his eyes flicker with something between anger and hurt, but there's also vulnerability. He's not just some cold, calculated businessman. There's more to him than the world knows. He's got layers and probably rivals an onion.

"So that's why you don't do relationships?" I ask gently.

He nods, his gaze meeting mine. "It's why I don't trust easily. Why I've avoided anything real for years. But you..."

I blink, caught off guard. "But me?"

"You're not like them. You're not in my world, and maybe that's why I find myself drawn to you. You're not polished or perfect, and thank God for that. You're *real*. And I don't want to screw that up."

My heart stumbles over itself. He likes me for me. Not because I'm some pawn in this fake dating game. Not because I'm convenient. But because he sees me, the real me, and likes that. My own parents don't even like me.

I couldn't help but smile, though my mind was still reeling from everything he'd just unloaded. I'd known this whole dinner arrangement wasn't normal, but hearing him explain why he didn't trust relationships, why he acted the way he did, made something click. He wasn't just a brooding, temperamental billionaire. He had layers, scars, things that haunted him just like anyone else. Strip away the extra zeroes in his bank account and he has just as much baggage as the rest of us.

But still. That didn't excuse his behavior tonight.

"Look, I get it," I said softly. "I get why you're jaded, why the idea of relationships freaks you out, especially when you've seen what people are capable of. But you can't push me away and then pull me back in whenever it suits you -- arrangement or not."

His eyes flickered, blue as the deep ocean, and for a moment, I wondered if he even heard me.

"I'm sorry, Violet," he said, his voice rough. "Tonight... it got to me. Seeing you with them, knowing how they think—how they see women—it just... messed with my head. And it's not because you're part of some game. I didn't expect to feel this... possessive."

Okay, now my heart is just forgetting how to beat entirely. Possessive. It shouldn't sound as good as it did. I should've been annoyed or turned off, but instead, it warmed me. Stupid, right?

"Well, that's flattering and all, but if you're going to pull this hot and cold routine every time we're around your business partners, we're going to have a problem."

He looked down, exhaling slowly. "I know. I know I screwed up."

"You left me with a table of strangers, Alex. That's not exactly what a 'boyfriend' does."

His lips twitched. "We're not *really* dating."

"Then stop acting like I am when it's convenient and ignoring me when it's not." I crossed my arms, staring him down, not caring that I was lying next to his half-nakedness. "You don't get to claim me one second and then act like I'm just arm candy the next. It's not fair and I'm no pushover."

He swallowed, his thumb brushing lazy circles over my hip. "You're right. I was a prick."

I raised an eyebrow. "Glad we agree on something."

He let out a low laugh, his eyes locking on mine again, more vulnerable than I'd ever seen them. "I didn't expect this. Any of it. I thought this arrangement would be easy. Straightforward. No feelings, no complications. But it's not. And it's because of you."

"Me?" I blinked, caught off guard.

"Yeah, you. You're... different. You're not like anyone I've ever met. And that confuses me."

I softened, biting back the urge to push more. Instead, I let the silence settle between us, letting his words sink in. He was scared, just like I was. But instead of shutting down, I wanted to face it head-on. That's the difference between us.

I leaned in slightly, our foreheads almost touching. "Maybe that's the point, Alex. Maybe you need someone different. Someone who won't screw you over or play the same old games."

He didn't say anything, just stared at me, those blue eyes burning with an intensity that made it feel like champagne bubbles were fizzing beneath my skin. And for a second, I thought he might kiss me. I kind of wanted him to. But instead, he brushed his thumb across my cheek, his touch softer than I ever imagined it could be.

"I don't want to mess this up, arrangement or not," he whispered.

I smiled, reaching up to place my hand over his. "Then don't."

I slide closer to him, resting my head against his chest, instantly comforted by the warmth of his body. "For what it's worth, Natalia was one seriously stupid woman. I mean, I've seen what's under those fancy suits. You're a total hottie."

He chuckles, his arm tightening around me, pulling me in. "You think that's all it takes?" he teases, but there's a tension in his voice like he wants to say something more. He lets out a sigh, his breath warm against my hair. "Listen..." He pauses as if deciding whether to let me in or not. "Never mind."

The urge to wrap my arm around him and nestle closer bubbles up, but before I can act on it, he shifts, rolling us to our sides. His arms lock around me, pulling me tight against him. My body molds to his like it's always meant to fit, and I can feel his breath growing heavier against the back of my neck.

It's like a brush of feathers, delicate, but electrifying.

"Alex?"

"Hmmm?"

"Next time... just promise you'll talk to me instead of being a complete prick?"

He laughs, the sound vibrating through his chest and against my back, and I can't help but smile too. His grip tightens slightly like he's holding on to the moment, to me. "Promise," he whispers.

Alex

THERE WERE ABOUT A hundred things I left out of that explanation to her that night. Mainly because if I couldn't sort through the mess in my head, what was the point of dumping it all on her like some chaotic salad of emotions, hoping she'd be the one to mix it into something that made sense? Even though I had started, I stopped myself.

What I should've told her was that I wanted her all to myself. How badly I want her has turned me into a moody bastard -- moodier than usual, which is saying something -- and the second it hit me that she wasn't mine, I lost it.

It's pathetic, really—how I acted, how I felt like some kid being denied candy at checkout. The way Violet's gotten under my skin so fast, in just a few days, is something I can't even put into words. "Dating" doesn't cover it. What I want is more than that. I want her attached to me—just me. I've never had this pull toward anyone until her.

And then there's the fact I've never slept better.

It's ironic. My bed costs more than her entire apartment, but lying there in her cramped studio, with her body pressed against mine, everything felt right. Like I could breathe. I slept like the dead. Well, that was after I told my body about five million times nothing was happening but sleeping.

When I woke, the sunlight streaming through the window stung my eyes, and I cursed under my breath. I'd overslept. Probably should've gotten out of there faster, but as I started to untangle myself from her, I paused. She was still asleep, those perfect lips slightly parted, her face so peaceful it almost made me forget how much of an asshole I was last night.

Almost.

That image of her asleep stayed with me all morning, even after I rushed out of her place, quickly getting ready for work. I'd texted Antonio to bring me a suit so I could change in the car. I also had to ignore his eyebrow wiggle when I did the walk of shame to the car where he waited. No way I was showing up at the office in yesterday's clothes, not when I was already running late. But even with the rush, I couldn't shake the sight of her. Peaceful, perfect, like everything was right when she was next to me.

At the elevator, my assistant—God bless her—was already waiting with a coffee. Five steps into my office, there's Dom, sitting across from my desk, clearly ready to interrogate me.

"Did you talk to her last night?" He doesn't waste time.

"I told her about Natalia. Why I got so pissed at dinner."

"And?" He arches an eyebrow. "Did you tell her how you feel?"

I stifle a groan. "Since when do we sit around talking about feelings?" Can't we be typical men and talk about the game or anything that ensures testosterone is flowing strong?

"So... that's a no."

I sigh, running a hand through my hair. "No, not exactly."

"Dude..." Dom leans back, giving me the *you're a complete idiot* look.

"I know, I know." I raise my hands, cutting him off before he can bring on the lecture. "I was going to tell her. That I want to date her for real, be exclusive... whatever. But it all got jumbled, and none of it came out the way I needed it to."

He tilts his head. "What exactly did you need to say? *'Hey, let's keep dating'* would've worked. Because technically, you are dating. You just throw the word *'fake'* in front of it to make it sound less real, but it doesn't change what's happening."

I unbutton my jacket, feeling way too hot all of a sudden. Talking about her does that—makes my skin burn as if thousands of tiny fireworks are bursting inside me. "It's more than that. Yeah, I want to keep dating her, but 'dating' feels... too light. It's not just about dinners or fake titles. I want her with me. All the time."

"So, you want her to be your girlfriend?" Dom deadpans.

"Jesus, what is this? High school?" I shoot him a glare. "No. I mean, yes... but no."

He shakes his head, fighting a grin. "You're confusing the hell out of me."

Trust me, I'm confusing myself.

"Yeah, try being in my head. It's a shit storm in there," I mutter, leaning back in my chair, the creak of the wood almost matching the noise in my brain.

Dom leans forward, an amused smirk tugging at his mouth. "You mean after you stormed out all pissy because men were looking at a woman you're obsessed with?"

I glare at him, seriously contemplating if I dare punch him even though my office is nothing but glass walls. Damn glass walls. Worst decision I ever made, letting Dom convince me we needed a 'modern, open feel.' Now, I'm like a goldfish on display for everyone in the office. "How many people do you think would notice if I knocked you out right now?"

"Probably all of them," he says with a laugh. "But dinner was fine if that's what you're asking. After you left, Jonathan didn't even blink. Why would he? He had Violet there, keeping him happy. Felt all warm and fuzzy with her at the table, probably because she has more charm in her pinky than you do in your entire body."

I roll my eyes, more annoyed than I want to admit. "Great, so what? Now they want her number to plan brunch dates with Samantha?"

"Actually, yeah," Dom says, shrugging. "Jonathan suggested it. Said you should tell Violet to get in touch with his wife. They'd be great friends."

"Over my dead body." The last thing I want is for Violet to get closer to anyone in that circle.

Especially Jonathan.

I'd rather Violet make friends with a pit viper.

Dom just shrugs again. "Well, they're fine for the next quarter, if that's what you're worried about. They got their little peep show, saw the 'girlfriend' you've supposedly been dating for a month, and now they're satisfied." He pauses, his voice dropping. "Although, man, Jonathan's a creep. His wife is sitting right there, and his eyes were glued to your...well, whatever she is to you."

My jaw tightens. *Whatever she is...*

Dom's words hit a nerve, probably because they're true. What the hell is Violet to me? I want her, no question there. I want to date her, but calling her my 'girlfriend' doesn't feel right either. If I don't get my head straight soon, I'm going to lose her before I figure out how to explain any of this.

And none of it matters if I don't talk to her.

"What are you thinking?" Dom asks, his voice cutting through my thoughts.

"Trying to think of a way to see her today..." I mutter, more than aware of how pathetic that sounds.

Dom raises an eyebrow. "I have an idea. Call her and ask if she wants to go to dinner with you."

I shake my head. "No."

He stares at me like I've seen him stare down his five-year-old. Now I know why the kid does what he's told. "You're hopeless. What's your plan? Just keep dragging her along to business dinners until you both magically fall into a relationship?"

I shrug. "That's... not the worst idea."

Dom groans, rubbing his temples. "For fuck's sake, ask her to lunch."

"Lunch is too casual," I cringe at the thought.

"Okay, dinner, jackass."

"I can't just ask her to dinner."

"Why not?" he says, incredulously.

"I don't know. Seems too soon after last night. Plus, I left her apartment this morning without saying anything," I admit, remembering how peaceful she looked sleeping. I didn't have it in me to wake her, though I wanted to kiss those lips and stay.

Dom holds up his hands, stopping me. "Wait, reverse. You stayed at her place?"

"Yes," I nod, "but like, I literally slept. No sex." Not that I didn't want to. Torture doesn't even begin to describe holding her all night without taking it further.

"And she let you? Just... sleepover?"

"Yeah."

Dom shakes his head, looking both amused and confused. "Dude, you're already dating her. Whether you've talked about it or not, you're in it. But, for the record, you should probably put a label on it. Not to sound like a teenage girl, but women need that clarity. They need to know where things are headed."

Apparently, *I'm the teenage girl* in this situation because I need that damn label just as much.

Even though I was the one who came up with this dating arrangement. Seems my plan has officially bitten me in the ass.

But first, I need to get her attention. And I have a few ideas...

Violet

WAKING UP TO AN empty bed wasn't exactly the morning I'd hoped for. The cold sheets told me Alex had left long before my alarm even went off. Disappointing, but not surprising, but there was a text waiting for me.

> Alex: Sorry I had to leave early, but you looked too peaceful to wake up. Sorry again for last night.

It wasn't much, but at least he acknowledged the mess that was dinner.

I made it to work on time, dropped off Margaret's lavender oat milk frothy disaster—which should honestly be classified as an insult to coffee—and dove headfirst into my day. Anything to keep from overthinking. But of course, he was on my mind.

Every time I tried to respond to Alex's message, I'd type something out, stare at it for a second, and then... delete it. What was I even supposed to say? Thanks for the cuddles? Sorry for storming out? Glad you didn't ruin my evening entirely? Nothing felt right, so I just left it alone.

Besides, I had bigger things to focus on today. Like the fact that I was determined not to overanalyze every interaction with him.

Yeah, right.

Max and I were deep into our eighth "coffee break" of the day, a term we used loosely. Did we drink eight actual cups of coffee? No. That would guarantee a heart attack—or at the very least, a marathon of trips to the bathroom. But the ritual of walking to the kitchen, grabbing a mug, and pretending to sip coffee was our way of taking casual breaks. Genius, right?

"So, he spent the night?" Max asked, blowing on his coffee like it wasn't for show. "But, no sex?"

"Nope. Nothing like that," I replied, leaning against the counter, trying to seem nonchalant about it.

"But he was in nothing but his underwear? God, I need to trade lives with you. No way I could've kept my hands to myself." He groaned.

"Trust me, it wasn't easy. I was mad enough to ignore it... mostly." Truth was, I did struggle. Who wouldn't? All that muscle lying next to me, his arm wrapped around my waist, his hand splayed across my stomach? I don't think I've ever slept so well. But still, the whole thing had me in knots.

And to top it off, I still hadn't texted him back. His message had been sitting there since morning, and now it was well into the afternoon.

"I don't even know what to say to him," I admitted, sipping water from my coffee mug—because we had to keep up the act. "Thanks for the snuggle session? Feels weird. Plus, his moods are all over the place. He was going to say something else last night, I could feel it. But then he just... stopped."

Max raised an eyebrow. "What do you think he was going to say?"

I shrugged. "No idea. But he wasn't ready to share it. I get why he got upset, I really do. His ex messed him up pretty badly. Honestly, his situation might be worse than what I went through with Jake. I mean, Jake cheated on me with my best friend, which was brutal, but Alex? He was engaged to Natalia, and she cheated with multiple people. That's... a whole other level."

Max nodded. "True. But you both barely know each other. Trust takes time, especially when you've been burned before. With what you've both been through, it's going to be harder than usual."

"Maybe," I sighed. But that didn't make it any easier to navigate the minefield that was Alex Bennetti and his moods.

Max studies me with that look—the one where he's assessing me like I'm some puzzle he's determined to solve. I hate that look. It's like he can see straight into my soul, and it's completely unfair because I'm an open book with all of the passages highlighted for him, but reading him?

Not so much.

"So, what happens after Friday?" he asks, raising an eyebrow.

I shrug.

"Honestly? No clue. He mentioned this arrangement would get us through the holidays, but hasn't said anything about events after the work party on Friday. Maybe that's his plan—go to the party, then just call it quits."

Max gives me a pointed look. "But he slept in your bed last night, and he made an effort to make sure you weren't upset. Plus, he told you about his ex-fiancée, which isn't exactly casual conversation. People don't usually open up like that if they're planning to ghost."

He's got a point. "Yeah, but could I date someone whose mood swings are that intense? I mean, one minute he's all-in—like, scorching hot—and the next, a glacier taking on human form. It's confusing."

Max twists his lips. "Rich man problems. Oh, to brood and still look hot. I brood and look like a toddler told it's nap time."

I burst out laughing, feeling some tension melt from my shoulder muscles.

I really should get back to work, but right now, I have a legitimate reason to take a break.

Margaret was reviewing the edits I'd just made to the recent submission, even though we both knew she'd waltz into Mr. Hartley's office later and brag about how she'd spent "countless hours" on it over her "busy weekend." Never mind that it was me who spent my Saturday hunched over it for her. And let's completely ignore the fact that I nearly face-planted into Antonio and his sleek black Lexus this morning as I rushed out the door to come to work.

"Mr. Bennetti has instructed me to tell you that you will get in the car and let me take you to work," were Antonio's exact words. Not asking. Just informing me. At least he smiled while doing it. I shot a glance at Max, who was standing next to me and shrugged. Who was I to argue? Walking on Mondays in Manhattan? No, thank you. It's like a circus had a baby with Comic Con—people in all kinds of outfits, and dramatic energy way too early in the day. I wasn't feeling it.

Antonio even made a stop at the coffee shop next to the office building, where I grabbed Margaret's dreaded lavender oat milk latte and a pumpkin spice for myself because, yes, I'm that cliché. As I thanked Antonio for the ride, he told me to text him when I was ready to go home and that he'd be nearby if I needed to run errands. I'm now under a billionaire's personal chauffeur service. Not complaining, though. Perks of fake dating a Bennetti, apparently.

I discovered Antonio's number had already been added to my phone—courtesy of Alex, no doubt. When did he even do that? Probably while I was dead to the world this morning -- and hopefully not drooling.

Walking into the office with both lattes and the manuscript I'd slaved over, I handed Margaret her drink. Her first words after taking a sip?

"How hard is this order, Violet?"

Apparently impossible, you wench.

I smiled through gritted teeth, apologized for the "mistake," and placed the manuscript in front of her, complete with red notes in the margins. I also let her know it was uploaded to the cloud, like the good little assistant I am. Then, I retreated to my desk.

I had this urge to text Alex. Something. Anything. But I didn't want to be that woman—the one who gets all clingy just because a guy spends the night. Even if it was strictly PG, minus his shirt and pants. Seriously though, that man's body should come with warning labels.

And yet, here I am, fighting the urge to send a simple text. Maybe "Thanks for the ride?" or "Nice abs, by the way"?

Yes, there's attraction, but this could blow up quickly. He may not even want a relationship, considering how his ex screwed him over, and that's probably why he offered up this arrangement any way. And me? I'm not sure I'm ready for one either. Yet, here I am, sitting at my desk, thinking about him all day. I don't want to be that woman—the one who falls head over heels after just a few days. Literal days, Violet!

Max and I had just finished that eighth coffee break, when a messenger arrived, our receptionist hot on his heels like one of those tiny, yappy dogs. You know, the kind people swear they love but just dress up because it's easier than having kids.

She was giving me that look of hers too. The I'd kill you to be in your shoes kind of look that made me incredibly uncomfortable, especially since I'd seen her nearly lose it when someone took her sandwich from the office fridge. She labels her food with semi-death threats and the way she attacks the printer when it jams? Yeah, I'm pretty sure she could take me in a fight. Too much pent-up rage there, and I'm not exactly scrappy.

"For you, Ms. Hart," she said, blushing and seething all at once, while the messenger emerged from behind her carrying a massive bouquet of peonies.

Blush pink and white, and all sorts of gorgeous.

Her evil glare wiped the smile off my face, but once she slithered back to the hole she came from, I allowed myself to breathe again and enjoy the moment. And it wasn't just a bouquet—it was a flower monster. I couldn't even see the messenger's head or chest until he set the arrangement on my desk. Half the admin pool stood up to gawk, and a few editors peeked out of their offices to see what came.

When the messenger heaved it onto my desk, it swallowed that entire half. I barely noticed anyone staring. My fingers were too busy smoothing over the soft petals, getting lost in their delicate texture.

Peonies are my favorite. It's not just because they are the divas of the flower world, blooming only for a few fabulous weeks and leaving us all wanting more. No, there is something irresistibly charming about their lush ruffled petals, the way they explode into riots of pink and white like floral fireworks on display. They are the flower that screams I'm here, I'm beautiful, I know it! Plus, they smell divine. A secret garden party everyone wants to be invited to, and I'm doing just that, sniffing the flowers and lost in garden lust without even looking to see who they are from.

"You lucky bitch," Max hissed, sliding up beside me and zeroing in on the massive bouquet, plucking the card from its delicate folds before I could even blink.

"Oh, it's from your hottie," he said, eyes dancing across the note, but I snatched it from his hand.

"Give me that!" I spun the card over, expecting something generic, but nope—his handwriting, clear as day. I recognized it from the notes he'd scribbled down the other day on that legal pad.

Miss you, beautiful.

My cheeks were on fire. Did he send these to make Jake jealous? Or were they really for me?

Does Alex actually think I'm beautiful?

It's official. I'm that pathetic.

I fumbled for my phone, finally ready to send a text after spending the entire day staring at the unsent message from this morning.

> Violet: "Miss you, beautiful?"

> Alex: Well, I'm not lying about the beautiful part... maybe not the miss you part either. I have a feeling you'd be more fun than this meeting I'm in.

Okay, heart? Chill.

> Violet: What, no roses?

> Alex: Did we not establish I don't do vanilla?

> Violet: Fair enough. They're gorgeous.

> Alex: Did you happen to open the other gift?

I blinked, glancing around my desk like he's secretly spying on me from some hidden camera. A black box sits quietly next to the sea of peonies. I hadn't even noticed it before. Max was practically glued to my side, way too deep in my bubble, but hey, Max was allowed.

The ribbon around the box was so perfectly tied that I hesitated before tugging on it, gently unwrapping it like it was some sacred artifact. The lid popped off, revealing a mound of white tissue paper.

I dug through the crinkling layers until my fingers brushed something cool—glass. I pulled it out, and there it was: a small picture frame, and inside? A ridiculously hot photo of Alex. Tasteful enough to be work-appropriate, but hot enough that I'd probably end up staring at it all day.

"Oh dear God." Max snatched it from my hands, eyes wide with admiration. "Does he have a twin? Cousin? Anyone single who looks even remotely like that?"

"You're drooling." I hand him a tissue, which he promptly tosses back at me.

But I was too busy gazing at the photo. Alex, in a cream sweater, not looking at the camera but laughing at something off-screen, all casual and unguarded. It was like a glimpse of the man behind the suit. And God, when he smiles? My entire body went haywire as if I were having some chemical reaction.

Pretty sure it's called lust, but semantics.

Violet: Is this your way of making sure I stare at you all day?

Alex: No woman of mine would ever want to stop looking at me.

Violet: Wow, you're really full of yourself, huh?

Alex: You wanted your ex to believe you had a boyfriend. What girlfriend doesn't have a picture of her man on her desk?

Violet: One who doesn't need to be claimed.

Alex: Too late. I already have a picture of you on my desk. It's quite lovely.

Violet: Do I want to know how you got a picture of me that isn't from the DMV?

Alex: Are DMV photos not acceptable for girlfriend pictures?

Violet: Not unless you're into "frazzled Violet with purple hair" vibes.

Alex: I've seen it. What was with the purple hair?

Violet: We don't know each other well enough to discuss that tragic phase. Show me the picture!

I waited, staring at my phone like it held the meaning of life. Just as I was about to give up, my phone buzzed, and I gasped.

It was me—wearing my old NYU sweatshirt, my hair in the messiest bun imaginable, laughing. Not even one of those cute, Instagram-worthy pictures. It was candid, pure, a moment where I wasn't trying to impress anyone.

> Violet: Stalk much?

> Alex: What can I say? You caught my eye.

It hit me. That was before we'd even met before I'd spilled my drink and plopped down at the bar. The bartender had cracked a joke to cheer me up, and I'd laughed, genuinely, for the first time that night. So Alex had seen me before he came up to me at the bar?

> Violet: Do all billionaires casually stalk women they don't know?

> Alex: Only the charming ones.

> Violet: Where did this picture of you come from, by the way?

> Alex: Do you want an honest answer?

> Violet: Nah, let's just start this fake relationship with a series of lies. That's solid relationship-building material.

> Alex: Technically, I already told your ex I was your boyfriend before you even knew my name. So, we're a bit late for honesty.

> Violet: Touché. Alright, spill. Where did the photo of you come from? Tell me the dirty secret.

> Alex: Wish there was something scandalous, but I couldn't decide. So, I asked my cousin Alena to pick one. She said it was her favorite. You can thank her for my thoughtful selection.

> Violet: She has excellent taste.

Alex: I almost sent the one of me in a swimsuit. Figured you'd want a closer look at my abs, but then I remembered you have work to do, so I went with the more "professional" option.

Violet: How considerate and arrogant of you at the same time.

Alex: I've got an image to uphold, Violet. It's a full-time job.

I couldn't help but laugh. The banter was easy, and natural, and it left me smiling, even though, realistically, we were in a weird, fake-but-possibly-not-fake situation. Yet, I couldn't deny that this "fake" thing felt more real than it probably should as each day ticked on by.

I was just about to reply to Alex when Mr. Hartley stepped out of the elevator, and suddenly, it was like a silent alarm went off. The entire office stiffened. Everyone skittered back to their desks, pretending to be busy. Even the senior editors, who normally acted like they owned the place, were suddenly typing away as if their lives depended on it. Margaret, in particular, was at her computer, fingers flying over the keys. But I wasn't fooled. She was probably typing gibberish into an open Word doc, like always.

I quickly placed Alex's picture on my desk, tucked the box under it, and forced myself to focus on the new manuscript in front of me. All the assistants were in the center of the room, our desks clumped together like a little island of chaos, while the senior editors lined the outer edge, hidden away in their cozy corner offices. Max, across the room, gave Mr. Hartley a quick nod before slipping back to his desk. I caught his sly smile as he settled in, coffee in hand, silently mocking the office scramble.

I sat a little taller, making sure I looked like I was working—pen in hand, screen filled with emails instead of my usual login page. If Mr. Hartley was coming my way, I needed to at least pretend I was earning this meager paycheck.

It wasn't uncommon for him to be down here. This was the editing floor, after all, and he often stopped by to talk with senior editors about manuscripts or drag them into the conference room for some secret meeting we were never invited to.

Jake's office was in the opposite corner, diagonal from mine. A few months ago, the idea of sitting here all day with a clear view of him would've killed me, but now? Now it was just another office to ignore.

I don't care that Jake has a front-row seat in my life now. Or that I can see him and Lisa practically licking each other's faces every day before heading out to lunch. Seriously, it's their daily PDA showcase, and trust me, my lunch threatens a return every day I see it.

Today was no different. Jake poked his head out just long enough to see the ridiculously oversized bouquet being dropped off at my desk, then slammed his office door shut like a toddler throwing a tantrum. Bonus points if this makes him jealous. I'm not complaining.

Let's get one thing clear: I would never, under any circumstances, get back with Jake. Aside from being the world's most unapologetic cheater, I wouldn't take him back even if hell froze over, pigs sprouted wings, and the Leaning Tower of Pisa did a perfect pirouette. Nope. I'd rather chew on tinfoil than give him another chance.

And, while we're on the subject, let's not forget how tragic he was in the bedroom. Calling it "awful" would be a generous compliment. It was like watching a bad movie—you're just counting down the minutes for it to end, praying to the universe that there's no sequel in the works. Zero passion. No fireworks. Just a lot of awkward fumbling and pauses, like we were both waiting for someone to yell 'cut.' I vividly remember the one time he asked, "Are you enjoying this?" and I caught myself thinking, *Does that mean it's over?*

I had my head buried in a manuscript that felt like it had to be over a thousand pages long. Seriously, if this wasn't a fantasy romance, I might die. Margaret must secretly enjoy torturing me. She knows I adore romance, so naturally, I never get to edit any. Nope. I get biographies, business, sci-fi, and historical fiction so dry it could turn a cactus into a puddle.

I flipped to the title page, already groaning internally, and reached for my trusty arsenal of red pens, highlighters, and sticky notes. That's when I saw it: *Corporate Love: How to Merge Your Heart with a Hostile Takeover.* For a brief, shining moment, I thought it might be a romance novel.

Spoiler alert: it wasn't.

All business. And just to twist the knife, the first chapter I flipped to was titled *Due Diligence.* Save me.

Mr. Hartley stopped at my desk, and I nervously looked up, bracing myself for whatever came next. He's an older man, his slicked-back black hair streaked with gray like he's auditioning for a role in a 1950s mob movie. His Bronx accent? Pure magic. It's the kind of voice that could make ordering a hot dog sound like either poetry or porn, depending on your feelings toward older men.

We don't chat much, but every time we do, he's unfailingly kind. There's something about him that feels larger than life like he's got the entire publishing world tucked into his back pocket. I'm not attracted to him—let's be clear. But he fascinates me. He's the head of one of the biggest publishing companies on the East Coast, and everything that comes through here has his stamp of approval. He has an eye for talent, the kind that can spot a diamond in the rough and make it shine.

Just the fact that he's within a six-foot radius of me? It feels like standing next to a literary god.

"Miss Hart," Mr. Hartley leans onto my desk, hands casually stuffed into the pockets of his suit.

I blink. He's never stopped to talk to me before, not like this. Is this a casual chat? Do CEOs even do casual chats with assistants? Normally, the only conversation we had consisted of *"fetch me another coffee,"* so this was a first.

He knows my name too...

Sweat prickles at the small of my back. No one wants the CEO to suddenly know their name when you're as low on the totem pole as I am.

"Hello, sir," I manage, shooting a glance at Max, who shrugs, wide-eyed. Naturally, the whole office is pretending to work but watching me like I'm about to step into a gladiator ring.

"Am I to understand that you are dating Alexander Bennetti?" Mr. Hartley asks, his tone casual, but the weight of his words hits like a wrecking ball.

Oh, that.

Of course, that rumor spread fast. I can only imagine who might've shared that piece of juicy gossip. *Looking at you, Jake.*

"I... uh... what?" I stammer, internally scolding myself. Come on, Violet. Get it together. "I mean, yes. Alex is my boyfriend."

I mentally high-fived myself for remembering to call him Alex. Like I'm part of some exclusive club now, considering very few people call him that.

Mr. Hartley raises a brow. "He and I do a lot of business together. I had no idea you two have been dating. Alex mentioned it when we chatted on the phone."

He told him? Alex called him? I had a million questions loaded, locked, and ready to aim, but I put a pin in that.

I nod, my brain still too frazzled to form any coherent words. First, my idol, the guy I daydream about reading and publishing my novel, is casually chatting with me. Now, he's apparently BFFs with my boyfriend who isn't really my boyfriend.

"Well, that's just great. Did he send you those?" Mr. Hartley nods toward the floral monstrosity taking up half my desk. You'd have to be legally blind not to notice it.

"Uh, yes sir," I manage. "Sorry, are they distracting? I can move them."

"No!" he practically yelps, making me jump. "Not at all, I mean. They're lovely. Mr. Bennetti has excellent taste. How do you like working for Miss Sinclair?"

Hate it.

She's a tyrant in high heels.

"Great. It's been an honor to work under such a talented editor," I say, forcing the words out and nearly gagging on the forced compliment. The taste of sarcasm lingers on my tongue and I must say spoiled milk would be better.

He squints at me like he can see right through the facade, but thankfully says nothing. "I see. Well, carry on," he adds before glancing down at the manuscript I've been suffering through.

And just like that, he strolls past me into Margaret's office, shutting the door behind him.

Great. Now he knows I'm the poor soul Margaret's torturing with that brick of a manuscript.

I immediately pick up my phone and fire off a message to my boyfriend—you know, the one who's apparently besties with my boss and conveniently forgot to mention that tiny detail.

> Violet: Did you forget to tell me that you're buddy-buddy with Mr. Hartley, or was that meant to be a fun surprise for me to figure out on my own?

> Alex: You know I have a job, right? Big CEO role. A whole company to run.

> Violet: Alex... what did you do?

> Alex: Nothing. Just thought it'd be a good time to catch up. Meeting you reminded me.

I stare at my phone, my heart racing. He spoke to my boss. Of all the people to casually "catch up" with, he chooses Mr. Hartley? The man who could make or break my career in two seconds flat. I could practically hear Alex's voice, smooth and nonchalant like this was no big deal. For him, it probably isn't.

But for me? This is huge, and now the panic is settling deep in the marrow of my bones.

> Violet: Please tell me you didn't say anything weird.

> Alex: Define weird.

I groan, rubbing my temples. Why do I feel like I'm about to regret this conversation?

> Violet: Alex, seriously. What did you say to him?

There's a long pause, which only makes my anxiety worse. I glance around the office, trying to appear casual while my insides mirrored that of a kettle on the verge of whistling at full boil. Everyone else seems oblivious, thankfully, and Margaret's still holed up in her office with Mr. Hartley.

> Alex: Relax. I didn't say anything to embarrass you. I just mentioned how lucky he is to have you on his team.

I blink at the screen, rereading his message. Did he just... compliment me to my boss? Is that supposed to make me feel better or worse?

I sit back, chewing my lip as a blush creeps up my neck. That's actually... kind of sweet. Unexpected, but sweet.

> Violet: You're really something, you know that?

> Alex: I aim to please, darling.

I roll my eyes, but there's a smile tugging at my lips.

Violet

I HEAR RAISED VOICES coming from behind me and tuck my phone away, pretending to focus on the absolute snoozefest of a manuscript in front of me. Seriously, who reads this stuff? Alex probably would. I make a mental note to convince him to read something with actual characters and, you know, emotions.

Margaret bursts out of her office in full-on diva mode, purse clutched in her hands. Each stomp amplifies her dramatic exit, and a small part of me hopes she snaps a heel.

She stops at my desk, fire blazing in her eyes. "Congratulations," the venom in that doesn't go unnoticed.

I blink. "What?"

Without another word, she storms off toward the elevators, jabbing the button like it personally offended her. The doors finally open, and she jumps in, mascara already streaking down her cheeks. By the time they close, I swear I hear her sobbing and it's not a pretty sound.

"Miss Hart," Mr. Hartley's voice calls from Margaret's office. "Can you join me, please?"

Oh no.

I stand slowly, dread curling up in my stomach. My feet move on autopilot, dragging me into the office Margaret just stormed out of, her overwhelming perfume still clinging to the air like bad karma. The office is the usual publishing chic—exposed brick, a solid oak desk, and comfy leather armchairs, though I doubt Margaret ever used them for editing.

Mr. Hartley stands leaning against the desk, arms folded. His eyes meet mine when I enter. "Mr. Bennetti mentioned that his girlfriend works very hard for this company and suggested I review her editing work. I was curious since you're not officially an editor, but I took a look at the manuscript he mentioned. Interestingly, Margaret's name is on it, but the editing history in the system? It's all you. Not a single change from her."

Oh. Crap.

I feel my heart drop into my stomach. I'm going to get fired, aren't I? Fired for doing someone else's job. Did I mess up something important? But if I had, Margaret would've scolded me in front of the whole office, as usual. And yet, here I am, getting called out by the boss. How did Mr. Hartley *not know* Margaret wasn't pulling her weight all this time? Everyone else knew.

"Uh, I'm not sure what you mean, sir." My voice comes out shaky, but I refuse to be the one to throw Margaret under the bus. I may hate the woman, but I'm no snitch.

Mr. Hartley raises an eyebrow. "I understand. You don't want to make waves. But let's be honest, the girlfriend of Alexander Bennetti doesn't go unnoticed."

Hold up. Being Alex's girlfriend suddenly earns me respect? Not the hard work I've put in for years?

Not the fact I've been busting my ass to figure out how to perfectly execute a lavender oat milk latte—which, now that I think about it, was never right because I forgot the honey stick.

Every time. Oh my God. That was the final touch she added and it seems my subconscious had been sabotaging Margaret's coffee all this time. Maybe there's a rabbit hole of psychological warfare here that I'll dive into later...

"So, congratulations, Miss Hart. You are now a senior editor with the company. You'll be stepping into Margaret's role, and we'll start sorting through some resumes for assistants. In the meantime, you can share Max."

Wait—what? My brain screeches to a halt. I stare at him, my insides buzzing like an active hive of bees. I'm pretty sure I'm going to vomit all over this man's very expensive shoes. Shoes I recognize because Alex has a pair just like them, and if they cost anything close to what I think they do, they're way out of my budget to replace.

"Sir, I'm sure there are other people more deserving of this promotion..." I manage to get out, my voice barely above a whisper.

He waves me off like I've just told him the sky is blue. "From what I've seen of the manuscripts, which I suspect you were the one truly editing, you're more than qualified." He gives me a reassuring pat on the shoulder, like this is just another Tuesday, and saunters out of the office, leaving me alone.

I stand there, frozen in what is now *my office*, though five minutes ago it was *hers*.

Can you haunt a place if you're not dead? Because I'm pretty sure Margaret's evil spirit is already staking a claim on this space.

I rush back to my desk, and all eyes are on me. Some sneers, a few amused grins from the Margaret-haters, and then there's Jake—arms crossed, leaning against the doorway of his office, smirking like he's just waiting for me to fall flat on my face. Well, the joke's on him because guess what? We're equals now. He's no longer my boss.

That part feels pretty damn good.

But the rest? Not so much.

Max rushes over, wide-eyed. "What the hell just happened?"

I grab my phone, doing my best to keep my cool despite the storm brewing inside me.

"Apparently, my boyfriend made a call, got Margaret fired for not doing her job, and now I've been promoted. Oh, and congratulations—you're now my assistant until they hire someone new."

Max bursts out laughing, and I slap his arm. "I need to meet a billionaire at a bar," he jokes.

"Go away," I hiss, already typing furiously into my phone.

> Violet: You can't just call my boss and get me promoted! People are going to think I didn't earn it, that I only got the job because I'm dating—but not really dating—you.

> Alex: There are worse reasons to move up in life.

> Violet: I'd like to move up based on my own merits, not because Mr. Infamous Bennetti made a random call about how much editing I've been doing. Cute move.

> Alex: So you think I'm cute now.

> Violet: Ugh, no. That's not what I said.

> Alex: And yet, that's how I'm taking it. Look, you did earn it. Just because they didn't notice you've been editing doesn't change the fact you have—and the success speaks for itself. Sometimes, people need a little nudge to see what's right in front of them. Most people say thank you at this point.

> Violet: Any other life-altering surprises I should brace for today?

> Alex: I've got a running list, and the day is still young.

I was just about to text Alex back when Jake sauntered over, dressed in a navy three-piece suit that screamed *"I think I'm better than you."* His annoyingly handsome face, complete with a fresh fake tan, scanned me from head to toe. Thank god I wore one of my nicer outfits today—because Jake, of all people, knows what high fashion is, and I didn't need him judging me. I had on a fitted black dress, black heels, and a deep purple belt cinched at my waist.

Classy, professional, but not an invitation for lingering stares—like the one Jake was giving me now. Because I didn't need the reminder that he's seen me naked.

"Wow, congratulations," he said nicely packaged with his signature fake charm. "Nice dress today. Didn't get a chance to tell you in the elevator."

Because I wouldn't care?

"Thanks," I replied, a little too casually. Then, just to twist the knife, I added, "Alex took me shopping this weekend. Insisted on all new clothes. Only the best for his girl."

Might as well use my fake billionaire boyfriend to my advantage, right?

Jake's eyes flicked to the giant bouquet on my desk—the one that looked like it belonged in a wedding, not an office—and the picture of Alex, now perched proudly on my desk. His jaw clenched, and I felt a small surge of satisfaction. Good. Let him simmer in that. Meanwhile, Max stood next to me, both of us waiting for Jake to go away so we could figure out this whole promotion situation.

Do I move right in? What's the etiquette for replacing your boss when they're fired on the spot?

"Well, good luck," Jake muttered before turning on his heel and slamming his office door behind him.

I leaned over to Max, barely whispering, "Was he jealous?"

Max nodded, stifling a laugh, as we quickly gathered my things from my old desk and moved them into my new office. The one that, not even ten minutes ago, belonged to Margaret.

As I stood in the doorway, I couldn't help but cringe. The entire place screamed Margaret. Ugly abstract art that looked like a toddler's attempt at modernism, framed photos of herself looking overly important, awards she probably didn't even earn. And don't get me started on her nail polish collection—why did she have so many shades of pink?

"Do we box this stuff up?" I asked, still processing the events. It was surreal that she hadn't been given time to clean out her office, but then again, making a dramatic exit was very on-brand for her, and taking the time to pack would have ruined the effect.

Max disappeared for a minute and came back with a trash bag. "This should do." He grinned, and I couldn't help but laugh as we started tossing her things into the bag, turning this Margaret shrine into something new. My office.

Once everything was cleared, it felt...bare. Except for the one photo of Alex I placed on my desk and the massive bouquet that now dominated the wooden counter behind me.

"Can I get you anything else, Miss Hart?" Max asks not hiding the sarcasm.

I shoot him a look. This is going to be unbearable. I love him, but Max as my assistant? He's going to have too much fun with it.

"Yes, a coffee—" I start, but then stop mid-sentence as the elevator dings open.

Of freaking course.

He steps out like it was timed perfectly, right after Hartley dropped the bomb on me. Alex strides across the office floor like he owns the place (which, let's be real, he could). Every woman in the room practically forgets how to breathe, their eyes trailing him like he's a celebrity waltzing down a red carpet. The receptionist nearly trips over herself as she leaps from her desk, all smiles and flirty hellos, but he doesn't even spare her a glance.

Max, of course, turns to watch Alex as if he's the second coming. "Damn, he's hotter than I remember."

Sadly, I can't argue. That perfectly tailored black three-piece suit? Yeah, it's doing things. And I've seen what's underneath that suit...

By the time Alex reaches my office, I hiss at Max, "Close your mouth." Max fixes his tie like he's about to meet royalty. "You know he's taken, right?"

"Doesn't mean I can't gawk," he grins, sliding out of the way just as Alex steps up. They greet each other like old friends, all part of the show, of course. If we'd been dating for a month, Max would definitely know him by now.

I glance at Jake's office out of the corner of my eye and spot him peeking through the crack in his door. Perfect. That's enough motivation for me to drop my scowl and replace it with the most radiant smile I can muster as Alex approaches.

"Well, hi, babe," I say, through gritted teeth, my jaw aching from the effort.

Alex raises an eyebrow, glancing briefly over his shoulder before leaning in, his voice a low murmur, "Oh, you're pissed but can't be, because everyone's watching, huh?"

Before I can even retort, he pulls me against him, one hand pressing into the small of my back, the other threading through my hair. And just like that, my body betrays me, melting into his like I'm a pad of butter hitting the pan. The scent of sandalwood and sweet spice wraps around me, making me momentarily forget that I'm raging, forget the office, and forget everything. It's clear Alex Bennetti has the cheat codes on my body.

He's not shy in the slightest as his lips crash into mine, parting my mouth with his tongue, kissing me like he's starved and I'm the only thing sustaining him. This is no cute, innocent peck that a boyfriend would give his girlfriend in an office full of people—no, this is a full-on, toe-curling, mind-numbing kiss.

And while I've felt his kiss before, back at the bar, this feels entirely different. We're at work, for heaven's sake, but he doesn't seem to care. Every gentle tug of his lips, the sweep of his tongue, the way his hand presses firmly against my lower back—I can't think straight. My thoughts? Gone. I'm not even sure I'm standing anymore; my body's slowly melting into liquid heat, and I'm struggling to hold on to what little bit of sense I have left.

When he finally pulls back, there's a smug smirk on his face, and I'm practically a puddle. I should be angry—should be furious—but all I can do is grab his tie, keeping him close. "I want to be mad. I really, really do," I whisper, breathless. "So just remember, I'm mad... just not right now. But later? Oh, I'm definitely going to be pissed."

"So, would you be mad if I took you to dinner to celebrate your promotion?" His lips brush against my ear as he asks. "And to make it up to you?" The warmth of his breath on my skin is downright sinful.

I tilt my head, suddenly hyper-aware of how close we are—his body pressed to mine, his fingers still tangled in my hair. It's like something straight out of one of those romance novels I always devour, the way he angles my head, firm but gentle, making me nothing but putty in his hands to mold. "You... want to take me to dinner?" I repeat as if the concept of basic human language has suddenly abandoned me.

"You're my girlfriend, right? Last I checked, good boyfriends take their girlfriends out to celebrate. You know, when they've got something to be proud of." He presses a soft kiss to my cheek, sending butterflies dancing in my stomach. "Believe it or not, Violet, I'm a good boyfriend."

He steps back slightly, giving me room to breathe, though it doesn't help the whole mushy-brain thing I've got going on. "And I figured I owed you a proper dinner after how last night went," he adds, the corner of his mouth twitching into a smirk.

I blink, still caught somewhere between wanting to rage at him and... well, wanting him. "I really, really want to be mad at you," I whisper.

"That's fine," he says with a casual shrug, "as long as it's after dinner. Hartley already agrees you should have the night off, anyway."

I groan, grabbing my bag and giving him one last narrowed glare before he holds out his hand. Reluctantly, I slip mine into his, feeling the heat of his fingers intertwine with mine, even as my frustration still simmers beneath the surface. We walk through the office, and Max, ever the troublemaker, gives me a wink. I subtly flip him off—well, as subtly as I can by offering him my pinky instead. Office etiquette, and all. HR would love me. Max just laughs, waving goodbye to Alex as if they're suddenly best friends.

"See you later, Alex!" Max chimes.

"Until next time," Alex responds like the two of them are going to grab drinks after this.

As we make our way toward the elevator, Jake is still standing in the doorway of his office, arms crossed and watching us with that annoying, broody stare. I flash him a fake smile, just for kicks, while Alex turns it up a notch.

"Oh, is that Jason?" Alex says loud enough for half the office to hear, a playful glint in his eye. A few assistants snicker as they pretend not to eavesdrop.

"It's Jake," Jake corrects stiffly from his little corner but Alex doesn't even look at him to acknowledge he heard it.

Alex tightens his grip on my hand, and before I can process it, he pulls me into a kiss. It's not showy, but there's something about the way his lips linger against mine that makes me forget we're in the middle of my workplace. "For good measure," he whispers, brushing his lips against my ear as he nips lightly at the lobe. If I wasn't already weak-kneed, I definitely am now.

By the time the elevator doors open, he tugs me inside, leaving me half-dazed, wondering how I'm ever supposed to be mad at him when he kisses like that.

Alex pulls out a handkerchief, dabbing at the corner of his mouth to remove the smear of my lip gloss. His brow arches as he asks, "Is that cherry-flavored?"

I groan, exasperated. "You cannot interfere with my job!"

His playful demeanor shifts. His eyes sharpen, losing that sweet, carefree glint and he's all business now. "I already told you, you earned it. Sometimes people just need to be pointed in the right direction."

"Promise you won't mess with my career again," I plead, my voice softer now. "I want to publish a book one day and know it wasn't because I dated you."

He raises a brow, eyes locked on mine. "Dated or are dating?"

I freeze. How do I even answer that? Are we dating? It's not like we've defined it. I mean, he is my date Friday for the work event, and I was his date Tuesday with his investors. And now he's taking me to dinner to celebrate my promotion... but does that mean anything? My mouth opens, then closes again as the question bubbles up but dies on my tongue.

The dreaded *What are we doing?* talk looms, but I refuse to be the one to bring it up.

Coming with me to my work party on Friday—part of our agreement. But showing up at my job, getting me promoted, and following it with that level of PDA? That's a whole other ball game, and one I'm not sure how to play. My brain is working overtime trying to piece it together.

Neither of us seems ready to break the silence as the elevator descends, so I guess we will just keep playing the game as it is for now.

Alex

I CAN'T BELIEVE I'M doing this. Every instinct in me screams that it's a bad idea, but here I am, crossing the line anyway. I pulled some strings to get her promoted. I don't make a habit of interfering with a person's career.

But, when I saw that stack of manuscripts on her desk the other day, it clicked. She wasn't just assisting; she was doing the actual editing, and that's not an assistant's job. She'd been pulling the weight for who knows how long, and no one cared enough to notice. That kind of managerial oversight—hell, laziness—infuriates me.

At first, I thought about calling Hartley and suggesting he expand the company, making more room for people like Violet to move up naturally. But then I realized it wasn't about needing more room; it was about recognizing who was already doing the work and who was coasting. Violet was being overshadowed by people who didn't deserve it.

So, yeah, I made a "casual" call to Hartley. And he promoted her based on merit like she should've been a long time ago. I'll stand by that decision, no matter how much it might piss her off. The world isn't fair, not black and white, and sometimes you have to push someone to see the value in what's right under their nose. That's all I did.

Sure, Violet might be furious, but at least now she's finally getting the recognition she deserves. Whether she knows it or not, this was for her. Besides, it was a rather quick and easy phone call compared to everything else I did today.

"Hey, Alexander, how's it going? It's been a while since the last charity gala. What was it for?" Hartley's fake Bronx accent grated on me, almost as bad as my cousin Eddie's exaggerated Italian one.

"Education or something," I replied, not bothering to recall which cause it was. I've attended so many events, that it's hard to keep track. I donate because I've got more money than I know what to do with. I could retire today, and live lavishly for the rest of my life, but why would I? I enjoy work. Even though, deep down, I know my staff would throw a party if I announced an early retirement.

The morning meeting had been the trigger. My board wasn't thrilled about my latest acquisitions—ones I've approved against their recommendations. Why? Because I can. Their role is mostly for show, there to reassure shareholders. But when I want something, I take it.

In response to their grumbling, I reminded them that I have the final vote, and I was not ignoring the latest acquisition, even if that meant yet another bidding war with Julian Stone. Another hour passed of listening to these suits argue about metrics and projections. I'd had enough. Slamming my laptop shut, the loud snap brought the room to dead silence. As CEO of Bennetti Innovations Group, my word was final, but it didn't make dealing with these clowns any less of a headache.

I stormed out, ignoring their disapproving looks. They think I'm just another rich kid who got handed the company on a silver platter, and I coasted on family connections. They couldn't be more wrong. I built this empire from scratch—my money, my vision. If they can't see that, too bad.

Unfortunately, now that we've gone public, I'm stuck dealing with a board of investors who think they know better than me. It's a constant tug-of-war between their outdated strategies and my drive to push things forward. It's infuriating, to say the least.

And that's how Hartley ended up on the receiving end of my frustration. He's the epitome of what I hate in business: a man in an expensive suit with fancy titles, but no real grasp on innovation. If only I could get a board filled with people who shared my vision—people with passion and drive, not these crotchety old men coasting on reputation and status.

As expected, the conversation with Hartley took the usual turn.

"I had been meaning to call you about grabbing drinks," Hartley said, the typical response from anyone in this world. Drinks, golf, the club, dinner—it's all just part of the same recycled conversation.

Perfect. My chance. "We could do dinner, absolutely. I'd love to bring my girlfriend along. You know her. Violet Hart? She works in your editing department."

There's a pause. I can almost hear the frantic typing on his end, likely looking up her name in his HR system. CEOs like him don't know half the people who work for them -- I should know. I'm one of them.

"Oh yes, Violet! Great woman, been here for years. I had no idea you two were dating."

Bet he couldn't pick her out of a lineup if he tried.

"She works hard," I said, leaning into the casual tone while still driving the point home. "Talks about how much she loves it there all the time. I'm surprised she hasn't been promoted to editor yet. With all the work she's been doing, I just assumed she had the title already. In four years, she's edited quite a few manuscripts for your company. Didn't realize that was part of an assistant's job. If you don't mind me asking since I'm new to this world, what do editors do if their assistants are handling the editing?"

The silence on the other end is priceless. I can practically hear the gears turning in his head, scrambling to come up with a response.

"Oh, well, sometimes they chip in to help when the editors have a backlog," he stammered. "We've been in high demand lately, as you know."

I didn't know. Nor did I care.

"Of course," I said smoothly. "I won't keep you, I know you're busy running things, but you should take a look at some of the work Violet's been doing. I was impressed. She's been editing over the weekend, off the clock. She's devoted, that's for sure."

That's my not-so-subtle way of pushing him to look into what Violet's been doing without spelling it out. Family name aside, people in my world like to keep me happy, and Hartley would line up with the rest to do just that.

"Absolutely," he said, back on his feet now. "Let's set up a time. I'll have my assistant call Penelope to schedule dinner for us."

I'll be too busy.

"Great, and hey, really appreciate you being such an inspiration for Violet. She's working on a novel herself, and I know being part of your team has helped her grow."

Total fluff. I had no idea if working there actually inspired her, but I knew Hartley's ego would eat it up, and stroking that man's ego was like greasing the wheels.

We wrapped up the call with the usual small talk. The kind where you smile through gritted teeth and pretend to care. "How's the club? Any new investments you're looking at?" The same tired questions we all ask, just to keep the conversation moving. It's part of the game, treading water until someone throws in the towel—or in my case, hitting the panic button for Penelope to come in with her well-timed excuse.

Right on cue, Penelope's voice filters through my office. "Mr. Bennetti, your next appointment is here," she says loud enough for Hartley to hear. *Perfect.*

"Ah, shoot. Looks like I've got to run," I say, feigning regret. "We'll talk soon."

And that's how business is done in Manhattan. Short, efficient, and just the right amount of bullshit.

I temporarily assigned Antonio to handle Violet's transportation, so today, Carlo will be driving us. He was my driver long before my private cook. Long story short, he wanted to cook and I will never regret allowing him to do so.

Leaving her office, we slid into the back seat of the car. Carlo greeted Violet with a nod and a warm smile before slipping into his driver mode, expertly navigating the chaos that is downtown traffic. Violet's fingers tapped a rapid rhythm against the leather seat, and while I found the sound oddly soothing, I knew better. It was her warning signal. Like the sirens that blare before a tornado hits? Yeah, I'd take the tornado over the storm I saw brewing in her eyes right now.

"We need to talk." She turned to face me those eyes like green flames.

I had prepared for this though. Ran through every possible version of this conversation in my head on the way over. "Alright, I'm listening."

Her gaze flicked to Carlo, clearly debating whether to have this conversation in front of him. I leaned in, keeping my voice low but firm. "He knows. Carlo has an ironclad NDA and the understanding that if he talks, he loses more than his job." I gave Carlo a wave, and he chuckled from the front seat.

"Oh, great. So now he gets to hear all of this too," she muttered, leaning back.

Shit. Probably not my best move.

She straightened up, her green eyes burning into me. "You can't just mess with my life, Alex. I didn't earn that promotion, and now everyone at the office will assume it's only because of you."

"And why is that bad?" I kept my tone smooth and calm, knowing that raising it would only send her straight to DEFCON 1. "People talk. Let them talk."

Her eyes flared, and I braced myself. "No one will respect me."

"Everyone respects you, Violet. They know the work you put in. Let them assume what they want. Assumptions get people nowhere." I leaned closer, my voice dropping lower. "Gossip? It's empty. It won't change the fact that you've been doing that job all along. The only difference now is that you're getting the credit for it."

She huffed, folding her arms, but I could tell she was thinking it over. Whether she admitted it or not, she deserved that promotion, and I wasn't about to let anyone convince her otherwise.

She's chewing on her lower lip again—a dead giveaway that her mind is running a marathon of thoughts. And right now, I'd give anything to know exactly what's spinning in that head of hers.

"Everyone's going to think I got the promotion because of you. What happens when we're not dating? You can't just barge into my life and change things without asking. You're sending drivers to pick me up, and no offense," she shoots a glance at Carlo, "but I can't have you controlling my life, Alex. Even if I was your—"

Nope. Not letting her finish that sentence.

We're already in some weird limbo with no label, and I'm not about to let her overthink it. So, I press my finger gently against her lips, cutting her off before she says something we'll both regret.

"I sent a driver because I care about your safety. Nothing more. Trust me, there are plenty of other things I'd love to do for you, but for now? It's just a driver." I pause, softening my tone a little, hoping it lands. "And I called Hartley because you deserve recognition for the work you've done. You edited those scripts that made him millions. People should get paid for the work they do. Now you've got a salary that pays you to edit the mating habits of sparrows or whatever other riveting material comes your way."

Her eyes soften, just a bit. A flicker of light green replaced that fiery emerald storm. I take it as a win and reach for a bottle of water. Twisting off the cap, I hand it to her with a smirk, enjoying the small moment of victory when she takes it without even thinking.

"Oh my god, you did that on purpose," she says after a sip, eyes narrowing.

"Did what?" I keep my face neutral, but the corner of my mouth twitches. I know exactly what she's talking about.

"You opened the water just to see if I'd drink it. I don't need you doing things for me," she snaps, poking me with her free hand.

I hold back a chuckle, thankful she doesn't throw the water in my face. "And yet, you drank it. Look at us, like an old married couple already. Bickering, me opening your water for you."

The idea excites me more than it should. Not the "old" part, but the ease of it, the feeling like we've been doing this for longer than a few days. There's something about her—something that feels... right.

"Stop doing things for me, Alex. If you want something changed in my life, you talk to me first. It's *my* life."

"Fair enough," I say simply.

Her eyes go wide, surprised that I agreed so easily. She wasn't expecting that. I did, after all, plan out all the possible ways this conversation could go. Hell, I even planned the water bottle trick. I never have water bottles just casually sitting in the back of the car.

The rest of the drive is a mix of Violet's silent stares, half-smiles, and scowls. One thing about Violet, though, is she loves to people-watch, and I'm thankful because the more the city sucks her in, the fewer nasty looks that head my way. I catch her eyeing every person we pass, from cabs to pedestrians, soaking up the city like it's something magical.

Manhattan's always been a mix of chaos and grime to me, but she's captivated by it like she sees beauty in the cracks and clutter that I don't.

By the time we reach the restaurant, I can finally unclench and step out of the car, straightening my suit jacket as I move to help her out. Penelope reserved the table in advance—this place is always packed with people pouring out of their offices, desperate for good food and a stiff drink.

The hostess spots me immediately, flashing her usual smile that fades the second she sees my hand laced with Violet's. She flirts every time I'm here, and every time, I tell her the same thing: I'm unavailable. But this time, I have undeniable proof right beside me.

"Mr. Bennetti, let me show you to your table," she says, her voice clipped.

I pull out Violet's chair, pushing her in gently before taking the seat next to her instead of across. No reason to sit far away when I'd rather be close enough to throw an arm around her chair and not give a damn who's watching.

"Still mad at me?" I ask, flipping through the wine list. I already know she doesn't like reds. The way her nose crinkled the other night made that clear. So, I'm searching for a white that won't be terrible with the steak I always get here.

Avoiding eye contact, I place the menu in one hand while casually reaching over with the other to rest it on her thigh. I expect her to flinch or push me away, but instead, she surprises me—her hand covers mine, warm and steady.

"A little," she teases, her eyes peeking at me over the top of her menu, playful but not giving me the satisfaction of seeing her full smile. Just those magical eyes.

She orders the same steak as me, especially after I mention the gorgonzola and pear that pair with it are phenomenal. Most women I've taken to dinner—rare as that is—stick with salads, chicken, or some barely-there fish dish. But Violet? She's comfortable with real food, which is refreshing.

We chatted about work, and she mentioned the manuscript she was working on before her promotion. Honestly? It sounds like something I'd read. She rolls her eyes at that like she can't believe it, but it's true. Our conversation flows smoothly until our plates arrive. And then I get an idea.

"Indulge me," I say, slicing a square of perfectly cooked steak, balancing the gorgonzola, pear, and spinach just right on the fork. I hold it out to her. "Try it all together. You'll see why I never order anything else here."

She hesitates, her eyes meeting mine with a flicker of curiosity. Then, without breaking eye contact, she wraps her fingers around my wrist and guides the fork into her mouth.

Worst. Decision. Ever.

Not because she didn't like the food—she loved it, if the way her eyes fluttered shut and the soft moan she makes are any indication. No, the problem is the way she takes the fork in her mouth, her lips slowly wrapping around the tines, pulling the food off and her cheeks hollowing out. It's downright erotic, and my cock reacts instantly, far too eager for a restaurant setting.

That moan? Yeah, it doesn't help my situation. It echoes in my mind, and suddenly, all I can think about is those lips on me. The thought of what else she could do with that mouth is now permanently lodged in my brain, and I have to shift in my seat to adjust myself before anyone notices. This wasn't her trying to get a rise out of me—she was just enjoying steak, for fuck's sake—but now I'm imagining a hundred other ways to hear those sounds again.

Needing a quick distraction, I bring up the one topic I'm sure will douse the fire that's currently burning between us—and maybe get me some clarity. Family is a cornerstone of my life, whether I like it or not. We're in each other's business every day, meeting for dinners every Sunday, and giving opinions on matters they have no right to weigh in on. But with Violet, it's like her family doesn't exist. No mentions, no calls, nothing. And yeah, I'm curious.

"Why don't you talk about your parents much?"

The smile that had been playing on her lips vanished instantly. Her eyes harden, and her whole body stiffens like I just flipped a switch. Her fork pauses midair before she sets it down slowly—thankfully not stabbing me in the process. She reaches for her wine, sipping slowly at first, then finishing the glass in a few long gulps, leaving only drops behind. I didn't expect that reaction.

"If it makes you uncomfortable," I start, though it's obvious it does. Maybe I should've steered away, but I've already opened the door, so now I have to walk through it. "We don't have to talk about it."

"Why do you even want to know?" The edge in her voice is sharp.

Her response catches me off guard. "Isn't that part of getting to know each other?"

She sets her glass down with a bit more force than necessary. "This isn't that kind of 'getting to know you' situation. If we were actually dating, maybe." Her voice drops as she leans in, her eyes locking with mine. "But we're not, right? This whole thing is just 'you help me, I help you.' We don't need to go digging into the past or uncovering skeletons. You don't need to know me like that."

Fair enough. Except I *do* want to know her like that.

I rub my hand over my jaw, staring at her. What *are* we? Because we're definitely not just friends. Friends don't imagine each other naked or wonder what the weekend would be like tangled up together. Should I just tell her? Lay it all out there—tell her I want to date her for real? It's risky, but maybe necessary. Dom was right; we've been doing this whole "dating" thing without actually calling it that. Maybe she doesn't want more.

Why the hell am I being such a teenage girl about this?

Still on the fence, I decided to just go for it. "Violet—"

"Violet, how lovely to see you!"

I instantly recognize the voice, though I barely know the woman it belongs to. The effect is immediate—Violet goes rigid in her seat, carefully dabbing her mouth with a napkin before plastering on the most unsettling, fake smile I've ever seen. It's the kind of smile that feels like something out of a horror movie—the one a creepy doll gives you right before it comes to life and kills you in your sleep.

And yet, despite the eerie vibe, I find myself both terrified and oddly turned on at the same time.

She turns to see what I'm already looking at. Lisa—though honestly, Barbie is a better fit. If there were ever a Barbie based on her, it'd be *Homewrecker Barbie* or *I Wear Chanel Better than You Barbie*. The possibilities are endless. Maybe I should pitch it to Mattel, and get some more realistic names out there.

Lisa, or Barbie, seems to be in the middle of some kind of girls' night because instead of her usual douche of the week, she's got two equally plastic-looking women flanking her. They're all dressed like they coordinated their outfits, drowning in makeup and perfume that could probably knock out a small animal. Lisa's gaze shifts to me, her friend on the right practically undressing me with her eyes. I scoot closer to Violet, draping my arm casually over her shoulder, feeling protective and—if I'm being honest—completely annoyed.

"Always a joy," Violet mutters, grabbing my glass of wine and taking a sip, effectively trying to end the conversation.

But of course, Barbie is too dense to take the hint. "I see you and Alexander are still together," she says, her eyes lingering on me like she's genuinely surprised. The way she says it irritates me more than it probably irritates Violet, and that's saying something.

I can tell Violet's about to respond, but before she can, I cut in. I'm going to pay for this later, but I can't help myself. "And why does that surprise you?" My fingers absentmindedly twist a strand of Violet's hair, coiling it around my finger while my other hand rests on hers, a casual yet territorial move.

Lisa places her manicured hand on her chest as if I've genuinely shocked her. "Oh gosh, I didn't mean for it to sound like that," she says, her voice dripping with fake innocence.

"You know what? You're right," I say, feeling Violet's sharp gaze flick toward me. She's going to kill me for this later, but I keep going, hoping to finish before I lose a limb. "I'm surprised too. Violet is by far the most beautiful woman I've ever seen—way out of my league, honestly. But here we are, celebrating her new promotion."

Lisa clicks her tongue and flashes a smile that's as fake as her tan. "I heard about your promotion. Jake told me all about it. Seems dating a Bennetti has its benefits."

I catch the glare she shoots me from the corner of her eye, and for the first time, I'm genuinely nervous that I might get my ass kicked later. I don't scare easily—my cousin's in the mafia, for fuck's sake. I've seen things most people wouldn't sleep over, but Violet? Yeah, I'm sweating a little, because this is the very reason she didn't want me to interfere with her job.

I turn my attention back to Lisa, forcing a smile that doesn't reach my eyes. "I'm sure Jake said plenty. But Violet earned that promotion. Remind me, Lisa, where are you working these days?"

That fake tan does nothing to hide the fact she's just paled about five shades. "I, uh... I'm between gigs at the moment."

Gigs? What are we, 21?

"That's a shame." I stand up, buttoning my jacket and holding out my hand to Violet. "Ready to go, baby?" She grabs my hand like it's a lifeline, squeezing so hard I feel it in my bones.

I glance back at Lisa, my voice laced with sarcasm. "Always a pleasure."

It's about as pleasant as having my balls waxed.

Lisa wiggles her fingers in some pathetic excuse for a wave, and I make a mental note to blacklist her so hard she couldn't get a job at a kiosk in Times Square, let alone anywhere respectable.

Waiting for Carlo to arrive, we stand under the valet station's cover. It's fall in New York, which means cold winds, relentless rain, and everything soaked in gray. While most people huddle under umbrellas or rush to escape the weather, Violet looks around like it's a masterpiece, as if the rain-soaked city is something worth admiring. I don't get it. No one sees New York like she does, and I doubt I ever will.

"So," I start, hands shoved in my pockets, bracing myself for whatever she's about to say. But she doesn't jump into it. Instead, she just turns to me.

Her eyes narrow, but there's something else there—half a smile, half a frown. She's a damn puzzle.

I've gotten good at reading people, knowing their tells. But Violet? I don't know her well enough to crack this expression. Is she mad? Sad? No, I've seen her pissed off and hurt, and this isn't either of those. And for the first time, I'm nervous because I can't read her, and that unfamiliar uncertainty is messing with my head.

Before I can even process it, Violet grabs my suit jacket and pulls me in, surprising the hell out of me. Despite wearing heels, she still has to get on her toes, and for some reason, that does things to me I'm not willing to admit. Instinct takes over, and I wrap an arm around her waist, yanking her closer.

"Shut. Up," she mutters before pressing her soft lips against mine.

Up until now, I've always been the one to initiate the kiss. But this time? She takes control, and I'm done for. Her hands fist my jacket, and I couldn't care less about the wrinkles. The second her mouth locks onto mine, I'm a goner. I bury my free hand in her hair, pulling her even closer, opening my mouth for her before she even needs to ask.

The way this woman kisses—it's like nothing else. She's both slow and hungry, sensual and commanding, deepening the kiss while I tug her against me. She pauses for a breath, her lips hovering just above mine, and then she smiles softly before diving back in.

I know exactly where we are—outside a fancy, crowded restaurant in the middle of Manhattan—and yet, I can't bring myself to care. My girlfriend is kissing me like she owns me, and for the first time in my life, I don't mind the idea of being owned.

I'm lost in the feel of her—those soft lips, the firm grip of her hands on my chest, the sweet taste of her mouth giving me a sugar high, and the way her body curves perfectly against mine. When she finally pulls back, her hands slowly release my jacket, smoothing the fabric, but her fingers linger on my chest, tracing the lines along the fabric.

I know she felt me, rock hard against her, and I don't care. My hand's still tangled in her hair, and if we weren't standing on a public sidewalk, there's no telling what I'd be doing right now. The things I want to do with her... definitely not safe for public consumption.

"What was that for?" I murmur, resting my forehead against hers, my arm loosely draped around her waist as if holding on any tighter might make her slip away.

Violet's green eyes flicker over my face, her lips parting like she's about to say something, but then she bites down on her lower lip. That lip. The same one I'm imagining kissing while she's naked beneath me. I groan internally, fighting the images that flood my brain.

She hesitates, then smirks slightly. "Just for show," she says, but we both know it's a lie. Still, I'll take it.

Alex

"Have you seen the article?"

I stop mid-stride the next morning, my coffee cup hovering at my lips, untouched. The second those words leave Dom's mouth, my brain switches gears. I don't own all the media outlets anymore, but I sold them to a friend. So if someone published something they shouldn't have, I could shut them down in ten minutes flat. "What article?"

Dom pulls out his phone, his fingers flying over the screen before turning it to face me. There's a picture. Of me and Violet from last night. The moment we were waiting outside the restaurant for Carlo, right after she grabbed me and kissed me out of nowhere. And I kissed her back, not giving a damn about the very public display of affection.

In the photo, her mouth is pressed to mine, my hand tangled in her hair, and my other arm wrapped possessively around her waist. We're smiling into the kiss like the rest of the world doesn't exist.

It looks...*real*.

My stomach twists. Because let's be honest—*it was real*. Only, neither of us has bothered to define what "real" actually means.

I glance down at the headline. *"Sorry Ladies, Looks Like One of New York's Hottest Bachelors is Off the Market."*

And I can't help but smirk.

Dom raises a brow, clearly amused, and I can see those lips tugging at the corner. "It's rather cute, huh?" he says.

I shoot him a look, sipping my coffee. "Don't think I've ever heard you use the word 'cute' around me, and I'd prefer to never hear it again."

I head into my corner office, coffee in hand, feeling the subtle shift in the air. A few people glance up from their desks, eyes flicking from their screens back to me. Yeah, they've seen the article.

Great. At least I don't have to make any phone calls today to deal with this.

I settle behind my desk—mahogany, not that cold glass-and-steel bullshit the rest of the office prefers. My space isn't sleek or sterile like everyone else's. It's rich wood, deep leather, warm tones, and shelves filled with books. Granted, they're all business books. Not a single fiction title to be found. I hadn't even noticed until Violet came into my world.

Dom drops into one of the cushioned chairs across from me, lounging like he owns the place. "So, did you put a label on it?" His voice is all teasing, and I don't miss the exaggerated pout he throws my way. "Because the media sure did. And you know once Mama sees this, she's gonna lose her mind."

I let out a frustrated breath, pulling up the article on my screen. "I tried to talk to her last night, but we were interrupted."

"By her mouth?" Dom grins, way too entertained by this.

I glare at him. "No. Well, yes. But I was actually about to have the conversation before that."

He's still grinning like a damn fool, and it only makes me more annoyed. How the hell am I supposed to put a label on this when every time I try, something—or someone—gets in the way? And now, with this article out there, everything feels even more complicated. And more real.

Dom leans back in his chair, all casual as he crosses one leg over the other. "Let me get this straight. You want to label whatever this is, but instead of using your words, you're out here just making out in front of every camera in Manhattan?"

I level him with a glare. "I didn't plan for that. It just... happened."

Dom's grin widens. "Right, because public PDA always just happens when you're with someone you're 'fake' dating."

He's not wrong, and that's what's driving me insane. I've been in control my whole life—my business, my decisions, my relationships. But with Violet, nothing is going according to plan. Every time I'm around her, my carefully built walls start to crack, and now I've gone and kissed her in the middle of the damn street for the whole world to see.

"I was going to talk to her," I mutter, staring at the article. "But every time I try, something gets in the way."

Dom's fake sympathy is all over his face. "Oh, poor baby. The billionaire can't get a moment alone to tell his girl he likes her. What a tragedy."

"Shut up." I run a hand through my hair, frustrated. "You don't get it. I don't do this whole feelings thing."

"Clearly."

I glance up at him, my jaw clenched. "I like her, Dom. That's the problem." Pulling up the link Dom sent, trying—and failing—not to smile at the picture staring back at me. It was cute. Damn it, did I seriously just think that?

Blame my brother and his habit of making me sit through too many of his son's Disney movies.

"You're looking at the article, aren't you?" Dom's voice was way too amused.

"Maybe," I muttered, scrolling through the rest of the page, not wanting to admit how much I liked seeing us like that.

"So... you probably have an hour before Mama calls. What are you gonna tell her?"

Good question. What do I tell her? My board already thinks I've been in a relationship for a month. My top investors met Violet and assumed she was the one. Her coworkers? They think I'm her boyfriend.

We've been playing this arrangement like a game, but now the tabloids have slapped a label on it. So I guess my mother will get the same party line.

Lying to my mother—now that makes me uncomfortable, and I don't get uncomfortable easily. But with any luck, after I talk to Violet, the lie will become the truth. At least, that's the plan.

I took another sip of my coffee, pretending to ignore Dom as I skimmed the rest of the article. Of course, it mentioned we'd been "discreetly dating" for about a month. Who leaked that? Not that it mattered; we gave them that story. But still, it was a reminder to have a conversation with Violet about how easily things slip out when you're around me.

"So," Dom drawled, still leaning against my desk like he wasn't planning on leaving anytime soon. "You gonna make it official with her or what? Seems like the media's already done it for you."

I grunted, closing the article. "I'll handle it."

But the truth was, I wasn't sure what "handling it" even looked like anymore.

Dom wasn't letting up. He sat there, tapping his fingers on the desk, a reminder of how much he enjoyed getting under my skin.

"I was there with Natalia, you know."

Just hearing her name tightened something in my chest. It wasn't just a casual mention; it brought a surge of anger, like a match scraping against the rough edge of my thoughts. "I'm aware, Dom," I said, voice tight.

"Just don't want to see you like that again," he said, and for a moment, he dropped the teasing.

I leaned forward, meeting his gaze head-on. Dom's my younger brother, but somehow, he's always managed to carry a sense of maturity that makes it feel like he's the older one. He also inherited Mama's uncanny ability to nag relentlessly. "It's not going to be like that with Violet." I meant every word. There was something about her—something different. "She's not... vanilla," I added, giving him a pointed look.

Dom raised a brow, then shook his head slowly, as I'd just made his point for him. "Oh, well then. Pardon me," he said with a drawl, leaning back, "but you, my dear big brother, are absolutely fucked."

I narrowed my eyes. "How so?"

Without missing a beat, he pulled out his phone again and flashed the screen at me. There it was: the picture of Violet and me from last night, lips locked, bodies pressed together like we couldn't get close enough. "Because that, my dear big brother," he said, dragging out each word for maximum effect, "is you looking all kinds of in love."

I scowled at the picture but couldn't deny what I saw.

Was I in love? No. But the idea of falling for her didn't scare me nearly as much as it should have.

Fuck. He's probably right.

Anyone else, I'd tell to get the hell out. But Dom? We've always been close. Even though he and Enrico are twins, Dom's always understood me better. Hell, he can read me better than he reads his twin.

"Not sure what you're getting at, Dom," I brush him off, which only makes him push harder. That annoying, knowing smirk playing on his face that says he's onto something and plans to drag it out.

"Sure, whatever you say, Alex. I've seen you kiss plenty of women, but I've never seen you wrapped up in one like that." He gestures to the article again. "Just promise me you're not going to get down on one knee tomorrow. Take it slow, get to know her."

If he only knew how little I actually knew about Violet... and how badly I wanted to know every damn detail. Like her favorite childhood stuffed animal, what snack she reaches for when she's stressed, or why her eyes shift colors depending on her mood like some kind of human mood ring.

"I can promise that." The words come out, but they feel hollow. Because if I'm being honest, I'm not sure I can.

My phone pings, and before I can stop it, a smile creeps across my face. Violet.

Dom catches it, of course, because he's still standing there, soaking in the moment like a damn victory lap. "Is that the infamous lady who's stolen you off the market?" he teases, wiggling his eyebrows before sauntering out of my office. "Holler if you need anything. One of us has to pretend like we work here."

I roll my eyes as he leaves, shaking my head. Fucking brothers.

VIOLET: Did you see that article?

ALEX: What article?

VIOLET: Us. After dinner last night. Quit screwing with me, I know you saw it.

ALEX: So what if I did? I am technically off the market.

I fired off the last message, letting it hang out there, half curious, half testing the waters. When no response came, I figured maybe she got caught up in work. Still, the silence gnawed at me, making it harder to focus on the emails piling up in my inbox. Normally, I wouldn't give a second thought to an unanswered text—I had a company to run, and it wasn't like I had time to analyze messages all day. But with Violet, it was different.

After a few minutes of pretending to work, I hit the intercom. "Penelope, can you come in?"

It didn't take long before she popped her head in, eyebrows raised in that way that suggested I was disturbing her unnecessarily early. "So soon? Need something already?"

I ignored her usual sass, tapping my desk lightly. "I need that photo from last night printed and framed. Send it to Violet's office."

She frowned, clearly confused. "Framed?"

"Yes, framed," I said, a bit sharper than intended. "She's decorating her office, thought I'd help her out."

Penelope's lips twitched, like she was biting back a comment, but she nodded. "Got it, boss."

Three hours later, my phone buzzed.

VIOLET: Thank you.

ALEX: For what?

VIOLET: The picture and flowers. Is this going to be a thing? Big bouquets and framed photos?

ALEX: Maybe. Can't have any man walking into your office without knowing you're off limits.

VIOLET: Didn't realize you were the possessive type.

ALEX: Very. What's mine is mine. You're mine.

I hit send, feeling that familiar thrill of risk. The possessive edge to my words wasn't something I'd normally throw out, but then again, everything about this was different. With her, it felt like I was constantly teetering between control and letting go.

Violet

LAST NIGHT WAS... DIFFERENT.

I'm not usually the kind of girl to make the first move—honestly, I don't even make the second or third—but standing outside in the cool night air, waiting for our car, something shifted. I wanted to kiss him. After the way he kissed me in the office earlier, my legs were still jelly, and my insides? Total goo.

And when I kissed him? God, I was giddy. I could've floated home. We joked in the car about him staying over again since we both slept so damn well the night before. Like some kind of addictive sleep aid, but one that involved warm arms and soft breathing. Except, half of me wasn't joking. Okay, maybe more than half. But I didn't invite him up. I wanted to. I really wanted to. But what *are* we doing? I have no idea.

This whole thing was supposed to be a fake dating arrangement. Yet here we are—talking every day, seeing each other constantly, kissing when there's no one around, no need to "perform," and he's sending me thoughtful gifts. I mean...we're dating, right? At least it feels like it.

But how do I feel about that? I'm not sure. Especially with a guy like Alex. The kind of guy who could date anyone. And somehow, I don't feel like I'm in the right league for him, despite all the sweet things he says. And now there's this stupid article making the rounds. The rest of Manhattan seems to think we're a couple, and I don't even know what *we* are.

So, like any mature adult facing confusion, I decided to bury it in work. If I ignore it long enough, maybe the confusion will magically disappear. Right?

The second I walk into the office, Max is waiting for me, his ever-present sarcastic smile firmly in place. He hands me a coffee with a dramatic bow as if I'm some sort of royalty.

"Miss Hart," he says, drawing out my last name with a mock reverence that earns him an eye roll from me.

I maneuver around his ridiculously tall frame blocking the doorway to my office. Stepping inside, I toss my purse into the armchair I added for decor purposes—or, more accurately, as a place to throw my stuff when I'm too frazzled to hang it up like a normal person. Crap. I forgot my jacket.

Max slides into the seat across from my desk before I even have a chance to sit down. "So, how did the dinner date go?" he asks, eyes gleaming with curiosity.

How did it go? Oh, you know, just a casual dinner filled with fake smiles, tension I could practically taste, and... a kiss. But not just any kiss. The kind that ruins you for all other kisses. Let's not even dive into the news article thanks. But unpacking *that* is a level of complicated I'm not emotionally prepared for before my first coffee.

I slump into my chair, smashing the keyboard until the login screen pops up. "Well," I start, drawing out the word like it's going to magically give me clarity. "We went to dinner. Lisa made an appearance, and Alex—" I pause, glancing at the framed photo of him now proudly sitting on my counter, "handled it... perfectly." The understatement of the century. "We even joked about him staying the night again, just to sleep."

"Wait, hold up," Max interjects, holding up a finger like he's about to deliver some groundbreaking analysis. "You had that man—" he points to the photo of Alex on the counter behind my desk, "basically naked in your bed, all wrapped around you, and you didn't have sex? And now you want to do it again? Just sleep?"

"Yes?" I reply, though my voice sounds more like a question. And honestly, I need more coffee—iced coffee—to handle this conversation. The image of Alex in nothing but briefs, his body pressed against mine, wrapped around me like he belonged there, is making my pulse race. And my thighs instinctively clench together.

A gentle knock at the door draws my attention. One of the assistants from upstairs is standing there, looking a little out of breath. "I'm sorry, Mr. Cooper, you weren't at your desk, but I have a new manuscript for Miss Hart. Mr. Hartley has requested that you put a rush on this one. They need to get it out before the end of the month."

My fingers are practically twitching with excitement. Please let this be something good. Now that I'm a senior editor, I'm hoping I'll finally get to work on manuscripts that interest me, or at least won't make me want to gouge my eyes out like Margaret's old assignments.

Max takes the envelope, his brow quirking in curiosity as he peeks inside. "A rush job?" he says, a slow grin spreading across his face.

"Oh my gosh, is it something I'll enjoy reading?" I squeal like a kid on Christmas, jumping up from my chair and practically sprinting around the desk to snatch the envelope from his hands.

I pull out the stack of papers, bracing myself for a thrilling escape into fiction. Until I see the title.

The Courtship Rituals of the Majestic Peacock.

Max must have caught the shift in my expression because he's doubled over, laughing so hard he can barely stand. "Are you serious?" I mutter, glaring at the offending manuscript like it personally wronged me.

"You've got to be kidding me," I groan, slumping back into my chair. The literary gods have forsaken me once again. What did I ever do to them?

Max wipes tears from his eyes, still chuckling as he straightens up. "At least the peacock is more majestic than a house sparrow, right?"

I shoot him a look, wishing he would spontaneously combust. Meanwhile, he strolls back to his desk—the one he commandeered outside my office, which is technically for assisting me, but easier access to come in and gossip whenever he pleases.

Great. So not only am I editing *The Courtship Rituals of the Majestic Peacock*, but now I get to hear Max make bird jokes all day.

The peacock may be getting some, but I'm definitely not.

My phone pings from across the office, pulling my attention. I cross the room and grab it from my purse.

> **Alex:** I feel like I made a mistake last night. I should have offered to help you sleep. I didn't sleep well at all. You fit perfectly next to me, and without you, sleep isn't the same. Just thought I should let you know that.

An aggravated sound escapes me—something between a groan and a growl—and it's loud enough that Max pokes his head into my office, his eyebrows raised in question.

"What's up?" he asks, his face a mix of curiosity and amusement.

Wordlessly, I hold out my phone for him to see.

He reads it and then gives me a soft smile. "Oh, that's cute."

"Is it though?" I mutter, flopping back into my chair. "We are... I don't even know what we're doing. Things like this just make it more complicated." I wave the phone in the air like it's the source of all my confusion. In a way, it is.

Max leans against the doorframe, folding his arms. "So, you two are fake dating but send texts like *that*?"

I sigh, resting my head in my hands. "Right? We're supposed to be fake dating for each other's... needs, or whatever. But honestly? It doesn't feel fake at all anymore."

Max raises an eyebrow. "So, what's the problem?"

"The problem is that we're supposed to be avoiding real feelings to keep things simple. And falling into a weird limbo is exactly how Jake and I became a thing. We both know how well that story ended." I let out another groan.

"He's sending messages you don't send to someone unless you have actual feelings for them." I sigh, more to myself than Max.

Max gives me a look that's half sympathy, half amusement. "So what's the plan, Violet?"

I slump deeper into my chair. "Am I seriously going to be that woman tomorrow at the party with watery eyes, pitifully asking, 'So, where do you see us going?'"

Max snorts, but he's holding back laughter. "Please tell me you won't. But if you do, at least wear waterproof mascara."

My fingers hover over my phone, nerves buzzing as I stare at Alex's message. "How do I respond without sounding like I also enjoyed sleeping next to him?" I mumble.

Max studies me, his smirk borderline amused. "Didn't you?"

"Of course I did!" I huff, throwing my hands in the air. It was *incredible*—too incredible. That's the problem.

Max steps closer, resting his hands on my shoulders like he's about to give me a pep talk. I always forget how tall he is until he looms over me like this, making me feel ridiculously small. "Then why are you freaking out?"

"Because this started as a simple date-exchange arrangement!" I glance behind him to make sure no one's eavesdropping. This is New York; privacy is a myth, even in an office. "Now it's obviously more. Especially when he sends messages like that! And I don't know if I'm ready to date someone like him. What if I get attached and he drops me for someone more his type? Someone like... I don't know, a supermodel?"

Max's eyes narrow, his grip on my shoulders tightening. "You're overthinking this. Getting a good night's sleep next to a hot guy isn't messy. It's glorious. Now, if you slept together—the naked, sweaty, let's-get-all-up-in-each-other kind—then sure, it might get a little complicated. But even then, I'd still cheer you on."

I bite my lip, trying not to laugh. Trust Max to make this sound simpler than it feels.

"And for the record," he adds, "just because you're not sleeping together doesn't mean you're not *dating* for real. You two just need to grow up, stop with the cute messages and innuendos, and talk. Like adults. Ask each other what you're doing so you don't do the Jake path again."

I blink at him, speechless for a second. As annoying as he is, Max has a point. I can't keep spiraling with these what-ifs. We can't keep dancing around the obvious tension, the constant flirting, the shared moments.

But I also can't have sex with him until I know what this is. Unfortunately, my heart and mind are all tangled up in this, while the rest of my body is loudly protesting, like a choir begging to be heard.

Even just sleeping in the same bed, with inches between us, was amazing. I was tucked against his ridiculously sculpted, tattooed chest, his arms wrapped around me like he never wanted to let go. I can still feel his breath against my hair, warm and steady as he slept. It was intimate in a way that left me feeling confused and... wanting. "You don't share a bed like that with someone unless you want more, right?" I mutter, unsure if I'm asking myself or Max at this point.

Max, ever the smartass, raises a brow. "I've shared a bed with you before, and we cuddled. Still just good friends." He says it like it's the most obvious thing in the world.

"Yeah, well, you also don't like vaginas," I shoot back, pushing myself off him and walking back to my desk. Max shrugs nonchalantly as if to say, *fair point.*

Sitting down, I stare at my phone, feeling Max's eyes burning holes into me. "You don't have to sit here and watch me text him," I groan.

"Oh, but I do," he says, fingers tapping rhythmically against his chin. "I need to make sure you don't say something stupid."

I throw him my best shocked face, complete with an exaggerated gasp. "*Me?* Say something stupid? Never."

Max just rolls his eyes. "Please. If I'm not monitoring you, you'll definitely do something dumb."

It's like I'm trapped in a bad soap opera—only, this is my life. And Max, as much as I hate to admit it, is right. Left to my own devices, I'll either say something I'll regret or spiral into a black hole of awkwardness. So, I set my phone down on the desk, the text thread with Alex wide open, taunting me like it holds all the answers to my mess of a situation.

"Just say something non-committal," Max leans over my desk, giving unsolicited advice.

"Like...?" I raise an eyebrow at him.

"You're the writer, Violet," he says with a shrug, smirking.

Ugh. Don't remind me.

I start typing, *Thank you for staying the night the other night and dinner last night.* Ugh, no, that sounds ridiculous. Delete.

Okay, maybe, *I enjoyed it too.* Wait. That sounds like I'm inviting him to stay over again. Which... do I want? Oh God, do I? Because now I'm freaking out that he won't, and I'm pretty sure my bed and sleep are forever ruined now that I know what it's like to have him next to me. I delete that too.

Max is watching me like a hawk, tapping his fingers on the desk. "You're spiraling. Hand it over before you overthink yourself into an ulcer." He stretches out his hand, wiggling his fingers knowing he's about to save me from myself.

Against my better judgment, I hand him my phone.

Max smirks and starts typing with way too much confidence.

> Violet: I enjoyed it too — thought you should know that.

I glance at the screen, gasping like I just witnessed someone kill a puppy. "Are you crazy? Now he's going to think I *enjoyed* it!"

Max stares at me like I've lost all common sense. "But you *did* enjoy it, Violet."

I slump back in my chair, spinning around in circles like I'm five, and just discovered the thrilling ride that is a swivel chair. "Yeah, but does he need to know that? What if he reads it, freaks out, and thinks we're moving too fast?" I'm chewing on my lip now, nerves eating at me. "Or worse—what if he doesn't stay over again? What if we've crossed some imaginary line?"

Before I can dig deeper into this spiral Max is so kindly pointing out, my phone pings in his hand. A wide, satisfied grin spreads across his face as he reads the reply. I don't know whether to be relieved or scared.

"What? What did he say?" I practically launch myself out of my chair, reaching across my desk to grab my phone, but Max is quicker, holding it just out of reach.

"First, what were you wearing when you slept over the other night?" He gives me a look, and I know where this is going.

I raise a brow, suspicious. "My usual sleep shorts and a T-shirt. Why?"

"The slutty ones that barely cover your ass?"

I glare at him, but it's not like he's wrong. "Maybe. Why?"

Max grins like a kid with a secret. "Just confirming."

Before I can react, his fingers fly over my phone, typing something I'm sure will ruin my life. I lunge across the desk, half crawling, half climbing over him, trying to wrestle it out of his hands. In my frantic effort, I end up half-sprawling across his lap, pinning his giant frame down, but it's too late. I hear the unmistakable *whoosh* of the text being sent, and I'm pretty sure that's the sound of my soul leaving my body.

"You're welcome," Max says smugly, finally handing me the phone.

I scowl, ready to chew him out, but then I see the message on the screen, and my stomach drops.

Alex: Well, what if you did that again tonight? At my place. I can make us dinner.

Violet: Only if you have a T-shirt I can borrow.

Oh. My. Gosh. I stare at the screen, half squinting, half glaring at Max, but I'm speechless. Just as I'm about to launch into a full-blown panic, my phone pings again. Max and I both look at the screen, me still straddling him, and I can feel the heat rising up my neck as we both read it.

Alex: Only if you promise that's all you'll be wearing.

Max fans himself dramatically. "Dear God, that's hot."

I groan, feeling like I need to dunk myself in an ice bucket. "He's going to expect me to actually sleep with him."

Max arches a brow. "Technically, you already did."

I press my fingers to my temple, feeling the impending doom settle in. "And now I'm apparently doing it again tonight."

"Yup." Max nods, entirely too pleased with himself.

"Sleeping," I mutter as if saying it enough will make it true. "Not sex. Just... sleeping."

Max smirks. "Sure. Keep telling yourself that, babe."

Alex

I HAD PLANNED TO hit the gym with one of the few people I consider a friend.

In Manhattan, the word "friend" gets tossed around too easily—everyone assumes you're close just because you run in the same circles. But real friends? Those are rare. Dante Pierce was one of the exceptions. We grew up together, and now he's the owner of Pierce Auto Group, a company that specializes in custom rebuilds and classic cars for Manhattan's elite.

We had a standing racquetball game—yes, I know, it's a cliché, but sometimes clichés are fun. We'd place bets, too, though the stakes have changed over the years. What started as $5 wagers at the local youth center over ping pong or tennis has evolved into thousands of dollars on who could win, with the occasional embarrassing dare thrown in for good measure.

Call it maturity, Manhattan-style.

Today, though, I was off my game. Every time Dante landed a shot I couldn't return, I muttered a string of curses under my breath. My focus was shot and I was glad the rooms at the club were soundproof because the last thing I needed was everyone passing by hearing just how frustrated I was getting. It wasn't uncommon for people to discuss business during these games—especially in a place like this, where privacy was practically a luxury amenity. But today, neither of us brought up work. I was too focused on trying to burn off this frustration.

Only problem? I wasn't burning off anything. The tension from last night—and from Violet—was still knotted tight in my chest, and no amount of racquetball was fixing it.

Dante and I have always been mistaken for brothers. We both have blue eyes, Italian roots, and similar builds, but his family took a different path. They changed their last name, and distanced themselves from the old Italian connections my family never let go of.

My mother wasn't Sicilian, something my grandparents never stopped grumbling about. But my dad? He didn't care. That's why I ended up with these blue eyes. Otherwise, I'd have inherited the brown hair, olive skin, and amber eyes like my brothers. Still, Papa's genes weren't completely overshadowed. The older I got, the more I saw it—same jawline, same nose, and the same shape of the eyes, even if they weren't the right color.

Dante ran his hand through his sweat-soaked hair as we walked over to the bench, grabbing towels and water. He raised an eyebrow at me, his usual smirk in place. "So, why didn't you tell me you were dating? Over a month. Thought we were close."

I shrugged, cursing internally. I had forgotten about Dante when I concocted this whole fake-dating plan. My family wouldn't be surprised. They expect me to keep my dating life under wraps until I'm serious about someone. Except now that I think about it, this situation with Violet *looks* serious. That article from last night for sure has reached my mama by now, and that means one thing.

Sunday dinner.

Shit.

It's one thing to play the game for the board, the press, and Manhattan's elite. I can keep up the charade no problem. But my mama? That woman is a force. The kind that raised three sons, held down the fort and never flinched while married to a man who didn't exactly operate on the right side of the law. Papa didn't just toe the line—he erased it entirely. And Mama, well… she's the one person I might not be able to fool. Even if my feelings weren't anywhere in the realm of fake for this woman.

"I meant to tell you, just got caught up," I mutter, taking a long swig of water, hoping to end the conversation.

"In her tongue?" Dante shoots me a smirk, clearly enjoying himself. I glare at him, knowing exactly what he's referring to—the damn photo. He throws up his hands, grinning like the idiot he is. "Hey, just saying, you looked pretty tied up there. And she's hot, man."

Dante, unlike half the fake friends in my circle, would never hit on someone I'm seeing. It's not his style. Besides, he's had a thing for my cousin for years but refuses to act on it. Makes him blind to every other woman throwing themselves at him.

"Is that article why you sucked so hard at ball today?" He's gearing up for another match, wiping the sweat from his brow but looking far too smug for my liking.

"What? No. Why would it?"

He shrugs, casually bouncing the ball on his racket. "Because usually you wipe the floor with me, and today I've won four games. Either your head's too caught up in that kiss or…whatever else you've been enjoying." He wiggles his eyebrows, earning a low growl from me.

"Watch it."

"Ah, so it *is* her," he shoots back, his smirk only growing as he tosses the ball in the air for a serve.

"Can we not talk about this right now?" I grip my racket, focusing on the ball like it's the only thing that matters.

I serve, hitting the ball hard, aiming for the perfect angle to send it flying past him. But Dante, as usual, is ready for it. Fucker.

"Nope. We *are* talking about this because you've been dating a woman for a month, and from what I'm seeing, you're already in that 'touch her and I'll bury you' phase. Which, knowing your family... well, let's just say it could happen." He laughs.

"It's not like that," I snap, cursing under my breath as the ball bounces back too high and Dante smacks it cleanly past me.

"Well, considering you can't serve for shit today, I'd say otherwise." He grins, setting up for another serve.

I rally the ball hard, trying to force it past him, but Dante's there, waiting, knocking it back with ease. My frustration boils over when I miss the return and the ball bounces twice. "Fuck!" I toss my racket aside, cursing louder this time.

Dante just chuckles.

"Okay, if I tell you, you can't say a word to anyone—*especially* not Alena. I'll fucking kill you." Alena is my cousin, and Dante's been secretly in love with her for years. If she finds out anything, it'll spread like wildfire straight to my mom, aunts, and my dad, and I do *not* need them prying into my personal life more than they already do.

Dante raises an eyebrow, holding up his racket. "Alright, but when Alena eventually finds out I didn't tell her, you better hook me up with the best plastic surgeon in Manhattan to sew my balls back on. And make sure they work."

I chuckle. He's not wrong—Alena is notorious for her temper. The Bennetti women are intense, and Alena, well, she takes crazy to a whole new level.

"So, she's not technically my girlfriend... not yet, I think."

"Come again?" Dante raises an eyebrow, looking like I've just told him the earth is flat.

I pick up the ball, tossing it lightly in my hand. "We met in a bar. I kissed her to make her ex jealous—it's a long story, one you don't need." No way am I going into detail about how I saw her and knew I had to have her the second I laid eyes on her. That makes me sound like a complete idiot... or worse, a creep. "Anyway, I had that investor dinner, and they've been on my case about dating. So, I brought her as my 'girlfriend'—even though she's not. I offered to be her fake boyfriend for a work event this Friday. We met last Friday, but to sell the story, I said we'd been dating secretly for a month. Only now I've spent every day with her since we met, except for Monday. This whole thing started as a fake dating arrangement, but now..." I trail off, feeling like an idiot.

"So what, you're friends with benefits? Please tell me you've at least fucked her. I saw the pictures from that article—the ones where you *weren't* sucking face. The woman is hot." Dante's holding the ball, looking at me like I've just handed him a puzzle. "And, seriously, *don't* say that to Alena. I like having my balls intact."

I laugh, grabbing the ball from him to serve. "No. No sex."

Dante groans. "But you *want* to have sex with her."

I smirk, lining up my shot. "I'm not dead, man."

"So, what's the reason you haven't sealed the deal yet?" Dante rallies a perfect return.

"*Assolutamente fottutamente ridicolo,*" I mutter, grabbing the ball and preparing to serve again.

Dante laughs. "You only bust out the Italian when you've got some serious blue balls, man. Must be bad." He's not wrong. I can speak the language fluently, but I only really use it around family—unless I'm pissed. And right now? Yeah, I'm definitely on edge.

I slam the ball, sending it his way. "I don't want to screw it up, alright? I actually *like* her. On Friday, I'm going to this work party with her to make her ex jealous, and I haven't told her yet, but... she's probably gonna have to come to Sunday dinner with my mama—"

Dante cuts me off, grinning. "Oh, I'm definitely showing up for that shit. Front row seat to see how that goes down."

I ignore him, rallying the ball hard. "I'm not even sure if she wants this to go beyond what we've got. If we sleep together, it's just gonna get... complicated." Or amazing. I can't deny that.

The ball bounces, but Dante doesn't even bother returning it. He just stands there, racket dangling at his side, looking at me like I've just said something insane. "Dude, if you think it's *not* already complicated, you're *più stupido di quanto pensassi.*"

I give him a side-eye. "Funny, coming from the guy who never uses Italian." Dante barely speaks the language, even with how much time he spends around my family.

He shrugs. "Just saying, man. You like her—obviously, with that possessive, scary-ass look you get every time I call her hot. Why don't you tell her you want to date for real? And for the love of God, get laid. Because a sex-deprived Alex? It's not pretty."

I was shoving my gear into my bag in the locker room, freshly showered, and pulling out my suit to get ready for the next meeting. We'd been at it for almost two hours—longer than I intended—but it's my permanently reserved court. I pay a hefty price to have it at the ready for days like this when I need to burn off the tension that can't be dealt with any other way. Something tells me I might be back tomorrow.

Pulling out my phone, I see a text from Violet.

VIOLET: *I can do that, but for the record, you're mine.*

Before I can react, Dante's leaning over my shoulder, still in a towel, snooping like the pain in the ass he is, and I shove him off.

"Well, *hello* there," he purrs, eyeing her message.

I roll my eyes and pull the phone away from him. "Mind your business."

"Just saying," he grins, reaching for his suit. "You should tell her what you actually want so you stop being a grumpy shit. You're already dating her."

It's like I'm reliving the same conversation I had with Dom. Are they coordinating this intervention? "I don't think she wants that. She's got a situation, like I did with Natalia. Only instead of it being everyone I worked with, it's her best friend."

"Oof. That's messed up."

"Yeah, maybe I'll just see where it goes," I mutter, buttoning up my shirt. "I like being around her. Hell, I haven't even known her for a week. We don't need to slap a label on this."

Dante smirks, adjusting his cufflinks. "You're Sicilian. Labels don't matter. We see what we want, know it's right, and we're in love. Days, minutes, hours—makes no difference. You're out here playing racquetball with me, pretending it's about blowing off steam, but really, you're avoiding the fact that you want her. So what are you running from? Sorry, I've heard your excuses, but they're weak."

I groan, pulling on my jacket and trying to ignore him. "Because if this turns into something real, and she doesn't stick around... I don't know if I could handle losing her."

Dante whistles low, running a hand through his damp hair. "Damn. That's it? You're scared?"

"Shut up," I mutter, shoving my gear into the locker.

He straightens his tie, looking all smug. "Dude, if *that's* your only excuse, you're already way past 'just dating' her."

Like I'm going to take dating advice from the guy who can't ask my cousin out on a date and comes to every family event just to be near her.

I realize the hypocrisy now considering the shit I've given him for not making a move, but I don't need to admit that to him.

Alex

SINCE THE ARTICLE DROPPED, I've dealt with no less than five calls from my mama, each one more insistent than the last. As expected, she's demanding I bring my "girlfriend" to a family dinner on Sunday. Since the rest of the world knows, it's time my family does too.

I'd hoped I'd have more time—time to figure out what exactly was happening with Violet and me, and more importantly, time to warn her about my family. They're...a lot.

Case in point, by the fifth call, my papa had joined the conversation, already asking when we were getting married.

What? "It's been a month, Mama," I managed, though it had technically been less than a week. And even that was a stretch. A week, a month—still too damn soon. The real issue wasn't even the timeframe; it was the fact that we weren't really dating.

Right. The 'us' conversation. The one I should've had days ago.

The lines between what's real and what's for show are blurring fast, and I'm not sure which side of the line I want to be on anymore. Seven days in and I'm confused as hell.

If it were just the family drama, I could deal. But reporters? Associates suddenly scheduling double dates, all looking for a way into my inner circle via Violet? That's where things get messy. The weird part? The only thing I like about any of this is hearing her referred to as *my* woman. *My* girlfriend.

And then there's work. Or rather, the fact that I haven't been doing much of it. Normally, when I'm stressed, I bury myself in my work. Hit the office by six, and stay until eleven if I need to.

But this week? The workaholic in me seems to have disappeared. Instead of living in my office, I've spent more time with Violet than anywhere else. I didn't even go in on Sunday. *Sunday*. The sacred work day. Instead, I was shopping with her.

Shopping.

Worse, I've become the guy I used to make fun of—the one who checks his phone every five minutes, hoping for a ping from his girlfriend.

Yeah. That guy is me now.

Last night has me wound tighter than a bowstring. I'll admit, I set myself up for this mess. Between the suggestive texts we exchanged and the fact that I invited her over, I figured something would happen.

Spoiler: it didn't.

Instead, I cooked her dinner—my infamous chicken parmesan. She'd loved it and now I wanted to make it for her again. It felt intimate. And that's saying something because I've never cooked for anyone before. Carlo, my chef, was practically floored when I told him I wouldn't need him for the evening.

Cooking felt different with Violet. As I set the plate in front of her, I realized I'd never even thought of cooking for someone like Natalia. She knew I could cook, sure, but she thrived on the idea of being pampered, of having a private chef cater to her every whim. She was a diva. Violet, on the other hand—her eyes went wide, full of awe, as if I was serving her magic on a plate. That reaction alone was worth more than I cared to admit.

We drank wine, talked, laughed. For a moment, it felt like we'd been dating for more than just a week—as this easy, comfortable rhythm had always existed between us.

Before I knew it, it was past one in the morning. I turned to say something to Violet and found her curled up on my couch, fast asleep, mid-conversation.

Sighing, I internally scolded myself for not bringing up the "we should go to bed" conversation earlier. But, of course, Violet had fallen asleep on the couch, leaving me with one hell of an internal debate: do I take her to a guest room or...my bed? In our texts, she'd said she was staying the night. So, I went with mine.

Thankfully, she was wearing leggings and a sweatshirt, so I didn't have to undress her. It was awkward enough just tucking her in and crawling into bed beside her while she was completely out.

I got amazing sleep, eventually, but only after I wrestled with the painful, throbbing erection from being this close to a woman I wasn't just physically attracted to—but mentally too. I can't even remember the last time I sat and talked for hours with anyone, not even Dante or my brothers. But with her, time disappeared.

At some point during the night, she shifted, her perfectly rounded ass brushing up against me, and I nearly groaned out loud. I had to will myself to inch away, desperately trying not to wake her up with...well, you know. The friction alone was driving me insane.

This morning, my alarm went off, jerking us both awake. My arm, which had been comfortably wrapped around her waist, slipped and grazed over her breast when she shifted and moaned at the sound of the alarm. Is there a part of this woman that *isn't* carved by the gods?

She's a walking—well, in this case, *laying*—case of epic blue balls.

Her intoxicating jasmine scent was all over my sheets, and I found myself half-tempted to never wash the pillowcases again. At least that way, if I woke up and she wasn't there, I could still breathe her in.

Despite sharing the bed two nights in a row now, I'd kept my hands to myself (minus the accidental graze this morning). The self-restraint? Excruciating. Physically painful. And the relief I found in a cold shower every morning—Arctic levels of cold—was the only thing keeping me somewhat sane.

Frankly, it was a miracle I survived work today. I got through the day snapping at just about everyone I ran into. By the time Dom strolled into my office, looking smug as ever, I was at my breaking point. He didn't seem to care, of course. He just casually sauntered in and plopped down in the chair across from my desk.

"I know you're the office prick, Alex, and it's a badge you wear proudly," Dom said, cocking his head to the side. "But today? You're in fine form."

I didn't even look at him, my eyes glued to the financial reports on my screen. My jaw was clenched so tight, it felt like it might snap. "Don't you have people to manage?"

He ignored that. "I take it you haven't talked to Violet yet?"

That did it. I slammed the laptop shut and finally looked up at him, my aggravation teetering on the edge. "What the hell is there to talk about?"

Dom raised an eyebrow, clearly not buying into my act. "I don't know, maybe the fact that you two have been playing house without admitting it to each other? You know, normal couple stuff."

I leaned back in my chair, running a hand through my hair. "Why does everyone keep saying that? We don't need to talk. We're already doing all the damn things couples do. She stayed over the other night. Nothing happened, but still. If everyone—including you—says we're already dating, what's the point in talking it out?"

Dom chuckled, leaning back in his chair with his arms crossed. "You think you're fooling anyone with that bullshit? You're avoiding it, Alex. You don't want to put a label on it because then she could reject you."

I shot him a glare. "I'm not avoiding anything."

"Uh-huh," he said, deadpan. "So you're saying you just *prefer* being aggravated and sexually frustrated? Because that's definitely what's going on here. You're a ticking time bomb, man."

I grit my teeth. Dom wasn't wrong, but I wasn't about to admit that out loud. "We're seeing where it goes. What's the rush to slap some label on it?"

"That's code for *'I'm scared to admit what's actually happening,'* and you know it." Dom leaned forward, all serious now. "Look, you like her. Hell, you probably more than like her at this point. You can play the 'wait and see' game all you want, but what happens when she asks where this is going, huh? You're gonna say 'I don't know' and just hope that works out?"

"I'm not avoiding it," I repeated, quieter this time like I was trying to convince myself. "Everyone already assumes we're together. Why complicate it?"

Dom sighed, shaking his head. "Because you're afraid of being rejected. And the longer you avoid it, the worse it's gonna feel if she walks away. You can't avoid that conversation forever, Alex."

Internally, I agreed with him. The gnawing insecurity was something I hadn't wanted to face. But I was too aggravated—and yeah, frustrated in more ways than one—to admit it.

"Why do I even talk to you?" I muttered, rubbing the back of my neck.

"Because I'm your brother and the only one who'll call you out on your shit," he said, standing up. "And also because I'm right." He started toward the door but paused, glancing back at me. "By the way, good luck at that work party tonight. You're gonna need it."

I groaned as he walked out, my mind spinning. The party was tonight. And whether I liked it or not, Dom had a point.

Tonight, I came home early, showered, shaved, and pulled on my favorite black three-piece suit. I guess I had a theme—black suits were my go-to. At least tuxedos weren't required for tonight, because the idea of wearing a bowtie made me want to gag. There's something about those damn penguin suits that's never sat right with me. Custom-made, finely tailored suits? Absolutely. Bowties? Hard pass.

I hadn't seen Violet yet, though I heard her come in and head straight to the guest room to get ready. Conveniently, the dress for tonight had *accidentally* been delivered to my place, which meant she had no choice but to come here from work. Antonio had driven her straight over, and I'd like to think there's a chance she might need to come back later to change... or just stay the night.

I know, I'm pathetic. But why do we have to sit down and talk about "us"? Why can't we just keep doing what we're doing and see where it goes?

Glancing at my watch, I realized we had about ten minutes before we needed to leave. I knocked on the guest room door. "Violet? We've got to go soon, and you know how I am with time."

She had a knack for making us late, and I swear she did it just to get under my skin. The crazy part? I liked it. No one ever pushed my buttons, but she—this woman who'd casually discussed bad orgasms and vanilla dirty talk with a stranger in a bar a week ago—had already figured out how to. She's broken through more of my barriers than anyone ever has.

And if she kept at it, I'd be completely screwed.

The door swung open, and for the first time in a long time, my breath caught in my throat. Violet stood there, draped in a deep emerald green evening gown that was perfectly tailored to her figure. It hugged her curves in a way that was both elegant and undeniably sexy, a rare balance that only someone like her could pull off. The gown was classic, sophisticated, like something out of an old Hollywood film—timeless, chic, and completely her.

Her vibrant green eyes sparkled, turning into the kind of emeralds that could make a man stop dead in his tracks. And I did. Her hair was swept back in a loose, effortlessly messy bun, with tendrils of curls framing her face. She wore the necklace and earrings I had given her to go with the dress, though I hadn't bothered to tell her they were custom-made. Now, seeing her in them, I knew it was all worth it. She looked... perfect.

I was staring, no doubt about it. And for once, I didn't give a damn. There was this odd tug in my chest as I took her in. She wasn't just beautiful—she was fucking mesmerizing. For a second, I completely forgot about the event we were already running late for. It was just Violet, standing there, a woman who had managed to turn my world upside down in a single week.

Violet

I DIDN'T REALIZE THE party was going to be this elaborate. The entire fifth floor of the office had been transformed into a massive dance and dining space, accommodating at least 400 people. When we arrived, a red carpet—an actual red carpet—was set up to honor the author of the book we were celebrating, along with critics and other authors basking in their moment of fame.

Alex wrapped his arm around my waist, pulling me in close as we smiled for the cameras. He was completely at ease in this world of flashing lights and attention. Me? Not so much. "How are you going to handle being a famous author if you can't handle a little press?" he whispered into my ear, his lips brushing the lobe, sending shivers racing down my spine. The October chill suddenly vanished, replaced by the heat that bloomed under my skin, radiating from the inside out.

I cringed, knowing the truth. "I never really thought I'd be a famous author." There. I admitted it. The words tasted like doubt, but they were real. My novel felt more like a distant dream at this point.

We made our way to a group of reporters, where a balding man with an unfortunate comb-over leaned in, phone poised to record. "Mr. Bennetti, you've kept your relationship secret for a month. Are there any *big* plans you're keeping under wraps?"

Oh. My. God. Did he... insinuate what I think he did?

"You'll never know," Alex replied smoothly, flashing a grin as a few other reporters jumped in, peppering him with questions. His arm around my waist tightened like he was anchoring me to him.

Then, a woman with a short-cropped blonde haircut muscled her way to the front, her phone extended like a sword she was about to wield. "Mr. Bennetti, are you and Julian Stone in another bidding war?"

Who the hell is Julian Stone? I didn't have to ask aloud because the second the name left her lips, I felt Alex's body stiffen. His jaw clenched, a muscle twitching just beneath his sharp cheekbone. The man looked like a superhero in that perfectly tailored suit, and now all I could picture was him as a Manhattan vigilante with his arch-nemesis, Julian Stone, lurking in the shadows.

Okay, maybe I do read too much fiction...

The moment the doors opened, servers with trays of champagne flutes greeted us, and without hesitation, I grabbed one and downed it in record time before snatching another. Nerves were shot. It wasn't just about putting on a good show for work, especially for Mr. Hartley, but also the look Alex had given me before we left his penthouse.

A look that screamed he was ready to devour dessert—and spoiler alert, I was the dessert.

Alex glanced at me, the only moment of peace before we were swarmed. "Oh my gosh, that article of you two was so cute!" gushed someone from the printing department—Chloe? Charlie? Caroline? I couldn't remember. Whoever she was, she was more focused on Alex than me anyway. The second she touched his arm, I felt my blood boil. But before I could react, Alex flinched away from her, smoothly wrapping his arm around my waist and kissing my neck softly.

When we were out of earshot, he stopped and turned me to face him. Leaning in, his lips brushed against my ear, the feather-light touch sending a slow, simmering heat pooling in my center. It was impossible not to imagine what it would be like if those lips touched... other places. "Kiss me," he whispered.

"What?" I blinked, thrown off by the sudden request.

He cleared his throat, shifting slightly like he was uncomfortable. I glanced around—was Jake watching? Lisa? My boss? He leaned closer, his breath hot against my skin. "Make it obvious I'm all yours."

Our eyes locked for a second, and it felt like he was searching for something deeper. Then, without another word, he kissed me. Gentle at first, a slow brush of his lips against mine, and just as quickly as he kissed me, he moved back to my ear. His voice dropped lower, a growl that had my entire body buzzing. "I'm a pretty possessive man, Violet, and I don't share. Every guy in this room has been eyeing you because they can see what I've got. And I've got no problem fucking you on that conference table, making sure they all hear you scream my name if that's what it takes to get them to stop staring at you."

My eyes locked with Max's from across the room, but I couldn't breathe. My cheeks were a new shade of red. Did Alex really say that? He stood there, casually sipping champagne like he didn't just drop that little bomb into the conversation.

"Well, I see you made it," came a voice I'd recognize anywhere, and my body had the same retching reaction every time it heard it.

I turned to face her, and there she was, clinging to Jake's arm like a parasite, her engagement ring blinding in all its oversized, gaudy glory. Not literally, but the thing was huge. Too huge for her bony, overly manicured fingers. She looked like a wicked witch hiding behind layers of makeup and Botox. Without all that effort, I knew what she looked like — it wasn't pretty.

Of course, Lisa wore a dress that left little to the imagination. Bright red because she naturally needed to be as subtle as a stop sign. Her lips matched the dress, and Jack, her accessory for the night, was decked out in a black suit with a red tie. The level of color coordination made me want to gag. Never would I be that *in love*—nor would I ever want to be. That wasn't love; that was tacky on a whole new level.

Alex turned with me, but instead of standing at my side, he came behind me, wrapping an arm around my waist and nuzzling my neck. The way he inhaled the scent of my hair, his lips grazing the sensitive skin along my neck, made everything else in the room disappear. It was just us. His touch was light and gentle, yet possessive in a way that had my body heating from the inside out. For a moment, it felt like no one else existed.

"Alexander," Lisa started, but Alex's head shot up from my neck, resting against the top of mine.

"I prefer Mr. Bennetti. Only close friends and colleagues use my first name." His voice was cool, calm, and authoritative, but definitely not friendly. It was the voice of a man who knew exactly how much power he held, and damn if that didn't make the room feel even hotter. Was it me, or had they cranked the heat up in here?

"Oh, of course, *Mr. Bennetti*," Lisa stammered, clearly taken aback. "I was surprised to find you here."

Alex cocked his head, giving Jake and Lisa a once-over while they stood there, clearly skeptical of our "relationship." They still didn't buy it. "Why would it be a surprise that I came to my girlfriend's work party? Mr. Hartley personally requested I make time for it."

Lisa's smug smile faltered for a second as she'd momentarily forgotten Alex's ties to her fiancé's boss.

Alex glanced down at their joined hands, his eyes catching on the massive engagement ring wrapped around Lisa's bony finger. "Beautiful ring," he said, though the tone made it clear it was anything but a compliment.

"Oh, thank you," Lisa blushed, too oblivious to catch the shade. Of course, she did.

"Poor cut, though. For a stone that size, you'd want much higher quality. I can give you my jeweler's name if you ever need an upgrade." He shrugged, casual as ever, but the insult landed hard. He leaned down, brushing his lips against my ear. "He made these earrings for Violet," he murmured loud enough for them to hear before grazing his teeth over the emeralds dangling from my lobes. "Custom work. Top-notch."

Custom-made? Seriously? My mind raced, but there was no way Alex was joking. His jeweler probably made these for real.

Jake's smirk didn't quite reach his eyes. He was definitely not enjoying the ego bruising. "Well, I suppose when your relationship gets more serious, she'll have a ring to show off, too."

"Oh, she will." Alex's hand rested on my stomach, his thumb lightly brushing back and forth like it was second nature. To anyone watching, we were just a couple lost in each other, but I was stuck between being furious and wanting to drag him into a dark corner and...well, things I shouldn't be thinking about at a work event.

When they were out of earshot, I turned to Alex, tugging at his tie to pull his face down to mine. "These were custom-made for me?"

"Maybe," he said, taking another slow sip of champagne, completely unbothered.

"That can't be cheap."

"My girlfriend doesn't wear cheap, and she doesn't wear the same jewelry every other person owns. She wears what's made just for her."

I swear it was like a hummingbird's wings were rapidly fluttering in my chest any time this man spoke to me like this.

Stop it, Violet. Don't be that girl.

In a flash, Mr. Hartley appeared at our side, dressed in a sharp black suit that matched Alex's, his wife on his arm. She smiled at us warmly, gripping my arm in that affectionate way people do when they're overly invested in something. "I saw that article! You both look *adorable* together."

"Thank you," I managed, hoping the genuine smile on my face covered the mild panic in my chest. Everyone thought we were this picture-perfect couple, even though I knew better. And did Alex seriously mention engagement rings?

Suddenly, the room felt too warm. "Excuse me for a second."

I slipped through the crowd, leaving Alex to chat with Mr. Hartley and his wife. The company's terrace became my escape, the November chill hitting me hard—like always, I'd forgotten a jacket. I wrapped my arms around myself, focusing on the crisp night air.

A few moments later, warmth draped over my shoulders. Alex. Of course. His coat settled around me just as he leaned against the railing beside me, that same casual stance I recognized from the bar the night we met.

"Engagement rings?" I shot him a side glance before looking back at the skyline, trying to keep my cool.

He shrugged like it was no big deal. "We have to make it believable. Just threw it out there for emphasis."

I raised an eyebrow. "You don't say *anything* without a reason."

"And you don't leave the house with a jacket, even though it's freezing outside," he shot back, smirking.

I couldn't help but snort at that, and before I knew it, he pulled me closer, his arm wrapping around me, enveloping me in his warmth. Together, we looked out at the glittering skyline.

"You know," he started, his voice dropping into that dangerously smooth tone, "we could make this more fun. Pretend we're engaged. Might even get my mama and papa off my back."

I blinked and turned to him. "I agreed to *girlfriend*—not fiancée. I'm not messing with that. I want a man on his knees, begging me to marry him because he loves me so much, he can't imagine a day without me."

He paused, his gaze flicking to mine with an unreadable expression. "So what's your dream proposal?"

I bit my lip, not having thought about it in detail. "I'm not sure."

He tilted his head, clearly amused. "For a hopeless romantic, you don't have a grand, elaborate plan?"

"It depends on the relationship," I admitted. "I just know I want it to be special. Something meaningful, not some cookie-cutter proposal that everyone else has. I want a story that's just ours. Something that's *us*—no one else."

His grip tightened slightly, and the teasing edge disappeared from his eyes for a second. But then, with a wry smile, he turned back to the skyline. "Good to know, in case I ever need that info."

He stayed silent after that, the tension from our earlier conversation lingering between us. We stood there for a few more minutes before I pulled back from the railing. I handed him his jacket, instantly regretting it when the cold air sank its teeth into my skin like a vengeful winter breeze, but I knew I needed to get back inside and mingle.

Our fingers naturally found each other as we walked back into the party, the warmth from his hand soothing the chill that lingered. Most of the attention was on Alex, which wasn't surprising. He had that magnetic aura about him—people wanted to be near him, hear him, know him. Still, whenever the conversation veered toward his business or personal accomplishments, he'd subtly redirect it, effortlessly guiding the attention back to me or publishing. It was his way of reminding everyone, including me, that tonight was my night. And I appreciated it more than he knew. It made me feel seen, not just like the arm candy on his side.

After three hours of schmoozing, nibbling on canapés, and sipping champagne, Alex leaned down to whisper in my ear. "Let's get out of here," his deep voice rippled through me. Truthfully, I had been ready to leave an hour before he suggested it. So, with a quiet sigh of relief, I let him tug me toward the elevator.

As soon as the doors closed, I gave a smile. "Must be nice being rich enough to leave parties whenever you want."

He chuckled a low sound that vibrated in the small space. "It has its perks, yes. I make an appearance, flash a smile, and whether I stay five minutes or five hours, everyone's satisfied."

Violet

ALEX SHOT ME A sideways smile on the ride back up to the penthouse. I hadn't planned on coming back here, but when Antonio asked where to go, the penthouse slipped out. The night was still young, after all.

"You really do look beautiful tonight," he murmured, his eyes dropping to his shoes like he wasn't used to giving out compliments.

I rolled my eyes, but a grin tugged at my lips. "I would tell you that you look handsome, but something tells me you're more than aware of that already." I paused, shifting my weight. "Do you think people find our relationship awkward because you're so... out of my league?"

His movement halted. He turned to face me, brows furrowed. "Why would anyone think that?"

I shrugged, trying to play it off, but I couldn't help the insecurity that crept in. "Because... you are. Look at you. You're the hottest bachelor in New York, rich, successful. You've got it all. I'm not exactly the kind of woman people picture with someone like you. Would you have asked me out if we hadn't run into each other at the bar that night? Like, for real?"

His grip tightened on the elevator railing, his knuckles going white. The silence stretched between us, and that silence was enough of an answer. I remembered how I must've looked that night—out of place, a little tipsy, a whole mess. I had known the moment I saw him that I wasn't the kind of woman someone like Alex would go for.

I swallowed the lump in my throat and forced a laugh. "It's fine, don't answer that."

I turned to face the elevator doors, watching the numbers blink by as we climbed higher and higher, each floor closer to the penthouse, each one making my chest feel tighter.

Then, before I could fully process what was happening, Alex moved. He pressed me against the cool elevator wall, his body firm against mine. His mouth crashed into mine, the kiss fierce, almost desperate. His tongue swept inside, claiming me in a way that made my head spin. One of his hands tangled in my hair, tugging gently, just as I liked, while the other arm wrapped around my waist, pulling me so close I could hardly breathe.

When he finally pulled back, his forehead rested against mine, both of us breathless, my lips tingling from the intensity of it.

"The moment I saw you in that bar, I already knew you were the most gorgeous woman I'd ever laid eyes on," Alex said, his voice low and rough. "Why do you think I took that picture? I didn't go there looking for a date. I was just curious about you, trying to figure you out. But when everything with your ex happened, it gave me the chance I needed."

His hand slid to my neck, his fingers warm against my skin. "I'm not out of your league, Violet. I asked you out because you're funny, sexy, and nothing like any woman I've ever met. Sure, there's a physical attraction," his lips quirked, "but I wanted more the second you opened your mouth. That's why I came back to kiss you. I was desperate to do something that would get me more time with you."

His lips brushed my cheek, trailing kisses to my ear, his breath hot against my skin. He pressed me harder against the elevator wall, and I could feel his erection, hard and insistent. "Do you feel that?" His hips rolled against mine, the heat between us practically igniting as I felt him against me. His mouth found my shoulder, then my collarbone, and I was positive my body was melting. His hands gripped my ass, pulling me tighter against him, making sure I felt every inch of him.

"You drive me insane," he murmured, his lips tracing my neck. "I've been dying to kiss you, touch you, feel myself inside you while you come around my cock." He ground his hips into me again, and I could barely hold back a whimper. The air between us was thick with desire, each kiss weakening my knees. "It's not just about fucking you, even though, hell, I'd take you against this elevator wall right now." His voice was a growl, filled with barely contained hunger. "I want more than that with you, and you know it."

His mouth crushed mine in an all-consuming kiss, a wild clash of lips, teeth, and tongue. It was raw and needy, his hands gripping me like he couldn't get enough. When the elevator dinged, signaling our floor, he broke the kiss, and I realized I was pressed so tight against him that my feet barely touched the ground.

As the doors opened, he let me slide down his body, gripping my hand and pulling me out of the elevator.

We barely made it through the penthouse doors before Alex grabbed me, lifting me off my feet and pressing me against the door. My fingers immediately fumbled with his suit jacket, yanking it off as he let out a low growl. His hands were everywhere—strong, demanding—as he carried me to the dining table, sitting me on the edge. He stepped back long enough to shrug off his vest and unbutton his shirt, exposing that chiseled, sculpted body I'd been dreaming about. My mouth went dry at the sight of him.

He leaned in, hands bracing on either side of my hips, his lips against mine with an intensity that left me breathless. His hands slipped beneath my dress, slowly hiking it up as his thumbs brushed against my inner thighs, sending delicious zaps to my senses.

"Alex?" I whispered against his lips, barely able to think straight.

"Mmm, yes, baby," he murmured, nipping at my neck.

"Is now a good time to tell you... I'm not wearing any panties?"

He froze for a split second, "Fucking hell," was all he said before shoving my dress higher. His eyes darkened as he looked down, his fingers immediately sliding along my center, teasing through the wetness already building. His touch sent a shockwave through me, and I arched into him as his fingers found my clit, circling slowly, deliberately.

"God, you're so wet," he rasped, his voice thick with desire. His lips crashed into mine again, one hand fisting in my hair, keeping me close while his other hand slipped a finger inside me. I gasped into his mouth, the sensation overwhelming, my greedy body already aching for more.

"I want to taste every inch of you," he whispered that sinful promise against my lips. His finger trailed up, brushing against my sensitive folds. "I'm going to slide my tongue here," he murmured, tracing the same path, "then suck on this," his finger pressed against my clit, making me moan. "While I fuck you with my fingers... watch you come and then lick up every drop."

Holy hell. This man was far from vanilla. His dirty mouth should come with a warning label, but instead of running, I wanted more. So much more.

"Alex..." His name came out in a breathless whisper as he laid me back on the table, his hands firm but gentle as they trailed over my body, tugging my evening gown down and exposing my breasts to the cool air. I could barely prop myself up on my elbows, my body becoming jelly beneath his touch. His fingers slid between my legs, spreading me wide as he stood between them, a wicked gleam in his eyes.

Then he thrust a finger inside me just as his mouth closed over my nipple, sucking hard enough to make me gasp. The combination of his fingers pumping slowly and the pull of his lips on my breast had me teetering on the edge of control. A second finger joined the first, and I moaned, my body arching off the table. His hands moved with purpose, one teasing and kneading my breasts while the other worked me into a frenzy.

His thumb pressed down on my clit, and I whimpered, his lips trailing down my ribs, brushing kisses along my stomach, making me tremble with every inch he moved lower. When his tongue dipped into my navel, I squirmed, the anticipation nearly killing me as he inched closer to where I wanted him most.

"Baby?" His voice was low, sending shivers through me.

"Yes?" I barely managed to get the word out, feeling like I sprinted five miles.

"Do me a favor..." His lips grazed my skin, hot and tantalizing. "Grip the sides of the table."

Before I could ask why, his mouth was on me, the flat of his tongue pressing against my core, licking a slow, deliberate path from bottom to top. My eyes fluttered shut, rolling back in my head as I gripped the table for dear life. The heat of his mouth, the way he worked me with his tongue—it was pure, unadulterated torture. And I loved every second of it.

He murmured something in Italian before his lips wrapped around my clit, his tongue swirling over the sensitive bundle of nerves making my thighs quake in anticipation. Heat and pleasure built in my core, rolling through every muscle in my body while he sat there feasting on me like a skilled artist working on a canvas. No man should be this good with his tongue.

When he slipped his fingers inside me, moving them in and out while he continued to suck and lick, I was positive I was going to pass out. Alex wasn't a man who did this for a woman's pleasure; it was apparent in every stroke that it was just as much for him as it was for me.

My fingers clung to the table's edge like my lifeline, anchoring me to reality while the rest of my world spiraled into bliss. My other hand was buried in Alex's hair, tugging, twisting, desperate to ground myself as his sinful tongue and magical fingers worked me over. Every flick, every curl of his fingers made my hips instinctively buck, but he kept me pinned in place with that strong, possessive grip. His tongue continued to lap at me, sucking and teasing at all the right spots until the pressure inside me broke. I came hard, gasping his name like a prayer, my entire body trembling, muscles obliterating. And he didn't stop.

"Alex..." I whimpered, barely able to form coherent thoughts.

He pressed a kiss to the inside of my thigh, his breath hot against my sensitive skin. "Look at me," he commanded softly. My head lifted, and when our eyes met, those mischievous, sexy blue eyes locked onto mine. I swear I forgot how to breathe. It was the most erotic sight I'd ever seen.

"I want one more," he said, his voice dark with promise, before he dipped his head again, his mouth finding that sensitive nub already overstimulated. His tongue flicked and swirled, and the intensity skyrocketed. Every stroke sent shockwaves through me, my entire body trembling from the overload of pleasure.

I didn't know if it was the way his eyes never left mine or how he turned something so wicked into pure ecstasy, but when that second orgasm ripped through me, I shattered. My body quaked, his mouth continuing to pull every last spasm of pleasure from me. I was on the edge of heaven, teetering on blissful oblivion, and the devil himself was between my thighs, dragging me under.

When he pulled his fingers out, he yanked my body to the edge of the table, his lips crashing down on mine. The taste of him mixed with me on his tongue sent a feral hunger surging through me. I needed more. My hands flew to his suit pants, unzipping and unbuckling as his tongue teased and tangled with mine, every kiss more desperate, more consuming.

When his cock sprang free, the heat pooling in my core flared, my body primed just from the sight of him. Reaching out, I wrapped my hand around him, stroking, marveling at how hard and thick he was. His grip on my hips tightened, pulling me closer, his kisses turning from hot to downright filthy, his tongue mimicking the same sinful flicks he used to wring two orgasms out of me.

"What do you want, Violet?" he growled against my ear, nipping at the lobe. His fingers dug into my hips, the way his body responded to mine driving me wild. I could feel him throbbing in my hand, impossibly huge. For a brief second, I wondered if he would fit, but that thought made me want him more.

My brain and my body were at war. I knew what I should want, but my whore of a pussy had a different idea, one that was begging for him to take me right there on that table. I could barely form a coherent thought, much less a decision. "What do you want?" I asked breathlessly, stalling for time as my desire continued to cloud my mind.

He pulled back just enough for our eyes to lock, his blue gaze dark and hooded, filled with something primal. My breath caught in my throat, my toes curling at the sheer intensity of his stare. "I want to fuck you on this table, hard and feel you come around my cock," yup, definitely not vanilla. "Then I'm going to take you to my room and fuck you slow all night until you can't walk."

I used to beg to find a man who would speak to me that way, and while Alex ticked that box and more, his words didn't shock me like you'd think they would. They only ignited me.

God, I wanted it all: every heated kiss, every teasing flick of his tongue, every inch of him. But that nagging voice in the back of my mind whispered *no*. The second we crossed that line, everything would change. I'd fall right into another Jake situation where one night becomes into friends-with-benefits and poor relationship choices. Boundaries were already a blur—sharing a bed, kissing like we couldn't get enough, and now this.

He just gave me back-to-back, mind-melting orgasms that left me wrecked in the best possible way. But diving into bed with him might wreck *us*.

He said all the right things in the elevator. But words in the heat of the moment don't always translate into reality, and I couldn't risk assuming that meant he wanted a real connection. And I needed that. Not just the passion or the mind-blowing chemistry but the foundation that came with trust and commitment.

I was trying to shut down the lust-fueled haze clouding my brain while the rational part of me scrambled to keep control. I didn't want to do something we'd both regret. Something that might ruin everything.

Alex

"Alex, I can't. I want to... God, do I want you," Violet whispered, her eyes flicking to the dining chair I'd kicked out of the way before making her my dessert on the table. Her taste still lingered on my lips, a perfect indulgence I wasn't ready to release anytime soon.

Her lips curved into a smile, but not the usual bright, sweet one I was used to. No, this was different. Bold. Confident. The same smirk she'd flashed me in the bar last week, three cocktails deep, when she rattled off her ideal type of dirty talk — if she thought tonight was my limit, I was barely scratching the surface.

"Sit." The command rolled off her tongue, and hell, I wasn't going to argue.

I dropped into the chair without protest, my gaze locked on her. She moved slowly, teasingly, sliding off the table. Her dress was a mess of silk and chiffon bunched around her waist, and she didn't seem to care. She owned it, letting the fabric cascade as she knelt before me.

Her green eyes gleamed with mischief as she settled between my legs, her hands resting on my thighs. That fire, that same fire I'd seen when we first met, was burning in her gaze again, and it ignited something primal inside me.

"What are you..." I didn't get the chance to think much as her hands ran up my thighs, gripping my cock as she licked the precum from the tip and made the sexiest fucking moan while doing it. I almost burst right there. Her hand took the base while she licked again, her tongue stroking the underside, going root to tip before swirling around the tip and sending heat straight to my balls.

When she took me in her mouth deep and without hesitation, I couldn't help but grip her hair, jerking and barking "shit!" at the contact. My balls are already drawing into my stomach, and my breathing makes me feel like I just ran a marathon.

Tears prick at the corner of her eyes as I gently rock my hips, sliding my length deeper down her throat. She doesn't resist it at all or even gag. Fuck me.

"Baby, I can't hold out much longer," I yank at her hair, but she grips me tighter, sucking harder as she looks up at me. Those green eyes were nearly molten, and her long lashes fluttered as her cheeks hollowed out. "Jesus Christ," was all I could say before I felt my cock swell and my release hit, but she only swallows and licks until I'm done. When she lifts her head, she licks her fucking lips, and I'm positive I'm hallucinating at this point.

My chest is heaving, and I grip her hands, yanking her onto my lap, a satisfied smirk across her face that is wicked and yet perfect on that sinful little mouth. "Tell me why I can't fuck you?"

"It complicates things," she says as her lips trail along my neck and suck, her body rubbing against mine. I'm still hard, and I know she feels every inch as she moves back and forth on me. If she doesn't want to have sex, she's going to have to stop what she's doing before I lose all control of myself.

"And this doesn't?" My hands grip her hips, not stopping her moving but almost helping her continue as she grinds on top of me. Jesus, what would this woman look like riding me? The way her hips swivel makes my head spin.

She shakes her head. "What you said in the elevator was sweet, and I'm not trying to downplay it at all, but I don't want to mess up what we have. We have needs, and we are physically attracted to one another."

"Clearly," I bit out, but before I could say anything else, she stopped rocking her hips and gripped my chin, forcing me to look at her.

"Maybe we just add this to our arrangement?" Her smile is coy as shit, and we both know there is no fucking arrangement right now.

"Add what exactly?" I lift a brow, looking down at her straddling my lap.

She shrugs, her hands gripping my shoulders, and then slowly, her fingers trace along until they're wrapping around the back of my neck, toying with my hair. "Maybe we can do this. Help each other out while we pretend...since we can't date anyone else." She sucks in her bottom lip, and I groan. "But no sex...not right now, at least."

My arms wrap around her waist when I dip my head to kiss her, but she pulls back. "I don't want it messy. I'm one of those girls that gets attached with sex. I know my limits. I can't get hurt."

"Why would I hurt you?"

"I'm not saying you would, but..." she doesn't finish.

Not going to lie, there's frustration building, but she did say not right now, as opposed to not ever. A fucking tease for sure, but I will take what I can get, especially if that means she's going to give me a repeat of what she just did.

"No sex," I nip at the soft flesh of her neck. "But I'm going to kiss you, and I'm going to taste that sweet pussy of yours—"

"Alex…" she whispers, but I can't tell if she's pleading for me to stop or keep going. When I kiss her, her fingers dig into the back of my neck, and she moans, her body flush against mine and every inch of my body tingling with need.

"No sex, but I have a condition," I say, and she leans back, eyes narrowing.

"Okay…" I can't help but allow my fingers to grip her ass, kneading it as I hold her against me.

"You're going to finish what you started and rub that wet little kitten of yours against my cock until you come," I kiss her, and it quickly goes from gentle to filthy and delicious. Practically fucking her mouth with my tongue to give myself an inkling of what I need right now.

Her hips roll against me, the wetness between her thighs creating the perfect friction against my throbbing shaft. As her grip tightens on my shoulders, fingernails biting into my flesh, I kiss her harder, not missing the tiny moans and mewls escaping her mouth as we both rock against one another.

"I don't think I have dry humped since I was a teenager," she says out of breath.

Biting the sensitive bit of her creamy, perfect skin where her neck meets her shoulder, I look at her. "Baby, nothing about this is dry. You're too wet for that…" she gasps, and I nip at her, waiting to do so much more but hold back. "We might not have sex right now, but trust me, I'm going to be deep inside of you soon."

"Shit…Alex…" her grip tightens as her pleasure builds, and I reach between us, massaging her clit until she comes apart, her nails digging into my shoulders and likely leaving a mark.

"Fuck…" I curse before kissing her slowly, my hand in her silky hair that I can't get enough of, worshiping her mouth for everything it's capable of and everything I want to explore. "You sure…no sex?" Can't blame a guy for double-checking.

"No…sex…" Though she can barely say it like she believes it and thank fuck for small miracles.

Violet

"So, LET ME GET this straight. The ridiculously hot guy you're fake dating—but not really—wants you and gave you what you think might be your first real orgasm? Woman, you're 29. Should I be concerned?" Max's voice drips with sarcasm, but I know he's only half-kidding.

Honestly, I've been worried about me much longer than Max has. Lost cause and all that.

I roll my eyes, holding my phone up while struggling to pick an outfit for dinner at Alex's parents' house. No pressure. I shouldn't be this nervous. I'm spiraling because I'm supposed to play the role of his doting girlfriend, but I can't even pick out a dress without second-guessing everything.

Alex's family is *close*. It's not the "how's it going? See you at Christmas" kind of close. No. They genuinely like each other, which is a foreign concept to me. My family is more the "good luck, you're on your own" type. And now I'm supposed to waltz into this dinner like I belong? What if they ask questions? What if they don't like me?

"I *may* have told him we could get each other off as part of our arrangement." I groan, still kicking myself for saying that out loud. Who even says that?

Max's deadpan face on FaceTime doesn't help. "Orally, too. Bravo. You're a real trail-blazer."

"Not helping," I huff, flipping through another clothes rack.

"Look, babe, you can call it an arrangement all you want, but you, me, and every breathing human knows it's not *just* an arrangement." He raises an eyebrow. "I mean, I'm also supposed to believe you two aren't having sex?"

"I *did* say no sex," I remind him, feeling less confident the more I think about it.

Max lets out a loud, dramatic sigh. "Yeah, I believe that as much as I believe Area 51's got all the aliens."

Ugh, last night. Three orgasms. One night. *Zero* sex. How is that even possible? I've officially been robbed for the last decade of my life.

"Please remind me why you didn't just jump him? If he can do *that* with his tongue, imagine what—"

"Max! Not helping!" I cut him off, my voice reaching a new pitch of desperation. I've been in a sexual tension rage since Friday night. To avoid Alex today, I even went to the gym with Max, which I *never* do.

"We were fake dating," I say, pacing in front of the massive mirror in Alex's penthouse. "Now... not? I don't know! It's complicated, and now I'm meeting his *family*!"

Max snickers. "Complicated doesn't even begin to cover this circus."

I narrow my eyes at him as much as I can through FaceTime. If we were in person right now, we'd be curled up with donuts and nearing a sugar coma while I panicked, but nope. I'm standing in a penthouse, surrounded by *my* clothes that are here, trying to figure out what to wear to meet Alex's family.

"Okay, what about this one?" I hold up a gray sweater dress paired with black leggings. "Perfect for fall. Not too slutty, but not boring either, right?"

Max raises an eyebrow, scrutinizing it like he's judging a runway show. "What shoes?"

Shoot. I hadn't thought that far ahead. "Uh, heels?"

He sighs dramatically, throwing his hands in the air. "Violet, I hate how terrible you are at fashion sometimes. Do you have boots that *don't* make you look like you're moon-lighting as a dominatrix?"

"Hey," I protest, half-defensive. I like my boots with a heel. They make me feel fierce. But, okay, maybe leather boots with stiletto heels might not scream 'meet the parents' vibes. Fine, I get it. They'd probably think Alex picked me up off the street for this occasion.

The irony isn't lost on me, though. Sure, I'm not a hooker, but let's be honest—I did meet a rich guy in a bar, he bought me a wardrobe, we're dating... sort of. If Julia Roberts can pull off her *Pretty Woman* fairytale with Richard Gere, maybe this isn't *that* different. However, Julia got laid on day one. My situation? It's a little more complicated.

But still, the vibe was there.

"I can see those gears turning, Violet. Spill it."

I toss the clothes onto the bed and collapse onto them, phone held high above my head. A dramatic sigh escapes me. "I don't know."

Lie. I know, but I'm not ready to dive into the emotional spiral yet. Still, I will combust if I don't get it off my chest.

"Meeting the family is way too much pressure. I don't even know how *normal* families act. You've met mine, Max. It's a dumpster fire. First impressions matter, and now I'm about to make one on my *fake* boyfriend's family, who isn't even fake anymore. I think."

"And let's not forget the 'make you disappear with the fishes' vibe his family gives off." Max's deadpan delivery does nothing to help my nerves.

I glare at the phone. "You're not helping."

Why was I so nervous? It wasn't like I'd never met a boyfriend's family before, but this? This felt different. Alex had only ever brought one other woman around, Natalia—and honestly, she should hook up with Jake and create a power couple of terrible people. And now, it's me. Except we've only been *real* for what? Less than 24 hours? Maybe?

And let's not forget the whole "this was supposed to be fake dating" part. Except the second his mouth was between my thighs, there was absolutely nothing fake about it. Otherwise, I'd really be leaning into full-blown hooker territory.

I've been at this for two hours, staring at outfits. Meanwhile, Alex is out in the living room, reading—an actual book. And I can tell he's suffering, but the man is making an effort. It's probably because of me... or because he's hoping for a repeat of what happened the other night. Either way, it's a win-win situation.

Sunday dinners are a sacred tradition in the Bennetti household, and while Alex managed to dodge it last week, there was no getting out of it this time, especially after *that* article. Yeah, I'm not exactly thrilled about meeting the family who's been linked to organized crime. But Alex swears the only ones still involved are his uncle and cousins. The rest? "Reformed," he says. Sure, let's hope the emphasis is on *reformed* sticks because I'm not trying to find myself in the middle of a mob family reunion.

Yesterday, I gave myself a gold star for avoiding Alex all day. It's impressive, really, considering we have this uncanny ability to be together all the time.

But when it came to bedtime, there he was, sliding under my covers like his own bed. And let's say things got *steamy*. We made out like teenagers, all hands and heat, and it was... well, *wow*. What that man can do with his tongue should be illegal in at least forty-nine states.

A knock on my door interrupted my thoughts, and Alex poked his head in just as I tried to figure out what to wear. I"One second, Max." Turning back to Alex, I sighed. "Sorry, I'm still deciding on an outfit. I'll be ready soon."

Alex gave me a once-over, his gaze flicking between the clothes scattered on the bed and the messy bun that screamed, "I'm totally not ready for dinner with your mob-adjacent family." He smirked. "You sure about that?"

I forced a nod, sitting up with what little dignity I had left. He lingered a second longer, clearly enjoying my frazzled state, before slipping out of the room.

Unmuting my phone, I sighed. "Alright, Max. Time to get serious."

Max's laugh echoed through the phone. "I'm living for this disaster. Can't wait to hear all the juicy details."

Rolling my eyes, I ended the call and set about getting ready. After some internal debate, I decided to leave my hair down. A few extra curls with the iron gave my natural waves a bit more bounce. I kept my makeup light enough to look polished but not like I was trying too hard. Alex might be a billionaire CEO, and we were headed to meet his family, but I wasn't about to cake my face with makeup for anyone. They were going to have to take me as I am.

Stepping out of the guest room, I stopped short. Alex was casually dressed in jeans—actual jeans. I never imagined him even owning a pair. He paired them with a button-up blue shirt under a cream sweater and loafers that screamed a preppy Hamptons vibe. He looked like he was headed to the country club, not a family dinner.

"Here goes nothing," I whispered to myself.

Violet

His parents owned a house in Greenwich because, of course, they lived there—only the super-duper rich owned property in that area.

The long winding driveway was lined with perfectly manicured hedges, the kind you see in architectural magazines—straight out of the "I-pay-someone-to-trim-these-daily" playbook. Stately trees flanked the drive until it opened into a grand circular courtyard with a fountain in the center. Oh, and cars. So many cars.

Panic settled over me like a heavy blanket. Then nausea. Lots of it.

"I thought this was Sunday dinner with your immediate family?" I glanced over at Alex, who was casually typing on his phone, completely oblivious to the fact I might vomit at any moment. He gave me a smile that only added to my rising anxiety.

"Well, if I told you what family dinner *really* was, you'd probably run for the hills," he replied far too calmly. "We're Sicilian, babe. Family is *big*. So... maybe two or three dozen people. Not counting the kids."

My mouth hung open, processing his words as Antonio got out to open my door. Two or three dozen? I thought "family dinner" meant a handful of people, not a tiny village.

And not counting the kids?!

"I can't go in there. Are you insane? Meeting that many family members? I don't know you well enough for that. What if they ask super personal questions about you?"

Alex nudged me gently, trying to coax me out of the car, but I pressed myself firmly against the leather seat. There was no way I was getting out.

"They won't," he said.

"They could ask about our sex life or something!" My voice rose, panic creeping in.

His eyebrow quirked, and he barely suppressed a smirk.

"Oh my God, they *would* ask about that, wouldn't they?"

I'm going to die. There's no way I'm surviving this. Not only do we not have a sex life, but who asks about that at family dinner?

Alex shrugged casually, like we weren't discussing the most mortifying thing possible. "They want grandkids. If anyone's going to press you about my sex life, it'll be Mama or Nonna."

"*Nonna*? As in, your grandmother?!"

He grinned that smug, sexy grin that always drove me insane.

I stared at him in disbelief. "Your grandmother would ask about our sex life?"

"Oh, definitely. She has no filter. My cousins are bad, but they learned from the best—Nonna. So, if you don't want to get grilled about our nonexistent sex life," he paused, letting those words hang in the air like a challenge. "Anyway..." he continued, dragging out the word, "I'd suggest not letting her corner you. And don't be fooled by her size—she's stealthy as fuck. If you get trapped, it's over. She'll also ask if you're on the pill."

I blinked at him, sure I hadn't heard that right. "Are you serious right now?"

"Dead serious. Nonna doesn't mess around. She once asked my cousin's girlfriend if she was still on the pill and then turned to Dante to ask if they were using condoms—*while* talking about a new Italian ice shop opening down the street."

Now I *know* I'm going to be sick.

He gestured for me to get out, and I groaned, sliding out of the car, my eyes glued to the massive mansion towering in front of me.

Holy crap, how big is this place?

In front of me was a sprawling sea of white, accented with a brick façade. The house had that grand Georgian-style architecture, all perfectly symmetrical, with columns framing the entrance like it was plucked straight out of a historical estate magazine. A few steps led up to a set of massive double mahogany doors, each intricately carved and flanked by shuttered windows. Above the door was a stunning pediment.

Yeah, I don't belong here.

This house was giving serious Stepford Wife vibes... with an Italian twist.

As I stood there, staring at the carvings on the door, Alex came up beside me, grabbing my hand. I latched onto it like it was a lifeline, which, honestly, it was.

"Don't you think it's weird that we've supposedly been dating for a month, and I haven't met your family yet?" I asked, glancing at him.

"Not at all. They know I'm private and don't bring women home unless it's serious."

Serious... but are we serious? I mean, what are we?

Before I could spiral into that thought, the doors revealed an actual butler, like a real-life penguin-suited butler.

Do people have butlers? These people do.

As much as I wanted to revel in the fact that butlers exist outside of TV shows, I was stopped dead in my tracks the moment I stepped into the foyer. A grand, sweeping staircase dominated the center of the space, with ornate wrought-iron railings that spiraled upward like something out of a fairy tale. A crystal chandelier the size of a small car hung high above, sparkling like it knew it was the room's crown jewel. The polished marble floors reflected everything—the light, the grandeur, and my wide-eyed expression.

And then there was the noise. Lots of noise.

Lots of people.

Alex tugged me to the right, pulling me through a hallway that opened into a living area. More marble floors and columns framed the entrance, and the room was filled with antique furnishings, velvet drapes, and elegant artwork. The ceilings stretched up impossibly high. Seriously, who cleaned those? Someone had to get up there and dust the cobwebs.

Before me was a sea of people, at least a dozen deep in conversation. Some lounged on the couches facing each other, others stood with drinks in hand, while kids zoomed around like they'd hit their daily sugar limit. But as Alex and I reached the entrance to the living room, all movement seemed to slow. I started counting heads but stopped when I hit twenty and realized there were still more.

An older woman with beautiful olive skin and sleek black hair pulled into a bun stood up from one of the sofas with a glass of wine. Her blue eyes—the same piercing ones Alex had—lit up as soon as she saw him.

Oh crap. This is *the* mother. The one I've been dreading meeting. My only reference for mothers is my own, and let's say she doesn't exactly scream "warm and fuzzy."

Panic bubbles up in my chest. I'm not ready. Nope, not at all.

But it's too late now. No backing out. We're in the lion's den.

She moves gracefully, crossing the room over plush rugs and expensive flooring. Her smile is wide and welcoming as she reaches out her hands.

"Ah, mio bambino, sono così felice che sei riuscito a venire," she says, pulling Alex into a hug so tight I think she might never let go. She holds him like he hasn't been home in years, which is both sweet and a little terrifying.

Don't get me wrong—men who love their mothers are great. But please tell me this strong, rich, alpha male doesn't turn into a full-blown mama's boy the second he's home.

Also, I thought his mother wasn't Italian. Yet here she is, speaking it so effortlessly, like the words were born on her tongue, and I have *no* clue what she just said.

She pulls back slightly, still holding Alex's arm, and her blue eyes flick to me. "E chi abbiamo qui, Alex?"

I catch the part where she says his name—everything else? Nada.

"Mama, English, please. Violet doesn't speak Italian." Alex's voice has that amused but firm tone..

His mother gives him a look, one of those clipped "I'm not mad, but I'm disappointed" looks, and I suddenly wonder if she's silently judging me for not speaking Italian. But she's not even Italian! Why do I care if it's a problem that I'm not?

"I'm sorry, Violet. It's wonderful to meet you. I've heard so much about you." Her voice is warm and genuine, and I can finally unclench, releasing the breath I didn't even know I was holding.

Have you heard so much about me? Before I can even process that, she pulls me into a tight hug—*tight*—like she's ensuring I'm not going anywhere. Her free arm wraps around me with the force that says, "Welcome to the family." I inhale her sweet, surprisingly pleasant perfume. Over her shoulder, I give Alex a wide-eyed look and mouth, *"Heard so much?"*

He shrugs like this is no big deal.

When she releases me, her eyes sweep over me appraisingly, and then she turns to Alex. "È davvero una bella ragazza, Alex," she says, motioning us further into the room.

Alex squeezes my hand, pulling me along, and I lean in, whispering, "What did she say?"

"You're beautiful."

I look at him, trying to gauge if he's teasing me, but no—he's smiling. Well, that's... nice.

"Come, come!" His mom waves us toward the living area, where all eyes are now firmly locked on me. "Everyone, this is Violet, Alex's girlfriend. Alex, don't be rude. Make the introductions."

Still gripping my hand like a lifeline, Alex smiles and starts rattling off names faster than my brain can process. His mom settles back into her seat next to his Nonna, who looks too young to be a grandmother. It must be those Italian genes because none of these women have aged past their late thirties.

As Alex recites a never-ending string of names, I smile, nod, and offer the obligatory "Nice to meet you" repeatedly. Some shake my hand, but most? Nope. They go straight in for the hug. Is this an Italian thing, or just his family's thing? Because I'm pretty sure I've just met my annual hug quota. Scratch that—*lifetime* hug quota.

And to my absolute horror, I catch sight of even more people out on the grand patio beyond the double glass doors.

Holy hell. There are so many people here.

"Oh, Alex, before you head outside," his mother grabs him, flashing an apologetic smile as she gently tugs him away from me. I watch, curiosity piqued, but before I can try to decode their expressions, Nonna—introduced as nothing else but that—hooks her arm around mine and insists I sit beside her.

I shot Alex a desperate *"Don't you dare leave me to* look," but the jerk just smiled. Bastard.

Nonna's accent is as thick and rich as freshly made pasta, and her voice makes me think of warm bread and cannolis. She brushes my hair gently with her fingers. "Your hair is gorgeous," she says, her eyes twinkling. "And those eyes. Beautiful." She plucks a wine glass from a passing tray and hands it to me. It's red. Not my favorite, but I smile and take a sip because, well, I can't be rude to Alex's Nonna.

"So, what do you do, Violet? By the way, I love your name." Her words are smooth, like honey, wrapping me in warmth. I could listen to her talk all day.

"I'm an editor at a publishing company," I say, glancing over at Alex. Whatever his mother is saying is not putting him in a good mood. His tanned skin is flushing a bit red, and his lips are pressed into a tight line.

"Publishing? Oh, books! How lovely," Nonna says, drawing my attention back to her.

"Yes," I reply. "Do you read much?"

"All the time! I wonder if I've read anything your company has published."

I rattle off a few titles, but she shakes her head, smiling politely. It was worth a try. I briefly considered telling her about the *Courtship Rituals of the Peacock* just for a laugh but decided against it. Although, with the way Alex hinted she loves talking about sex, maybe that wouldn't be the worst idea if there's an awkward pause.

Alex is back at my side, his mother trailing behind him. "Come on, we must introduce you to Papa before he throws a fit for not meeting you in the first five minutes."

His mother gave me a strange good-luck smile and waved us off.

We step out onto the patio, and I'm blown away. If I thought the front of the house was impressive, the back is on a whole other level.

There are immaculate gardens, a massive seating area with a table that could easily seat thirty, outdoor sofas and loungers, and, of course, a pool so clear it looks like it's made of glass.

We go to the seating area where a few men are lounging, holding tumblers filled with amber liquid and puffing on cigars. It's like a scene from a very manly, old-school movie, and I feel even more out of place. As they all stand to greet us, the awkwardness skyrockets. One man, with black hair streaked with gray—basically Alex's future twin in twenty or thirty years—steps forward.

"Alex, who do we have here?" He smiles warmly at me. "Is this the Violet we've been hearing so much about?"

Hearing *so much* about? We've been fake-dating, semi-dating, for barely over a week. What exactly have they heard?

"Yes, Papa. Meet Violet. Violet, this is my father, Ricardo," Alex says, introducing us.

I instinctively reach out to shake Ricardo's hand, but he leans in, giving me a hug and a kiss on the cheek. Well, okay then.

Ricardo then introduced me to the other men seated with him, though I barely caught any of their names. Half of them seem to be named Vincent or something close.

Then, one man stands, but he doesn't quite look like he belongs to the immediate family. But the woman beside him—tall, elegant, and related to the family with her dark features—catches my attention.

"So, this is Violet," the man says—no thick Italian accent like the others.

But again, he knows me. How many people here have heard of me?

He's dressed in slacks and a button-down shirt, a little more casual than I expected, but the woman with him? She's in a slinky black gown and sky-high heels that scream *high fashion*. Am I underdressed? Everyone inside seemed casual, but she looked ready for a night at the club.

"Violet, this is my cousin Alena, and this is Dante, my best friend. Though, honestly, he's more like a brother." Alex introduces them, and I give a small wave, trying not to feel completely overwhelmed by all the names.

Just then, another man strolls over, wrapping an arm around Alex's shoulders. "Don't forget to introduce your *real* brothers—no offense," he adds, glancing at Dante, who shrugs with a small smile. Then the new guy turns his attention to me, and wow—another Italian god. He has the same features as Alex, but his eyes are amber, not blue, and they practically sparkle in the evening light.

"I'm Rico, the youngest brother," he says.

Right, Alex has brothers. I remember meeting one last week. But I'm confused. "Youngest brother?" I cock my head and look at Alex. "I thought you said your brothers were twins?"

We are. Dominic was born a few minutes before me." He says it nicely but so matter-of-fact-like at the same time.

"Ah, got it," I say.

I glance around, expecting to see Dom, but Alex says, "Dominic's out of town this weekend. You'll see him next Sunday. His son, Luca, is somewhere around here, though. He's staying with my parents while Dom's away for work."

Wait... Dom's a single dad? And did Alex say *next* Sunday?

So, I'm officially part of this weekly family adventure now?

Luckily, my head nods as I sip my wine, trying not to choke under the weight of Dante and Rico's curious gazes. Do they know something? Everyone seems to have heard about me, but how much has Alex told these two?

"Did your Mama tell you?" Dante asks, side-eyeing Alex before offering me a small, almost apologetic smile.

"Tell me what?" I ask, hoping this isn't some mafia secret.

Alex rubs his temples, which screams *I'm already over this.* "Natalia is coming for dinner."

My heart drops. "As in...?"

"Yup." His tone is flat.

Dante grins like this is the best news he's heard all day. "This is going to be glorious," he teases, relishing the drama.

"Fuck off," Alex mutters, not even trying to hide his irritation.

Wait—why the hell is *she* here? Alex's ex showing up at a family dinner? I remember him telling me that she had some connection to his family, but she comes to Sunday dinners? These are supposed to be family events, right?

"She's dating my cousin, Eddie," Alex explains, his voice tight. "He's bringing her."

Dante, still rubbing his jaw and barely containing his amusement, looks like he's enjoying this way too much. Even Alex's cousin Alena smirks. Are they entertained for my sake, Alex's, or both?

And just like that, as if someone flipped a switch, a voice that's too sweet and smooth for comfort chirps behind us. "Oh my gosh, Alex! So wonderful to see you."

I can almost feel Alex tense beside me, and before he even turns around, a "Fuck," slips out under his breath. He pulls me closer, practically fusing me to his side as if to shield me—or himself. "Natalia..." he says flatly. No smile. Just... *Natalia.*

And wow. That's *Natalia?*

She looks like she just walked off a runway—tall, legs for days, with perky breasts, and a designer dress that probably costs more than my rent. And the heels. *Who even wears those to a family dinner?* I recognize the man she's with—Eddie, I now assume—from the bar. Is Alex upset because she's dating his cousin or because she's here at all? Either way, this is awkward with a capital *A.*

Natalia glides over like she owns the place, breaking away from Eddie, who heads to the bar. She's flawless. I mean *flawless.* Perfect skin, makeup that looks airbrushed, and a smile that sparkles even in the dim lighting of the patio. She barely glances at me, zero acknowledgment of the fact that I'm glued to Alex's side, and instead places her manicured hand on his bicep. "It's been too long," she purrs, lips slightly pouted.

Does she not notice me? I'm practically a human accessory pinned to Alex's sweater. And I'm pretty sure I'm glaring daggers at her.

Alex immediately pulls his arm away and tightens his grip on me and says, "And thank fuck for that."

Oh, okay, so no *"I miss you"* vibes there. Got it.

Eddie saunters over, and Natalia links her arm with his, ignoring Alex's frosty demeanor. Then she turns her attention to me, her eyes raking over me in a way that screams *judgment.* It's giving Lisa energy, and now I hate her. Like, she's already on my permanent blacklist for what she did to Alex, but now, with that whole *I'm-too-good-for-you* vibe, she's skyrocketed to *punchable* status.

And believe me, I would—if I weren't so short. I'd have to aim up, but her tits would be an easy target. She's practically flaunting them in that sequined dress, glistening like a disco ball with every move.

"Oh, how rude of me. Who's this?" Her voice is sweet—too sweet. It's giving fake sugar and arsenic vibes.

Yup. Definitely Lisa's long-lost twin.

Before I can even open my mouth, Alex steps in, pulling me tighter against him like he's afraid I might evaporate. "This is Violet. My girlfriend."

Girlfriend. That word rings in the air like a challenge. Natalia's amber eyes narrow slightly, but she keeps that picture-perfect smile. "I see..."

God, she even talks like Lisa. It's unnerving. Her eyes, while admittedly gorgeous, have the same cold, calculating look. If she were a snake, she'd have struck by now, fangs bared. I half expect her to hiss.

"Pleasure," I say through gritted teeth because I'm a grown woman and will *not* stoop to her level, no matter how much she makes me want to channel my inner bitch.

"Well, I need to introduce Violet to the rest of the family," Alex cuts in.

Natalia purrs, "I didn't know you brought women you dated home." She's practically baiting him, her tone dripping with faux innocence.

Alex doesn't flinch. Instead, he stops, looks down at me, and cups my cheek, his thumb brushing gently over my skin in a way that feels too intimate. "Only the important ones," he says, his voice soft, but I can tell it's a dig aimed at her.

My heart does a little somersault at that, while my logical part reminds me this is all probably for show. But still, *important*?

Before Natalia can fire back with those perfectly painted lips, Alex turns us away, effectively ending the conversation. Out of the corner of my eye, I catch Dante grinning like he's watching his favorite drama unfold.

As we head back inside, Alex introduces me to the rest of the family, but all I can think is: *Was that for real? Or was I just his pawn in this weird ex-girlfriend' family chess match?*

Finally, we have a moment alone, nestled together on a lounger by the pool while plates of food are set out on the table nearby. Some are left inside, for those who prefer the dining room over the cool evening air. Alex's face is completely unreadable, and I wish I knew him well enough to figure out what's running through his mind right now. Is he brooding? Pissed? Preparing to snap back into his icy businessman mode like he did at dinner the other night?

Reckless as always, I go for it.

"So, I assume you didn't know she'd be here?"

"Nope."

"And... do you want to talk about how that makes you feel?" *Oh great,* I'm officially channeling my inner therapist.

"Nope."

Okay, then. It's going to be *one of those nights.* Awesome. I came here to charm his family, and now I'm probably going to be left alone, awkwardly introducing myself, making small talk like a moron. If he pulls a disappearing act for a 40-minute business call? I'm done.

While my brain is busy cranking out worst-case scenarios, Alex moves fast—so fast, I barely register it before his hand is on the back of my neck, pulling me toward him. For a split second, I think this is just for show. Maybe Natalia is watching, and he's putting on the act. But then his lips meet mine, and this is no chaste, *let's impress the family* kiss. This is a full-on, deep, all-consuming kiss.

His fingers thread through my hair, his other hand resting firmly on my lower back, anchoring me to him. My hands grip his sweater as his tongue explores my mouth like he's starved and I'm the only thing that can satisfy his hunger. And, holy hell, I am not stopping this.

When the kiss slows, I think he will pull away, but instead, he hovers just a breath away, his blue eyes locking with mine, filled with something I haven't seen before. A raw, intense longing. Then he crashes his mouth into mine again, this time with even more heat, more need. It's the hottest kiss we've ever shared, and we're at his *parents' house.*

I have no idea what his family thinks of this public display of affection, but Alex clearly doesn't care.

Someone yells out that dinner's ready, and Alex finally pulls away. I blink, trying to clear the fog of lust from my brain, my heart galloping.

"And that kiss was for...?" I ask, still dazed, trying to regain my composure.

He shrugs like it was nothing. "I'm happy you're here tonight. If you weren't, I would've left. Being around her brings up a lot, and you put up with my mood swings..." He trails off, running a hand through his hair before standing up, leaving the rest of the sentence unfinished.

Holding his hand out, I take it, and he pulls me to my feet, immediately wrapping me in his arms for another kiss.

And just like that, the world disappears. It's not for show this time, not for anyone but us. The way he kisses me, with that desperate intensity, it feels like he genuinely wants me. Like he needs me. Like he'd fall apart if he couldn't have this.

I've never had anyone kiss me like that and never had anyone crave me like he does.

"Are you hungry?" Alex asks, pulling back from the kiss, his breath still mingling with mine. One of his cousins—probably one of the Vincents—lets out a whistle from across the patio, but Alex ignores him.

"Starving," I reply, though only half of that is about food. The way his smirk tilts up on one side tells me he knows exactly what I mean. He leads me to the long dining table, pulling out my chair like the perfect gentleman, before sitting beside me. Most of the family is gathered outside, but apparently, Nonna refuses to dine in the chilly air, heaters or not. Meanwhile, Natalia has planted herself directly across from us, like she's auditioning for an episode of *The Real Housewives of Sicily*.

Alex starts filling my plate with food I can't quite identify, and I pray I'm not about to eat something wild, like chicken hearts. He adds a generous serving of rigatoni, passing the platter around the table. Then, without warning, he leans in and presses a soft kiss to my cheek, causing my face to heat.

I get that he's laying it on thick for the benefit of his cheating ex-fiancée, but *wow*.

Under the table, his hand finds its way to my thigh, his fingers moving in slow, deliberate strokes up and down. It's subtle, something Natalia can't see, but I'm sure she senses exactly where his hand is.

And the food—oh, *my god*, the food. I am ruined for all future Italian restaurants. The spices and the sauces—it's like I've been transported to a party in Sicily, and my taste buds are dancing.

Natalia sips her red wine, her eyes darting between me and Alex before zeroing in on him. "Alex, non sapevo che stessi frequentando qualcuno. E una cosa seria o volevi solo vedere come avrei reagito?" she purrs toward him.

Alex, ever the gentleman, doesn't even blink. He responds in perfect English, which is likely for my benefit. "Believe it or not, Natalia," he starts, his voice smooth and cold, "I had no idea you'd be here. I brought Violet to meet my family. I don't give a shit how you feel about it."

Eddie, sitting next to Natalia, looks like he'd rather crawl under the table than deal with whatever drama she's trying to stir up. Poor guy. He's not in charge of this relationship, and I can't help but see the Lisa parallel—another woman who bulldozes her way through everything, getting what she wants at any cost.

An awkward silence falls over the table, punctuated only by a few coughs, as Alex takes his time chewing his food, giving Natalia a look that clearly says *I'm done with your bullshit.* When the tension finally lifts, conversation resumes around the table, much more casual now as if everyone's relieved the standoff is over.

Ricardo sits at the head of the table, his gaze settling on me with a warm smile. "So, Violet, I hear you're working on a novel. Alex mentioned you're hoping to become an author?"

Wait, what? My eyes dart to Alex, who looks entirely too comfortable with the conversation he's set up. Great. Now I feel like my life's ambitions are on display—the pressure knots in my stomach.

"Oh, yes," I say, trying to sound casual. "I'm juggling a few projects right now, but hopefully, I'll finish one soon."

"That's fascinating," Ricardo says, leaning back in his chair, surprising me. "I've always admired writers. I barely have the patience to answer emails, let alone craft a story. Finishing a book is a real accomplishment."

Well... shit.

I was prepared for them to judge me. I mean, I don't come from money; I'm not some high-powered executive, and my dream is to write novels—a career my parents practically rolled their eyes at. But Ricardo's compliment hits me sideways, and now I'm all kinds of confused.

Alex

FUCKING NATALIA.

She's at the top of the list of people who shouldn't be here. But leave it to my dumbass cousin Eddie, who'll stick his dick anywhere, to bring her along. She'll use him like every other man, and when she's done, she'll dump him, leaving him a blubbering mess—his damn fault.

Natalia is like a villain straight out of a Disney movie—Wicked Witch of the West and Cruella de Vil mashed into one. Every glance from her feels like a dark spell, her laugh grating on my nerves. If there's a casting call for the next evil queen, she's got the part locked down.

And the fact that she touched me? Like we're friends who exchange holiday cards or chat over brunch? Please. She knew Violet would be here, and I'm sure Mama warned her not to cause a scene in front of my "girlfriend." For the record, I've cut all contact with Natalia. She's called me and begged me to return, but that's not happening. The day I return to her is when the Leaning Tower of Pisa straightens up and tap-dances down the street.

I haven't answered her calls or given her the time of day because Natalia doesn't want me. She wants the idea of me—the corporate mogul, the lifestyle. But she doesn't want *me*.

And now she's here, invading my one sanctuary. Sunday dinners with my family are the only time I'm not *the CEO*, not the business powerhouse. I'm just Alex. I laugh, relax, and enjoy the time with family and friends, and now she's tainted that.

I shot Dante a warning glance because he could've texted me to say she was here. Next week, he's going to be the damn racquetball.

Alena was sitting next to Violet, deep in conversation, completely immersed in talking about fall. Alena loved it, and apparently, so did Violet. Who knew? I certainly didn't. But hearing Violet talk about how much she adored the changing colors, her walks through

Central Park, and how autumn inspired her writing made me pause. Her voice lit up when she spoke about it being the most romantic time of the year in Manhattan.

This woman. Hell, she was perfect.

She fit in with my family, chatting with my cousin like they were old friends. Natalia, on the other hand—everyone knew her, but no one was connected to her anymore, except for Eddie and whatever the hell that situation was. She never cared enough to engage with my cousins and never made an effort. Violet? She was different. Even my mother had called her beautiful—something she'd never said about anyone I'd brought home. However, Violet probably thought it insulting since my mother said it in Italian.

And then, my father had to open his mouth, leaning back with that damn knowing grin of his as he sipped his drink. "So, Alex, how serious is this relationship between you and Violet?"

Fuck. I knew this was coming. I had warned Violet that talks of marriage and babies were bound to happen, but not like this—not at the table in front of everyone.

"Very," I answered, squeezing Violet's thigh under the table. Her leg felt like an anchor, keeping me grounded in this madness. I didn't let go. I didn't want to.

My father's grin widened, glancing between us. "Quando hai intenzione di chiederle di sposarti?"

Yeah, he just asked when I was planning to propose. And from the way Violet's hand froze mid-motion with her fork, I knew she had caught onto enough of that. She might not have understood the words, but the meaning? Loud and clear.

To them, we'd been dating for over a month, more than enough time in my parents' world to expect a proposal and babies shortly. They'd gotten married within months themselves, so why wouldn't I? It's just how they were. But this wasn't the same. Not by a long shot. A month to me and Violet... technically, it hadn't been that long since we'd met in that bar.

I shifted my gaze from my father to Natalia, sitting there with her perfectly curated sneer, and then back to Violet. She didn't get it, but those eyes—damn, those eyes. They weren't just green. They were everything. Honest. Deep. Real.

I smirked, turning back to my father. "Presto, sto pensando molto presto," I said, laying it on thick for good measure.

Out of the corner of my eye, I saw Natalia's face lose its color while my father's grin grew wider as he glanced over at Violet, thrilled with my response.

I knew exactly what I'd just told him. I told myself it was only to get him off my back and stop my family's inevitable questions about Violet. But what bothered me wasn't that I'd said it—that those words came out quickly. I'd just told my father I would propose to Violet soon, and part of me almost meant it. It didn't feel like a lie. It didn't feel like something I'd said to smooth things over.

It took me months to even consider proposing to Natalia. And in hindsight, the signs that I shouldn't have were right there, clear as day. But with Violet? Everything was different. Since I met her, it's felt like I'm moving at G-force speeds. I knew I wanted her to be mine the second I saw her, not as a casual fling or some one-night stand. I wanted her to be mine for good.

And that thought didn't freak me out, which was unnerving. My rational part had thrown caution to the wind the second Violet entered my life. I hadn't even slept with her, barely known her for two weeks, yet here I was, so deeply attached to her that it didn't feel like I was moving too fast. No hesitation. No second-guessing.

Under the table, Violet's hand stayed wrapped in mine as we ate. The warmth of her palm against mine grounded me, even as my family's chaotic conversations whirled around us. From who was pregnant again to who's getting married next, to the weather and the family business, the topics jumped like a deck of cards in a never-ending game of Uno on speed.

The women cleared the plates, a tradition I've never liked but one that still stands in my family. Violet offered to help, even though Mama told her she didn't need to, especially since it was her first time here. "It's no problem at all," she waved off my mother's protest, effortlessly slipping into the routine and helping clear the dishes like she'd been part of this family forever.

Meanwhile, my father, Dante, and a few cousins headed to the lounge area on the patio. Despite the crisp October air, the outdoor fireplace and heat lamps made it bearable. I purposely chose a seat that gave me a view of the kitchen, where I could keep an eye on Violet and hopefully save her from Nonna cornering her.

Luca, my five-year-old nephew, crawled up between me and Dante, his Nintendo Switch in hand, volume blaring. I reached over, turned the sound down, and wrapped my arms around him, helping him through a particularly tricky part of *Mario Party*. Since when did video games get this tough?

Luca's Dominic's son. Dom's a single dad, and Luca stays with Rico, my parents, or occasionally me when he's away for work. Not as often as I'd like, given how married I am to my job, but whenever I do, it's always good to have him around.

Every few minutes, my eyes drifted back to the kitchen. Violet was drying dishes with my aunt, chatting like it was the most natural thing in the world. My family has three dishwashers and a small army of maids, but on family night, tradition ruled—everyone pitched in, and every dish was washed by hand. And Violet? No hesitation. She was laughing with my aunts and cousins, even my mother, like she belonged there. The nerves she had when we first arrived were long gone, replaced with easy smiles and genuine warmth.

I couldn't help it.

I realized something while sitting there. I could ask her to marry me. Not now—I still had some grasp of sanity left. At least, I think I do. But watching her, being part of my family like this, it was different.

When Natalia used to come over, she did the bare minimum. She'd duck out of the kitchen to avoid getting her perfectly manicured nails dirty. She never stayed to help or chat and didn't care for the gossip or the wine my aunts loved to pour. But Violet? She fit right in.

I glanced over at the patio. Sure enough, Natalia was already out here, sipping her drink and avoiding any actual work. Typical.

Luca and I were close to beating this level, but Mario botched it again. "This game is rigged," I grumble, handing the Switch back to Luca as Dante leans in to help.

"Alex?"

I glance up to see Natalia standing there, looking down at me. Great.

My father raises a brow, and I know exactly what he's thinking. Everyone in my family knows I've been weak regarding her in the past. Our breakup was a complete disaster. There was no clean break—just us trying to make it work, failing repeatedly. Even after she slept with half the people I worked with, I told myself I could fix it, that I could still have the marriage, the kids, the whole damn dream.

Yeah, it's not exactly what you'd expect from me, but every Sunday dinner, watching my cousins with their kids and seeing the happiness on their faces messes with my head. Call me sentimental.

Reluctantly, I follow Natalia to the far end of the patio, into the shadows.

"What?" My tone is cold, my hands shoved deep in my pockets, and my expression is as blank as I can manage—there is no way I want her misreading anything here.

"I just thought we could catch up," she says, giving me that familiar smile. "It's been a while."

I take a page from Violet's book and lay it out bluntly. "Yeah, well, after you fucked half my colleagues, there wasn't much left to talk about."

Her face tightens, but she quickly recovers, stepping closer and touching my chest. "Alex, that was in the past. Let's start over."

A few months ago, I would've caved and fallen right back into her web. But not now. I grab her wrist, moving her hand off me like I'm flicking away a piece of lint.

"Don't touch me, Natalia. I have a girlfriend now. Did you miss what I said at dinner?"

She snorts, tapping her heel against the concrete, arms crossed in a way that makes it obvious she's trying to push her chest up for attention. But I'm not interested. Not even a little. I've seen better—on a green-eyed beauty helping my Mama and Nonna with dishes inside.

"So, you're going to ask her to marry you?" she asks, eyes narrowed in disbelief.

"Yup," I reply, unbothered. "Believe it or not, there are women out there who don't sleep with half the city. She's one of them. You wouldn't know about that, though, right?"

We're standing way too close for comfort when I catch movement out of the corner of my eye. Violet rounded the corner, her gaze flicking between me and Natalia.

Shit.

I hope she doesn't misunderstand this because nothing could be further from what it looks like.

"Sorry... your mama—who insisted I call her that, by the way," Violet's voice carried a playful lilt as she smiled up at me. I couldn't help but smirk. My mama never even hinted that Natalia should call her anything close to that. "She told me to come grab you for dessert duty," Violet added, her eyes flicking between me and Natalia.

"Gladly, babe." I didn't waste another second. I grabbed her hand and walked us back inside.

"You two are so adorable!" Mama cooed before kissing my cheek and pulling Violet into one of those enthusiastic hugs she reserved for people she already considered family.

"Mama," I said, a chuckle escaping, "what do you need me to do?"

"Finish the caramel sauce for the panna cotta," she replied, still beaming as if she'd won the lottery just seeing Violet and me together.

I rolled up my sleeves, glancing at Violet as she followed me toward the stove where everything was prepped.

"So," she teased, standing beside me, "you can cook more than just chicken parmesan?"

I started adding butter to the saucepan, smirking. "I'm Sicilian. If you can't cook, they pretty much disown you."

Violet laughed, that sound like sunshine on a dreary day.

"Do you cook much, Violet?" Nonna asked, wiping her hands on a dish towel while surveying the kitchen, ensuring everything was in order.

Violet shook her head. "I wish I did. My parents weren't big on teaching me how. I can manage a few things, but nothing like what you all made tonight."

My cousin Valeria, who had been lounging against the counter, perked up. "Well, you should come over for our cooking nights!"

"Cooking nights?" Violet turned to me, eyebrows raised.

I shrugged, stirring the sugar in the pan, trying to hide my grin because, right on cue, Natalia strolled into the kitchen. And guess who was never invited to cooking nights?

Yup. You guessed it.

Cooking nights were a weekly tradition, every Wednesday without fail. Mama, Nonna, and all the women in the family gathered to share recipes, gossip, and teach each other new kitchen techniques. It was their way of bonding, and now, Violet was being pulled into the mix.

"You'll learn to cook fast," my cousin Valeria assured her with a grin. "Trust me, I couldn't even boil water for pasta when I was younger. Now? I can cook just about anything. Except for the famous caramel sauce. That's the one recipe someone won't share." She shot me a pointed look.

She wasn't wrong. My caramel sauce recipe was a well-guarded secret, passed down from Nonna but perfected by me. The secret? Chili pepper. Simple, but why ruin the fun when everyone's still trying to guess?

Violet wandered over to me, leaving the women to their conversation. I could feel their eyes on us, but I didn't care. "So, this is your recipe?" she asked, curiosity bright in her eyes.

"Yes and no," I said, leaning against the counter. "It's based on Nonna's, but I made a few tweaks. Gave it my spin." I tilted my head toward the stove, then grinned. "Want to give it a try?"

She nodded, and I couldn't resist. I pulled her close so her back pressed into my chest, her body perfectly nestled against mine. My hands guided hers, holding the spoon as we hovered over the bubbling caramel. "You have to stir constantly," I said softly, my breath teasing her ear. "Feel that resistance? That's the sugar caramelizing. We don't want it to burn, so you must scrape the bottom, but be careful not to let any get on the sides. It'll crystallize."

Her jasmine scent wrapped around me, and as ridiculous as it sounded, watching her stir caramel drove me insane. Her hands, her focus, the way she fit perfectly into me—it wasn't just the sauce that had me heated.

"How am I doing?" she asked, looking over her shoulder at me, her lips so close I could almost taste them.

I trapped her between my arms, leaning in just enough to make her feel how much I was holding back. "Perfect," I whispered, my voice rougher than I intended. And I wasn't just talking about the sauce.

Mama walks over, her face lighting up with a smile. "Avrete entrambi i bambini più carini," she clasps her hands together like she's already planning a nursery. I help Violet finish the sauce, showing her how to pour it into a dish before she takes the pot to the sink. Valeria jumps in, insisting she'll handle the cleanup, practically shooing us out to eat.

As we step outside, Violet mutters, "I wish I knew Italian."

I chuckle. "Trust me, they've been nothing but sweet. All compliments."

"Oh really?" Her eyebrow quirks up as she side-eyes me. "What did your mom say back in the kitchen?"

I hesitate, knowing that telling her exactly what Mama said might send her running for the hills. Not every woman is ready to hear about future babies, especially not when things are still...fresh. But then again, it's Violet. She can handle it — hopefully. "She said we'd have the cutest babies," I say, giving her a casual shrug, but I can't deny that thought's crossed my mind more than once, especially if they look like her.

We take our seats back outside at the table, the warmth from the heaters doing their best, but let's face it—it's October, and it's cold as hell. Nonna and a few others have smartly stayed indoors, but I grab a plate of panna cotta to share—no point in fighting the chill when I can focus on the woman next to me.

"What exactly is panna cotta?" Violet asks as she eyes the plate.

"It's like a creamy custard," I explain, a grin tugging at my lips. "Smooth, tastes like vanilla."

She smirked at me with mischief in her eyes. "But we don't do vanilla, remember?"

I lean in closer, my gaze trailing down to her lips, lingering on the dusting of freckles across her nose. "There's one way I will," I say, my voice low and teasing. Without giving her a chance to respond, I dip my finger into the panna cotta and caramel sauce, offering it to her.

She takes my finger into her mouth, slow and deliberate. Her lips wrap around it, her tongue sliding over the caramel as she licks it clean. But she doesn't stop there. The way she sucks gently, pulling my finger out with a slight grip on my wrist—it's impossible not to remember how those lips felt somewhere far more enjoyable.

I know she said no sex, but there are plenty of other things we could do—and have done. The temptation to take some of this caramel sauce home and lick it off every inch of her skin is getting stronger by the second.

It's probably not my most brilliant idea, though, because now I'm hard as a rock, but honestly? I don't care. Especially if it means watching her suck the sauce off my finger or, better yet, feeding it to her myself. The way her lips part, eyes closing as she moans softly... Fuck.

Back inside, Violet insists on helping clean up, of course. She's over by the counter with Nonna while I'm leaning against the other side of the island, doing my best to talk business with my father—though my attention is elsewhere.

Then, out of nowhere, I hear Nonna ask, "So, is my Alex everything you hoped for in bed?"

Violet doesn't spit out her coffee, which is impressive, but she does shoot me a look. You know the kind—promising pain, injury, and possibly death.

I barely hold back a laugh while my father chuckles beside me, obviously amused. In all fairness, I had warned her before we got here.

Nonna, completely oblivious—or more likely, not caring—keeps going. "He's so handsome, and I know all the ladies want our Alex, but he picked you. You must be able to keep up with him, creatura vivace."

I pinch the bridge of my nose, silently begging for it to stop. Nonna never had boundaries. Or better said, she didn't care.

For a second, I think Violet might stay quiet and let it roll off. But when she squints at me, I know I'm screwed.

"Oh, he's the best," she says, sweet as honey but with an edge that makes my pulse race. "Definitely more than just muscle, and very good with his tongue." She even licks her lips while saying it, locking eyes with me.

Is she trying to kill me?

Nonna beams, clearly satisfied. "Ah, wonderful! Then you'll have no problem starting a family. Alex's Nonno, rest his soul, and I had fun making babies every day, a few times a day!"

"Nonna!" I hiss, trying to save Violet from picturing that. "Violet doesn't know you well enough to be scarred for life."

Mama walks in just in time, chuckling as she catches the end of the conversation. "Nonna, let's not scare Violet off with your stories. Give her a chance to know us first."

Nonna waves her off with a dismissive hand, clearly unfazed. "Bah, I'm just being honest. Not my fault my son married a prude."

Violet stifles a laugh, and I can't help but smile.

Before I know it, it's past ten, and I'm making the rounds, saying our goodbyes. Violet is deep in conversation with Valeria, making plans for Wednesday's cooking night when Dante pulls me aside.

"Are you seriously going to propose to her?" he asks, not even trying to lower his voice.

"What? No. Not now," I say, lowering mine. "I just needed to get Papa off my back. You know how he is. Toss him something, and he'll let up for a week or two."

Dante narrows his eyes. "I thought this was fake."

"Things changed." I shrug, trying to brush it off.

He crosses his arms, not buying it. "You realize every woman in the family is already planning your wedding, right? The second you told Papa that, you weren't just throwing him a bone. You weren't lying."

I glare at him. "What, you a mind reader now? Maybe quit selling luxury cars and go run a psychic hotline."

He doesn't even flinch. "I've seen you in love before, and it sure wasn't with Natalia. The way you've been looking at Violet all night, your eyes haven't left her—even when she's in the other room."

I check my watch, then pull out my phone. Twenty texts. Dozens of emails. All piling up while I'm here. "It's not like that," I muttered, distracted. "We haven't known each other long enough. You're confusing lust for love."

Dante smirks, leaning closer. "I know the difference between 'I want to fuck her' eyes and 'I want her to carry my babies' eyes."

I squint at him, but his words hit a bit too close.

Violet

The week started slow, and while I still saw Alex, I could tell something was off. He seemed more stressed than usual. When he surprised me with a lunch date today, I was excited—until I saw his mood.

He barely touched his food, and the color on his face was paler than usual. There was something heavy weighing on him. I figured work was getting to him. I knew he had another acquisition on the horizon, and Julian Stone was causing trouble, monopolizing his time. Alex hadn't discussed it with me, but I picked up bits and pieces from overhearing conversations, especially when he left me alone at dinner with his associates.

He and Stone were in a brutal bidding war over a company. Alex needed the company's proprietary software, while Julian Stone—this corporate vulture—was more interested in buying failing companies, gutting them, and selling off the parts. If Stone won, Alex would have to pay double, maybe triple, to get the coding from him instead of buying the company outright. The details went way over my head, but I could tell it was serious. Most evenings, when I came to his house, he was either buried in contracts or stuck on a late-night call with Australia, given the time zone difference. Their mornings were our nights.

I'd already been to two family dinners, and time flew faster than expected. While those dinners added more "real" dates to cross off the list of the fake ones we'd claimed to have, I still felt like I'd barely scratched the surface with Alex. Every night, we'd fall asleep talking, sometimes about mundane things like our day and sometimes about more profound, personal topics. Even though we'd only been dating for a few weeks, I was grateful he asked me to join him for lunch and a walk today. Maybe we'd talk, maybe we wouldn't—there was a comfort in the silence between us. Being near each other was enough to remove whatever stress was building outside the "us" bubble.

Most nights, he was exhausted by the time we got to bed, leaving little room for conversation beyond a quick recap of the day. I suppose that should have been a relief. If we weren't diving into conversations, it meant less temptation for...other things. Things I wasn't ready for yet. The fact that we'd made it this far without crossing that line? The man deserved a medal for restraint.

The tension between Alex and me grew each day, and resisting him got harder. Especially when he'd crawl into bed at night wearing nothing but his boxer briefs while I lounged in his t-shirt. There wasn't much fabric separating our most intimate parts, and waking up every morning with his rock-hard erection pressing against me was becoming more difficult to ignore. And yes, we've shared a bed every night since this started. How we've managed to do that without tearing each other's clothes off? I have no idea.

A few mornings ago, I nearly lost the battle. I was so close to rolling over, straddling him, and letting things go wherever they wanted. And as if he could read my mind, he beat me to it. I found myself flipped over, his body pressed against mine, his erection snug between my legs as his lips traced hot, lazy kisses down my neck. His hands were everywhere—kneading my breasts, making me ache for more. We'd agreed on no sex, opting to please each other in other ways instead. And while he was amazing—honestly, the man was a god with his hands and mouth—there's only so long a girl can go without wanting the whole experience.

Now we're walking through Central Park, ice cream cones in hand despite the chilly November afternoon. I know it is not the most practical choice for the weather, but I always go for ice cream when given the option. We stroll along the path, hand in hand, while I do what I always do in the park—people watch.

Central Park is a melting pot of personalities. You've got everything from fashion elites rushing through in designer coats to kids on bikes and exercise junkies jogging by, "stretching" at benches as they scope out the dating scene. But my favorite to watch? Couples. There's something heartwarming about seeing them together. We pass an older couple huddled on a bench, sharing a cup of hot cocoa, which makes way more sense in this weather, but still... ice cream.

"So, why don't you come over earlier on Saturdays?" Alex breaks the silence, pulling me out of my people-watching trance. And thank God for that, because a few more minutes of watching his tongue swirl around that ice cream cone—slowly, methodically—lapping up his vanilla like he was making a show of it... Well, let's say it reminded me exactly what that tongue is capable of.

Alex had been asking me to come over earlier on Saturdays for a while now, but I'd always show up closer to dinner. We had fallen into this routine—dinners together, then bed—and while that sounds sweet and innocent, the sexual tension between us was thicker than fudge sauce. But there were two reasons I resisted coming over earlier.

First, the longer I was with him, the harder it was not to throw him on top of me after he rocked my world with one of his mind-blowing orgasms.

Second? My parents.

Every Saturday morning, like clockwork, my mom calls. It's her weekly "check-in," and by check-in, I mean she finds something to criticize. I still haven't told her about my promotion because, in her mind, I've been a senior editor for years. Could you imagine the horror if she found out I'd been "just" an assistant this whole time? I can already hear her voice laced with disappointment. Sometimes, a little lie was necessary to preserve what little sanity I had left when dealing with the two people who gave me life.

"Saturday mornings, my mom calls," I shrug, taking another lick of my lemon sorbet. It's so good—tangy lemon with real zest mixed with creamy vanilla. Heaven in a cone. "It's mostly her, anyway. Just checking in."

Alex glances over at me, his brows furrowed. "Isn't that a good thing? You get to catch up."

I roll my eyes. Of course, he wouldn't understand. His family was like a warm, never-ending hug wrapped in homemade pasta. They had their Sunday dinners, their cooking nights—full of jokes and support. They never criticized, never tore each other down. I've seen it firsthand, and while it's sweet, it's also foreign. My family? It's a whole different story.

I lick my sorbet again, trying to find the right words. "No, these calls aren't like that. They're draining. Every week, it's just more disappointment."

He frowns, his eyes searching mine. "Disappointed in what?"

I let out a breath, focusing on a runner passing us by. "To them, I should have accomplished more. Even the things I have done, the achievements—they're never enough."

He looks at me for a long moment, clearly confused. "That's... insane. My family is the opposite. Sure, they'd never let someone talk to them like that. Once, I told Alena she was disappointing me, and my cousins practically tore me apart. Do you stand up to your parents?"

I huff a little laugh, shaking my head. "It's not that simple. You don't know what it's like to grow up with people who constantly make you feel small... like you're not enough, no matter what you do."

Alex pauses by the trash can, tossing his cone in and wiping his hands with a napkin. He glances at me, his expression tight. "Violet, don't take this wrong, but you need to start standing up for yourself. You can't let people walk all over you, even your parents. It's the same with your job. Margaret treated you like a doormat for years because you let her. How different would things have been if you just told her no? You let Jake and Lisa treat you like some personal punching bag." He cringes after he says it.

I feel a flash of heat rise in my chest. "That's not fair, Alex. You don't know what it's like for me. I'm trying. I'm doing my best, but you've only been in my life for a few weeks. You haven't seen the rest of it. You don't get to judge." My voice shakes, but I hold firm.

"Maybe that's the problem, Violet. You *are* doing your best, but sometimes that's not enough. You're better than this. You deserve *more*." He reaches for my hand, but I pull away, the sting of his words hitting harder than I expected. "You didn't get promoted because you let everyone walk over you."

I narrow my eyes. "I got promoted because *you* made a phone call," I snap, the words biting hard.

He sighs, and this time, he pulls me toward him, his grip firm but gentle. "Yes, I called to push you in the right direction, the direction you *deserve* to go. But it would be best to learn to stand up for yourself, Violet. I won't always be there to push back for you." His voice softens, but I catch how his face flinches at the words, as if he's already seeing an end I hadn't anticipated.

His words sting, and suddenly, the truth I've been avoiding hits me like a brick. I shove him away, blinking back the tears that are already forming. He doesn't understand, and I've never let him see what I deal with. Only Max knows, and it took years for him to pry that out of me.

"You're right, Alex. You *won't* be there forever. Whatever *this* is, it'll be over once you get what you need from me. You'll return to your life, your perfect family, and I'll be left to pick up the pieces. Why am I even trying to get close to them? The closer I get, the worse it will hurt when it's over, when *you* don't need me anymore. You have everything—money, success, a family that loves you. You don't know what it's like to live my life. To have parents who remind you at every turn that you're a failure. To be a *failed* writer who can't even finish a damn novel because her mess weighs her down."

The moment the words spill out, I see the regret in his eyes, but I'm feeling too raw now. "Violet, I didn't mean—"

"No, Alex. You've said enough." My voice is sharp, knifing through whatever explanation he's trying to give. "Enjoy the rest of your afternoon. I need to get back to my 'mediocre' job and try not to fail at being a pushover today."

I don't wait for him to respond, turning on my heel and walking away. My steps are quick, and even though I hear him calling my name behind me, I refuse to turn around. Not now. Not when the tears are threatening to fall.

"Violet..." His voice is softer now, pleading, but I can't stop. When he grabs my arm to get me to face him, I shake him off, my voice breaking.

"I have to get to work."

Max is on my heels when I return to the office, closing the door with an exaggerated huff. "What happened? I thought you were on a lunch date with Alex."

"Well," I sigh, flipping through a random stack of papers, my fingers shaking just enough that I'm grateful they're hidden behind my desk. "We had a little... disagreement. And now I'm ready to immerse myself in it." I glance down at the manuscript title and holy hell; *this* is what's waiting for me.

Clearing my throat, I grab a tissue to dab at my under-eye area, praying my mascara hasn't betrayed me. I look up at Max with as much seriousness as I can muster. "I needed to rush back to the office. After all, I urgently need to dive into *The Flirtatious Fantasies of the Playful Parrot*." Usually, I'd burst out laughing at the absurdity of that title, but right now, it's the only thing keeping me from spiraling into a full-blown meltdown.

Max crosses his arms, eyes narrowing as he takes in my appearance—my blotchy face, trembling lip, and the overall disaster that is me. "Violet, what happened at lunch?"

"Nothing." I sound way too chipper. I yank open my desk drawer, now stuffed with editing essentials—highlighters, red pens, sticky notes. Anything to look busy. "Hartley wants this book done before Friday, so here I am, being a responsible editor, getting an early start."

Tapping my pen against the manuscript, I blink up at him, hoping he'll drop it. But, of course, he doesn't budge. He's standing there like he's waiting for me to crack, arms crossed, and I know he's not leaving until I spill. But if I start talking about what went down during lunch, I won't stop. And I sure don't want to cry at work.

My phone pings, and a name flashes across the screen. I ignore it, even though I know exactly who it is.

"Aren't you going to check that?" Max arches a brow, looking far too smug for someone not involved in my personal life.

"Nope." I snatch my red pen, flicking the cap off so hard it flies across the room. But I ignore it, acting like I'm the picture of calm, professional composure.

Max knows me too well, forcing me to add a new life rule mentally: never let friends get to know you this well. Because instead of leaving me alone, he plops down in the armchair across from my desk, casually tossing my purse onto the floor. Then, he grabs my phone. "I'm going to take a wild guess here and say you're not checking your phone because you know it's Alex, and something happened at lunch that has you all twisted up. Maybe you're a little mad at him, a little mad at yourself, and instead of dealing with it, you've buried yourself in work."

I stare at the manuscript before me, pretending to absorb *The Flirtatious Fantasies of the Playful Parrot* like a literary masterpiece. Honestly, these titles are starting to toe the line between creativity and... bird porn for the birdwatchers of the world. Why do I keep getting these? Did I accidentally sign up to be the editor for all things avian erotica?

Max is watching me. I can feel it. His gaze, his presence, even the annoying tap of his foot. It's like he's waiting for me to crack, to spill the entire lunch debacle spinning around in my head.

Not today, Max. Not today.

"So, what was the fight about?" he finally asks, in that tone he uses when he already knows the answer.

"How do you even know there was a fight?" I snapped, instantly regretting that I had just confirmed what he was fishing for. Damn him.

A mischievous smile tugs at the corners of his lips, and at this moment, I hate him just a little bit. "Alex might've called while you were storming back here." He pauses, savoring the dramatic moment. "Seemed a little... concerned."

Of course, Alex called.

Tapping my pen, pretending to work, is useless now. I toss it on the manuscript, which will surely be the most thrilling content I've ever enjoyed editing. Then, I lean back in my chair and square off with Max, knowing full well he's got a lecture or some life lesson brewing. "Okay, go ahead. Let's hear it. Give me your thoughts."

I don't even ask why Alex called him, as Alex is everywhere. In my life, in my business—literally when it comes to work—so why would I be surprised he reached out to my best friend after we disagreed?

Max leans back, stretching the moment like he's about to deliver an Oscar-worthy speech. "Well... I know he feels bad about how he worded things."

I clap my hands together. "Great, we're all on the same page. He said something stupid, I'm mad, I'll get over it. Can I get back to work now?" I eye the pen cap that went flying earlier and rolled next to my snack-filled filing cabinet.

Deciding to retrieve it, I slip off my boots and kneel to grab the cap. Honestly, shouldn't Max be doing this? He is my assistant, and today, I feel like being that kind of boss. "He made some valid points. Points I've told you myself, but probably with more tact," Max says casually.

My fingers pause, just touching the cap. I sit up on my knees, likely tearing a hole in my stockings. "Wait—you agree with him?"

Max shrugs, all nonchalant like it's no big deal. "He's not wrong, Violet. It would be best if you had been promoted years ago, but instead, you drank your lavender latte and never stood up for yourself. Worked yourself into the ground for what? You're the one who answers the phone when your mother calls, knowing damn well she's going to criticize you. Alex feels bad for phrasing things that way, but you know what I told him?"

I roll my eyes. "I'm not exactly dying to know." I grab the cap and return to my desk, giving myself a high-five for accomplishing something today. *Cap retrieval award: me.*

"He asked me how he could make it up to you."

"I'll be fine. I'm just pissed right now."

"And I told him that, but you're missing the point." Max, ever the nosy friend, slides my phone out of my purse and unlocks it easily, even though I change the passcode religiously.

"Clearly." I push my desk chair back up, gripping my pen like I'm about to edit the hell out of this parrot-mating manuscript and turn it into the rockstar of... what? The nature section? I had no idea where they put these kinds of books in the bookstore, so I started Googling to figure out where these masterpieces were shelved. Top shelf? Bottom shelf? Maybe in the hidden, never-been-touched section?

But then I stumble across something that makes me pause. Mr. Birdman, Mating Specialist, the author of this mind-boggling series, has sold *a lot* of books.

What. The. Actual. Hell.

This guy has to be raking in a hefty paycheck from royalties on bird sex. No wonder he's cranking them out like his life depends on it. Maybe I'm in the wrong genre. Forget romance novels—maybe I need to start writing about the dramatic love life of a parrot and a lonely house sparrow.

A parrot with abandonment issues meets an emotionally unavailable house sparrow. That could sell.

"Violet?" Max interrupts, pulling me back from the brink of this brilliant career shift.

"Oh, right. Sorry, what's up? I'm very busy with this incredibly riveting manuscript on avian intimacy."

I quickly scribble "bird romance novel" on a sticky note, alongside "research why bird mating books are so popular," because that's information I never thought I'd need.

Max sighs dramatically. "Do guys who aren't serious about a woman typically call their girlfriend's best friend to figure out how to fix things? Especially when they didn't even do anything *wrong*?"

I pause, blinking. "No, but... what exactly are you getting at?"

Between the shocking success of Mr. Birdman's love life and the rediscovery of my pen cap, I've lost the thread of this conversation entirely.

Max stands up, tossing my purse back onto the armchair like he's had enough of my nonsense. He grabs my phone and places it gently on my desk like it's a ticking time bomb. "Tell him it's fine and that you'll be there tonight. Because, Violet, that man, for whatever reason, is in love with you. No guy goes to that much trouble or worries about upsetting you if they weren't head over heels."

And with that, Max spins on his heels and leaves me alone in the chaos of my thoughts—Alex, bird mating, and a love story about birds that were never meant to be... but maybe could be if the stars aligned just right.

Crap. Am I the house sparrow, and Alex is the parrot? No, wait. Alex is a peacock. Doesn't matter. We're the birds.

Alex

AFTER THE WALK IN the park—which felt less like a casual stroll and more like a trip down memory lane—I returned to the office in an exceptionally sour mood. It didn't help that I returned knowing I had to deal with my brothers about how Julian Stone was continuing to underbid us, but all I could think about was Violet and the way she reacted to what I said.

Why the hell did I tell her I wouldn't always be around? That's not what I meant. I wanted her to know she couldn't rely on me to fight all her battles, but... I plan on being around her until I die. Things had been going well between us—better than I expected, honestly—and now we had our first real fight. The last thing I wanted to do was sit here and talk business.

But I had no choice. Julian Stone was undercutting us at every turn, and it was starting to feel personal. That's two companies in a row he's started bidding on—both ones I needed, and both at the exact moment he had no business even knowing about. There's a rat somewhere, and I'm going to find it.

Rico and Dom were already in my office, and the door closed. There's no point in bringing the board into this mess—they're too jumpy, and one of them might be feeding Stone for all I know.

"I want all the computers and company phones swept," I told Rico, who nodded, his expression as blank as ever. He could've been a statue. Even now, when he should be livid or at least concerned, there's nothing. Rico could probably win at poker against the Devil himself.

"Think someone in the company flipped?" Dom asked, leaning back in his chair, his face shadowed with worry.

"Has to be someone on the inside. How else would Stone know which one we're after instead of the decoy?" I'd been at this long enough to know the game. Julian Stone buys companies, guts them for parts, and sells off the remains for profit. Usually, he overbids on the decoys I throw out there, but lately, he's been one step ahead, targeting the ones I want. "It's got to be someone in acquisitions. Maybe even the board. They're the only ones who would know the real target versus the bait."

Dom rubbed his jaw, looking as frustrated as I felt. "Our people are solid. I don't see someone flipping."

It had to be someone. No one else had access to that level of detail. I'm always careful when I talk business, even at home with family. I never mention specific company names, and I refer to them as 'acquisitions' in case anyone is listening. Paranoid? Maybe. But that paranoia has saved my ass more times than I can count.

"The guy's a snake. It wouldn't surprise me if he found a way in here," Rico finally chimed in, his voice sounding more like he was rebooting from sleep mode.

I turned to him, my brother, and our tech guru and asked, "How long will it take to sweep all the company computers and phones?"

Rico gave a nonchalant shrug. "I can have it done by tomorrow."

Of course, that meant he'd work through the night, but Rico had nothing better to do. He was at the office or working from home if he wasn't scheduling his weekly Wednesday one-night stand like a routine. The guy was a machine.

Rico's always been closed off, the strong, silent type. Women found it sexy, but Dom and I knew better—he didn't like people. Conversations were tedious, and he'd communicate with lines of code rather than human beings.

"Get it done," I said, waving him off before standing up from my desk, a small smile tugging at my lips despite everything happening.

Dom raised an eyebrow. "And that look is for...?"

I shrugged, but the reason behind the smile was clear in my head. "Violet and I fought. I need to make it up to her."

Dom chuckled, shaking his head. "Yeah, you're not hung up on her at all."

"Fuck off," I shot back, but even as I said it, I couldn't shake the thought of her.

Violet

"WHERE ARE YOU OFF to?" Alex asks as I step into the living room, rocking a pair of skinny jeans and a light sweater. My hair is thrown into a messy bun to keep it out of the way for tonight's cooking plans. It hits me only when I step into the kitchen—I haven't been home in days. All my clothes are at Alex's penthouse. It's like I've practically moved in without even realizing it. We've fallen into this comfortable rhythm, waking up and going to bed together, sharing the space like it's second nature.

I glance up, spotting Alex at the dining room table, typing away on his laptop. And he's only wearing sweats. Just sweats. His abs—six-pack, maybe eight-pack, I've honestly lost count—are on full display, along with the tattoos that weave across his chest. My fingers have memorized those patterns, tracing them while lying in bed at night. It's become a lullaby, the smooth whirls of ink coaxing me to sleep.

"It's Wednesday," I say with a shrug as if that explains everything.

"You went last week." His eyes lifted from the screen, and his brow arched.

He's not wrong. I went to cooking night right after family dinner on Sunday last Wednesday, then again this past Sunday when Valeria practically dragged me to learn her lasagna recipe. I have to admit, I'm having fun. It's more than just cooking. I've learned recipes and laughed with his family. None of them have teased me for needing extra help, and they're all so welcoming.

At first, the idea of going without Alex made me nervous. But tonight? I'm not even a little worried.

"I love your family. They're so much fun! Plus, you're busy with the whole acquisition thing, and learning to cook is always a win," I say, flashing a smile as I lean against the counter.

Alex glances up from his laptop, pausing for a second. "I know you guys don't just cook," he says, giving me a knowing look.

Okay, fair. We do have a few drinks. Maybe gossip a bit, but thanks to Alex, I have a driver, so it's all under control. The gossip is light, though, nothing scandalous. Aside from celebrity dirt, no one bad-mouths the family. There's... a lot of sex talk. And I mean *a lot*.

I didn't realize just how open Alex's family is about their sex lives—especially Nonna. And not just her. Everyone's sharing stories like it's a therapy session, and there's me, keeping it PG because I've got nothing that compares to their stories. When I get home, I practically sprint to the shower. Not because of the "food smell," like I tell Alex, but because I need to cool off. Desperately.

Sleeping next to him every night has become a test of pure willpower. I think I've held strong... mostly. But last night? Last night, I lost a few points.

He held my back to his front, his arm draped over my waist, fingers tracing lazy circles on my stomach. Slow at first, innocent. But those circles started drifting lower. Then *lower*. And before I could even say his name, his hand slipped under my underwear. "Alex..." I whispered, trying to keep my cool, but his fingers found me wet and waiting, and then he started saying the filthiest, hottest things.

One finger slid in. Then two. I was panting, pressing myself back against his rock-hard erection, feeling it throb against me as his mouth left wet, open-mouthed kisses on my neck. His voice, low and rough, told me all the things he'd do if he were inside me. Then, when he added a third finger, my body trembled, stretched most deliciously, and I couldn't help but whimper. When he whispered, "Just getting you ready, Bella... every inch of me, buried inside your perfect cunt," I came undone.

Just thinking about it and catching a glimpse of the faint bruise in the foyer mirror, I pressed my legs together.

Sorry, lady bits, you don't run the show.

But let's be honest, they do, especially when Alex strolls around the house looking like *that*. All casual, shirtless, with abs that should have a separate zip code. It's getting harder and harder to resist him. The feel of his skin against mine every night, the fact that I've moved in—it all makes it a little absurd that we haven't just given in.

But... there's something about holding back that's deepened everything between us. Removing sex from the equation, for now, has made me get to know Alex on a different level. There's no foggy glass of lust clouding things. I'm not saying no sex is a magic cure for relationships, but there's something to be said about taking your time, and at least I can assure myself it isn't the same spiral that happened with Jake.

That being said, I'm *more* than ready for the next step.

Alex stood up from the table, stretching, all toned muscles and mind-numbing good-ness. "You really enjoy going to these cooking nights?" He almost sounded surprised, like I was doing it for him.

"This is all me, babe. I love it!" And I wasn't lying. It's something I genuinely look forward to. After the first night, Valeria gave me her number and even checked on Monday to ensure I'd still come. "I'm expected now. Mama says it's tradition."

He smiled, coming closer as I stood by the front door. There was something in that smile: a little knowing and amused.

"What?" I asked, raising a brow.

"You usually say *your* mama... but now you're just calling her Mama."

Huh. That *was* interesting.

Alex hooks a finger through one of the belt loops on my jeans, tugging me closer. I think he will kiss me for a second, but no—he takes his time. Pressing into me, he moves slowly until my back bumps against the door. His finger slides out of the loop, his hand curling around my hip.

"Do you like my family?" he asks, voice low.

It's not what I was expecting in this position, but okay, I'll bite. "I do. A lot, actually." And it's true. They're fun, warm, and welcoming—nothing like the emotional landmines that are my own family, who usually make me want to dive under the covers with a pint of ice cream after any interaction.

He makes a soft hum, resting his forehead against mine. "Am I selfish for saying that even though you're out having fun, I miss having you here?"

Oh, come on. If I were writing this tender moment in one of my books, I'd say this man was in love. But that can't be right... can it? You don't get these feelings without... well, you know. Being *intimate*. Right? No, I think it's more that we've gotten used to each other. We have this rhythm, this comfortable routine, and while I'm not mad about the space Wednesday nights give me, they're probably just throwing a wrench in that. Until I'm ready for the next step — emotionally and not giving into the physical part of me screaming it's more than prepared to go — a little time apart from the sex god currently in front of me is probably a good idea.

"A little," I smile, looking up at him. His blue eyes are locked on mine, intense. The heat of his body seeps into me, his grip tightening on my hip, making everything inside me melt into a hot, swirling mess. He looks like he's about to kiss me. I'm sure of it. But instead, he leans in and presses a soft kiss on my forehead.

"Okay then," he says, pulling away. "Have a good time. Antonio's already downstairs waiting."

I will need Antonio to crank up the air conditioning when I get in the car.

Violet

I WAS SO DEEP into editing this ridiculous manuscript about bird mating habits that I didn't even hear the door open until there was an awkward cough. Glancing up, I see Jake leaning in the doorway, arms crossed, trying to look... stoic. Is that what he's going for? Whatever it is, he's failing miserably.

A wave of regret hits me. How did I ever date this guy? Especially now that I've known Alex for barely a month, and he's managed to give me more orgasms with just his tongue and fingers than Jake ever did with... well, anything.

The mere thought of going further with Alex has me shifting uncomfortably in my chair, crossing and uncrossing my legs like my body is trying to figure out how to calm itself. It's a losing battle.

Last night, after my shower, I found Alex waiting for me in bed, reading. The whole thing felt so... domestic. Like we'd slipped into some cozy, old married couple routine. One of us always waits for the other, and once we're both in bed, he wraps his body around mine, holding me close until we fall asleep.

If this thing between us ever ends, I'm convinced I'll never sleep well again. But I force myself to ignore that dark corner of my brain—the part that spirals into all the what-ifs. No use going down that rabbit hole today.

"Did I interrupt?" Was Jake's voice always this grating?

"Hmmm?" I barely pull myself from the depths of bird mating habits to face him.

Jake's eyes sweep the counter behind me, zeroing in on the fresh bouquet Alex sends me daily. Not a single rose, because of course, Alex would never be that cliché. The sight of it makes my lips twitch up into a smile.

"Well, your man sure likes to remind everyone you're taken," Jake says, still leaning against the door frame like he's trying out for the next GQ cover. Spoiler: he's not landing that gig anytime soon.

"What can I say? He knows what he's got and treats it right." Was that a jab? Yes. Did he deserve it? Absolutely.

"So, you suddenly have a rich boyfriend and got promoted... what's next on your grand life plan?"

I tap my red pen against the manuscript—yep, still editing the fascinating world of bird mating—and squint at him, trying to see what's rattling around in that pea-sized brain of his. If I squint hard enough, maybe I'll find crickets.

Do crickets even chirp? Mental note: look that up. I should know if I'm going to throw it into a book.

"Did you need something? Kind of a busy day." I glanced pointedly down at the manuscript, then back at him. "Trying to get this done before Friday."

"Oh, plans with Mr. Moneybags, huh?" The way he says it makes my skin itch. No, worse—it's like a full-on rash forming from pure annoyance.

"Yes. We're going to a friend's wedding."

"You love weddings." Ugh. Why does he have to remember things from our barely memorable relationship?

"That I do." Short answers. Let's speed this conversation up before I throw my pen at him.

Jake snorts. "Speaking of weddings... any idea how The Gardens suddenly canceled our reservation?"

That makes me look up.

I blink, keeping my face as neutral as possible. "I'm sorry, what?"

"At the bar, your boyfriend asked where we were getting married. A week later, our reservation was canceled. And guess what? He owns The Gardens."

I shrug, though inside, I'm doing mental cartwheels. "He owns a lot of businesses, Jake. I doubt he's personally involved. That's what boards and, you know, teams of people are for. He's way too busy to deal with your wedding drama."

Wait—does Alex own The Gardens? He never said anything about it at the bar. I want to smile, maybe even giggle, because... wow. Sweet or not, it's oddly satisfying. The Gardens is *the* venue, my dream wedding spot. Ever since I saw a friend get married there, I imagined myself walking down that aisle draped in white and rose gold. A fairy tale. A fantasy I never thought I'd get to live.

And Lisa? Oh, she knew. She knew The Gardens was my dream. She chose to rub it in my face, along with Jake. Typical Lisa—she probably even copied my color palette because she can't help but mimic everything I do. Jake included.

"Talk to the wedding coordinator. They might know what happened. I promise you, Alex had nothing to do with it. He's too busy for petty stuff like this," I say, already pulling out my phone to text Alex and subtly ask about *The Gardens*.

Jake stands there, giving me that look—the one he thinks makes him seem intimidating. I stare right back, not blinking. Is this a staring contest? Fine. Game on.

After a moment, he huffs and walks away.

I win.

I pulled up the text thread with Alex and typed out a quick message.

Violet: You didn't tell me you owned *The Gardens*.

Alex: I didn't... until a few weeks ago.

Violet: Oh my God. Please tell me you didn't buy the venue just to cancel Jake and Lisa's wedding. Who does that? Do you have that much money to just toss around?

Alex: I'm not sure I should answer that question.

Violet: Tell me.

Alex: Are you mad?

Violet: No. Oddly, I'm rather entertained.

Alex: Then yes, I did buy it. To do that.

Violet: You realize most boyfriends send flowers. Once. Not daily. And definitely not by buying venues to settle their girlfriend's score.

Alex: Maybe some boyfriends do, but you're dating me, Violet. A woman like you deserves to feel special. Speaking of which, did today's flowers arrive?

Violet: Yes. What's with the cactus?

Alex: I have to change it up. Keep you on your toes. It had a blossom, so it counts.

Violet: Except it's the only thing that *won't* die. So now I have a spiky death trap in my office.

Alex: Do you plan to fall into the pot?

Violet: Well, no.

Alex: Then I think you're safe. I'll have to come up with something new for tomorrow. Gotta go. Board meeting. You know, that thing called work.

Violet: You and I both know you text me during those anyway.

Alex: I admit nothing.

Smiling, I set my phone down and glanced at the cactus. It was the oddest thing to get this morning. Even the receptionist gave me a look like she was questioning every life choice that led her to deliver plants for a living. She used to be excited about the daily flower deliveries. Now? Pure annoyance. The sneer she wore as she handed me the cactus was new. And impressive.

Max stood at my office door, but instead of hovering, he stepped inside and closed it behind him. His look screamed curiosity.

"What did Jake want?"

I leaned back in my chair, a smirk playing on my lips. "No idea. He was ranting about how his wedding reservation at *The Gardens* got canceled." I couldn't help it; the smirk widened. Alex bought the venue to cancel it before we were even officially together. Why did that make me feel all warm and gooey inside?

Max raised an eyebrow. "What's that look for?"

I propped my head on my hand, still clutching the red pen I'd been using. "Hmm? Oh, nothing."

"You're practically glowing, and it's making me a little nauseous, to be honest."

"Okay, fine." I exaggerated a scowl. "Better?"

"It's more natural," he deadpanned, leaning back in the chair and lacing his hands behind his head. Max always looked put together, like he'd just walked out of a photoshoot. Even though he was technically my assistant, his sharp suits said otherwise. Today, it was black with a cream-colored shirt—impeccably fitted. How he didn't have a boyfriend was beyond me. He was tall, dreamy brown eyes, dark hair, and a permanent five o'clock shadow that made him look like a rom-com heartthrob. And, because he's my gay best friend, I've seen him naked—trust me, it's all good under there.

He gave me an odd look, his mouth quirking to the side. "So, the family dinner went well. And you've been to his mom's house alone twice now? Hanging out with the ladies of the family?"

"Yeah?" I answered, unsure where this was going.

"I'm worried about you."

My brows shot up. "Why?"

"Because, Violet, you like the guy. You're withholding sex, and we both know why."

I sighed and dropped the pen, letting it roll across the desk. "Yeah, I know. I'm afraid that once I cross that line, I'll be vulnerable. And we both know half my heart resides in my vagina."

Max made a face at the word, cringing. "But you're still sharing a bed with him, right?"

"You can share a bed and not have feelings," I say, lying through my teeth. I mean, I'm trying to believe it. Except, my heart leaps every time Alex pulls me close at night, so there's *that*.

Max gives me a look. You know, the *sure, Jan* one. "Uh-huh. And all this 'helping each other out in other ways' isn't making your..." He waves his hand, wiggling his eyebrows like a cartoon villain. He hates saying the word *vagina*—claims it might burn him if he does.

I roll my eyes to save him the agony. "We're not having sex until I'm ready to be vulnerable."

Max's head tilts as he stares out the window, doing that dramatic, deep-thinking thing. "No one is ever ready for that, Vi. I don't want you to get hurt again." He turns back, pinning me with *the* look. The one that's worse than my mother's death stare. "When you fall, you fall hard. And I just don't want you crashing this time, only to end up on my couch for three weeks, eating all my kettle corn while rewatching the same three rom-coms. So, I guess you taking your time is just saving me from reliving that nightmare."

"First, kettle corn is a gift from the snack gods. Sweet, salty, crunchy perfection." Now I want kettle corn. Great. "And second, I wasn't heartbroken over Jake. I was in shock."

Not just shock—horrified. He didn't just cheat on me with my best friend; he wrecked me. Took something precious that wasn't his to ruin, and I hated myself for letting him get that close. For thinking he felt the same way when I was fooling myself.

I know I need to be careful around Alex because, let's be honest, Max is right. When I fall, I fall hard, like a "lovesick puppy." I start cooing, all heart-eyes and butterflies. Then, inevitably, my heart gets broken, and I'm left trying to piece myself back together with Max's couch, an endless supply of kettle corn, and my favorite rom-coms. It's a messy, predictable cycle.

But with Alex? If he broke me, I wouldn't just be in pieces. I'd be shattered. There wouldn't be enough kettle corn or Nicholas Sparks movies to fix that damage. I'd have to rebuild myself from scratch, like one of those art projects where you make the clay and sculpt it into something new. Maybe I'm being a little dramatic, but you get the idea.

While I'm lost in this thought—probably veering too far into the land of denial—my phone buzzes. I assume it's Alex, but nope, it's my mother. I hold the screen out toward Max, who sighs but doesn't budge from his chair.

It's not Saturday, and she never calls midweek. My mom is the poster child for predictability. So, what is she doing calling in the middle of the workweek? This can't be good.

"Mom, so nice to hear from you." I try to keep my voice light as I say it, and Max lifts a brow in silent question. I shrug back. What else am I supposed to say? *Hey, Mom, calling to tell me how much I've failed you this week?* That feels more fitting but less polite.

"Violet, why didn't you tell us?" Her tone immediately makes my spine straighten.

"Tell you what, Mom?" I'm already bracing myself.

"That you had a boyfriend!"

Oh. *That*? How the hell do they know? My parents live in California, and I've made zero effort to broadcast my personal life. Thank god for that distance—it adds a nice buffer zone between me and the inevitable disappointment parade.

"Uh, yeah, I do... how did you find out?" My voice is casual, but I'm panicking inside.

"There's an article, Violet. With a photo of you two kissing in public." My mom sounds scandalized. PDA is her sworn enemy. Is *that* what she's upset about? Because honestly, I wouldn't be shocked if she was more horrified by me kissing my boyfriend in public than by the fact I didn't tell her I had one.

"Oh... that." It wasn't like I kissed him that night, planning to be the news tomorrow.

"But you're dating Alexander Bennetti." She says his name like he's some A-list celebrity.

"Yes, Mom. I am. For almost two months now." I try not to cringe at how surreal it sounds to say it out loud, knowing she's probably already Googling his net worth.

"Well, Vi, I'm upset I had to find out by reading it online." *Of course you are, Mom.* "Your father and I will be in New York on Sunday, so we wanted to take you and your boyfriend out for dinner."

Oh, you've got to be kidding me.

I press the phone against my forehead, gritting my teeth. "Sunday? Well, he's a big deal CEO, you know? He might be busy. Plus, we usually go to his parents' house for dinner." The second the words leave my mouth, I regret it. Why did I have to mention *that*? I can already picture my mom riding that statement like a wave in Malibu.

And, right on cue, she pounces. "Violet, you can skip your boyfriend's parents and spend time with your family. We haven't seen you in months."

She says it like it devastates her. Please. This woman could go a year without seeing me and wouldn't flinch. We've done it before—no big deal.

"Okay, I'll see if he's available, but no promises, Mom." I hang up before she can say more. We don't usually bother with "bye" or "I love you." Those words never entirely made it into our family's vocabulary.

I honestly can't remember the last time my parents said anything remotely affectionate or, god forbid, a compliment. Is that normal? Probably not.

Spending time with Alex's family has made me painfully aware of how dysfunctional mine is. No hugs, no family dinners, no real closeness. I have cousins I've never even met. Meanwhile, Alex's family is practically a small village. Sure, they're in each other's business, but in a caring way. It's not like they're gathering ammo to throw at you later.

"Sunday dinner with your parents *and* Alex?" Max raises a brow, leaning forward. "That's going to be..."

"Torture. I'd rather peel my skin off." I deadpan, slumping in my chair.

"Okay, dramatic much? I was going to say interesting."

Interesting? It's more like a nightmare.

"Now I have to warn Alex about my parents." A groan escapes me, thinking about the chaos that's about to unfold.

"I'm sure he's used to dealing with people like them." Max is too confident.

"Yeah, *he* might be, but I'm not." Every time my parents visit, I'm guaranteed to be an emotional train wreck. I spiral for at least a week, trying to shake off the feeling of inadequacy they always seem to leave behind. It's like I ate a bad taco, and it's taking its sweet time to work out of my system.

No matter what I achieve or how much progress I make, they always leave me feeling... empty. And I don't have the luxury of a weeklong pity party right now with two looming deadlines and Thanksgiving around the corner. Sitting on Max's couch, wallowing in self-pity, this time is not on the agenda.

Max stands up, leans over my desk, and softly kisses my forehead. "Good luck with that. I'll be waiting for the post-dinner horror stories."

Violet: My parents are coming into town and want to go to dinner with us on Sunday.

Alex: Oh, we're at the *meet the parents* stage now? Is this relationship getting serious?

Violet: Listen…

How do I even begin to explain this? He knows the basics about my parents, but knowing and *experiencing* them are very different. He's about to see the circus, which is my family. His family radiates warmth and togetherness. Mine? A cold, distant mess. And let's be honest, how long will he want to stick around after that?

I mean, I don't even see my parents for the holidays. They never ask me to come to California. I'm lucky if I get a "Merry Christmas" text, which usually shows up a week late. Two years ago, my mom forgot my birthday entirely. Instead, she texted me the next day to ask if I'd finished writing my book. Yeah, it's super festive. Happy birthday to me.

Alex: Still waiting over here for you to finish that thought…

Violet: My parents aren't like yours. We'll talk about it later.

Alex: Okay. Are you still going dress shopping with Alena today?

Violet: Yup, she needs a dress too.

Alex: If Alena's coming, she will make you spend a fortune. And you'll end up in something expensive.

Violet: Something tells me you can afford it.

Alex: It's not the money I'm worried about. I told you I want *some* cleavage, but Alena's going to make you look *too* good. I can't legally gouge out eyes at a wedding, no matter how many people are staring at my woman.

Violet: Maybe look into an anger management course before the wedding?

Alex: Just... don't let her talk you into anything that'll get me arrested.

Violet: No promises.

Alex: Hell...

I laugh, shaking my head. Alena's style is anything but tame. I've seen her outfits, and subtle is not in her vocabulary. But she's going as Dante's date to the wedding, which will be entertaining. Dante's dealership rents high-end cars to the Harringtons—a group of New York's elite—so he snagged an invite.

Now, I might be new to the dynamics of Alex's family, but something is brewing between Alena and Dante. They aren't *together*, but they're never apart. It's like watching a romantic drama unfold in real-time.

Still, I'm glad for the friendly faces. Alex will get pulled into business talk every five minutes at this wedding. It's inevitable. But lately, he's been glued to my side like I'm his buffer. And honestly? I don't hate it. Whether he's shielding himself from saying something regrettable or likes having me there, I'm not complaining.

Violet

TONIGHT'S ITINERARY: WEDDING FOLLOWED by doom tomorrow...meeting the parents. Pick your poison.

I'm standing in a dress that Alena and Valeria swore I had to have, and now here I am, wearing what costs more than a BMW. Alex paid before I could even think about escaping the price tag. It's a custom piece by some big-name designer I've never heard of.

But I won't lie—this dress is stunning. Rose gold is my ultimate weakness. The bodice fits like it was poured onto me, intricate lace weaving delicately across, catching the light with tiny sequins that add a soft sparkle. A sweetheart neckline gives just the right hint of cleavage, satisfying Alex's one request. The skirt flows in layers of soft tulle and organza, elegant without being over the top. Rose gold accents are woven through the fabric, with a hem that brushes the floor, finishing in a soft train.

I catch myself in the mirror and take in the back: a tasteful, low V-cut with rose-gold buttons trailing down from the waist. Let's say getting myself buttoned into this masterpiece took some severe gymnastics. I nearly asked Alex for help, but with the tension between us these days, chances are he wouldn't be buttoning anything up—more like tearing it off.

Glancing at the clock tells me he hasn't come knocking yet, but we've both been giving each other space. It is a smart move, considering our proximity lately has been nothing short of volatile.

When I left the guest room, he was in the foyer, adjusting his cufflinks.

Damn.

He didn't just look good; he looked unfairly gorgeous. Sexy. Sharp. A whole three-course meal wrapped in a perfectly tailored tux. Add a bow, and he might as well be my personal Christmas gift.

When his eyes landed on me, he froze, hand still on the cufflink. "Well, I'd say that was worth every penny." His gaze raked over me from head to toe, and I felt every inch of it. I'd gone all out tonight: more makeup than usual, a loose twist in my hair with a few strands framing my face. After all, this was a grand billionaire's wedding, and I had to look at the part.

"You don't look half bad yourself." I smiled, stepping forward to help with his cufflink.

The tension between us? Palpable. Like a warm blanket on a scorching day. It flushed through me as we stood there, close enough to feel each other's breaths, lingering in a way that made my heart skip. But then he blinked, took a small step back, and offered me his arm, guiding us to the car with a reserved but knowing smile.

Billionaire weddings are another level entirely. Like a red carpet event — press, flashing cameras, crowds. It's surreal. There must be at least 400 people here. I laugh a little as we walk in because a Harrington is getting married at the Grand Harrington, Manhattan's most luxurious hotel. If you own it, why not make it the wedding venue, right?

We weave through the crowd, occasionally pausing as someone stops Alex. He handles the introductions, giving his usual "This is Violet," and we move on. His hand stays on the small of my back, a warm, steady presence. As we near the ballroom, he wraps his arm around my waist, pulling me closer, and I feel that familiar thrill in my stomach.

We find our seats, which are somehow close to the altar. How well does he know this Griffin guy? Just as I settle in, excitement bubbles up in me, and I let out a little squeal.

"You seem more excited than the bride," Alex murmurs, settling beside me.

"I told you, I love weddings." I turn to give him a playful scowl, but he's just staring at me, blue eyes soft and glued to my mouth. I face forward again, soaking in the aisle lined with candles, silk tapestries, and flowers. Everything is like something out of a fairy tale. "It's so beautiful," I whisper as the lights dim, signaling the start.

He leans in close, his voice low. "What is it that makes you love them so much?"

"Other than being every romance writer's dream ending?" I smile, but he nudges me to go on.

"There's the bride, having her perfect day, her father with that tearful look as he gives her away." I pause, knowing I'll never experience that, but there's no need to ruin the moment. "And then the groom's reaction. Seeing their bride walk down the aisle does something to them, no matter how tough they are. Their real feelings come to the surface, raw and true. When they lock eyes... it's just magical."

He watches me as I gaze down the aisle. I hear his soft "I see," but my focus snaps to the doors opening. Charlotte Prescott appears, her father at her side, looking more nervous than she does.

"Wow, she's gorgeous," I murmur, half to myself. The woman beside me smiles, nodding in agreement. It's finally time for my favorite part. My eyes dart between Charlotte and her soon-to-be husband—Griffin, right? It's a weird name, but I'm here for the romance, not the names. I watch them like a hawk, waiting for that moment when they lock eyes, and the world disappears.

Alex's hand settles on my thigh, warm and steady. I look down, catching his hand curling around me while his other arm slips around my shoulders, pulling me close. I return to the ceremony, trying to focus, but his arm around me, all protective and adorable, makes it very hard to care about anything else. He's set a new wedding standard: cozy cuddles required.

Griffin spots Charlotte and suddenly stands taller, his face lighting up. When she meets his gaze, any nervousness melts off her face, her cheeks flush, eyes sparkling. I swear my heart's racing, and I'm just the spectator here.

Alex leans in, gently kissing my cheek, making me turn to him. His hand comes up, thumb grazing my cheek, and then he kisses my lips softly before returning to the ceremony like it's no big deal. This man...

The ceremony is beautiful, and soon, we're off to cocktails in the lobby while they prep the ballroom for the reception. Champagne in hand, I hang around as Alex talks business with associates, trying to make sense of it all. I'm piecing it together, though. He's got his hand in everything, but most of his billions are nestled in tech—cybersecurity firms here and abroad.

I'm introduced to so many people with names I'll never remember and wives who insist we'll "absolutely have to grab coffee soon," which we both know will never happen. Let's be honest—these women will forget my name the second they leave.

Finally, the reception kicks off, and thank god, because I'm starving. My genius self decided to barely eat yesterday just to fit into this overpriced dress. No way was I risking bloat in something worth more than my rent.

As we find our table, I can't help but gawk at the extravagant centerpieces and gold-plated everything. Alex, on the other hand, practically growls.

"What?" I ask, curious.

He leans in, lips brushing my ear. "Julian Stone's at our table. Griffin thinks he's funny."

"So... you two aren't exactly pals?"

"Far from it."

"Well, this should be fun," I whisper, grinning.

We take our seats, and Alex makes zero effort to hide his distaste. Across from us sits Julian, the poster boy for bad decisions, wrapped in a designer suit. His eyes—sharp silver-gray and a little too assessing—seem to gleam with some private joke only he's in on. Slicked-back hair, a cocky smirk, and that air of *"I'm better than you"* that oozes from every pore. Trouble, top to bottom. His date looks thrilled to be here, eyeing every man within range while he's blatantly checking out the scenery. Classy gal.

"Alex, nice to see you." Julian's voice is all smooth edges, but we both know he'd rather be anywhere else. Men in this world are pros at dressing up insults as pleasantries. Exhausting if you ask me.

"And you too," Alex replies, voice clipped.

Julian's gaze slides my way. "Care to introduce us to your date?"

Alex leans back, draping an arm over my chair, all casual possessiveness. "This is Violet Hart, my girlfriend."

"Oh, I know. Hard to miss those articles gushing over you two. It seems like there are already betting pools on wedding bells."

Alex raises a brow. "And what's your money on, Julian?"

Julian smirks, head cocked in that oh-so-condescending way. "Knowing you? Betting she'd say no the minute you asked."

Yeah... I wouldn't.

Did I say that to myself?

Julian's sharp gaze zeroes in on me, his eyes raking over me like he's sizing up prey. He's good-looking, sure—classic villain vibes with those razor-sharp cheekbones and a suit as black as his intentions. But his smile? It doesn't reach those cold, calculating eyes. It's like staring down a real-life Disney villain, only much less charming.

"So, Violet," he says, letting my name roll off his tongue with a slimy smoothness. I'm ready to change my name if it means never hearing him repeat it. "Your guy and I have been in a bidding war lately. I'm sure he's filled you in?"

He hasn't exactly spilled the details, but I nod anyway. Alex only mentions this man's name when he's deep in business talk, and I'm pretty sure he avoids it outside of work because the mere thought of Julian probably raises his blood pressure. Glancing at Alex, I catch that clenched jaw and the slight tick in his cheek.

Yeah, he hates this guy.

Julian dusts off an imaginary speck on his jacket before flicking his gaze back to me. "I know Alex isn't enjoying our little game. I, for one, am having a blast. Too bad your board had to reel you in and pull your bid."

Alex leans forward, propping his forearms on the table, hands clasped, his gaze locking on Julian with a force that sends a chill down my spine. "I don't make it a habit to overinflate prices just to entertain myself. If you want to burn cash on companies barely worth their valuation, that's your choice."

Something shifts in his expression—a flash of cold calculation, and it's like seeing another side of him, the one reserved for boardrooms and negotiations. "The fun part,

Julian," he says, voice low and measured, "was baiting you. Data Synthesis wasn't even on my radar. I wanted 64 Bit Securities, and guess who got it for a steal while you drove up the price of a company worth half of what you paid?"

His smile? It's this dangerously sexy, deadly smile—one part thrilling, two parts terrifying. And right now, I'm unsure if I should fan myself or hide.

Julian's smile falters just a fraction. Clearly, he didn't expect Alex to pull one over on him, but something about him screams that he won't let it happen again. Not that Alex seems fazed.

He leans back, adjusting his suit jacket with an infuriating calm. "My board? They don't tell me what to do. I ensured it leaked that they 'pulled the bid' so you'd pour money into the wrong company while I secured what I wanted." He pauses, the corner of his mouth lifting. "But don't worry, Julian. I'm sure we'll play again soon."

I make a mental note to ask Alex later what all that corporate lingo even means, but for now, I'm content with the aftermath.

Alex gives Julian one last subtle smirk, then stands and extends his hand to me. "Let's go mingle with some of the more important guests," he says, not even sparing Julian a glance as he helps me up.

Who knew the business world was so dramatic?

Alena spots me from across the room and, practically dragging Dante along, beelines in my direction. I've never seen a woman move so fast in five-inch heels. She makes it look as natural as sneakers.

"There you are!" she squeals, finally reaching us. One glance at her dress has me thanking my lucky stars. I didn't let her talk me into something similar. She's rocking this powder-blue number that clings to her like shrink wrap, barely grazing her thighs and holding up by the thinnest straps. It's all curves and cleavage, and she owns it. I... would not.

Dante takes a sip of his drink and shakes his head. "Still can't believe a woman agreed to marry Griffin," he mutters.

I don't know much about the groom, but how he looked at his bride almost made me swoon. "Is he that bad?"

Alex lets out a low chuckle. "You have no idea. The guy's a robot. They call him the Monster of Manhattan—and no, it's not a cute nickname."

"And yet, you're friends?" I raise an eyebrow.

Alex shrugs. "Friends enough for a wedding invitation, I guess. I know his brothers a bit better. They're... more human."

Dante nods, his expression unreadable.

From what I saw, the guy wasn't all that monstrous. But if he's earned that nickname in this cutthroat city, what's he done to deserve it?

Alex

"YOU HIRED ISABELLA MORETTI to make Violet's dress?" Alena's voice slices through the bar's low hum, hands on her hips, staring me down like I just offended fashion itself. Violet's nowhere in sight, so Alena's cornering me for answers. Perfect.

I shrug, playing it cool. "Uh, maybe?" I know she'll piece it together — Alena recognizes a custom Moretti dress on sight, and those don't happen unless it's for a hefty price tag or a particular order. I may have arranged a little surprise, choosing the dress in a color Violet would love, knowing she'd never buy it herself. She'd probably faint if she knew the cost.

And I'm not lying: the dress was worth every cent.

Alena taps her foot, eyes narrowing as she holds her gaze. Dante, beside me, raises an eyebrow, clearly entertained. He and my brothers knew about the arrangement with Violet, but Alena was out of the loop. She can't keep a secret to save her life; if she knew, all of Manhattan would, too, by now.

"Interesting..." Dante smirks, giving me a look with that damn eyebrow wiggle.

I'll admit, the whole thing's not exactly on brand for me. It may have been a touch extra, cashing in a favor from Isabella to rush the order. But hey, it was for the wedding—technically business attire, right? Besides, any doubts evaporated the second Violet walked out in that dress. A crime worth committing.

"Was Violet upset?" I ask, scanning the room for her as if she'd miraculously appeared.

"No," Alena says, crossing her arms. "I'm the one upset. I didn't tell her the dress was custom-made or that you paid god knows how much to have it done in record time." She grabs Dante's drink, downing it in one quick gulp. "The fact I didn't spill it is a miracle."

"Don't worry, babe," Dante cuts in, taking his drink back with a smirk. "He's only overcompensating with fancy dresses 'cause he can't just tell her he loves her, so this is his version of saying it."

I glare at Dante, then turn to Alena. "You told her?"

Alena rolls her eyes, undeterred. "Please, Alex. You bring home no one, then suddenly show up with some gorgeous girl? Of course, I hounded Dante until he cracked." She looks at him, and he shrugs unapologetically, his grin smug. Dante wants to be in my cousin's pants, so I'm sure he cracked under the slightest bit of pressure. "Don't worry, I'm not telling your mama or anyone else. They're already obsessed with her."

"Good," I mutter, knowing Mama would personally ensure I never saw another family dinner, and if I did, my balls would not be joining me.

"It's not just an arrangement anymore. We're dating," I clarify, needing Alena to understand that this isn't some convenient fling.

"Sure," Dante drawls. "But let's be real, you were just as smitten back when you still called it an 'agreement.' The only difference now is you look like a puppy with separation anxiety every time she leaves the room."

Alena snickers, clearly enjoying the show, and I turn to the bartender, signaling for another scotch to endure this conversation.

"Where is she, anyway?" I scanned the room, wondering why she hadn't returned with Alena from the ladies' room.

That's when Alena's lips twist into a grin I've known since childhood. The kind that means she's done something completely underhanded, and I will pay for it.

"Oh, I may have introduced her to Theo Harrington," she says, pointing across the room. "See? Just over there."

I follow her gaze, and there's Theo, looking far too interested, and Violet, giving him her full attention.

Dante shakes his head, but Alena beams. "You need a push, Alex. I've seen the way you look at her. You'd pee a circle around her if you could. And Theo's got a shot if you won't do anything. He's hot."

"Unbelievable," I grit out, my blood boiling as I watch Theo lean in, his attention locked on *my girlfriend.*

Yeah, fuck it, I said it. *My girlfriend.*

She's sipping champagne, head tipped back in laughter at whatever Theo just said. He's a good guy, and he's funny too. But right now? I'd be fine strangling him. He's got everything going for him—closer to her age, rich, good-looking, and, unlike me, he probably doesn't have to arrange fake dates to get a woman in his life either. But every possessive bone in my body screams that Violet's mine and the entire room should know it.

"I can practically see the wheels turning," Alena says from behind me, not missing a beat.

"You mean, watching him plot out how to punch Theo? Because that's what I'm seeing," Dante mutters, grabbing my arm just before I move. "Not my idea, by the way, just for the record in case shit goes down."

"Wow, way to support the team, Dante." Alena rolls her eyes, looking back at me, all sorts of wicked on that face. "Well, Romeo, go claim your girl before a rich, hot Harrington does."

"I hate you both," I mutter, but I'm already halfway across the ballroom, dodging people trying to get a minute of my time. Violet spots me first, her eyes locking on mine, and she gives me this smile that melts through whatever guarded layer I've got left. Hell, she's beautiful.

Theo turns as I approach. "Oh, hey! We were talking about you." He offers his hand, and I shake it, resisting every urge to do anything more because—despite myself—I like the guy. "I figured the gossip columns were just throwing out rumors, but you're actually in a relationship. After Natalia, I'm happy for you."

Damn it. Now, I can't hate him *or* hit him.

"Appreciate that," I say, slipping my arm around Violet's waist, lifting the champagne flute from her hand, and taking a sip before giving it back. "If you don't mind, I'd like to steal Violet for a dance."

"Of course," Theo says with a nod. "Let's catch up soon. We just acquired Prescott's hotel line, and there could be some potential for network security deals."

I flash a quick smile. "Set it up with my assistant." And with Violet in my arms, I lead her toward the dance floor. Now I get why Griffin Harrington got married.

"What?" Violet asks, her face upturned as I lead her to the dance floor. She's soft in my arms like she was meant to fit here, with her hands slipping naturally around my neck while I settle one hand against her lower back, pulling her close. Close enough that there's no room for anyone—or anything—else between us. Our faces are inches apart, and I swear I'm in trouble.

"Just thinking," I murmur, "we were all trying to figure out how Griffin convinced someone to marry him. It's probably a business move. Merger of sorts."

She gives me a horrified look. "Like... married to merge?"

I smirk, keeping my eyes locked on hers as we sway. "Arranged marriages are more common in our world than you'd think." She's so petite in my arms, so close, it feels like I could hold her there all night. "So, thinking of snagging yourself a Harrington? They have businesses in tropical spots, which are more fun than mine."

She rolls her eyes, clearly trying not to laugh. "A few months ago, maybe. He's hot."

I stop us, hand tightening on her back, pulling her flush against me as she bursts into laughter. She grabs my face, her fingers warm against my jaw, forcing me to meet my gaze. "Besides, he has no chance."

"Oh yeah?" I tilt my head, amused. "What's stopping you?"

"Developed a taste for Italian lately. And I'm not done yet." Her voice is low, teasing.

Dear god, this woman.

Not for show.

Not for cameras all over us.

Not for those on the dance floor watching us.

I take her face in my hands, brushing my lips against hers before I press in deeper, letting the kiss linger, slow and sure. My fingers hold her chin, guiding her as I slip my tongue into her mouth, tasting her warmth and sweetness. Her arms loop around my neck, pulling me closer, meeting me with a softness that just might kill me. This isn't the kind of kiss that devours or demands; it's deliberate, steady. It's every feeling I haven't put into words yet, pouring into her with every slow movement, and from the way she's kissing me back, I wonder if she feels the same.

When I finally pull away, I look into her eyes, and she gives me a mischievous smile. "What?" I murmur.

She tilts her head, eyes glinting. "Told you, I'm developing a taste for Italian."

Fucking hell if that look isn't the most mischievous thing I've ever seen. Those green eyes of hers were practically a cauldron of trouble.

I lean close, letting my lips graze her ear, and ask, "How much are you craving right now?"

She tilts her head, putting on that thoughtful expression that drives me crazy, but then rises on her tiptoes, her mouth so close to my ear I can feel the heat of her words. "Let's just say... I wouldn't mind dessert. Every. Single. Inch. I can get."

Fuck me.

That confident, sexy Violet from the bar is right in front of me in complete form and then some.

If my body hasn't betrayed me already, it's right on the edge, taking every last shred of control to keep it together. If we weren't on a crowded dance floor, there'd be no question about where this would end up.

"Then I'd say we need to get you your dessert. Now."

She licks her lips, and that wicked spark in her eyes makes it harder for me to keep any trace of composure. I'm like a teenager again with how quickly my cock twitches as her tongue sweeps across those lips. "I think we should."

I can barely swallow. I've never been this close to losing my mind.

Violet

Maybe it was how he looked at me before we left or that possessive glint in his eyes that found me in the crowd, but something snapped inside me. Screw skirting around it. I'm dating a ridiculously hot man, and I have needs.

Emotionally, this might wreck me, but right now? I want him. Need him. Crave him. You get it.

He's given me more orgasms than I thought possible, and I have a feeling that if he takes things to the level I just not-so-subtly hinted at? I'm done for. If he fucks anything like what he does with that mouth, I'm a goner.

The second we're in the car, his mouth is on mine, fiery and unrestrained. The kiss is hot and hungry, pulling every shred of self-control from my body and replacing it with pure heat. His hands tangle in my hair, letting it spill free, and I swear this is the hottest make-out session of my life. One second it's intense and all-consuming; the next, he's slowing it down, making it sweet, almost reverent. Every nerve in my body is lit up, and I don't even register the car stopping until Antonio clears his throat, giving us a cough that pulls us back to reality.

Well. That's awkward. But it was worth every second. I'll find a way to look Antonio in the eye again another day.

Alex thanked Antonio, and we managed to pull ourselves together, but the moment the elevator doors closed, his restraint unraveled. He pressed me against the wall, his leg slipping between mine, anchoring me in place as his mouth claimed mine all the way to the penthouse. Each floor only seemed to build the tension higher, and by the time we reached his door, I was grateful the elevator opened practically at his front step.

The second the door clicked shut, I felt myself pressed against it, my back to his chest. His lips traced a slow path up my neck, along my shoulder, and right back up to my ear. At first, his hands stayed on my hips, keeping me tight against him, but soon, they were at the buttons of my dress, fumbling with each one.

"Remind me never to buy you a dress with so many damn buttons," he muttered, frustration clear in his tone, and I couldn't help but laugh, squirming under his touch as he took his time with each one. When the fabric finally slid off my shoulders, pooling at my feet, he spun me around to face him. His gaze dropped to my black lace lingerie, lingering on each tantalizing inch of exposed skin.

"Fuck," he growled, fingers tracing down my ribs and up to the lace cupping my breasts. His eyes darkened as he took in every barely covered, totally not innocent detail. "While we're making reminders, don't forget to stock up on this...exclusively."

The way he bit his lower lip had my thighs clenching, heat pooling as his gaze traveled down my body. His fingers traced over my hips, hooking into the straps of my thong, his thumb teasing along the delicate string as if he was debating—rip it off or slowly slide it down.

"Alex?" I whispered, my voice barely steady.

"Hmm?" He didn't take his eyes off that one stubborn piece of fabric until I pressed myself against him, one hand firm on his chest, the other tangled in the hair at his neck. His gaze snapped up, and then his mouth crashed into mine, a hard, claiming kiss. Before I could catch my breath, his hands gripped my ass, lifting me as my legs wrapped around him, and he carried me into the bedroom, setting me down at the foot of the bed.

He ripped off his tie as I fumbled with the buttons on his jacket, our mouths colliding whenever we could manage between tugging off clothes. Piece by piece, fabric hit the floor until he stood in only briefs, his body on full display—muscles cut like marble. That tattoo snaked across his side, giving him a rugged edge, contradicting his always-in-control CEO demeanor.

I was still in my heels when he unhooked my bra, flinging it across the room before slipping a finger under my thong. He pulled it down slowly, trailing kisses along my thighs that made my skin tingle. When he reached my ankles, he glanced up with a smirk and gave me a playful shove, making me fall back onto the bed.

"As much as I want to fuck you with these on, that's for another time," he murmured, sliding the heels off one by one, followed by the thong. He stood, tugging me closer to the edge of the bed until my face was level with his chiseled chest.

Seriously, how does a man have pecs like that? All those early mornings at the gym paid off; now, that body was mine to explore. I'd be lying if I said I wasn't tempted to run my tongue over every hard line and curve of his skin.

His hands gripped my hips, firm and possessive, as I stood completely naked before him for the first time. My fingers hooked into the waistband of his boxer briefs, and I tugged them down, watching them fall to the floor. Our breaths mingled, ragged and heavy with anticipation. Then, he wrapped his arms around my waist, lifting me effortlessly further up the bed. His body covered mine, and when our skin finally pressed together, I gasped. We'd played around plenty, but this? This was uncharted territory—no barriers, no distractions—just heat and hunger.

His fingers trailed between my thighs, teasing my folds, and he hissed, "Already so wet," while his mouth latched onto my nipple, making me arch against him.

Reality smacked into me like a cold wave. This was happening. And I knew myself. I'm the kind of person who thinks and feels with her whole heart and, yes, her body, too. Once I crossed this line with Alex, there'd be no going back for me. It wouldn't be just a hookup; it would mean more to me, regardless of his feelings.

"Alex, wait," I whispered, feeling the nerves twist inside me as his fingers tangled in my hair.

He paused, his intense eyes searching mine, burning with a heat that made me shiver. "What is it?" His voice was low, rough around the edges, like he was fighting for control.

I bit my lip. My timing was the worst. "I can't... We can't do this if it's just something casual. I know we haven't exactly defined what we are, but—"

He put a hand over my mouth, his lips brushing my ear as he leaned in. "We both know we've been something since I met you. I don't just want you, Violet. I need you."

His words melted every bit of hesitation, especially when he kissed me again—slow, deliberate like he was sealing a promise with his lips. He pulled back just enough to look me in the eyes, his forehead resting against mine. "I want to take my time with you, but right now... I have zero control."

You and me both.

A moan slipped out as his fingers teased my entrance, sliding inside me while his thumb pressed against my swollen clit. His mouth crashed into mine, swallowing every sound that escaped like he needed to taste the effect he had on me.

Then he paused, reaching for the nightstand. "I need one thing first," he muttered, voice rough with need. "Condom."

I grabbed his wrist, pulling him back. "I'm on the pill."

He froze, eyes locked on mine, searching. "I've never... fuck it," he said, his resolve slipping away. He moved between us, slowly dragging the tip of his cock through my wetness, savoring every inch before lining himself up. His lips brushed against mine, a whisper of a kiss, as he eased just the tip inside, teasing and torturously slow.

I knew he was big, but as he was slowly stretching me, a delicious combination of burn and pleasure, I realized just how big he was. Every second of being stretched has turned my brain to mush and anything else that belongs to my body.

"Fuck you're tight," his hand gripping my hip as his other tangles in my hair. His mouth is on mine, his kiss deep, hungry, like every tether of control he has is slipping, and he needs to kiss me to keep himself calm. Our kiss was like tongue delivered Xanax, every ounce of tension leaking from my body, each lingering swipe kept me centered. He slides in another inch, and it's torturous. Not the stretching but the pace. Like he needs to draw out the experience, and I welcome it, wanting to savor every second of this first time, knowing very well that he won't keep it slow much longer.

I kiss him back just as deeply, loving how he groans, his hips moving gently as he presses himself in, his back muscles tensing under my grip, and wet heat flooding my channel. Every muscle of his body shutters as he tries hard to hold back, not wanting to take it at the pace I know he needs. He's not the only one overwhelmed with that carnal need. My body hums, my pussy throbbing as that flame inside of me starts to lick and nip at me, begging for him to let go.

When our mouths part, it isn't far; his lips are so close to mine that I can brush mine across his. "It's okay..." I look at his gorgeous blue eyes, eyes full of lust and crazed. He's been very patient, and I know he has little self-control left. "Fuck me, Alex," I whisper against his mouth, and he obliges, thrusting himself into me hard, deep, and when every inch of him fills me so quickly, I arch my body into his, gripping his shoulders with my nails and probably leaving marks. He was still on top of me, kissing me and giving me a minute before his hips slowly rolled into me, making circles, stretching me to adjust to him.

"Oh god, Alex..." I whimper it into his ear with each movement.

Cupping my face, he said into my mouth, "I'm going to fuck you hard, but if you think that's all you're getting tonight, you're wrong." He groans into my ear. "You feel too fucking good..."

I couldn't respond with anything more than a whimper because I wanted it.

His thighs keep my legs open, even though I try to squeeze myself around him with them as he slides himself out and drives back in. With every pull and thrust, my body rewards him with more wet heat.

"Alex..." I moaned into his ear, gripping his shoulders as the force of him consumed me. Every inch of him was too much, yet he was just right.

"Can I tell you something?"

Are we talking while doing this? I guess we are.

"Ye....Yes..." I gasped as he thrust into me again.

"I've never done this without a condom," he thrust again harder. "I'm never wearing one with you, that's for fucking sure." He practically growls it out between gritted teeth, his length pumping in and out of me at a fierce pace, my breath barely having time to fill my lungs before he plunges deeper, harder.

Pleasure builds so intensely, and I've never gotten off during sex. I don't know if it's his size or the way his body is taking me hard, claiming me most intimately, but an orgasm builds, tingling through my body, spiraling into my stomach and through my spine. When he pushes deeper, he rubs against something so deep inside of me that I can feel my body pulling apart thread by thread, and when his hand grips my throat, applying just enough pressure to hold me, it is so dominating, and god, it is incredibly sexy, I unravel completely.

I arch as a violent orgasm tears through me like a Kansas tornado tears through the plains, my body convulsing around him. I can feel every inch and ripple of his cock as he slows his pace, pumping himself just right to milk out every spasm of my orgasm before he says something in Italian, his hand gripping my hip for leverage as he thrusts into me deeper and harder, his cock swelling as he comes with me, his grip so tight on my hip I'm going to have a bruise and I don't care, even as his hips continue rolling into me as he empties himself inside of me.

We're both panting, breaths mingling as he cradles my face, kissing me slow and sweet like he's savoring every second. It's a stark contrast to the way he just took me—brutal, relentless, and utterly mind-blowing—but the sheen of sweat on both of us gives it all away. He's still inside me, body heavy against mine like he can't bear to let go, and honestly, I'm not complaining.

I thread my fingers through his hair, pulling him closer and deepening the kiss. No one has ever taken me like that before, and even if I'll be sore later, it's a small price to pay.

Something is intoxicating about how he presses his weight into me, his lips brushing mine like this is more than just physical. It feels like the start of something that could matter and that we are both on the same page for the first time.

Alex

I'VE HAD SEX WITH women before, but never have I felt this kind of unbearable need—this raw, consuming hunger. I wanted to be slow, to savor her, to coax every moan and sigh out of her. But after weeks of teasing and tension, I couldn't hold back. I devoured her. And now, without a condom between us, I'm ruined for life.

Feeling her—every inch, every pulse—made it clear that I'll never want anyone else. I've known it since the moment she walked into that bar. But admitting that out loud? She'd think I was crazy. Honestly, I'm thinking it myself, but that doesn't change a damn thing.

I made good on my promise, finding myself hard not even ten minutes after having her because I couldn't get enough. This time, though, I slowed down. I took my time. Went deep. And every sound she made, every gasp and breathy moan, just drove me wilder.

I needed more of her.

Always more.

She moved beneath me, her body arching and writhing, nails dragging down my back and pulling at my hair. It was maddening and addictive. I gripped her hand, intertwining our fingers and pressing it down beside her head. My other hand tangled in her hair, that wild mess I couldn't get enough of. My mouth barely left hers—I couldn't breathe without tasting her. Her moans vibrated against my lips, filling my lungs with a rush I'd never felt before.

Fucking hell, I am in love with this woman. And it's not because of the sex—it's everything but that. It's like going without it for so long made us see each other, really see each other, and this? This just solidified what was already there.

I keep my movements slow, my hips rolling into hers, drawing out every moan that slips from her lips. It's torturous in the best way.

I want to linger on that edge, to savor every second. I wasn't wrong when I thought she'd be the woman you could lose yourself in for days. Now that I have her, I don't want it to end. Each thrust sends a jolt through me as I feel her tighten around me, our bodies slick with sweat, the room filled with the sounds of her arousal and my deep, steady rhythm.

When she finally tumbles over that edge, I follow her, pressing my cock in deep, letting myself get lost in the way she breathes my name, the way her body spasms around me as I come with her. I grip the comforter, anchoring myself as I release inside her, shuddering with a force I've never felt before.

I knew it would be good with her—hell, I knew it'd be mind-blowing—but I didn't expect it to feel like this. Like a missing puzzle piece snapping into place, that last edge piece you never knew you needed until you find it. And now that it's here, everything makes sense.

Emotionally and mentally, I was already in too deep. I told myself the physical part was just lust, but it's more. It's her. I've never felt a connection like this, like she's electric in my arms, charging every nerve in my body. My chest still heaves as I roll us to our sides, pulling her against me, holding her like she might vanish if I let go. Maybe it's primal or crazy, but I can't seem to loosen my grip.

Her face nestles into my chest, her breath warm against my skin, and I keep her close, my arm wrapped around her while my other hand traces gentle patterns up and down her back. Her skin is like silk under my fingertips, and I try—unsuccessfully—to ignore the way my body reacts, my cock going from semi-hard to throbbing just from touching her. I have a month to compensate for, and my body is cashing in the favor.

Waiting a month to have her like this nearly drove me insane. I've never been easy in the boardroom—I mean, you don't build an empire in New York by being a teddy bear—but lately, even Penelope has pointed out my attitude. She claims I should be the happiest guy around, given I'm "off the market" now. And okay, she has a point. But each week that went by, with this maddening tension between Violet and me, only added to a mountain of frustration that no amount of...personal relief could fix. I was a storm waiting to happen, and everyone knew better than to test me.

Maybe Monday, I'll be less of an ass. Doubtful. But I might be a little less...on edge.

"Alex?" Her voice is soft against my chest, barely a whisper, and she snuggles closer. Her arms wrap around me, and something inside me loosens, even as it makes me uneasy. Vulnerability isn't my thing, yet here I am, thinking about how I wouldn't mind being tangled up with her forever. Dangerous thoughts. Ones that could leave me open to getting wrecked.

"Hmmm?" I murmur, tightening my hold just a bit. She shifts, not to escape, but to pull back enough to look at me, and I'm done for. Completely. Physically, emotionally, all of it.

The first time I saw her, I thought she was stunning—one of the most beautiful women I'd ever laid eyes on. But seeing her like this, cheeks flushed, hair tousled, glowing from being freshly fucked... I'm pretty sure that image is seared into my mind for life.

No one else is ever going to see her like this if I have a say in it. She's mine, whether she knows it or not.

"You have a deliciously dirty mouth," she says, and even in the dim light, I catch the glint in those green eyes of hers. It's that look that undoes me—sweet, but with a hint of something wicked beneath the surface.

"Is that so?" I try to play it cool, though my pulse is anything but. She hasn't heard half of the things I want to say to her, but I'd gladly spill every thought in my head if she asked.

She bites her lip, that coy smile curving her lips. "No vanilla dirty talk from you."

I grip her hips, rolling her onto her back, kissing her deeply, feeling the unspoken words stuck in my throat. They're right there, but I hold them back, self-preservation kicking in now that the haze of the best sex of my life has cleared just a bit.

"How sore are you, baby?" I ask, trying to keep my voice steady.

She raises an eyebrow, a smirk playing on her lips. "Baby? That what we're calling me now?"

I shrug, playing it off like it's no big deal, even though it slipped out without me even thinking. I'm not the type for pet names—they usually make me cringe—but for her, I'd call her my sun, moon, and stars if it'd make her smile.

Nudging against her with my still-hard length, I smile, letting my fingers trace over her thighs, feeling the heat of her skin. "How sore are you?" I nip at her bottom lip, rubbing my tip against her, feeling her slickness as I get ready to push inside her again. I've already come twice, and it's nowhere near enough. "I have a few more dirty words I want to share..."

She scrunches her brows, pretending to think it over, and damn, she's adorable.

"Not that sore," she finally says, a playful edge in her voice.

"Thank fuck for that," I murmur because there's no way I'm holding back now. Foreplay can wait—I need to be inside her. I don't give her a chance to say anything more before I thrust into her, hard and deep.

She's addictive, a need that's burrowed deep inside me, and I'm pretty sure I'll never get enough. Every moan, every gasp fuels me, my hands roaming her curves, gripping her ass, guiding her leg around my hip until I find that perfect spot. When she arches off the bed, crying out my name, I know I've found heaven. Even as she's coming down, I keep moving, slow and steady, letting the pleasure build again, feeling the tension coil inside me. Her body clenches around me, and I'm right there with her, a release that steals the air from my lungs. I collapse against her, still buried deep, my chest heaving as I whisper her name like a prayer.

And even now, with us tangled together, my need for her doesn't fade. It only deepens. Mentally, emotionally, physically—I want more. Always more.

Alex

"Okay, so clearly you got laid, but I don't think I should have to pay up on the bet. You hustled me." Dante leans against the locker, tossing a towel over his shoulder, irritated he bet like a cocky bastard and lost.

I wipe the last droplets from my face, toweling off after my shower at the club. "How do you figure that?"

"Because as far as I knew, you were walking around with a permanent case of blue balls. If I'd known you were, you know, *relieved*, I wouldn't have bet a grand a game."

I try to keep my grin in check, but my mind drifts back to the shower earlier this morning, and Violet—wet, soapy, utterly irresistible. "A man should always know what he's getting into before placing a bet. Consider it a life lesson." I toss the towel into the laundry bin and pull on my clothes.

"You're a dick." Dante shakes his head but reaches for his phone to Venmo me the money. Friend or not, we always settle our bets. And after he'd cleaned me out the past few weeks when my mind was anywhere but the game, I'm soaking up every dollar sign that pings on my phone now.

I was surprised he won today, even with the tension relieved. Sure, I wasn't distracted by my previous frustrations anymore, but my head was still full of Violet—every way she'd made me forget the world outside my bed. And how many ways I'd like to make her forget it, too.

I glance at my phone and see the Venmo notification with a not-so-subtle emoji in the note. "Real mature," I mutter, smirking as I slip on my suit jacket.

I knew this match would bleed into the afternoon, and with dinner looming with Violet and her parents, I'd come prepared. I told her I'd meet her at the restaurant—no sense keeping her waiting when the only place I want to be right now is by her side.

I knew Violet wasn't close with her parents, but I hadn't expected the relationship to be this toxic. I didn't realize just how deep the damage ran until Violet started opening up.

Sure, my family had their expectations, but if I'd told them I wanted to quit everything and become a street poet, they wouldn't act like I didn't exist. They'd at least pretend to support me or make a joke about it over Sunday dinner. But Violet? Her parents practically erased her the moment she veered off their chosen path. They stripped away her confidence, leaving scars she's still trying to cover up.

She wants to be a writer. I see those wheels turning in her head every time she drifts off mid-conversation, already plotting some new story. She's intelligent, witty, and if anyone could write a damn good book, it's her. And who decides being an author isn't a real career? Even if I don't read romance, I know half the world does. If she wants to take a swing at it, why shouldn't she? No parent should withhold love and affection because their child didn't squeeze into a box made up solely of their expectations.

I haven't even met these people yet and already dislike them.

"What's that look for?" Dante's voice snaps me back, and I realize I'm frowning as I adjust my tie, reaching for my jacket.

"What look?"

He's already dressed, of course. The man could win a gold medal for the fastest transformation from a towel to a three-piece suit. I swear, he times himself just for fun. Meanwhile, I'm here trying to figure out how to put on my best poker face for two people who don't deserve to be in the same room as Violet, let alone call her their daughter.

"Meeting Violet's parents today for dinner," I say, and Dante probably hears a different kind of reluctance in my tone. He thinks I'm nervous about the "meet the parents" milestone, but that's not it. I'm not afraid of what meeting them means for us. Hell, I'm committed to this relationship. No, what grates on me is that I despise toxic people, and Violet's parents sound like they wrote the book on it.

I knew Violet wanted to talk this morning. Hell, I'd wanted to have an honest conversation last night, but then she went and got naked, and suddenly, talking wasn't on my list of priorities. I need her fully clothed and at least three feet away to have a serious discussion. My self-control is hanging by a thread, and the idea of sitting next to her at dinner tonight brings up way too many dirty thoughts—thoughts I'm failing to hide, judging by the way Dante is eyeing me like I've lost my mind.

"Care to elaborate on that?" He gestures up and down my face, clearly noticing my smirk.

"Her parents are... a piece of work," I reply. "Not exactly looking forward to meeting them."

A thought strikes me, one that I quickly try to shove into a mental box labeled *way too soon*: If I ever want to marry this woman, would she want the whole traditional thing—like me asking her dad for permission? The idea of me asking *them* for anything makes my teeth clench. But then I wonder if it even matters to her. We've talked about a lot but haven't touched on family traditions or what she sees in her future. The fact that I'm even entertaining the idea has my mind running in a million different directions.

On paper, we've been together two months—solid enough to be serious but not epic, not a grand love story... yet. But the reality? It's just been a little over a month. We've spent countless nights together, shared dinners, and too many conversations that went way past midnight. She practically lives in my house now. A month might be just over 700 hours, but I know those numbers because time has always been precious.

Except now, those minutes and hours can slip through my fingers whenever she's around. Time that used to be carefully measured and managed is now tangled up with thoughts of her—her laugh, the way she brushes her hair out of her face when she's focused, the way her eyes light up when she talks about her favorite books. And somehow, all those precious seconds I used to guard so carefully feel like a damn good investment when I'm spending them on her.

I'm a walking game of racquetball. One moment, I'm ready to say screw it and confess to Violet that I'm in love with her—yes, even though it's only been a month. But it's been one hell of a month. Then, the ball ricochets against the rational part of my brain, reminding me it's too soon.

So, where will the ball land now versus five minutes from now? Hell if I know. This morning, I almost let it slip that I love her. Truly, head-over-heels. But I caught myself, knowing she might think it's just the physical side talking—the lust that built up over weeks, the craving that finally snapped last night. But the truth is, I realized I loved her long before we hit the sheets. The sex just... cemented it and made me certain I wasn't getting out of this.

Securing my locker, I try to refocus and tamp down the chaos in my head. My mood is decent—better than it has been, even with the emotional whirlpool I'd rather not dive into right now.

That is until I turn and spot Julian.

I run into Julian often, but lately, it's like he's taken up permanent residence in my life since Violet showed up. It's almost like the universe decided to balance the good she brings with the toxic sludge he embodies.

"Fucking hell," I mutter, not bothering to hide the words as he steps up to Dante and me. Dante despises Julian as much as I do and doesn't hide it either.

"You boys enjoy playing with your balls?" Julian's smirk is as slimy as ever.

"That's the best you've got? 'Playing with our balls'? Come on, Julian, try a little harder. Maybe reference our *very large* balls next time," I shoot back, deadpan. Dante snorts beside me, barely holding back his amusement.

Julian's smirk doesn't falter as he pivots. "How's Violet?"

Just hearing her name from his mouth makes my fists itch. Of all people to know about my history with Natalia, it's him—because he was one of the ones she slept with while she was supposed to be my fiancée. And she wasn't just sharing her body; she was sharing my business secrets, too. So, my hatred for Julian? It goes way beyond his sleazy business practices. The guy has zero integrity.

"She's great," I reply, keeping my tone flat, then gesture behind me. "On my way to meet her and her parents for dinner." I pull my phone from my jacket pocket, scrolling through emails that don't interest me in the slightest—because anything is better than talking to Julian.

He raises a brow, amusement flickering in his eyes. "Oh, that serious, huh? Maybe I'll lose that bet after all."

I'll make damn sure of it.

"Pleasure as always," I lie smoothly, tucking my phone away and stepping past him without another glance.

Dante trails behind me, muttering, "How you keep your cool around him should earn you a medal. He says two words to me, and I'm ready to deck him."

"Yeah, well, some things are worth the restraint," I reply, thinking of Violet. And tonight, even with her parents on the horizon, I'm determined to keep things under control—for her.

Trust me, I know better. If it weren't for the gossip columns constantly sniffing around—especially now that my relationship has become prime clickbait for bloggers and media vultures—I'd have no problem rearranging Julian's smug face in the locker room. But I have to think about the company image. It is never a good look when the CEO gets arrested for assault, no matter how satisfying it might be.

So, instead, I keep playing the game. I am baiting Julian with companies I don't care about to see how far I can push him to overpay. The last one? Total dick move, and I had to explain it to Violet later. She's adorable when trying to grasp the nuances of business transactions, asking questions with those wide, curious eyes. I didn't share much detail. I've been permanently closed about my company, especially after what happened with Natalia.

Every man Natalia slept with got a piece of my business, shared through pillow talk. Half my staff became jobless because she wrangled company secrets out of them and handed them straight to my competitors. It's not that I don't trust Violet—hell, I trust her more than I've trusted anyone in years. But I've learned that mixing business and pleasure can go very wrong.

But I explained the cat-and-mouse game I play with Julian, mostly because she seemed intrigued after the wedding. She laughed when I told her about it. And I mean really laughed. Her giggle—it's pure, unfiltered joy, and for some reason, it's only endearing coming from her. Any other woman might've sounded clueless, but with Violet, it's different. That's who she is, and I wouldn't change a damn thing about it.

Alex

Antonio pulls up in front of the restaurant, and I step out, buttoning my coat. He holds the door open with a smile. "What?" I ask, eyeing him suspiciously.

"I dropped off Miss Hart earlier," he says, using her formal name with that old-school formality. He and I both know she insists on being called Violet, but he wouldn't dare in my presence. One of the many things I want Violet to embrace is that respect isn't optional. In this city, using a last name carries weight. You reserve the privilege of first-name familiarity for those who earn it.

"And how was she?" I ask, even though I know she's dreading this dinner as much as I am.

"Nervous. She rambled the entire way, from wanting to cancel to saying never mind. It took her five minutes to convince herself to leave the car."

Damn. If I'd realized how worked up she'd be, I wouldn't have let her face this alone. I should've picked her up instead of letting her come here solo while I met her. But I nod at Antonio, accepting this as another moment where I should've done better, and head inside.

I made the reservation myself, and while there's usually a six-month waitlist, a few name drops and a reminder of old favors got us a table right away. I know this place is far from the trendy, modern spot Violet initially suggested. It's not that the restaurant she picked was bad, but it wouldn't cut it for this particular dinner.

First, her billionaire boyfriend wasn't about to be seen in some Instagrammable eatery. Second, I wanted her parents to see she was not the failure they thought she was. They needed to step into a place where they'd never get a table themselves—where they'd see that Violet, their so-called "disappointment," was doing just fine without them. Maybe it's a bit over the top, but I'll take my wins where I can get them, especially when it means proving a point.

Or maybe I'm just projecting my issues with status onto this dinner. Either way, it's too late for second-guessing now.

The hostess recognizes me immediately. "Mr. Bennetti, your party is already waiting for you at the table."

I glance at my watch. Am I late? Regret hits me for leaving Violet alone with her parents for even a minute. I follow the hostess through the dining area, nodding at a few familiar faces along the way, and then we reach the back, where the more private tables are tucked away. Relief washes over me when I see only Violet there, nursing a large glass of white wine—half gone already. She's wearing this simple yet stunning black dress, and despite the nerves radiating off her, she looks perfect.

I place my hand on her bare back, feeling the warmth of her skin against mine, a welcome contrast to the cold tension I'd carried in. Her head snaps, and when those green eyes land on me, they light up. Before I can think twice, she's up, wrapping her arms around me, and I kiss her, not caring if the hostess is left fumbling with the wine menu behind us. I only pull away when I feel the tension ease from her shoulders, her smile becoming a little less forced.

But even as she smiles, I see that brightness fading from her eyes—like a candle flickering before going out. It's the same look she gets whenever her parents come up in a conversation. And it hits me right in the gut how these people drain the life from her, leaving her deflated and small.

I cup her cheek, forcing her to look into my eyes. "We don't have to do this. We can leave right now. I have... other ways to make you feel better." My voice drops, and the blush that rushes to her cheeks tells me she knows exactly what I'm suggesting. Hell, if I don't control myself, I'll pull her into a corner of this restaurant, and I don't think either of us would mind.

Before I can decide whether to make good on that thought, she freezes, her face paling as she looks over my shoulder. It's like someone just flipped a switch, draining all the color from her. I turn to see what—or who—has caused her to shut down like that, and my grip on her hand tightens, intertwining our fingers. Two people walk toward us, and I know, without needing an introduction, that these must be her parents.

Her mother is striking, with the same wavy brown hair and green eyes as Violet. The resemblance is impossible to miss. But where Violet's eyes are vibrant and alive, hers feel like shards of glass—sharp and cutting. Or maybe that's just my bias talking because, honestly, I don't like her. The sour curve of her lips isn't helping her case either. Trailing behind her is an older man, hair a mix of gray and stubborn streaks of black, his beard neatly trimmed. He's tanned, probably from their sunny California lifestyle, and stands about my height. Their outfits scream California chic—more relaxed than you'd find in

Manhattan. But I've never judged by clothes. I size up the attitude, the aura they bring into a room. And these two? They're bringing a storm.

"There you are, dear. I was impressed to hear you managed to get a reservation here. But of course, I'm sure your... friend had something to do with that," her mother says, her gaze sliding to me with a practiced smile that feels more like a challenge than a greeting. It's time to put on my game face. I return her smile, feeling Violet's hand tighten around mine like she's hanging on for dear life.

"I wanted only the best for my Violet." I might've laid it on thick with the possessive edge, but I'm not letting these people think they can waltz in and treat her like she's lesser. She's mine—my world—and they'd better respect that if they plan on making it through dinner without regret.

Her mother extends a hand, introducing herself as Victoria with a practiced ease. Her father doesn't even glance at Violet, which has my blood simmering. He looks straight at me, offers a handshake, and introduces himself as Richard. I grip his hand firmly, keeping my expression neutral. "Pleasure to meet you both," I reply smoothly, then turn to pull out Violet's chair, helping her settle in before I take my place beside her.

The dining area is just how I wanted it—exclusive, with only three tables on this level and a server ready to jump at our slightest nod. The space between tables ensures no one can eavesdrop, making it the perfect spot for a conversation that might get uncomfortable.

Under the table, I rest my hand on Violet's thigh, feeling the tension in her body. Her small, clammy hand covers mine, trying to keep steady, but I can feel the anxiety thrumming through her. It's like she's bracing for impact, and we haven't even ordered food yet. The more I watch her unravel in the presence of her parents, the more I realize just how deep those scars go.

I order a bottle of their best red and white, figuring we'll need a little extra liquid courage before this ends. My focus stays on her, even as I make the request. I can see her jaw clenched and her gaze fixed downward as she twists the edge of the tablecloth between her fingers. The sight of her like this—so tense, unlike the woman I know—makes me wish I could sweep her out of here and remind her that she's worth more than whatever these two think of her.

"So, Mr. Bennetti," her father starts, his voice smooth and measured, the kind you'd expect from a man who plays the part of the polished gentleman but has a hidden edge. I recognize that tone because I've used it, masking the darkness beneath a polished smile. "I was surprised to hear you and my daughter were dating."

Seriously? That's the opening line?

I lean back in my chair, shifting slightly, trying to calm myself and keep the heat of irritation from creeping up my neck. I lift our intertwined hands, kiss her knuckles, and feel Violet's tension ease a bit. When the wine arrives, I take my glass, swirling the deep red liquid before sipping. "And why is it that you're so surprised?"

He gives a tight-lipped smile that doesn't reach those judgmental eyes. "Well, you're a successful CEO here in Manhattan. I wouldn't expect you and our Vi to run in the same circles. I'm just curious how you two even crossed paths, let alone started dating."

I'd love to spin some romantic tale about how I fell for her the moment I saw her in that bar, but that's not the narrative that'll fly with this guy. Instead, I lean forward, setting my glass on the table, keeping my tone smooth and controlled. Violet's hand tightens in mine, and I give her a reassuring squeeze. "To be honest, sir, there's no one quite like your daughter. Maybe we don't come from the same social circle, but that's exactly why I'm so drawn to her. No other woman compares to what Violet has—her spirit, her smile, the way she holds herself. I don't date much. I tend to focus on my work but with Violet? I'd sell my company if it meant I could spend just five more minutes with her daily."

I can feel Violet's eyes on me, wide and curious, but I don't look at her. Those words were real, not just some carefully crafted line to impress her parents, and I was not ready to face her reaction to hearing it aloud.

Her father studies me, then glances at Violet with a stiff smile. "I see. It sounds like you found yourself a good man, Vi."

His backhanded praise irks me like Violet's worth is tied up in landing someone like me.

I lean back, giving him a measured look, keeping my voice calm but firm. "Actually, I'm the lucky one. She's the one who finally gave in after I spent plenty of time trying to convince her I was worth it." It's not entirely true—I knew I wanted more from the moment I met her—but I'm not letting him think she's the one who should feel grateful here. Because if anyone is lucky in this scenario, it's me.

A heavy and brittle silence settled over the table, with Violet taking far more sips of her wine than usual. Meanwhile, her mother watched her with that pointed look that twisted something inside me.

"So, Violet, how is the book coming?"

Under normal circumstances, a question like that from a parent might sound supportive, even caring. But coming from her mother, it was a barb disguised as curiosity. I could practically see her trying to poke holes in Violet's confidence, and now my patience was hanging by a thread.

"It's... it's a work in progress," Violet replied, her fingers clenching the tablecloth so tightly her knuckles turned white.

Her mother gave a dismissive huff. "It always is."

I snapped. "What's your problem?"

There it was. I didn't bother to hold back. Maybe I should have, but I didn't care anymore. In the short time I'd been sitting here, these people hadn't made eye contact with their daughter. I'd watched the light drain from Violet's eyes, her shoulders shrink, and they'd slipped in more than a few digs at her. I'd had enough.

Victoria placed a hand on her chest, eyes wide like I'm the asshole here. "Excuse me?"

I leaned in, lowering my voice but ensuring every word dripped with condescension. "I said, what is your problem?"

"Our daughter has always had unrealistic dreams, Mr. Bennetti: art, writing, all that nonsense. We want the best for her," Richard chimed in, trying to smooth things over, but he still couldn't even glance at Violet. She was shrinking into herself, and it made my blood boil.

I locked eyes with him, my tone cold. "As do I. But I support her in those dreams."

Richard's eyes narrowed, but he kept his smile tight. "You've been dating our daughter for what? A few months? How serious could this be?"

"Serious enough that I plan to marry her," I shot back without thinking. "Then I suppose her being a Bennetti would be enough for you, right? Something for you to brag about to your friends?" Yeah, that came out before I could fully think it through, but I didn't care. I meant every word.

Violet's head snapped toward me, her eyes wide in shock. I met her gaze and softened my expression into a gentle smile.

"So, you're getting married?" Victoria's eyes darted between us, suddenly alert.

I was about to answer, but Violet straightened, finally letting go of her death grip on the tablecloth, leaving a crumpled line where she'd pinched it. She lifted her chin, meeting her mother's gaze head-on. "Yes. Alex fully supports my writing, and I will finish my book, Mother. Whether it sells or not doesn't matter. I'll have achieved my dream."

"And what, you'll just have your rich husband support you while you tinker away at the same book you've worked on since college?"

My patience is usually rock solid. I've faced down entire boardrooms filled with arrogant pricks who think they're untouchable just because of their last names. But these two? They're testing my limits, grinding them down to dust.

I push back my chair, the legs scraping against the polished floor, and I reach for Violet's hand, pulling her gently to her feet. "She's not using me for my money. I'm lucky enough to support her, desperate to give her whatever she needs to make her dream a reality." My voice drops, cutting through the tension. "And don't expect an invitation to the wedding. My father's more than happy to walk her down the aisle, and my family's embraced her with more warmth in a few weeks than you've shown at this dinner."

I hold their stunned gazes, then add, "I'll cover the bill since I doubt either of you could. But if you contact her again, you better make an apology. And if you ever insult the woman I love again, I'll make sure you regret it."

I don't give them time to respond. I guide Violet out of the restaurant, keeping her hand tightly in mine.

Thankfully, I anticipated this disaster, so Antonio's waiting at the curb, car ready to go. Her hands tremble as I lead her into the backseat, and I know it's not from the cold. I shrug off my jacket and drape it over her shoulders before leaning forward to turn up the heat. After buckling us both in, I wrap an arm around her, pulling her closer.

"Well, that went well, don't you think?" I give her a small smile, trying to break the tension, and she surprises me by bursting into laughter.

"I'm not going to be your fake fiancée now," she says, looking at me with a mix of gratitude, the dullness in her eyes slowly fading to something warmer.

I cup her chin, our faces so close I can almost taste the honey on her lips. "I don't want you to be. I want you to be the real one... when you're ready." And before she can process what I just admitted, I kiss her—deep and unhurried—trying to pour everything I can't yet say into that one moment, even as I mentally kick myself for putting it out there like that — but for some reason when I'm with this woman, I say the dumb shit I'd never say to anyone else.

Violet

Every time I see my parents, it's the same. A weekend phone call can ruin my day, but an in-person visit? That sends me into a full-blown spiral. Tonight was no exception. Alex stood up for me, saying things I never thought I'd hear anyone say in my defense, least of all to my parents. And while it helped, a numbness still settled in, stubborn and unshakable.

When we got home, I didn't want to talk about it, and he didn't push, which I appreciated more than I could say. Instead, I lost myself in him, letting him work his magic with his tongue, fingers, and every inch of his body. Part of me wonders if he did it to silence the storm in my head. His touch switched from raw, deliciously brutal to slow, intimate lovemaking, leaving me breathless and drained. I fell asleep wrapped in his arms, completely spent, and woke to him bringing me coffee—something he's been doing since that night.

The next few days blurred together, each one a mix of work, reviewing manuscripts, and getting lost in other people's words—words that flowed beautifully across the page, words I envied. Why could I help others shape their stories, but I couldn't get out? I'd come home determined to prove my parents wrong. I'd open my laptop, ready to write, but the words stayed locked in my head like they were trapped behind a net that refused to let them stretch onto the page. After staring at the screen, I'd snap it shut, feeling like a failure.

Alex never pressed me about it. Instead, he'd watch me with those concerned eyes, his handsome face creased with worry. I'd put on a brave face, insisting it was okay, just a phase. "I'll get over it in a few days," I'd say, even though I didn't fully believe it.

Most nights followed the same routine. I'd come home, shower, and Alex would join me if he was there—often offering a distraction of the steamy variety. He knew it was the only thing to pull me out of my head. And honestly? He wasn't wrong. For those brief moments, lost in lust, I forgot about the nagging voice that told me I wasn't good enough.

I forgot my parents' condescending remarks, the way they couldn't fathom how someone like Alex could fall for someone like me.

How we met wasn't exactly conventional, but I deserve happiness. I deserve him. Yet they acted like he was settling like I was lucky he gave me the time of day, while still managing to express their disappointment in everything I hadn't accomplished.

Tonight, I was in the shower, washing the day off me, scrubbing away the residual grime my parents left behind in my mind—part of the emotional tailspin they always put me in. Alex had texted earlier, saying he'd be at the club (which I now knew meant racquetball), but wanted to have dinner with me. He even had his private chef whip up something special. Not wanting to ruin the surprise, I headed straight to our room now. As the water ran over me, I tried to wash away the frustration, the anger not just at them but at myself for letting them get to me, for not standing up to them. But deep down, I knew why I didn't. It feels like no matter what I do, it'll never be enough for them. And maybe that's what hurts the most.

I don't hear him come in, but suddenly, his warm body wraps around mine, hands roaming over my back, kneading my ass, then gliding up my front. His fingers trail up to my breasts, kneading gently as he pulls me tighter against him. A gasp slips out when I feel his erection pressing into my lower back.

He chuckles against my neck, his breath warm and teasing. One hand wanders down, skimming the sensitive skin of my inner thigh before sliding through my wetness. "I'll never get tired of you being surprised when I'm hard for you," he murmurs, nipping at my neck. "And just so you know, that's not going away anytime soon." He kisses my neck, sucking gently, his teeth grazing my skin. "Thinking about you all day makes the boardroom... challenging." His lips move to my ear, sucking on the lobe.

"Yeah, I'm sure it's hard to explain that you're just really excited about your latest merger," I quip, earning a low growl from him. His hand leaves my breast, sliding up to my throat, his strong fingers curling around my jaw as his other hand slides one, then two fingers inside me.

"Always so wet for me," he whispers, curling his fingers just right, hitting that spot that sends a shiver up my spine, making the hot shower water feel almost icy in comparison.

"I am... in the shower," I manage between shaky breaths as his thumb presses against my clit, making my knees weak.

Without another word, he reaches past me, shutting off the water before pulling me closer, a smirk playing on his lips. "Guess we'll just have to see if it's the water," he teases. Grabbing a fluffy white towel, he wraps it around me, leaving himself gloriously naked. In one smooth motion, he pulls me into the bedroom and tosses me onto the bed, his grin downright wicked. He takes his time exploring my body.

With every touch, he gets bolder and more sinful, and I soak up every dirty word that spills from his lips. My breaths come in short, desperate bursts as his fingers work like an art form, precise and perfect. The tension snaps, and I shatter beneath him, trembling as he keeps going, licking and teasing until I'm quivering with oversensitivity.

He kisses his way back up, swirling his tongue in my belly button with a move that should not be as erotic as it is. When his mouth finally meets mine, the taste of him mingles with the remnants of me on his tongue, heady and intoxicating. His grip tightens on my thighs, fingers digging into the sensitive skin of my ass, and then he's thrusting into me, hard and urgent.

"I couldn't wait," he growls in my ear, his voice thick with desire as he rolls his hips, taking me in deep. He holds my hips, controlling the pace—fast, rough, desperate. He can read me, knowing exactly when I crave that feral edge over slow tenderness. Right now, I want it all—harder, deeper, unrestrained. His body slapping against mine fills the room with an oddly satisfying rhythm, and I can't get enough of it.

"God, baby, you're always so tight. Perfect, every time," he groans, voice rough and breathless as he drives into me, each thrust a delicious mix of pleasure and pain, reaching depths I didn't even know were there. "Give me one more," he rasps, his hand sliding from my hip to my clit, massaging it in rhythm with his movements.

My nails dig into the hard muscles of his shoulders, feeling every flex and tremor as he edges closer. I love him like this—wild and unrestrained, surrendering just enough control to me, knowing that if I asked him to slow, he would. But I don't. I crave every second of this. One more press on my swollen clit, and I unravel, my body clenching around him as I cry out his name. Heat blooms through me like fireworks, and the waves of release crash over me, leaving me breathless and trembling.

"Fucking hell," he groans into my ear, never slowing, pushing through every shudder that rocks me. His eyes flash with raw need as he pulls out and flips me over. Before I can catch my breath, he's behind me, pushing me onto my knees, ass in the air. His hands grip my hips, and he's inside me again, stretching me, filling every inch. I moan at the pressure, loving the way he holds me steady, pounding into me until he reaches his release. He wraps his arm around my waist, pulling me back against his chest, his lips pressing hot, lingering kisses against my neck as he rides out every last wave, his hand holding my throat gently.

When the storm finally settles, he doesn't let go. He keeps me close, his mouth still nuzzling my neck, the kisses turning soft.

"Talk to me, Violet. Please." His voice is barely a whisper, almost a plea.

I sigh, trying to steady my breathing. "I'm fine. My parents take a lot out of me." I shift away, but he holds me tighter, his arm locking around my waist.

"Are you mad about what I said to them?"

"What? No. Not at all." I turn, catching his gaze, his eyes searching mine like he's expecting something worse. Leaning back, I angle up for a kiss, our lips brushing awkwardly but sweetly. "What you said was the sweetest thing. No one has ever stood up for me like that. I'm just... lost in my head."

He studies me for a moment longer, and then his grip tightens, grounding me. "How can I help?"

"Well, normally, I'd sit on Max's couch and contemplate my questionable life choices, but he found a new boy toy, so I don't want to intrude." I guess my time with Alex gave Max the freedom to find someone. Part of me feels guilty like maybe Max was single for so long because he was too busy keeping my messy self glued together.

Alex doesn't let me go, "Well, pretend I'm Max. Okay, don't give me that look, you know what I mean. If I were Max, how would I help?"

"You want me to sit on your couch and wallow in self-pity while you bring me my favorite latte and pastries that I shouldn't eat?"

He grins, that devilish, charming smile. "Baby, you can and *should* eat more. I'm Sicilian, and we like our women's curvy. Even Mama wants you to have larger hips for *i miei futuri bambini.*"

I blink, processing that. "Did you just say your future babies?"

"Oh, so now we speak Italian?" he teases.

"No, but hanging out with your family and texting Valeria daily means I've picked up a few words."

He gently pushes me forward, grabbing the towel to clean us up before disappearing briefly. When he returns, he's holding one of his robes, wrapping me in the silky fabric, and I melt into its softness. He props me up against the pillows, draping a throw over my legs.

"What are you—" I start, but he silences me with a finger to his lips.

I clamp my mouth shut, watching him move around the penthouse. I hear him shuffling through the living room, the clink of dishes in the kitchen, and a brief phone call that's too low for me to catch. When he returns ten minutes later, he's holding a book and a glass of water and wearing the biggest, most self-satisfied smile.

Violet

ALEX IS STILL IN his boxers, and I can't help but appreciate the view—or notice he's not entirely calmed down yet. With an exasperated laugh, he catches my gaze and heads to the dresser to pull on some sweatpants. As he ties the drawstring, I pout.

"That was for me too, you know."

He shakes his head, climbing onto the bed beside me and sliding under the throw. "Not right now," he says, then holds up my well-worn copy of *Pride & Prejudice*. "It's late for a latte, but I've already arranged for it to arrive in the morning. Until then, you have two options. We can watch your favorite movie or read this book together. And when the pastries arrive, we will eat them and wallow together until you feel better."

And damn it, how could I not fall a little harder for this man?

No one's ever done this for me before, and here he is to ensure I feel seen and cared for. I lean in, cupping his cheek, pressing a soft kiss to his lips. "I think, Mr. Bennetti, I'm falling in love with you. And it's okay if you don't feel the same—even if you're talking about babies and marriage. We can do it backward, I guess."

He laughs, deep and rich, kissing me back. "Baby, I have been falling in love with you too. Have been for longer than I should admit." There's this boyish smile tugging at his lips, the kind that makes my insides go all gooey.

"Try me," I challenge as he pours a glass of wine.

He settles in beside me, glass in hand, studying me with a look like he's weighing how much he should spill. "Honestly? The moment I saw you. I wasn't in love yet, but I knew I would be. Ridiculous, right? But I couldn't help it. I had to talk to you and learn everything about you, and once I got a taste, there was no going back. No woman could ever beat you."

"Well, aren't you the romantic," I tease, swirling my wine, trying to act like that didn't just melt every last bit of me.

He arches a brow, but before he can fire back with some snarky retort, I cut him off with a kiss.

When the pastries arrive, I'm the one raising my eyebrows. He ordered nearly two dozen different kinds like he wasn't sure which sugary treat could fix my broken mood. It's all from the fancy French bakery down the street, and I zero in on an éclair with vanilla filling. Alex smirks when I dip my finger into the creamy center, sucking it off slowly, knowing exactly what I'm doing.

"Knock that off. I'm trying to be a sweet boyfriend, not fuck you hoarse." His voice goes rough, sending a shiver down my spine—because, honestly, how does he manage to say something so filthy and make my heart flutter all at once?

For now, I manage to resist him and settle into the bed with him, turning my attention to the TV. He queues up my favorite movie on Netflix, and we lean back together. I can't help the little smile that sneaks onto my face. I've seen this movie a dozen times—okay, maybe three dozen—but it's his first time.

As the opening credits roll, I stop teasing and let my romance-loving soul take over. God, I adore this movie. No matter how often I've watched it, I'm always on the edge of my seat. How Mr. Darcy looks at Elizabeth, the tension between them, the heartbreak when she rejects him, and how he changes—melting into this swoony, selfless puddle of a man, willing to do anything to make her happy.

It's kind of like the guy sitting next to me.

It's like a shiver rippling up my spine, making me rethink everything. Alex had feelings for me from the start, right from the moment he first saw me. And he didn't just sit on them—he acted. He knew I was miserable at work and did something about it, just for me. He stood up to my parents, defending me, but it felt like one of those big romantic gestures. Sort of like Mr. Darcy defying his aunt and choosing Elizabeth anyway—though wasn't it weird that he was supposed to marry his cousin? It was a thing for the old money types back then, but...ew.

I shift back to thoughts of Alex and our relationship, especially while Jane is on the screen, finally getting her happily-ever-after proposal from Mr. Bingley. And even though it's cheesy, I want that. I want to be the girl who goes all teary-eyed when the guy she loves gets down on one knee.

I must've gotten lost in my thoughts for longer than I realized because, suddenly, the credits are rolling. Alex is looking down at me, his expression soft. "Feeling any better? If not, we can watch it again."

I smile, snuggling deeper into his arms, the throw draped over us, the box of pastries I overindulged in sitting on the nightstand. "Don't be ridiculous. I'd make you watch *The Notebook* if I needed a second round."

"Mind if I ask you something?" He shifts until he's sitting up against the headboard, pulling me up with him, his gaze searching mine with those ridiculously blue eyes. Seriously, how did they get so blue? His dad's eyes are a warm amber, and his mom's are a pale blue, but his? They're like they were custom-made just for him.

"Sure..." I reply, noting the way his expression is hard to read. His jaw is tight, but he's not clenching it, and his eyes are almost...nervous.

"Why do you let your parents get to you like that? Let them talk to you that way. I know they're your parents, but if my mama or papa spoke to me like that, I wouldn't think twice about walking away."

I shrug, trying to explain. "You've got a big family that's almost *too* involved in your life," I say, thinking about how often his cousins text me. Especially Valeria, who has no problem asking if Alex is keeping up with his 'responsibilities' in the bedroom. Boundaries are foreign to his family. "And even though you already have two brothers, all those cousins are like siblings too. You're all close. I never had that. No siblings, no cousins, no Sunday family dinners. Just...my parents."

I take a breath, the truth slipping out. "I guess that's why I always answer their calls and meet them whenever they're in town." And let's be honest—it's never *for* me. They come on business, and I'm the last-minute addition, the afterthought. It wouldn't surprise me if they'd been in New York for weeks without telling me. "Every time, I just hope maybe they'll be proud."

One day, I wish to sit down with my parents, tell them something I've done, and see pride in their eyes. Even just for a few seconds before that familiar look of disappointment creeps back in, reminding me of all the ways I don't measure up. But then reality hits—I'm never going to make them happy. Even if I become a best-selling author, writing the stories I want to write it still wouldn't be enough. I didn't follow their path or live up to their expectations. Maybe if I did get famous, they'd brag about me at their fancy parties, but I'd always be the failure in private.

Alex shifts, sliding down the headboard until he rests on his pillow. "My family likes you," he says, his voice low and comforting. "My cousins can't wait to read all that 'porn stuff' you write." He grins, and I can't help but laugh because that's the same thing my mom would call any romance with a hint of spice.

"Yeah, but your cousins aren't exactly shy. Alena had no problem telling me about how she went down on Dante during the ride to the wedding, and they're not even together yet?"

Alex groans, a hint of exasperation in his voice. "Please, I don't need that image of my cousin and best friend. But yeah, they're still playing the 'friends with benefits' game, even though everyone in the family knows it's more than that."

I roll my eyes, recalling some of the conversations I've overheard. "Let's just say cooking night has been a crash course in oversharing. I've got mental images that might require actual eye bleach."

He laughs, the sound deep and warm. "Oh, I can believe it. Nonna is the worst. When I turned sixteen, she asked if I'd 'popped a cherry'. I thought she meant *actual* cherries, so I told her I'd eaten them plenty of times. She nearly died laughing."

I smirk, raising a brow. "What, the girls weren't falling over you at sixteen?"

He snorts, and it's an unguarded, honest sound that I love. "Not even close. At sixteen, I was a skinny kid with braces and acne—all those awkward teenage clichés. College is when I started to fill out, ditch the braces, and thank God, the acne finally cleared up. My first kiss wasn't until I was seventeen, and it was with a friend. We were just practicing so we wouldn't look like total idiots when we kissed someone."

Alex, the billionaire CEO, one of the city's most eligible bachelors, hadn't kissed a girl until seventeen? That's... adorable. And unexpected.

"So, when was your first *real* kiss?"

He smiles, the motion tugging at his lips as his fingers run soothing circles on my arm. "A few months after that. Still a hot mess, though."

"Okay, fair is fair. My turn. I was fourteen."

He quirks a brow. "Well, weren't you a little vixen?"

I laugh, shaking my head. "Hardly. It was just a quick peck from my neighbor. He dared me."

He grins, that teasing look in his eyes. "You fell for the dare trick?"

"Yup." I let my eyes wander over his perfectly chiseled torso, struggling to imagine him ever *not* being hot. "Okay, so when did you lose your virginity?"

He scrunches his brows. "Twenty."

"No way!"

"Yes, way," he says, sounding like a teenage girl sharing juicy gossip. I can't help but laugh. "I didn't grow into myself until college. I wasn't exactly turning heads back then. Even in college, I didn't do the whole party scene. No one-night stands, no hookups. It's not my style, despite what the gossip columns love to say. They think I must've been with half the city since I wasn't in a serious relationship. But honestly, most of those women were just... dates."

I bite my lip, suddenly feeling like a bit of a cliché. "Well, I was sixteen, and let's just say it was neither romantic nor memorable." I sigh, cringing internally at the awkwardness of it all. First boyfriend and everything. "How many relationships have you had besides Natalia?"

"And you?" He shifts closer, flashing that easy smile. "Relationships? Two. Including you."

"What?" I pull back, propping myself up on my elbow, staring at him like he just told me he's from another planet. "How is that even possible? You're like... well, older."

"Are we calling me old now?" He hooks his hand behind his head, giving me a playful smirk. "I told you, I wasn't looking for anything serious. I went on dates, but nothing clicked. I won't keep dating someone to tick a box."

I let out a small huff. "I'm the opposite. I kept giving the same guys chance after chance, thinking maybe a spark would magically appear. Even with Jake, it started as a one-night mistake that somehow turned into a relationship. I kept convincing myself it might become something real, and we all know how that turned out."

"I'd say it worked out in my favor." He smirks, making me want to punch and kiss him simultaneously. Before I can come up with a witty response, he lunges at me, rolling me onto my back and pinning me beneath him. "I have a rule..." He nips at my neck, and somehow, the way he's got me pinned down is the most thrilling thing ever.

"What's the rule?" I manage, breathless, as his fingers start to part my thighs.

"No other men's names in this bed," he growls, fingers hooking into the sides of my thong, dragging the fabric down with a deliberate slowness that has my skin tingling.

"And why's that?" I challenge.

With my panties gone, his hands trail up my legs with agonizing patience before he presses himself between my thighs, hard and ready.

"I'm a jealous man. What's mine is mine. I hear another man's name on your lips, which does things to me." His voice drops to a dangerous whisper, sending a shiver down my spine.

I reach for his waistband, my fingers slipping inside, wrapping around him as he groans into my ear. His hand wraps up in my hair while the other finds my center, teasing my slick folds.

"I'm going to fuck this wet pussy until the only cock you remember is mine."

His kiss is savage, lips crashing against mine like he's claiming every inch of me, and I meet his intensity head-on, biting his lower lip. That unleashes something primal. His grip tightens in my hair, pulling my head back as he nips at my neck. He shoves his sweats off, rolling his hard length against my slick heat, positioning himself at my entrance.

"This is not going to be gentle," he warns, voice rough.

"Did I ask you to be?" I challenge, feeling the edges of a smirk tug at my lips.

He snarls a sound I've never heard before, and in a single, brutal thrust, he fills me. The air rushes from my lungs, the sharp mix of pain and pleasure bringing tears to my eyes as he pulls my hair, setting a punishing rhythm. His grip on my hip is unyielding, holding me in place, ensuring I take every inch of him, and I know I'll feel his fingers bruising my skin tomorrow.

"Fuck!" He groans, taking my breast into his mouth, his thrusts relentless. Then, his lips crash back to mine, devouring me in a kiss that's all teeth and hunger, like he's consuming me whole. It's rough and raw; somehow, it feels like a claim and promise.

Without warning, he pulls out, flips me onto my stomach, and yanks my hips up to meet him. One hard thrust has him buried deep, and I can't hold back the scream that tears through me. His fingers grip my hair, arching my back, and he hauls me upright against his chest. His other hand wraps around my throat as he drives into me, his voice low and dangerous in my ear. "Come for me, baby. Let me feel that sweet, tight pussy clench around me before I fill you up."

He releases my hip and lands a sharp smack on my ass, sending a stinging heat through my skin, only to smooth over it right after.

Dear... God.

Then he shoves me forward, keeping a tight hold on my hair, and the wild pace he sets shreds my control. A terrifyingly powerful orgasm rips through me like a lightning strike, seizing every muscle.

As I gasp his name, I practically see stars. His grip eases, sliding to my waist, and he plunges deeper, his body shuddering against mine as he reaches his release. My limbs are still trembling when he flips me onto my back like I'm weightless. Not that I'm complaining—I couldn't move if I tried. He cups my chin, kissing me like he's trying to catch his breath, slow and steady, until his lips soften against mine.

"Just remember who made you come," he whispers before heading to the bathroom.

Yeah, that's not something I'll forget anytime soon.

When he returns, he's got a warm washcloth, cleaning me up before tossing it across the room. He slides under the covers, pulling me close to his solid, unyielding body.

Men like him can't be real. He's rich, gorgeous, sweet, and talks about his feelings now that he's out of his shell. I drift off, convinced I'm delusional because this has to be fantasy. I'll wake up any moment now, and the last month will be just another story my romance-obsessed mind cooked up.

Violet

"WILL THIS DO?" I leave our closet, swaying a little in a long, silky purple evening gown. The heels are between stripper and classy—if that's a category.

Alex's eyes darkened, his gaze trailing over me like he was already picturing peeling the dress off. "Yes, if you intend not to go tonight and have that ripped off you."

Ignoring the heat in his stare, I brush past him into the foyer, feeling the familiar thrill run through me. It's been two weeks since the Harrington wedding, and we still can't seem to keep our hands off each other. Not that I'm complaining.

A few days after my parents' visit, when I finally pulled myself back together, Alex insisted on moving all my stuff into his room. He refused to let me keep anything in the guest room, claiming it made it feel like I had one foot out the door. It was ridiculous—okay, maybe a little sweet, too—so I let it slide. After what Natalia put him through, I understood his need for reassurance.

Now, I'm in the bathroom, carefully applying my makeup. And, of course, Alex is leaning against the doorframe, watching me like I'm a movie he doesn't want to miss. I know he loves seeing me get ready, and he pouts when I pull my hair back into a bun. It's the little things with him.

Tonight, we're headed to a charity event.

Being in Alex's world means being expected to go to these kinds of things. Honestly, I always wonder how much of the money spent on these lavish parties makes it to the charity. But that's probably too logical for this crowd.

For the past few days, I've been opening my laptop without that familiar knot in my stomach. It no longer feels like a machine built to mock me. For once, my parents' voices aren't echoing in the back of my mind while I type. I'm finally making progress.

I'm not the plotter type; honestly, I don't want to be. I tried it before. After all those creative writing courses, I told myself I *had* to have a plot, an outline, and that elusive three-act structure for perfect pacing. But every time I forced myself down that road, it became a dead end.

So, I did the best thing I could think of: I wiped the slate clean. I took one of my story ideas, the one I love the most, with the cutest meet-cute, and I sent its outline to my computer's recycle bin.

No outlines.

No rigid structure.

Just me, the keyboard, and the flow of the story.

And honestly, it's liberating. It's like letting my words spill out onto the page and letting the story breathe and grow into its own rough, wild shape. The first draft? Rough doesn't even begin to cover it. It's full of cringe-worthy moments that make me wince when I read them back. But underneath all the chaos, the story is there. The foundation, some of the framework—maybe even a window or two. Now, I get to go back, work on the structure, refine the details, and add those finishing touches. Building it like a house, brick by brick, or whatever they use to make those classic New York brownstones. Are they brick, or is it all just a façade? I've always wondered.

Alex occasionally peers over my shoulder as I write, and I nudge him away with a playful scowl. He pouts, which, strangely enough, I find sexy, and then sits across from me at the dining table. He knows it's my favorite spot to write. There are two reasons for that:

First, the view. An entire panorama of Manhattan unfolds before me, and I swear this city has magic all its own. Why is Manhattan so damn inspiring? Why does it feel like the ultimate backdrop for every romance story? It's like the city whispers to you, *"Hey, dream big!"*

Maybe it's the skyscrapers that stretch up to tickle the clouds or the constant hum of life below—taxis, chatty pedestrians, and street performers with dreams of making it big. Only in Manhattan can you sit on a park bench in Central Park and watch the world unfold. And this old guy feeds the pigeons every morning—I'm convinced those birds are plotting a coup.

The characters here practically write themselves. Like the guy in a three-piece suit serenading his pug with an accordion. What's his story? I don't know, but it's definitely not dull. And the coffee shops—don't even get me started. Each one feels like a mini oasis where you can order a drink with an extra shot of inspiration.

Manhattan is a character all its own. It's a melting pot of dreams, ambitions, and questionable fashion choices, and I wouldn't change a thing about it. Anything feels possible here.

Look at the man sitting across from me —he's pure inspiration. He's the man you can't write into a story because he's too good to be believable. Sure, he's got quirks and flaws, but I'm more than okay with them. They're nothing I can't handle.

Reason two: why do I love writing here? Well, it's him. He sits two chairs over, strategically not blocking my view and giving me those looks—the kind that screams exactly what he wants to do when the laptop closes. He thinks I don't notice, but oh, I do. Still, he ensures not to mess with my creative process—a gentleman... and a tease.

I adjusted my new diamond earrings—Alex surprised me with them. They probably cost more than my entire wardrobe combined, but he just shrugged and said he saw them and thought of me. Who buys diamonds on a whim for their girlfriend? This man, that's who. My dreamboat, no shame in saying it.

And trust me, we're *that* couple right now. You know, the kind that makes you roll your eyes, but secretly, you can't help but root for. We're like a walking rom-com, doing all the cliché things: finishing each other's sentences, gazing into each other's eyes like we're the only ones in the room, on the planet, in the entire freaking universe. I giggle at the silly things he says, and he laughs at my jokes like I'm the next Tina Fey. If he weren't who he was, we'd probably have been kicked out of a few places by now for being too touchy.

Our texts are filled with hearts and all sorts of wildly inappropriate things that make my knees go weak. A simple walk through the city becomes an adventure, stealing kisses under every tree and light pole. And at work? I'm daydreaming more than I should be, zoning out over manuscripts, and then scrambling to catch up. Yesterday, I caught myself doodling a heart in a staff meeting. Max took one look, rolled his eyes, and scribbled "You disgust me" next to it. Yeah, we're disgustingly cute, and I'm not even sorry.

And don't get me started on how Alex looks at me. When he does, it's like I'm the only woman in the world. We go out to dinner, and sure, people notice him—he's gorgeous. But he's got his hand wrapped around mine or his arm snug around my waist like he's showing the world I'm his. It's heady, the kind of thing that makes my heart race.

Tonight, Alex promised we'd stay long enough to smile for the board members and shake a few hands before escaping. He even hinted at a reward if I behaved myself. It almost makes me want to misbehave to see what kind of punishment he'd come up with.

Not that I haven't been pushing his buttons all day. I've sent him risqué texts during his board meetings to mess with him. I know his schedule inside and out, and I get a thrill knowing I'm why he's squirming in front of his advisors. His messages back? Let's say they're equally dirty and delightfully frustrated.

Alex sneaks up behind me as I finish my makeup, pressing a soft kiss to the back of my neck. He's obsessed with that spot—if he's not gripping it while he's inside me, he's running his lips over it, making me clench my thighs just from the feel of him. It's almost enough to make me abandon this event altogether.

But not tonight. I spin around, pinning him against the wall with a hand on his chest. "Mess up my hair or makeup, and I will be so mad," I whisper, brushing my lips just over his, teasing him right back.

His voice drops, that smirk tugging at his lips. "I don't need your lips or hair to do what I want to do to you."

Yeah, that kind of talk makes my resolve wobble, heat pooling low at the mere thought of his plan. *Focus, Violet. Stay on task.*

I give his chest a playful pat, resisting the urge to tear that suit right off him. "Be a good boy, stop turning me on, and when we get home, I'll let you show me exactly what you have in mind." With a wink, I head for the door, imagining how this night will end.

Alex

EVERYONE KNOWS VIOLET'S MINE. But I'd prefer to make it official—give her my last name or, at the very least, put a diamond on her finger that's big enough to blind NASA. Yeah, I'm possessive. It's a male ego thing. I can't help it.

When we enter the charity gala, I clock every guy who dares glance her way. My fists itch, but I rein it in. Most attendees work for one of my companies or are family, but a few are outsiders. It's not just my name on the event; I run the board, though I've already saved a seat for my future wife. Would she freak out if she knew that? She's a hopeless romantic, those wide eyes practically glowing with love. But she might think I'm nuts if I told her how serious I am.

Things have moved fast between us—too fast for someone like me. But I don't regret it, not for a second. What I worry about is how much she's gotten under my skin. She's shattered my walls and left me vulnerable. The idea of losing her? It makes my chest tighten, and my mind spirals.

"Your event, and you show up late?" Dante strolls over, handing a champagne flute to Violet and barely acknowledging me. Great, thanks. I wave over to a server for my drink.

I spot the faint flush on Violet's cheeks. It's the aftermath of our little limo escapade—her leaning back against the leather, my mouth between her thighs. I might've left myself with blue balls, but seeing her like this? Worth it.

Dante, in his usual three-piece suit, sighs. "No Alena?"

"She'll be here soon. Something about Valeria and Gloria helping her with a dress emergency. I left before they dragged me into it. Those three together are a handful." Dante's gaze shifts to Violet. "You look nice."

My hand drifts down Violet's back, grazing her lower spine, where the dress dips dangerously low. It's my territory, and I hate that everyone else can see it.

Leaning closer, I whisper into her ear, trying to make it look sweet. "Are you seriously not wearing any panties?"

She tugs at my lapels, pulling me in tighter. "Says the man who took them off in the limo," she purrs, her voice a seductive challenge. "Figured it'd drive you wild."

It's taking every ounce of willpower not to drag her into a secluded hallway right now. But I have a charity to run and a room of people expecting me to play host.

The Bennetti Foundation for Future Leaders—my baby. I started it to give kids from challenging backgrounds a chance, mentor them, and ensure they get opportunities I never had to fight for. I didn't grow up poor, but I know what feeling alone is like. This is my way of giving back, and I want Violet to be a part of it, to help me expand it beyond New York and Miami. I imagine her sitting beside me on the board, guiding the future together.

As always, Mama appears like a ghost, sneaking up on me with her uncanny timing. She's here to whisk Violet away, her smile innocent, but her grip is anything but. I watch them disappear into the crowd, Violet throwing me a desperate look over her shoulder, and I can't help but laugh softly.

Dante nudges me. "So, when are you two getting married?"

Before I can respond, Julian saunters over with his usual smug look and a whiskey in hand, making me want to punch him in his pinstriped suit. Dante and I exchange a glance. He's already downing his champagne, probably looking for an exit strategy.

Spotting Evander Harrington—one of the more decent Harringtons—across the room, I seize my chance. "I need to catch Evander," I say, ditching Julian without a backward glance.

Evander welcomes me with a handshake. He's unlike his brother Griffin, who's colder than a New York winter. Evander's brilliant in tech, focusing on private security, while I stick to corporate. We make a good show of being rivals, but it's more of a friendly competition.

As I reach for my drink, Evander nods toward the bar. "You see who Julian brought tonight?"

I follow his gaze, and my stomach drops. Natalia. Wearing a gold dress that screams, "I'm all about your money," she drapes herself over some poor guy who looks like he wants to run for the hills.

"You've got to be kidding me," I mutter. "She was dating my cousin a minute ago."

Evander smirks. "Well, she's always had... eclectic taste."

Ignoring her, I try to refocus, but then I see Violet and Valeria at the bar. Natalia zeroes in on them like a shark. Evander's eyes light up with amusement. "Oh, this is gonna be good."

But Violet, ever the classy one, smiles politely and turns back to Valeria—my girl.

Natalia, however, isn't done. She catches my eye, then slinks over.

"Alex," she purrs, her voice dripping with fake sweetness. "Saw you alone and thought maybe things ended with you and Violet."

I resist every urge to shove her away. "Why would I end things with the woman who hasn't slept with half of Manhattan?"

She leans in, her breath hot against my ear. "When you're done playing house, you know where to find me."

I pull back, my patience fraying. "Sorry, Natalia, I'm not looking to book a trip to your homeland of hell."

Evander barely hides his laugh. But then I see Violet approaching, and my gut twists. I brace myself. "It's not what it looks like."

Violet raises an eyebrow. "And what does it look like?"

I step closer, cupping her face. "You saw her being touchy, but trust me, I wasn't interested."

She doesn't back down. "Funny, she made it sound like you two were on great terms."

I let out a frustrated sigh. "I'm not about to embarrass you, Violet. If something were going on with her, I'd tell you. Straight up."

I lean in, kissing her lips, making it clear to everyone in the room who I'm with. When she pulls me in closer, I lose myself in the moment, uncaring of the onlookers.

"Get a room," Dante quips from behind, earning himself a glare.

Violet shoots him a look. "I need some air," she says, striding toward the veranda, leaving me with a knot in my chest.

I'm still leaning against the table, trying to keep my cool, when Dante glances at me. "You know she's gonna make you work for it, right?"

"Yeah, I know," I mutter, feeling the weight of the ring box in my pocket. I pull it out, showing him the oval-cut diamond, waiting for the right moment.

Dante whistles. "Damn. Tonight?"

I shake my head. "No plan yet. ... keep it close. In case the moment's right."

Alena appears, snatching the box from my hand. "Oh, my god, this is stunning! Are you seriously going to do it tonight?"

"No," I admit. "But I want to be ready when the right moment comes." Thinking back on how Violet said she always pictured something special and unique. Something no one else could claim.

She clutches her chest like she's just watched a Hallmark movie. "You're gonna make us all look bad, you know that?"

Dante smirks, but there's a warmth in his gaze. "Just don't screw it up, man. She's a good one."

I pocket the ring again, my mind drifting back to the woman standing on the veranda, the one who's turned my world upside down. "Yeah, she is."

Violet

SAYING I NEEDED AIR was an understatement. These events have never been my scene; tonight, everything felt off. Between the fancy crowd, the ex-girlfriend draping herself over Alex like he's a last meal, and Alex's recent weird mood, I was way out of my element.

The veranda was freezing—classic New York almost-December, with the chill sinking into my bones. I hovered by the doors, letting the faint warmth from inside chase away the cold. No snow yet, but you could feel it coming.

And then I heard *that* voice. The one that made me want to both sprint away and retch at the same time. Julian. "Violet, you look stunning tonight," he drawled, sounding like he was trying too hard. Scratch that. I want to vomit.

I turned to face him, rolling my eyes. "Wow, Julian, compliments from you? What's the catch?"

He pressed a hand to his chest, all mock offense. "You wound me. No catch, just genuine interest." The way he dragged out *genuine* made me want to gag. "How's everything going with Alex? Any ambitious plans he's cooking up?"

Oh, he's fishing. I could practically see the desperation in his smirk. I plastered on my best sarcastic smile and leaned in like I had a secret to share. "Oh, definitely. You know Alex—taking over the world one business at a time. Relentless."

He inched closer, and the sharp tang of his cologne hit me, making my skin crawl. His whole aura was just off—like he came with a built-in warning siren. "Sounds like him. Any big moves I should be on the lookout for?"

I looked out at the city lights, smirking. "If I told you, I'd have to kill you. But I'm sure he's three steps ahead of whatever you plot. I don't know, driving up a company's price to watch you pay more than you should."

"I bet. Come on, Violet, give me just a taste," Julian's voice drips with sleaze, and the way he licks his lips makes me want to bolt. "How does he stay ahead of competitors? You know his family and what they are like. You're telling me he doesn't lean on the family name—or his Uncle Tony—to get ahead?"

I know all about Uncle Tony, the real mafia guy in the family. But Alex? He keeps his distance. His uncle might have connections, but Alex doesn't dip into that pool—at least, not that I know. I shrug, crossing my arms tight over my chest. It's not just the winter air making me shiver; Julian's slim and unnerving presence. "Julian, do you honestly think I'd tell you even if I knew anything? Hypothetically speaking, he's got creative ideas. But he's just brilliant like that."

Julian's grin grows more predatory, and I can practically see the gears turning behind those calculating eyes. "What kind of ideas?"

I force a laugh, going for the most sarcastic tone I can muster. "Oh, you know, replacing his staff with robots. That's high on the list."

He tries to keep a straight face. "Innovative guy. So, has he talked to you about Alton Technical?"

"Not a word," I snap back, my patience thin. The longer I'm out here, the more I regret it. I came for fresh air, and instead, I'm stuck breathing in his cologne, which now smells like pure toxicity. If this were a cartoon, he'd have a green cloud of poison swirling around him.

He raises his hands, stepping back with a mocking smile. "Okay, fair enough. Always enlightening, Violet." He pauses, throwing one last parting shot over his shoulder. "Oh, and Violet, when you get bored of our boy, you know where to find me."

"Julian, I'm thinking more about when pigs fly, hell freezes over, and the earth opens into a giant crater—then I might consider it."

His smile lingers a little too long for comfort, and there's something about it that feels off, but I shrug it off, assuming that's just the vibe this man gives. Turning back to face the city lights, I focus on what makes me feel alive, letting the chill air clear my head.

Violet

It took me a week to shake off Julian Stone and that creepy conversation on the veranda. Thanksgiving sped up the process. It's wild to think that Alex and I have been together, like *really* together, for almost two months. With my family barely acknowledging my existence, choosing where to spend the holidays wasn't hard. So here I am, wrapped up in his world instead.

Alex has been working longer hours and making many whispered phone calls. From the bits I've gathered, someone in his company feeds Stone's info, which complicates his latest deals. He doesn't bring it up much at home, though. He's more interested in taking my clothes off and finding other ways to relieve his stress. Not that I'm complaining.

Home.

It's funny how quickly it happened—how *he* happened. For the first time, I feel like I belong somewhere. I come home from work, and he's there shortly after. We have dinner, relax in the hot tub, and get lost in movies or deep conversations. And, of course, there's the sex. I never felt this kind of chemistry with someone—explosive, electric, and somehow better every time.

Today, we arrived at his parents' house for Thanksgiving, and if I thought Sunday dinners were a lot, I wasn't ready for this. Do Sicilians even celebrate Thanksgiving? Well, they sure do here. The place is packed—family members I've never met, and even more, I'm sure I'll forget by the end of the night.

I'm halfway through my first glass of wine, watching Alex talk animatedly with an aunt from Sicily. Dom sidles up next to me, nudging my shoulder as we lean against the wall, observing the chaos. I've always been a people-watcher, and Alex's family is like its own reality TV show—full of passion, noise, and quirks I never knew existed.

I love watching Alex's family in action—their lively voices, the flow of Italian back and forth, the kids zooming around like tiny tornadoes. You'll often find me with them, laughing and playing along. Dom's son, Luca, has become one of my little buddies. When

Dom is out of town, I even insist Luca stays with us, and it's been eye-opening to see Alex around him. He's a natural—a man who would make an incredible dad.

Cue my ovaries doing somersaults as Alex's cousin hands him her baby across the room, and he takes the little guy without a second thought. He cradles the baby against his shoulder, smiling and chatting away like he's done this a million times. It's impossible not to swoon. He's perfect.

"Stop drooling," Dom teases, snapping me out of my thoughts. Over the past few weeks, Dom and I have become close. He's always around the penthouse or making me laugh during Sunday dinners.

I roll my eyes and focus on Dante and Alena across the room. "How long has he been pining after her?" Dante's practically glued to her side on the couch, his arm casually draped over the back. But he's itching to do more than sit there.

Dom rubs his jaw, a smirk tugging at his lips. "Ten years... at least. As long as we've known."

"Ten *years*?" I glance back at them, eyes widening. Alena is talking animatedly, oblivious to how Dante is soaking up every word like she's the only person in the room. "And why haven't they...?"

Dom grins. "Oh, we've got bets going. I lost mine two years ago. Shame, too. The pot's getting big. I think Dante is just shy."

I raise an eyebrow. "Dante? Shy? Please."

"Okay, maybe not shy in general," Dom admits. "But shy around her."

"Why? She's always his date for everything."

"Yeah, but she thinks they're just friends."

"Ooooh, so he's stuck in the friend zone?" I say, smirking. I know they've crossed some lines that most friends wouldn't, but I keep that tidbit to myself.

Dom nods. "Yup. And he's got no balls to get out of it. He's afraid it'll mess up the family dynamic, even though Nonna has repeatedly told him to grow a pair and ask her out. Not like she's seeing anyone else."

"Think she's waiting for him?" I ask, glancing back at them. Ten years... that's a seriously long wait.

"Possibly. They have this weird, push-and-pull dynamic I've given up trying to understand. Like two New Year's ago—they took their midnight kiss way too far and pretended it never happened the next day."

"And what about you, Dom? Anyone special in your life?" I nudge him playfully, knowing his answer before he even says it.

Dom gives me a flat look that screams, *please.* We've become good friends, especially since I get along better with him than his twin, Rico. It's almost mind-boggling that they're related, let alone twins. Rico is closed off and moody, like trying to talk to a very attractive brick wall. I've tried, but no dice. Alex and Dom have both reassured me it's not that Rico dislikes me; it's just his nature. The guy struggles with people, and it's obvious there's more beneath the surface that they're not ready to share.

"Luca and work keep me busy enough. Especially now without a nanny." He sighs, running a hand through his hair.

I smack his arm, mock scolding him. "Again? You fired another one?"

Dom shrugs like it's no big deal. "She didn't stick to my schedule."

Oh god, *the* schedule. Dom has a meticulous, stick-up-your-ass level routine for Luca, right down to the minute the kid gets his morning multivitamins and the precise brand of gummies he'll allow. I roll my eyes, unable to hide my exasperation. "So, who's the next victim?"

"Well, the nanny agency I was using cut ties. I've gone through too many. I might have to look overseas. There are a few international agencies."

"Oooh, like the whole au pair thing? How fancy of you."

He snorts. "Please."

While he talks, my attention keeps drifting back to Alex. He's cradling a baby from one of his many cousins across the room, bouncing him gently. The sight does dangerous things to my ovaries.

"So, you and Alex. Things moved pretty fast, huh?" Dom leans in, smirking like he's got a secret.

I raise an eyebrow. "How do you figure?"

"Well, you went from not dating to full-on relationship mode overnight."

"Think it's too fast?" I've wondered if we're speeding along faster than our hearts can keep up.

"Nah. We're Sicilian. We move fast, and when we love, we love hard."

His words hit me like a one-two punch—excitement and nerves tangled together. On one hand, it feels like everything's falling into place. But on the other, I wonder if we're rushing into something that could burn out. We've admitted falling for each other, but we haven't dropped those three big words yet. Do near-admissions even count?

Dom catches my expression and winces. "Oh, sorry. Maybe you guys aren't there yet."

I snort. "You're a terrible liar, Dom."

"So... you do love him?"

I look down at my empty wine glass and frown, thinking I could use a refill. "Maybe."

He chuckles. "You gonna tell him?"

"Uh, no way. He's stubborn as a mule. He has to say it first."

Dom rolls his eyes. "Great, another couple spending a decade tiptoeing around their feelings."

Oh, hell no. Not letting that happen. "He's already mentioned marriage and babies more than once, so don't bet on ten years."

A sly grin spreads across his face. "I didn't. I bet on Christmas."

I squint at him. "Christmas is over a month away."

He leans closer like we're co-conspirators. "Not for the 'I love you'..." Then, with a wink, he saunters off, leaving me a little stunned.

Oh.

Alex

I SIT IN MY office, buried in a mountain of emails. Seriously, why does everyone insist on emailing?

Half of these back-and-forth exchanges could be resolved with a ten-minute phone call, but no, we all have to hide behind our keyboards. I've got days' worth of replies to get through because I let them pile up while I was wrapped up in Violet. I'd trade all these messages for just one more hour with her. But I regret not knocking these out sooner—now it's turning into a marathon of pointless replies.

Penelope's voice crackles over the intercom, interrupting my self-imposed isolation. I'd told her to hold all interruptions so I could finally dig through this email avalanche. But, of course, my peace never lasts.

"Mr. Stone is here and insists on seeing you," she says, her tone carrying that edge that she's serious.

I groan and run a hand down my face. "Penelope, when I say I don't want to be disturbed except for extenuating circumstances, Stone is not one of those, right?"

I hear the frustration in her tapping pen. Through the glass walls of my office, I catch a glimpse of her shooting me a death glare. That woman could turn stone into dust with a look. "He says it's about Violet," she replies.

That snaps me out of my email haze. I look up, and sure enough, Julian stands over her desk with that infuriating smirk, wiggling his fingers in a smug little wave. My jaw tightens. "Fine. Send him in," I bite out.

The sight of him makes my skin crawl. Julian Stone is like a bad penny—he keeps turning up. Always with that smug smile, even though I've beaten him out of two ac-quisitions recently. He thought he was being clever, playing a bidding war I orchestrated, only to watch me snatch the companies he had his eye on. Yet, he's still getting inside info—just not all of it. He figured out my decoy move on the third deal, which means his little informant isn't close enough to know the actual play. Great. It only makes finding the mole that much harder. But we'll get there. And when we do, Julian Stone won't have that smug as shit look on his face.

Julian strolls into my office like he's stepping into his living room, not mine. He drops into the chair across from me, unbuttoning his hideous striped suit. Stripes. Really? Of course, Julian would go for that. He's the kind of guy who thinks pinstripes make him look like a 1920s gangster, but he misses the class by a mile.

"Julian, to what do I owe the pleasure?" I lean back in my chair, injecting as much sarcasm into the question as possible. It's a shame he's too dense to hear it. Nothing about him or his overpowering cologne makes his presence enjoyable.

He flashes that slimy smile, pulling out his phone. "Your girlfriend is something else," he says, eyes fixed on his screen.

I hold back an eye roll. "Did you come all this way just to state the obvious? I'm well aware." I return my focus to my emails, hoping he'll take the hint and slither out. But instead, my laptop pings with a new text message—from Julian, of all people. I don't even want to know how he got my number.

"You're texting me while sitting right in front of me?" I ask, irritation edging my voice.

"Open it," he replies, his smug smirk firmly in place, chin propped on his hand like he's lounging. His way of looking at you feels like a thousand invisible spiders crawling under your skin. I'm not afraid of him—far from it. It's more a reaction of pure disgust.

Fine. If opening whatever this is will get him out of my office sooner, I'll play along. I pulled out my phone and clicked on the message, noticing an attached audio file. I raise a brow. "What's this?"

He stands, straightening his suit jacket like he's preparing for a photo shoot, then picks at an invisible speck of lint on his sleeve before leaning against my desk. I suppress a groan, picturing the disinfectant wipes I'll need to sanitize whatever he touches. He's like a human contagion I'd rather not catch.

"Consider it an early Christmas present," he says, fingers drumming on my desk with too much satisfaction. "Always a pleasure, Alex."

Not even a little bit.

I don't say a word as I stare at the recording. With a click, Violet's voice fills the air, mingled with Julian's smooth, sickly-sweet tone. It's the kind of voice he probably thinks sounds charming, but to me, it's all creep and sleaze. I can hear the rustling, like he's recording her on the sly, probably using some cheap device in his pocket. Pathetic.

But then, the conversation filters through, and each word lands like a punch to the gut. The world seems to slow, every second dragging like a weight. I replay it, needing to catch every word, hoping I've misunderstood.

What. The. Hell.

It's a recording of Violet and Julian, but she's laughing—almost playfully—and spilling details about my business. Her voice, so casual, so open, twists in my chest like a knife. I replay it again. And again. Each time, my grip tightens around my phone until my knuckles go white, my mind racing with disbelief and something that feels a hell of a lot like betrayal.

I jab the intercom button with a shaking hand. "Penelope, I'm leaving for the day," I manage, barely holding myself together.

As I'm shoving things into my briefcase, Dom saunters in, his usual laid-back attitude shifting when he notices my expression. "What did he want?" Dom shudders, glancing over his shoulder as if Julian's presence still lingers in the room. "That guy creeps me out. They don't call him the Grim Reaper for nothing."

I don't answer. I can't. Words are tangled up with the fire in my chest, burning too hot to let out.

Dom's brows pull together, concern in his voice. "You good?"

I look up sharply, barely restraining the rage. "I know who's been leaking information," I bite out. And that's all I say before storming out, my chest heaving like I've been punched.

I tell Antonio to drive me home, knowing Violet will already be there. She'll be waiting, like always, but today... today, everything has changed.

Alex

I LEAVE THE CAR, and the elevator ride up feels like a slow, torturous countdown. Each tick of the floor number grates on my nerves, winding me tighter with every passing second. By the time I reach the penthouse, I'm ready to explode.

When I push open the door, there she is—Violet, sitting on the couch, a book in her lap. Her smile lights up the room when she sees me, warm and bright, like nothing's wrong.

She's *smiling* at me? Seriously?

I freeze, caught between the past and the present. The memory of that night in the bar when she first caught my eye collides with the recording I had listened to earlier. The woman who captivated me—whose laugh I craved, whose body I memorized, whose soul I thought I understood—now sits there, looking at me like she hasn't done anything.

She blinks at me, the smile fading as silence stretches between us. Her expression shifts, worry replacing the ease like she's picking up on the crackling energy in the air. Did Julian plant her from the start? He's twisted enough to do something like that, but again, I pursued her. How could he have known I'd choose her?

Or did he get to her later, once we got close? It's a tangled mess in my head; the only things that make sense are the hot threads of anger, betrayal, and hurt burning through me.

"Alex, is everything okay?" she asks, her voice soft but cautious.

Is she serious right now?

"What did you say to Julian at the event the other night?" My voice comes out hard, sharper than I intended.

She freezes, her face paling. "What do you mean?"

Her body stiffens, and I see the shift in her eyes—the concern morphing into confusion, then panic. She's scanning me like she's trying to find a clue, a lifeline. Is she scrambling for a story? A lie? She doesn't know she was recorded.

"What did you say to Julian?" I press, each word dripping with barely restrained fury.

Why am I even asking? I have the recording. Maybe, deep down, I want to hear it from her. I wanted to listen to her admit she had gone behind my back. Hear from those perfect lips that have whispered my name, that I've kissed more times than I can count. I want her to say it so I can figure out if any of this—any of *us*—was ever real.

"I... I don't know," she stammers, and it's almost impressive how easily she slips into that role, but it only makes my blood boil hotter. "We chatted about the gala... he asked about your work. We didn't talk about much. He creeps me out, so I tried to keep it short."

Unbelievable.

I move closer, and she backs up, scrambling to the edge of the couch like a cornered animal. When I'm standing right over her, I lean down, trapping her with an arm on each side. "Don't lie to me, Violet. I know what you said. I have a recording."

Her eyes widen, panic flashing across her face. "A recording?"

It's amazing how people react when they're caught in a lie.

"Stop lying, and tell me what you talked about with Julian." My voice is ice-cold. Controlled, but barely. It's a miracle I'm not shouting.

Her green eyes blink rapidly, and she bites her lower lip, probably scrambling for a way out of this mess. I ignore the tears starting to well up in the corners of her eyes—right now, I don't have room for sympathy.

"I don't know. He asked me questions, but I didn't tell him anything. I swear."

I scoff, stepping closer, my voice dripping with contempt. "So, you're still going to lie, even after I told you I have a recording? You mentioned *Alton Technical*. Now he's playing hardball, avoiding my traps because *you* clued him in on the one company I want. We thought the leak was from someone in my company. Didn't realize it was the woman I loved screwing me over." The words burn in my throat, and I know I'll never repeat them.

I push away from her, looming over her petite frame. "I don't know what you think I said or what Julian twisted, but—"

"You *suggested* I use my family's mafia connections, and you flirted with him. You're still denying it, even though I have the proof. It's all on that damn recording, Violet. And guess what? He plans to release it to the media. Especially the part where you imply that my family's business is tied up with mine. You know how hard I've worked to keep those worlds separate."

My voice reverberates through the room, every word sharp enough to cut. Her face is pale, eyes wide with fear and confusion. But I'm beyond caring about the tears spilling down her cheeks. All I see is the betrayal, the cracks in the foundation I thought we were building.

She blinks rapidly, her face shifting from shock to anger as she stands. "I would never flirt with that creep, and you know I wouldn't say that about you and your family," she insists, shaking her head like she's trying to convince herself as much as me. "I wouldn't. I don't care what the recording says—you heard it wrong."

You have got to be kidding me. Is she delusional?

"Oh, I heard it just fine, Violet. Why don't I play it for you? Then you can stand there and keep lying to my face." My voice comes out cold, harder than I intend, but I can't reel it back now.

She crosses her arms, tears glossing over her eyes, and a doubt flares in my chest for a fleeting moment. What if she... no. It's on tape. It's on the damn tape, and I can't let myself forget that.

I pull out my phone, my thumb hovering over the play button, and then press it. The recording plays in the room, every word I've memorized pounding like a drumbeat. Only now is it worse, hearing it with her right here—denying it with those fake tears.

Julian: Violet, you look absolutely stunning tonight. How's your night treating you?

Violet: Oh Julian, compliments from you? What's the catch tonight?

Julian: You wound me. No catch. Just genuine interest. *A laugh from Violet*

Julian: So, how's everything going with Alex these days? Any new ambitious plans he has in the works?

Violet: *Laughs* You know him. He's relentless.

Julian: C'mon Violet, give me just a taste. You know his family and what they are. You telling me he doesn't lean on the family name to stay ahead?

Violet: I'd tell you... he's brilliant like that. Of course, the family is involved. The Bennetti name carries weight, and then some. Alex is smart enough to use it just enough to get what he needs.

Julian: So, has he talked to you about Alton Technical?

Violet: Oh, you know already... driving up the price so you pay more, but we both know what he's really after.

Julian: *Laughs* Fair enough. Thanks for the chat, Violet. Oh, and Violet, when you get bored of our boy, you know where to find me.

Violet: *Laugh* Julian, I just might consider that.

As the recording ends, her face goes ghostly pale. She looks like someone just pulled the ground from beneath her feet. Every word hits, and with each one, she opens her mouth like she will say something to explain, but nothing comes out. Is she working on an excuse?

"I swear... I swear that's not the conversation I had with him. I promise you." Her voice is barely a whisper, trembling, her eyes wide and glassy. Damn, she's good—a world-class actress, right in front of me. But I'm done playing her games.

I close the distance between us, slow and deliberate until she's backed up against the wall, trapped between my arms. My hands press against the wall on either side of her head, caging her in. Her breath hitches. "It's a fucking recording, Violet. Don't lie to me."

"I'm not!" she cries, her voice cracking as tears stream down her cheeks. "I swear, I didn't say those things. I mean, some of them, but not like that. That wasn't the conversation. I don't know what's going on!" She grips my shirt, fingers clutching tight, but I rip her hands away, shoving them back toward her. "Please, please, I need you to believe me. I didn't say it like that."

"But you're not denying you spoke to him, are you?"

"I did, but he's a creep! I hate him more than you do. I didn't say those things, Alex. I can't even explain it. I don't know how or what happened. Please, please believe me."

"It's recorded, Violet." My voice is cold and unyielding, and I shake my head, disgust twisting in my gut. "You know, this is what I get. You don't know this world, and maybe Julian planted you from the start to mess with me, but it doesn't even matter anymore." I push off the wall, turning my back on her. "You didn't just betray me. You handed over my business—my life—to him. And then you flirted with him?"

I stalked down the hall toward our bedroom, her following behind. I ignored her and threw open the closet, grabbing a suitcase. It landed on the bed with a thud, and I started tossing her clothes inside, my movements rough and angry.

"You know, I was going to ask you to marry me. Thank fuck I didn't." The words taste bitter as they leave my mouth, and I throw more of her things into the bag, not caring how they land.

"What are you doing? Alex, please!" Her voice cracks, but I ignore her, heading into the bathroom to grab whatever toiletries she might need and tossing them in without a second thought. Pulling out my wallet, I throw $500 onto the bed beside the suitcase.

"Take that. Use it for a cab, or a hotel, or wherever the hell you want to go. But don't come back."

Her mascara runs in black streaks down her face, and the sobs racking her body twist something in my chest, but I force myself to look away. She gave up her apartment to move here, but that's not my problem now. She can figure it out.

"Alex," she whispers, reaching out, but I yank my arm free, causing her to stumble back into the dresser.

"Do. Not. Fucking. Touch. Me." I am seething with every ounce of anger I have. "Get out. Go find someone else to use."

She straightens, her eyes wild, the desperation replaced by fury. "So, you're not even going to believe me?"

"It's recorded, Violet. What do you expect me to believe?"

"Maybe you loved me," she snaps, her voice raw and broken. "You knew me well enough to realize I wouldn't do this. But I guess you never really knew me at all. So you know what, Alex? Fuck you."

She zips up the suitcase with shaky hands, yanking sneakers from the closet and slipping them on alongside a hoodie. I watch her gather her laptop, shoving it into her bag before slinging her purse over her shoulder. She doesn't look back as she drags her suitcase to the front door, the sound of it scraping against the floor more grating than it should be like it's etching the moment permanently. The door slams shut, the lock clicking behind her, sealing the emptiness she's left behind.

I stand there, listening to the silence momentarily before I make my way to the bed. I don't bother to watch her leave from the window. Instead, I sit on the edge, staring at the chaos of clothes and sheets, her scent still clinging to the air, making breathing hard.

Just another Natalia. Just another woman out to serve herself.

I walk back to the living room, intending to pour myself a drink, but I grab the whole bottle instead. I head to the guest room, loosening my tie as I collapse onto the bed, drinking straight from the bottle like it might drown out the thoughts.

But it doesn't. I pull out my phone, open the recording app, and replay it repeatedly, each word scraping against the raw edges of my heart.

She's such a fucking liar. It's all right there—every damn word.

Alex

I'VE NEVER MISSED A day of work. Ever.

Barely alive with the flu? I'm in the office.

Suffering the world's worst food poisoning after Dante convinced me to try some sketchy taco cart? Still in the office.

But getting betrayed, used again, and realizing I was stupid enough to let it happen for a second time? *That* kept me home.

Now, I'm here on my couch, making my way through the liquor cabinet, replaying every second of last night—her face, the shock, the tears—unbelievable. For a split second, I almost bought it. Almost. I cut off that line of thinking fast because the evidence was sitting on my phone, taunting me—that recording, those words, replaying repeatedly as I take another swig straight from the bottle.

And sure, I didn't show up at the office, but that didn't mean I wasn't working. I tried reviewing reports, but every word blurred, and every number looked like another lie. Rational thought? Out the window. I don't even know how often I've called Penelope, berating her over things that had nothing to do with her. And I'm pretty sure a few of those calls happened while I was slurring.

Eventually, she snapped. "Call me when you're sober and when you can speak like an adult," she'd said before hanging up on me. My assistant, who never wavers, hung up on me. I can't even blame her.

I tried Dominic next, thinking he'd back me up. But he only told me I was being irrational, that I was screwing up. "Irrational? I have a fucking recording!" I'd shouted back, but Dom sighed, probably rolling his eyes on the other end.

I'm trapped in this pit of anger, bitterness, and self-pity. No matter how many times I replay it, whether I'm drunk or stone-cold sober, I can't claw my way out of it.

At least in this state of numbness, I don't feel anything. But as soon as it fades, everything rushes back in.

It's been forty-eight hours since she left, and I stare at my phone as if it will magically give me answers. Why would I expect her to call? And even if she did, what would she say? Apologize? Beg for forgiveness?

It wouldn't matter. I wouldn't believe a word of it. I didn't believe her before, so what will change now? So why does this knot in my chest keep tightening? She betrayed me, and I told her to go. End of story. Right?

A sharp knock at the door interrupts my thoughts, but I plan to ignore it until it turns into pounding.

"Jesus Christ, knock it off!" I drag myself off the couch, still in the same sweats and T-shirt I've been living in, and yank open the door.

Dante's standing in a suit, looking like he's stepped off a magazine cover, only makes me more aware of how disheveled I am. Behind him, Dom pushes his way in, right along with Dante. Dante's expression is neutral, but Dom's? He looks like he's about to wring my neck. Great. It figures she'd turn my blood against me.

"Please, come inside," I mutter sarcastically, stumbling back to the couch. It's pathetic how this couch, which I barely used before, now feels like it's molding itself to me. I've never been home this much—usually, I'm working, barely spending time in this penthouse. Until she moved in. Then suddenly, this place felt like a home, not just a crash pad.

Dante takes the armchair on my left, and Dom sits to my right, unbuttoning his jacket as he scans the empty bottles across the coffee table. "You want to talk about it?"

"Do I look like I need to talk about it?" I snap, taking another swig straight from the bottle.

He shrugs. It's not the reaction I hoped for, but it's typical Dante.

Dom sighs, leaning in, and I can see the wheels turning in his head. "You want to hear my thoughts?"

"No." I know it won't stop him. Dom says whatever he wants, whether I ask for it or not.

He rubs his jaw, glancing at me before looking away, like he's picking his words carefully. That's never a good sign. "Just spit it out, Dom," I mutter, feeling the burn of the liquor as I take another drink.

He leans forward, voice firm. "I don't think she did it."

I laugh, but there's no humor in it. "Are you kidding me with this shit?" I pull out my phone, bring up the recording I've tortured myself with and hit play. I hold it out, letting the voices echo through the room—each word like a jab to the gut. "Go on, tell me how she didn't say that."

Dom shrugs again. "Julian's a snake. Maybe he baited her. Maybe he doctored the tape. She denied it, didn't she?"

I down another long pull from the bottle, willing myself to get drunk enough to drown out his voice. Because the alternative—listening to him, letting that tiny seed of doubt sprout—is too dangerous to consider.

"I saw them talking at the event on the terrace. That's when this recording was made. She was talking to him," I say, gripping the bottle like it's my only lifeline.

Dante shoots up from his seat, swiping the bottle from my hand with a speed that catches me off guard. He sets it down gently on the coffee table, his usual easygoing demeanor nowhere to be found. "You've had enough."

I narrow my eyes at him. "I don't need you to come here and play life coach. I've got this handled."

"Do you, though?" His voice is sharper than I've ever heard, cutting through the haze. Dante, pissed off, is a rare sight. He's the steady one, the calm in the storm—even with a Sicilian temper lurking beneath. It takes a lot to set him off, and now he's staring at me like he doesn't recognize the man sitting in front of him.

He leans back in the armchair, chin propped on his hand, looking like he's about to deliver a verdict. "Right now, you're being a complete asshole. You're taking the word of that snake Julian over her? It makes me question why I've respected you for this long." He stands, buttoning his suit jacket with a snap, his eyes hard as he glares down at me. "Maybe it's for the best. If this is how you're going to treat her, you didn't deserve her in the first place."

"Oh, screw off," I mutter, not even looking at him.

"Gladly. You do you, Alex. Like you always have." He storms out, the door slamming behind him, leaving a trail of frustration in his wake.

Dom stands up next, shaking his head slowly like he's disappointed but not surprised. "She didn't do it, Alex. I know it. I don't care what you think you heard or what Julian spun for you, but you never deserved her if you let her go that fast."

I scoff, but my throat feels tight. "We knew someone was feeding information. She practically handed him everything—told him exactly which company I was after."

Dom crosses his arms, eyes narrowing as he watches me stumble over my conviction. "Did she? Or are you just hearing what Julian wants you to hear? How many other companies did you talk to her about? Did you ever give her the names of the decoy companies?"

My head feels foggy, swimming in a mix of alcohol and doubt. I can't recall every detail, every conversation. Maybe I mentioned acquisitions, but specifics? I shake my head, forcing the thoughts away. No. I must have told her the names. She was on that tape, after all. It's proof.

"It's on tape, Dom," I snap, my voice unsteady, the desperation bleeding through.

Dom shakes his head, disgust clear on his face. "If that's what helps you sleep, brother, then you're more lost than I thought."

"It does," I take another swig of my alcohol, and my brother stands there, nothing but disgust on his face before he storms out.

Alex

I DO NOT KNOW how they got into my house, but someone on my security team is getting fired when my parents leave. My papa yanks open the curtains, flooding the room with blinding light, while my mama rips the covers off me, utterly unbothered by the fact that I'm lying there, stark naked in my guest room, with three empty bottles on the nightstand.

"What the hell are you doing?" I groan, my voice barely more than a rasp, my head pounding like a drum. Everything sounds like echoes, a muffled noise until I catch the rapid-fire Italian curses. That's when I realized it was Mama. Of course, it is.

"Mama, get out," I grumble, pressing a pillow over my head, trying to drown out the world, not caring that she's probably getting an eyeful.

"Like hell I am," she snapped back, her voice sharp enough to pierce through my skull. I don't have the energy to handle her right now.

"Dom told me what happened," she says firmly.

I groan louder, rolling over and burying my face deeper into the pillow, ignoring the fact that my ass is entirely on display. She barged in here—her problem, not mine.

"Dude, get up." Dante's voice cuts through the chaos, loud and booming. Just great. How many people are in my room now? He's seen worse, so I don't even bother to care.

"Sei un fottuto idiota," Papa mutters as he grabs my wrist and hauls me upright with surprising strength for his size.

I groan, clutching the covers around my waist, slumping against the headboard, barely managing to keep my eyes open against the pounding in my head. What a way to start the day.

"You haven't been at work," Dom says, voice flat. I can't tell if he's irritated because he's been picking up my slack or just concerned, but I'm too busy figuring out how to get the four of them out of my house—or at least get a drink in my hand to chase away this hangover.

"No shit. Taking a few sick days."

"More like embracing your new career as an alcoholic," Dom shoots back, while Mama mutters under her breath in Italian, gathering up the empty bottles and hauling them to the kitchen.

Papa's voice cuts through the haze in my brain, rough and unforgiving. "Where is Violet?"

"Gone. I ended it. She betrayed me." The words come out harsh, but they sting even more on the way out.

Dante settles himself on the edge of the bed, dangerously close, considering the thin sheet is all that separates him from a full view of my bare ass. He tosses an envelope at me, and it lands on my chest.

"I want to understand something. You're choosing to believe Julian—an absolute snake—over Violet?"

I grab my phone from the nightstand, but it's dead. Still, I hold it up, my hand trembling with irritation. "You heard the damn recording when you came over the other day."

Dante's eyes darken, his expression angrier than I've ever seen. He picks up the envelope and shoves it right in my face. "Yeah, I heard it, but I decided to do some digging while you ran off to ruin your life. I went to Evander Harrington."

I freeze, my focus narrowing on him. "Why would you do that?"

His voice is pure frustration, a growl of disbelief. "Because, unlike you, I believe Violet. Hell, everyone in this room does. So while you've been holed up here playing the brooding idiot, Dom's been running the business, Rico's been working on figuring out Julian's game, and I've been trying to prove you're a damn fool."

Great. My family is constantly swooping in with their brutal honesty and unwanted interventions.

"But why Evander?" I demand, the question tumbling out before I can stop it. *Seriously? That's what I'm focusing on right now.* "Now he knows stuff he doesn't need to. Why didn't you go to Holmes?"

Dante stares down at me, one brow arched in that infuriating way he has. "Holmes doesn't pick up his phone after midnight, and you know it. Besides, Evander owed me a favor."

I shake my head. I don't even want to know how Dante managed to get a favor from Evander Harrington. The Harringtons don't dish out favors lightly, especially Evander. And now, because Dante cashed in that favor with one of the best hackers in the game, I owe him big time. And Dante isn't the type to let go of a favor until he's ready to collect, and he'll squeeze every last drop when he does.

I rip open the envelope, my hands unsteady, and pull out a stack of papers. Metadata, call logs, timestamps—all from Julian's phone. "What is this?"

Dante's eyes harden. "Julian made the recording at the charity event but edited it that same night. Evander hacked into his phone and computers and pulled the original conversation."

My stomach lurches. *"Original conversation"* hits me like a punch to the gut. It means what I heard was doctored, twisted beyond recognition, and every drop of alcohol I've consumed over the past two days seems to claw its way back up my throat.

"Oh, just now realizing that maybe that prick Julian lied to you?" Dante flips another page of the report. "Evander transcribed the original conversation and analyzed the recording. He even detailed where each word, laugh, and comment was cut and pasted into that new version you've repeatedly listened to."

Dante stands, raking his fingers through his hair as he buttons his jacket. Meanwhile, Papa stands there, arms crossed, eyes hard. "You read this?" I ask, my voice rough as gravel.

Dom's face is darker and angrier than I've ever seen him, which says a lot, considering he's the guy who can watch cartoons with his five-year-old son all day without flinching.

"My gut told me to have Dante look into it after I heard what went down. That woman didn't seem like the type to do this." My papa's voice is stern, his eyes boring into mine with an edge I've never seen before—disappointment. It's a knife to the gut, one I hadn't expected, and damn, it hurts.

Great. It's just what I needed.

My hands tremble as I flip through the pages of the original transcript. It's a mix of dehydration, a hangover pounding through my skull, and the brutal realization that maybe, just maybe, I was wrong. Mama shoves an electrolyte drink into my hands, but there's no warmth in her voice when she speaks. "Drink it, you fucking moron," she hisses before disappearing out of the room.

So much for motherly love.

I take a shaky sip, the taste almost as bitter as the mess I've made, and reach for my phone—dead, of course. "Give me your phone," I bark, holding my hand to Dante.

He doesn't budge. "You can't call her."

I freeze, glaring up at him. "And why the hell not?"

"She's gone, Alex. I had to bring in Uncle Tony's men to track her down. She's off the grid—no phone, no trace. Evander tried to ping her location, but her phone had been disconnected. I even talked to her parents, but they had no clue where she was. They didn't seem to care much either, so take that as you will."

My mind races. "She wouldn't go back to them. It's complicated, and I don't have time to explain." I rub my temples with the edge of the papers, not doing myself any favors with the headache. "Holmes. Did you get him on it? And what about Max? He's her best friend—he might know."

"No dice," Dante says, crossing his arms. "Max claims he has no idea where she is, and honestly? If he does, he sure as hell isn't telling you."

I scowl. "Give me your damn phone."

With a heavy sigh, Dante hands it over, and I dial Holmes, praying he's got something up his sleeve.

"Dante, my man, what do you need?" Holmes's voice crackles through the speaker, full of casual amusement.

"It's Alex, using Dante's phone."

"Oh," he snorts, and I can practically hear the eye roll through the line. I'll ignore that for now.

"I need you to track down Violet. She left three days ago, her phone's off. Can you find her?"

Holmes chuckles, but there's an edge to it. "This isn't going to be one of those creepy stalking things, is it?"

"Just do it, Holmes!" I snap, hanging up before he can get another word in. I plug in my phone, shoving the charger into the wall like it might make the damn thing boot up faster.

When I turn back around, still stark naked, Dante stares at me. "Shower first, Alex."

Dom smirks, shaking his head. "Make that two showers. And a good scrub. You smell like a bar that caught fire and forgot to burn down."

Alex

Holmes tracked Violet's last calls and texts to Valeria's before she vanished completely. Now, here I am, standing in my cousin's living room, surrounded by her curated chaos while she lounges on the couch, cool as ice. Dante tagged along, probably for the sheer entertainment of watching me suffer. Dom had to pick Luca up from preschool, but he's already told Dante to keep him updated.

Valeria reclines on her sofa, her eyes glued to some reality TV nonsense while my patience hangs by a thread, my head pounding from the worst hangover of my life. She swirls her wine, taking slow, savoring sips like she's at a spa retreat instead of holed up in her overpriced apartment.

"Valeria..." It's the third time I've tried to get her attention, my tone a razor's edge. She lifts a perfectly manicured, blood-red fingernail in the air, motioning for me to zip it until the commercials.

I try to channel all that breathing and meditation nonsense Violet used to preach about. But honestly, I'm two seconds away from snapping, and in my current state of shit sleep and lack of food, she'd probably have me on the floor before I could land a single punch. That would be the final humiliation, and I'm not signing up for that.

"Fucking hell," Dante finally snaps, striding over to the glass coffee table cluttered with Valeria's stack of trashy magazines. He grabs the remote and clicks the TV off before she can even make a sound.

Thank God. My headache sends Dante a silent thank you while Valeria unleashes a storm of Italian curses.

"Where's Violet?" I grind out, rubbing my temples as if it'll magically make all this disappear.

She cocks an eyebrow, her face the picture of innocence. "I don't know what you mean."

Oh, she wants to play games? Fine. Let's play.

I lunge forward, closing the space between us, caging her in with an arm on each side as she scoots back on the leather couch like a cowering poodle. My face is inches from hers, and I know damn well those manicured claws of hers are sharper than any knife in her designer-filled apartment. "Where. Is. My. Girlfriend?"

Valeria taps her lips with those nails, drawing out every second to get under my skin.

"Last I heard, she wasn't your girlfriend because you're a stupid jackass."

Of course, the entire family knows. Why wouldn't they? They've probably all been gossiping about my screw-up. I push away from the couch, smoothing the front of my suit. Formal attire felt like the right choice today. You never know where the day will take you, and I can't show up looking like I just crawled out of a three-day bender, even if that's exactly what I did.

"Valeria... I'm running out of patience. Just tell me. Please."

She studies me, then her eyes narrow, lips curling into a smirk. "Do you love her?"

That's the question she decides to ask. Now?

"Of course I do. Why else would I be here?"

"Then why didn't you believe her?"

"I'm not in the mood for this—"

She stands, tugging down her mini skirt, and I catch Antonio, my bodyguard, checking her out. She gives him a flirty smile. I shoot him a glare, and suddenly, he finds the ceiling and the carpet far more interesting. "No fun, cousin," she mutters, stepping closer, adjusting my tie like this is some casual chat. "If I tell you, you erase all favors I owe you, and you owe me a favor. One."

Desperation twists inside me, making me agree before I think it through. "Fine," I bite out, and Dante whistles under his breath like he's watching a soap opera unfold.

She leans closer, her voice dropping. "I gave her to Marco. To keep her safe."

I freeze, every muscle locking tight as her words sink in. Dante's face pales, and he takes a few steps back, muttering curses.

"Valeria, say that again and think really hard about how much sense it makes. You gave her to Marco to keep her safe? Do you remember who Marco is?" My voice rises, edged with disbelief. My mind is already running through the scenarios, and none are good.

She rolls her eyes. "Well aware. Trust me, he wouldn't touch your woman. He knows the rules."

I stare at her, fury and dread churning in my gut. "Then again," she continues, crossing her arms and giving me that smug tilt, "she's not your woman anymore, is she? Not after you threw her out and handed her cab fare?"

The image flashes through my mind—me tossing money at Violet, telling her to get out like some heartless jerk. Yeah, I'm an asshole, but that doesn't mean she should be with Marco right now. He might know the rules, but Marco bends them to his will. He does whatever he damn well pleases.

Valeria shrugs, hopping back onto the sofa with a smirk. "You'll have to deal with Marco to find out where he took her, and honestly, I don't pity you. Maybe I even did this to teach you a lesson."

Of course, she would. Typical.

The last thing I want to do is deal with Marco. I tolerate him at best. Now, I've got to ask him where he's stashed my girlfriend. Marco wouldn't hurt her—he knows she's important to the family, and even Uncle Tony wouldn't dare cross my father. But that doesn't mean I trust him with her.

I tried calling Marco, but he sent me straight to voicemail. Asshole. So, I pull up my text messages instead, tapping out the frustration with each keystroke.

Alex: Where the fuck is she? If you touch her, I will end you.

Marco: Always love our chats, cousin.

Alex: ...

Marco: She's hot. Never thought I'd say that about a chick who's not Sicilian, but damn. Those curves. Is she sure she doesn't have some Italian in her?

I clench my jaw, tapping my phone against my forehead, trying to think of a way to get answers from him without making this explode into a full-blown family feud.

Alex: I screwed up. I need to know where she is.

Marco: I put her up in one of my places, but she asked me not to tell you.

Alex: Since when have you respected anyone's wishes, especially a woman's?

Marco: Since they're smoking hot, and she had good reasons. Wasn't even scared of me. Mouthed off to me like it was nothing. Kind of makes me question the vibes I'm putting off. Might need to work on my intimidating factor.

Alex: This isn't about your ego right now.

Marco: Should be, but nah, I'm sticking to my word. She doesn't want to be found, and while you're family, I'm a man of my word.

Alex: Since when?

Marco: You really want to question me right now?

Alex: I'm family.

Marco: A word's a word—family or not.

Alex: Go to hell.

Marco: Got a guy on her. Chill. She knows how to get in touch when she's ready to leave. It's up to her if she wants to see you.

Alex: When did you become the noble type?

Marco: Never, but Valeria cashed in a favor.

Alex: Let me cash in one of mine, and you can tell me where she is.

Marco: Love you, cousin. See you at Christmas.

Without thinking, I hurl my phone across the room. It shatters against one of Valeria's ridiculous purple-painted walls. "Fuck!" The sound echoes through the living room, followed by an awkward silence.

Valeria arches a brow, unfazed. "Marco playing games?"

No, for once, he's decent, which makes it worse. "She's gone. She doesn't want to be found, and Marco's honoring it."

Dante crosses his arms, his face a mask of contemplation. "Holmes can still look."

I shake my head. "He won't find her. Marco's too good at hiding people, secrets, and anything he wants to stay buried. Alive or not."

I feel the words burn in my throat as the reality sinks in. She's gone. She doesn't want to be found.

Violet

I'd never been to Miami, and trust me, this is not how I pictured seeing it for the first time. But desperate times, right? After leaving Alex's house with my suitcase and no real plan, I tried calling Max, but he didn't pick up. So, I turned to the next person I could think of, Valeria.

The second I stepped into her apartment, I practically crumbled into her arms. Thank God she's stronger than she looks because I was a pile of nothing but sobs.

"What happened?!" she demanded, holding me tight as I curled up on her foyer floor, suitcase behind me, tears streaming down my face. She didn't even ask why I had it.

I don't know how long I stayed there, crying until my eyes felt filled with sandpaper. Eventually, I told Valeria everything. The gala. The conversation I thought I'd had with Julian. The tape. And, of course, what Alex said to me when he threw me out. For the record, I left the money he gave me on the bed—*not our bed anymore.*

Valeria cupped my face with those claws she calls nails, her grip both firm and weirdly comforting. "He's my cousin, and I love him, but he's a jackass," she said before kissing my forehead. "Stay here."

I shook my head. "No, I need to get away. He knows we're close, and I don't want to risk running into him. I need distance. I can't go home." My voice cracked, and I bit my lip hard. Valeria knows a little about my relationship with my parents but not the whole story. "I can't go to my parents. Is there somewhere I can go where Alex can't find me? I just... I need to be far away."

Not that I think he'd come looking for me—he made it pretty clear where he stood. But the idea of being in the same zip code as him, of feeling that tight, crushing ache in my chest every time I think about running into him, was unbearable.

And let's not even get started on the media. Once word got out that Alex and I split, they'd be all over me like vultures, and I'm not sure I'm strong enough to handle that right now.

So, yeah. The thought of seeing Alex again? It's enough to make me run as far as I can. Hearing his voice, seeing his face, feeling that familiar pang in my chest—it's all too much.

"I know someone..." Valeria taps a perfectly manicured nail against her lips, clearly thinking. "It's my cousin, Marco."

As in *mafia* Marco? My stomach flips. "I... I don't know about that, Valeria."

She waves dismissively like we're discussing weekend plans, not trusting a mafia guy. "Marco's many things, but he's still family. *My* family. I trust him, so you can too. Let me call him."

A little while later, Marco arrives, flanked by a human mountain. Seriously, this guy makes Antonio look like a friendly neighborhood bouncer. He's stuffed into a suit that barely contains him, with a face so expressionless I wonder if his muscles even know how to move. It's unsettling, to say the least.

Worse, Marco's resemblance to Alex is uncanny—same strong jawline, same dark hair. But while Alex's eyes are a piercing sky blue, Marco's are a deep brown, shadowed with something far less friendly. The sight tightens my chest with mixed emotions I can't untangle. How exactly does one greet a mafia boss? Handshake? Awkward wave? Secret handshake? I'm frozen, clueless.

Valeria, thankfully, takes the lead. "This is Marco, and behind him is also Marco," she smirks.

I raise a brow, trying to keep up. "Uh, what?"

Marco cracks a small smile—just barely. "Yes, it's confusing. You can call him Marcello when we're both around. It'll save us all some headaches."

I nod, trying to absorb everything without letting my nerves show.

There isn't much conversation after that. Marcello gathers my things, Valeria pulls me into a tight hug, and before I know it, I'm whisked onto a private jet—*Marco's* private jet, to be specific. The guy can summon a jet whenever he feels like it—whether that's a perk of his money or his mafia connections, I'm not about to ask.

Buckled in, I try to wrap my head around what's happening. A flight attendant hands me a tumbler filled with amber liquid that smells like oak and spice.

"Drink," Marco says, settling into the seat across from me.

I shake my head. "I'm not much of a drinker."

"You need it," he replies, shoving the glass closer until I take it. Reluctantly, I take a sip. It burns, but this warm, honeyed aftertaste almost makes it go down smooth. As the warmth spreads through me, I realize how cold I've felt for the past 24 hours—like the heat is finally thawing me out. At least enough to function.

"Give me your phone," Marco says abruptly.

"Excuse me?"

"Your phone. Before that shit Holmes tracks you."

I have no clue who Holmes is, but from the look on Marco's face, I'm not about to argue. I dig my phone out of my bag and hand it over. Marcello takes it, pops it open, yanks out a chip, and smashes it under his heel like he's stomping out a cigarette.

Marcello handed me a new phone, which was much more basic than my old one. "This is your new device. My number, Valeria's, and Marcello's are preprogrammed. Use it to reach us if you need anything."

I stare at him, trying to process this new reality—a burner phone. It's like I'm in some spy movie, except there's no glamorous soundtrack playing in the background.

Sighing, Marco rubs a hand over his jaw like he's dealing with a stubborn child. "It's a burner phone, sweetheart. It can't be traced."

I never thought I'd be here—using a burner phone on a mafia jet, feeling like an extra in a crime drama. Life, you've got a weird sense of humor.

"Where are you taking me?" I ask, staring out the window at nothing but darkness. The hum of the plane engine fills the silence, my nerves buzzing just as loudly.

Marco glances over, casual as ever. "I have a place in Miami I don't use often. Alex doesn't know about it. I bought it a few months back. You'll be comfortable there." He jerks a thumb toward Marcello, the human mountain who's made himself look even bigger in the cramped jet seat. "He'll stay with you. You don't leave without him, don't go anywhere without him, and if you need something, you ask him. He's there to keep an eye on you."

Do I need protection? The question clings to my tongue, but I swallow it down. Instead, I nod, closing my eyes as the whiskey warmth settles deeper into my bones. Letting it work its magic, I give in to the exhaustion pulling me under.

***

TWO DAYS LATER

I've been crumpled up on Marco's Miami penthouse couch for what feels like forever. Sleep? Not happening. In just a few short months, I forgot how to sleep without Alex beside me. I even tried stacking pillows behind me, hoping they'd mimic the warmth and pressure of his body. Spoiler: they didn't. So, I've resigned myself to the couch, hoping it'll offer some comfort.

Showering? Nope.

Washing my face? Not in days.

I've been parked here, binging every rom-com ever made—yes, even the really bad ones that should have stayed buried in a studio vault somewhere. But at this point, I'll take any dose of happily-ever-after I can get, even if it's wrapped in cheesy dialogue and unrealistic plot twists.

Am I wallowing in self-pity? Oh, definitely.

This has to be rock bottom. I am hiding out in a mafia man's penthouse, using a burner phone, with a bodyguard who watches me like I'm some rare species. Marcello, for the most part, keeps his distance. He brings groceries and drops off meals, and one night, when I was ugly-crying so loudly I probably made him uncomfortable, he left a pint of Ben & Jerry's outside my door—the guy's got layers.

But the worst part, the part that crushes me, is knowing I still love Alex. Love doesn't just vanish like that, no matter how badly I wish it would. Denial is a lovely fantasy, but even I have to admit the truth—I still care about him. I'm not stupid.

My phone pings, the burner was glowing with a text from Max.

> **Max:** How are you holding up?

> **Violet:** It's been two days, and I've watched over a dozen movies. I'm crying so much that Marcello had to buy more tissues. And he brought me ice cream.

> **Max:** I wish I were there, babe.

> **Violet:** I know. I wish you were too. Did you get the pictures I sent you? The ones of the penthouse like you asked?

> **Max:** Yes, and I'd kill to be in that penthouse in Miami... with Marcello. Damn, that man is hot.

Trust Max to zero in on my stoic, brick wall of a bodyguard. After checking with Marco, I gave Max the number and sent him photos of my temporary hideout. Of course, the second Max saw a photo of Marcello, he went full heart eyes. Since his latest relationship crashed and burned, he's been back on the market, and apparently, Marcello is now his prime target.

I mean, sure, Marcello's got the whole muscle-bound, brooding thing going on, but I can't see myself casually asking him if he's into dudes. Yeah, right. That conversation would be as smooth as the ice cream he left at my door.

Max: Look on the bright side, Vi. At least your parents can't call you every Saturday to tear you down anymore.

Violet: True. That's definitely one of the pros on my list.

Max: Oh God, no. Tell me you're not making a pros and cons list. You always do that when you're spiraling.

Violet: I'm not *starting* to spiral, Max. I'm already there.

Max: You know what I mean. Hit me with the pros.

Violet: Well, not having to talk to my parents ranked pretty high. Plus, Alex is in another state—far, far away. He can't reach me. And hey, I found out who he truly is before things got even messier. And then there's the whole penthouse situation. Marco said I could stay as long as I wanted, and there was a pool and a sauna. Oh, and of course, I have you.

Max: I better be higher on that list than the pool and sauna.

Violet: Duh, I wasn't listing them in order. You're definitely a top pick.

Max: Just so you know, he's called me a few times. Begging me to tell him where you are. I told him I don't know because, well, it's true. I only know you're in Miami.

Violet: Please don't tell him.

Max: I won't.

Violet: How did he sound?

Max: Are you sure you want to know?

> **Violet:** ...

Max: Like hell. I'm pretty sure he was drunk a few times when he called. Sober a few others. But it's always the same. He's begging me to help him find you so he can apologize. It's hard to keep saying no. He really does love you.

> **Violet:** Yeah, well, he didn't love me enough to believe me.

Max: I get it, babe, I do. But maybe, just maybe, you should hear him out—when you're ready on your terms.

> **Violet:** I'm not ready.

Max: Then don't talk to him. And I won't spill a thing.

The rest of that first week in Miami, I drowned myself in movies, books, and endless replays of the gala night in my head. I kept going over every detail, wondering if I might've had one too many glasses of champagne, and said something I shouldn't have. But the way I laughed and the stuff I supposedly said to Julian didn't add up. I wouldn't flirt with him.

The guy gives off serious creeper vibes, like the kind that makes you want to scrub your hands after shaking his and sharing business info with him. Yeah, right. I knew enough to know he was a competitor, and when he asked me about that one tech firm, I didn't even understand the significance.

None of that matters now, though. I put myself out there for Alex, and he didn't believe me.

Alex didn't believe me.

Sure, I know he's been burned before. But when he had the chance to trust me, dig deeper, and see me for who I am—he chose not to. So, I had to leave, far away from his connections, endless resources, and the press in case they found out. That's why I ended up with Marco and his... *associates.* If anyone could help me vanish, it was them.

Now, here I am, hiding out in Miami, letting the mafia keep me off the radar. If this isn't rock bottom, then I'm not sure what it is, and I'm not eager to find out what's below this.

**

THE HOLIDAYS

The holidays have always been my thing—twinkling lights, cheerful music, the magic in the air—especially in New York. The city glows like it's dipped in Christmas spirit. Usually, I soak it all in, letting that joy and warmth seep into my soul.

But this year? It's like a beautifully wrapped gift that's empty inside. The lights don't sparkle the same, and every cheery song feels like a taunt.

Everywhere I look, I see couples—holding hands, laughing, sneaking kisses under mistletoe. Yes, even on the beach, which honestly is kind of hilarious. But each sweet moment I see feels like a jab, a reminder of what I no longer have. I've spent the holidays alone before, but this time, it's different. There's a chill that even Miami's warmth can't touch, sinking into my bones.

Christmas Eve rolls in, and I stare out the window, watching raindrops splatter onto the balcony and into the pool. I wish they were snowflakes. Manhattan's getting a white Christmas this year, and I'd give anything to be there. Every raindrop on the pavement feels like a little nudge, reminding me of Alex. His smile, the warmth of his touch, the way he looked at me like I was his whole world. God, I was so lucky to have that—to have *him*—even if it didn't last. I can still hear his voice, those sweet things that made me melt... and the harsher words that shattered me.

My phone buzzes, cutting through the silence. It's Max. Of course, it's Max.

"Hey, you. How're you holding up?"

"I'm okay. Today's rough. Tomorrow might be, too. But after that, it'll get easier." At least, that's what I keep telling myself.

"Did you get my gift?"

Max gave a gift to Valeria, who then gave it to Marco, who eventually got it to me. It's a scarf we found while shopping earlier this year. I'd called it the perfect Christmas scarf, and he'd remembered.

"I did. Thank you. It's perfect." A real smile tugs at my lips for the first time in days.

I hear voices in the background on his end. "Are you busy right now?" I ask, glancing at the clock. It's eight at night.

"Yeah, I'm at a family dinner, but I always have time for you."

My heart squeezes. I wouldn't be with my family right now—no way in hell. But I'd be with Alex and his family, probably in some warm, bustling room, with kids running around, ripping open presents, and adults chatting away. His family felt at home. I tasted what it was like to be wrapped up in love, no strings attached. To be hugged without any judgment and no questions about my life choices. His mom believed in my writing dreams more than my own ever did. And how pathetic is it that I'm mourning the loss of his family almost as much as I'm mourning him?

Yeah, this Christmas feels colder than any I've ever known.

Christmas morning is a special kind of torture. I wake up to the deafening silence of Marco's penthouse, with a sad little tree that Marcello and I decorated. There are no gifts underneath, no laughter filling the space, just quiet. Too much quiet. I spend the day reading, escaping into old movies, and trying to get lost in someone else's happy ending. Thoughts of what could have been with Alex creep in, but I shove them away. I'm getting better at that, little by little.

But New Year's Eve? That's even worse. The last days of the year drag on, each feeling like an eternity, as if time itself wants to rub my loneliness in my face. I've cried myself to sleep more nights than I can count, replaying every memory with Alex and wishing for things that will never be. Facing a new year without him feels like a weight pressing on my chest. But here I am. Alone.

As midnight approaches, I sit in the living room, clutching a glass of wine. Marcello joins me, looking like he'd rather be elsewhere. The TV blares with the crowds in Times Square, the energy of the city I love so much counting down to midnight. I take a deep breath, the kind that steadies your soul, and make a promise to myself.

This is it, Violet. This is the last day you cry over Alex. You're not starting another year with tears and shattered dreams. You deserve better, and you're going to find it.

The countdown ends, the cheers echo through the screen, and I wipe away one last rogue tear. Marcello clinks his glass to mine, giving me a small, almost awkward smile.

No more wishes, no more what-ifs. This is my reality now. It's time to pick up the pieces, find my path, and rebuild.

Happy New Year, Violet. You've got this.

***

ONE MONTH AND ONE WEEK LATER

At first, I worried that being without the New York skyline while working on my novel would kill whatever writing mojo I had going. Turns out, it didn't. Instead, I traded the concrete jungle for a tropical twist—downtown Miami's skyline and the ocean's sparkling blue stretching out beside me. When I needed a break from the city view, I'd swivel my chair and let the waves do the inspiring.

So, I wrote. And wrote. And wrote some more. Day and night, I buried myself in the story through Christmas and New Year's. In Miami, it didn't even feel like winter. No snow, no freezing air. Just sun, sand, and swimming in January. The festive cheer of New York felt a world away, but honestly, that was the point.

Since the first of January, I've thrown myself into finishing this book. No more binge-watching rom-coms or devouring other people's stories. I'm all in. If I'm going to rebuild myself, I must do it right. And for me, that means being a writer again. It's like laying down that first brick of my new life. A little piece of who I am.

Some days, I typed so hard I was sure my fingers would bleed. My pointer finger even got a blister from all the keyboard abuse. In his typical tough-guy fashion, Marcello tossed a box of band-aids at me, then gave me that look—like I was the biggest wimp he'd ever seen. He doesn't understand the actual pain of a keyboard-induced blister.

> **Max:** So, you finished it?

> **Violet:** Finally! First draft done! I'm taking a week off from it before diving into edits. Marco says he knows an agent who owes him a favor and can get it to them. Not gonna lie, I'm a little scared about what that "favor" might have involved.

> **Max:** Considering his background, it's probably better you don't ask.

> **Violet:** Oh, I'm sticking to a strict "don't ask, don't tell" policy these days. It's been working out pretty well.

> **Max:** Smart. Have you spoken to…

Max—and even Marco, who might be some mafia kingpin, mob boss, or whatever—knows better than to say his name around me. I don't care if it means I'd end up "swimming with the fishes" like in the movies; I'd still punch Marco in the face if he let that name slip. And the guy had the audacity to find that cute, calling me "adorable" and saying I'm about as threatening as a "baby chick." But hey, he kept his word. No name-dropping. So, I'm counting it as a win.

Violet: I have no intention of reaching out. He didn't believe me. Told me to get out of his life, so I did.

Max: He's contacted me daily, Vi. Every. Single. Day. Sometimes twice. He keeps asking if I've heard from you, and honestly, it's getting hard to lie. I like Alex.

Violet: You and the rest of the world.

Max: And you *love* him. Don't you think you should at least let him know you're okay?

Violet: Marco already told him I'm safe and taken care of. That's all he gets to know for now. Besides, the first and only time he told me he loved me was when he was kicking me out of his life.

Max: Fine. I'll check in later. Enjoy your break.

Violet: Miss you.

Max: Miss you too.

I shut my laptop with a satisfied smile. A finished first draft. It's a huge deal. I've never had a complete book in front of me before, and yeah, I'll need to edit, review, and tweak it, but the story is there. It's written. The characters, the plot—every little piece. And when I typed that final sentence, it felt like a vise around my chest finally let go. All the tension, all the pain, released. I could breathe.

You're not a failure. You finished a book. You wrote the first draft!

So, I decided to take the next week off. My plan? Sunbathe by the pool right outside the penthouse. Who needs a pool on the roof when the beach is right there? Marco thinks it's a good idea. But, of course, I'm not allowed on the actual beach. Something about this being "someone else's territory" and me needing to stay out of sight. Sure, I could shop or do other things, but sunbathing on the beach is a no-go in Marco's rulebook.

I slipped into the new bathing suit Marcello bought me—imagine the poor guy's adventure trying to pick that out—and grabbed a towel from the closet. The Miami sun felt like heaven as I stretched out by the pool. I don't know how long I soaked up the rays, but I drifted off to sleep at some point.

When I woke up, the sun was low on the horizon, casting everything in a warm, orange glow. It's different from Manhattan sunsets. There, everything turns a mix of gray and purple, with occasional bursts of orange between the skyscrapers, like the city itself is hiding secrets. I miss that. But this—this is pure, golden warmth.

Grabbing my towel and empty wine glass, I cursed as the hot concrete scorched my feet, making me skitter inside like a crab avoiding a beach bonfire. As soon as I stepped into the penthouse, I spotted a figure sprawled out on the leather sofa. I yelped, nearly dropping everything. A stack of papers slipped off his face, revealing Marco lounging like he owned the place.

Well, he *does* own the place, but still.

"What are you doing here?" I gasp, practically out of breath from nearly suffering my first heart attack.

Marco raises a brow. Yeah, okay, dumb question. He owns the place. A stack of papers sits before him, a few scattered across the coffee table. And wait—hold up—is that *my* manuscript?

I rush over, snatching the pages from his hands, fully aware I might've just given a mafia man a paper cut. "Oh my god, you're reading my manuscript!"

He leans back, fingers interlaced behind his head, looking far too amused. "It's good stuff. Not usually my thing, but if I'd known romance books had women with perfect tits and this much... activity, I might have reconsidered."

I roll my eyes, gathering up the pages. "It's not done. It's just a first draft. It still needs editing before it's anywhere near ready." I shuffle the messy bundle of papers, trying to balance them with my towel as I stumble over to the dining table.

Behind me, I hear him moving around, raiding the fridge. Marco has this weird obsession with sparkling water, so Marcello keeps it stocked. He pulls out a raspberry vanilla flavor, and I must bite my tongue to keep from laughing. Big, bad mafia boss sipping on raspberry-vanilla sparkling water? Not exactly the image I had in mind.

I press my lips together, fighting back a smile as I cross my arms and face him. "Why are you here? Usually, you give me a heads-up."

He shrugs. "I told Marcello, but he said you were asleep."

"Okay, but seriously, why?"

"Bella, I *own* the place. I can come and go as I please. I had some business down here, but I'm flying back soon. Too humid for my taste."

The first time he brought me here, I'd asked him why he kept a penthouse in Miami if he hated the place. He gave me some cryptic explanation about needing multiple residences under various aliases so he could move around without being tracked. I didn't push for more details.

"Well, nice to see you too," I say, trying to keep my tone light.

"Not the reason I stopped by, though I could get used to a hot woman in a bikini greeting me in my penthouse," he smirks, giving me that look. It's unsettling how much he resembles Alex—with the same jawline, olive skin, and smirk with dimples. But while Alex's eyes are piercing blue, Marco's are an intense amber, and his accent's thicker.

He waves a hand between us, gesturing to the space. "Alex called me. Again. You see, Bella, before all this," he motions between us, "I spoke to my cousin during holidays, maybe once a year, if that. Now? I've got him blowing up my phone daily."

"See? I brought you two closer," I quip, flashing a grin.

He snorts, the sound rougher than a laugh. "Hardly, Bella. My cousin is driving me up the wall, and here's the kicker—I owe him a favor."

Of course, the Bennetti family and their endless favors. Valeria's favor got me in with Marco, and she used it to make sure Alex couldn't find me. It's like favors are the family's currency. They don't just trade them with outsiders; it's like a whole stock market of favors among themselves.

"Okay, and what does this favor involve?" I ask, genuinely curious.

He shakes his head, smirking like I just missed the point. "That's not how it works. You do something for someone, no matter how small, and now they owe you. When you decide to cash it in, they pay up."

"So, like, if I asked you to kill someone, I'd have to be ready to do the same for you later?"

He nearly chokes on his fancy raspberry vanilla sparkling water, his laugh deep and rough. "Jesus, Bella. I don't just go around killing people. And no, it's not like that. A favor can be anything, cashed in at any time."

I bite my lip, thinking it over. "But don't you think that's a little... unreasonable? Like, what if you did something as small as, I don't know, dog-sitting—"

"I don't dog-sit."

I roll my eyes. "Okay, fine. Can I finish?" Marco nods, motioning for me to go on. "Anyway, say you hypothetically dog-sit for someone, and now they owe you a favor. But then they turn around and ask for, I don't know, a million dollars. That doesn't seem fair."

He shrugs, leaning back like this is the most obvious thing in the world. "Then I loan them the million."

The nonchalance in his voice makes me pause. "But that's not an even trade!"

"Exactly. Which is why you don't give out favors to just anyone. You only offer them to those you trust and won't abuse them. If someone asks me for something, and I don't want to owe them later, I tell them to go fuck themselves."

"I see..." Then the realization hits, a pit forming in my stomach. "Wait, do I owe you a favor?"

He shakes his head, a smirk tugging at his lips. "If you did, you'd know. I make it crystal clear when I do something for you that earns a favor. So no, you don't owe me." He glances at me, that smirk widening. "Unless you *want* to."

I roll my eyes and turn back to the dining table, wrapping my towel tighter around me before gathering up my scattered manuscript pages.

"You going to work on it more? It was pretty good before you so rudely interrupted my reading." Marco strolls out of the kitchen, dropping into a chair at the table. His laid-back look—jeans and a black shirt—makes him seem worlds apart from Alex's polished three-piece suits.

"I planned to take a week off before diving into edits," I reply, not looking up as I organize the pages, stacking them neatly with my trusty red pen on top, ready for when I'm back in the editing zone.

"No." His voice shifts, turning sharp, almost commanding.

I glance up, catching him polishing off the last of his sparkling water. "Excuse me?"

He leans forward, forearms pressed against the glass-topped table, leaving smudges that will drive me nuts later. "I said no. No week. You finish it *now*."

"But I need a break. It's part of the process—"

"That's stupid. It's fresh in your mind, Bella. Edit it. I want it on my desk Friday to send to my friend." He stands, tossing the empty bottle into the trash and blowing a mock kiss as he heads for the door. "Friday, Bella."

I gape after him. "But it's Tuesday..."

He doesn't turn around and throws a lazy wave over his shoulder. "Better get to work then."

Alex

DESPITE CALLING MARCO DAILY and pressing Max for information, no one would give me anything. Max swore he hadn't heard from her, but the lack of concern in his voice told me otherwise. Someone should tell him he's a terrible liar, but I couldn't blame him for protecting his friend. Hell, I almost respected him for it.

Board meetings blurred into a dull hum. The gossip columns hadn't caught wind of our breakup—thankfully, no one had turned it into a headline yet. But I knew the next event I attended would bring questions, and I'd have to admit the truth. For now, I stuck to telling people she was "away, working on her novel." It was the only thing I could cling to, a thread of hope that wherever Marco had stashed her, maybe she really was writing.

Pathetically enough, I watched *Pride & Prejudice*—her favorite—every week. Yeah, a grown man, reciting lines alongside Mr. Darcy, imagining her reaction, the way she'd light up at her favorite parts. The way her face softened during those grand declarations of love. When Dom caught me watching it one night, he looked at me like I'd lost my mind.

And maybe I had.

I'd been hurt before. Natalia had cut me deep, and for a while, I convinced myself I had every right to assume the worst when history seemed to repeat itself. But it wasn't fair to judge Violet by someone else's mistakes. She deserved better than my knee-jerk assumptions. She deserved my trust and a chance to explain.

I could've asked Holmes or Evander to investigate the recording from the start, but I concluded that she had betrayed me instead. Of all people, Dante dug deeper and proved that Julian was the snake I already knew him to be. I didn't even give Violet the benefit of the doubt. I just pushed her away.

Now, I'm the fool scrambling to find her, calling in favors, practically begging. She left my life because I told her to, and I can't even blame her.

I know she won't forgive me. Why would she? But I must apologize, even if it's just for my conscience. Maybe that makes me selfish, trying to clear my guilt. But some part of me believes she deserves to hear it. She deserves to know that I realize how wrong I was, even if it's too late, even if no apology can erase the hurt I caused.

***

THE HOLIDAYS

I had a whole Christmas planned with Violet. I imagined a tree, presents, and the moment she'd unwrap the ring I'd hidden just for her on Christmas morning. What a joke. How could I go from being ready to dive in headfirst to doubting everything at the slightest hint of trouble?

Christmas with my family turned into a disaster. The conversations went silent the second I stepped through the door on Christmas Eve. Mama and Papa were the first to greet me—Papa with that look of disappointment, Mama with a worried smile as she hugged me tightly. No one dared to mention her name. I'm pretty sure Mama told them to leave it alone. But it was clear—everyone knew what happened, right down to me falling for a fake tape from a piece of trash like Julian. They could see through me, and they weren't impressed.

My family adored her—Violet. And I could see in their eyes they were angry with me, disappointed. They love me, sure. They tolerate me. But they're pissed I let her slip away.

And then there was Natalia—back again, like a bad memory that refuses to stay buried. Maybe she's some ghost haunting me. She's back with Eddie, the poor guy who never grew a spine. I managed to avoid her during Christmas, but she corners me on New Year's Eve, dressed in something that barely qualifies as fabric. It makes me question everything I ever saw in her. How in the hell did I ever think she was attractive?

All I could think about was how Violet would've shown up—elegant, understated, wearing something classy that didn't try so hard. She could've worn a paper sack, and her beautiful smile and those green eyes would still light up a room. She never dressed to show off and never had to prove anything. But Natalia? She's got a dress so short it's barely legal, and her chest practically spilling out of the top. She clinks her champagne glass against my sparkling water, and I sigh.

I haven't touched alcohol since that bender after Violet left. I want to feel every emotion, every ounce of regret and pain, because I deserve it. For the things I said to her. For the way I threw money on the bed and told her to leave, like she was some cheap fling. Five hundred dollars like that could sum up her worth. There isn't an amount in the world that could.

The words I threw at her, the way I dismissed her, replay in my head like a broken record. Guilt coils tight in my chest, a constant, gnawing ache that makes looking in the mirror feel like a punch to the gut. I can't even imagine how she must have felt, and the thought keeps creeping in—did she think about me during the holidays? Did she wish to start the new year with me, with a clean slate?

She's been gone for over a month, and every day feels like a new shade of regret. Holmes tried to track her down, but I knew he wouldn't have any luck. Whatever shady tactics man uses, they're nothing compared to Marco's resources.

"I heard you and Violet broke up." Natalia's voice slithers through the noise of the party, and she wedges herself closer to me, practically pressing against my side. For every inch she moves in, I step back. She gives me a pout that she probably thinks is endearing.

I'm sure you were just devastated.

I don't respond. I sip my sparkling water, wishing the glass was full of something more potent. The clock will strike midnight in an hour, and the idea of starting a new year without Violet claws at my insides. It feels wrong, empty.

Then, I feel her hand—Natalia's perfectly manicured fingers sliding against my arm, slow and deliberate. My jaw tightens as I glance down at her, wondering if she's serious. Stroking my arm like we're in some secret corner while my cousin, her current boyfriend, stands just twenty feet away. She cheated on me before, and now she thinks I'll let her do it again—with me, no less?

Unbelievable.

Worse, she was there that night. How much of a role did she play in everything that happened? I fucked it up. I take that blame and will go to my grave. But did she give Julian the idea? I'd put nothing past her.

"Do you mind?" I snap, glaring down at her fingers as they creep along my arm. "If you need something to stroke, your boyfriend is over there." I jerk my chin toward Eddie, who is oblivious and clueless.

She makes this annoying cooing sound that makes my stomach churn. "Oh, Alex, we were so good together. Maybe we could try again now that Violet's out of the picture?"

Last I looked, hell hadn't frozen over yet. So, that's a hard pass.

I reach over, grabbing her hand. She gasps like she's won, but I pluck her hand off me like she's a stray piece of lint. "Natalia, there will never be an 'us.' We were never good together. Touch me again, and I'll personally make sure Nonna throws your ass out. We both know she's itching to do it."

Her face falls, but I don't give her the satisfaction of sticking around to see the reaction play out. I head outside to the patio, letting the cold air slap against my skin. The sounds of everyone inside cheering and wishing each other a happy new year fade into the background as I stare out at night, wondering where Violet is right now in the world. And what she's doing.

And if, somehow, she's thinking about me too. Sadly, if she is, they aren't good thoughts.

***

A MONTH LATER

"Ah, Alex! To what do I owe the pleasure?" Marco's cocky voice filters through the line, and I swear, if he were closer, I'd be tempted to drive to his brownstone and knock that smirk right off his face.

"You know exactly why I'm calling."

"Do I now?" He's playing dumb, like always.

"Marco…"

"You call every damn day, Alex. I tell you the same thing every time. What makes you think that I will change my tune just because it's a new year?"

I smirk, leaning back in my chair. "Because I'm calling in my favor."

There was a pause, then a muttered curse. "Fuck. Do you really want to burn that favor on this? There are a million better ways to use it, cousin."

"This is the most important thing right now."

There is a beat of silence, and then he breaks into a laugh that grates on my nerves. "So you're really whipped, huh? Never thought I'd see the day." I hope he chokes on his laughter like he did when we were kids.

"Marco, enough. The favor."

"Cousin, I made a promise. Even with our little favor system, I can't just spill it. But… I'll work on it. Give me some time, and I'll figure out how to let you cash it in. Not right now, but eventually."

I pinch the bridge of my nose, trying to keep my cool. "What's the point of a favor if you're not going to honor it now?"

"Because, despite everything, I made a promise to her. And while I'm an asshole, I still value family."

"I'm your family, dickhead. Not her."

"We both know your mama and papa practically adopted her. Even my father called, threatening to take a finger if anything happened to her on my watch. So, yeah, la mia famiglia and all that."

I grind my teeth, frustrated. "So when can I cash it in?"

"When she's ready, Alex. Not a moment sooner."

"She might never be ready to see me again," I mutter, my eyes fixed on the photo of her on my desk—the one I snapped that night at the bar. She's smiling, that carefree, contagious smile I can still feel in my chest. When I returned to the office, I shoved it in a drawer, thinking out of sight, out of mind. But that was a joke. I ended up opening the damn drawer every chance I got just to catch a glimpse. So, I gave up on pretending. It stays on my desk now, right where it belongs.

Marco pauses on the other end, his voice softening, almost uncharacteristically gentle. "She'll come around. Maybe she won't say it directly, but when she's ready, I'll know. And then I'll tell you."

It gnaws at me—how Marco seems so sure he can read her that he thinks he understands her well enough to know when she'll be ready. But I've got no leverage here, no argument to make, so I clench my jaw and hang up, falling back into this haze of living without her.

My days blur together. I wake up, work out, eat, and work. I sit through endless meetings, pushing through each one like a robot. I bury myself in work, staying late until the building is empty, hoping exhaustion will drown out my thoughts of her. I work out again, eat, sleep, and repeat. Days stack up into weeks and then months. Two months. Three.

She's probably moved on by now. And every day without a word from Marco or Max, that thought becomes more challenging to ignore.

Violet

Violet: You actually read the whole thing, right? Like, you're sure it's good?

Max: I love you, but a man can only repeat himself so many times before he loses his mind.

Violet: It's been a month! They're going to reject it. I just know it.

Max: I'd say no news is good news.

Violet: You think so?

Max: Literally told you the same thing four hours ago, Violet.

Violet: Sorry! I'm bored out of my mind. A girl can only sit by the pool and watch so much daytime TV. Marcello refuses to play Uno with me anymore. He said I get too competitive.

Max: You are borderline psychotic over that game. I don't blame him.

Violet: You're missing the point.

Max: No, I think we've hit a solid growth opportunity here. Maybe... don't take Uno so seriously?

Violet: There's nothing else to do while I'm waiting for them to get back to me!

Max: What about Monopoly? Poker? Regular, human conversation? The fact that a mafia guy is too scared to play Uno with you kinda proves my point. But seriously, you'll hear back soon.

Violet: I hope so. This is my last chance at true happiness. If they say yes, I'll finally feel accomplished.

Max: You really think this is going to be the thing that makes you whole?

Violet: Don't start with that again.

Max: Fine, I won't, but just know that when you finish this and still feel like something's missing, I'll be ready for you to admit I was right.

Violet: You're going to enjoy my misery?

Max: No, I'm just going to enjoy you realizing that writing a book might be your dream, but deep down, you know what you're really missing.

Violet: It doesn't matter. Please, just drop it.

MARCO SET ME UP, as promised, with a literary agent he knew in Chicago. So, there I was, sitting in the agent's office, Marco and Marcello on either side of me, looking like they were ready to terrify the poor guy into submission. Hey, whatever works, right? I submitted my manuscript a month ago, spending every single day since I was convinced I'd get a rejection. Then Marco called, saying his friend wanted to meet—in person.

A few hours later, I found myself on a private jet, wearing an outfit Marco picked out. I expected something... questionable. But to my surprise, he handed me a tasteful blouse, a pencil skirt, and heels that didn't threaten my ankles.

"Please, those other dresses were for fun," he said, catching the look on my face.

"Really? I don't find a dress that's a set of crisscross straps over my entire chest *fun,*" I shot back.

"I did," he smirked.

I rolled my eyes. He didn't see anything because I refused to leave the room in that... thing.

Now, I'm sitting across from Mr. Timberlieve, fiddling with my fingers. He doesn't look like anyone Marco would associate with—more like a stuffy professor than a mob boss contact. The guy's older, with a balding head and gray hair, slicked over in a sad attempt to hide it. His glasses were practically magnifying lenses on that beak of a nose.

"Thank you for coming, Miss Hart," he croaks out, coughing in a way that makes me fight back a cringe while plastering on my most polite, totally-not-terrified smile. In front of him was my manuscript, printed out and marked up, so he'd clearly given it a thorough read. "We were impressed. I heard you were a senior editor at Hartley & Co., so I'm surprised you didn't bring this to them."

Right, why didn't I?

Oh, yeah. That's where my ex works—who definitely despises me—and it's in the same city where the guy I thought loved me ended up breaking my heart. It's not exactly the setting for my new chapter. So, I put on my best bluff. "I just wanted to make sure there was no favoritism since I worked there for so long."

Marco's eyebrows shot up in amusement, but thankfully, he kept his mouth shut.

For someone who throws around words like "boss" and talks like he owns the world, Marco never entirely managed to make the mafia thing sink in for me. It's like my brain refuses to connect the dots between the guy who helped me run away to finish my book and the reality of what he does. Denial? Maybe. But it's a lot easier to live in a world where your biggest supporter isn't also a guy people whisper about in fear.

And, honestly, he's... nice. He's way more sociable than you'd expect from a guy with his reputation. He'd swing by the penthouse now and then, noticing if I seemed down, and he'd talk to me—like, real conversations. Once, he even spent a Wednesday night with me watching rom-coms, laughing at all the cheesy lines, and sharing popcorn. The world fears him, but somehow, I don't.

Yes, he's stupidly attractive—like, lethal-level hot where "if looks could kill" almost feels literal—but there's nothing there for me, not like that. My heart still stubbornly clings to someone else, no matter how much time I've spent hiding away in a world of love stories and guaranteed happily-ever-afters.

Why? Because my life? Yeah, it's far from a rom-com right now.

"I called you in because, unlike most of my competitors who just send off an email, I'm old-school." Mr. Timberlieve's voice snaps me back to reality, and I bite my lip to hold back a laugh. The man practically screams vintage—sitting there with my printed manuscript before him, probably having read it cover-to-cover in paper form. His office looks like it's been untouched since the 70s, with wood-paneled walls and retro carpet that could double as a time capsule. The desk? Definitely older than me.

"I enjoyed your book," he continues, and my heart skips a beat. "So, I've sent it to a few publishers, and we've already received several offers."

He pulls out a file and hands me a stack of papers. Faxes. *Actual faxes.*

Who even faxes anymore? Can you even buy fax machines?

I'm aware this isn't the time to wonder these things.

I stare down at the faxed offers, trying to get past the fact that they arrived by *fax*. There, in front of me, are actual offers from multiple publishers—upfront payments, royalty terms, print runs. The numbers blur together as I skim through hardcover copies, e-book editions, and royalty rates. My heart races, and I swear it's getting hotter in this room.

People want to publish my book. Multiple publishers. Six of them.

I must look like I'm on the verge of a meltdown because Marco, sitting there all cool and collected with his hands clasped, glances at Mr. Timberlieve. "Which offer is the best?" he asks, his tone leaving no room for nonsense.

My hands tremble as I pass the stack to the agent, who barely glances through before pulling out a specific page. "This one," he says, sliding it back to me. "They're a smaller publisher based in New York, relatively new, but they specialize in romance. Their social media presence is top-notch, and they've been steadily growing."

Okay, hold up—Mr. Fax Machine knows what social media is? Now, *that's* a twist.

Marco nods like he's sealing a business deal, which, I guess, he is. "She'll take that one. My lawyer will handle the paperwork, but I want it published by the end of the month."

Mr. Timberlieve removes his glasses, looking like he's just been slapped with a cold wind. "It typically takes months—editing, cover design—"

Marco lifts a hand, and I swear the room temperature drops ten degrees. "End of the month," he repeats, his voice cutting through the air. "I'm sure you can make it happen. Give the publisher my contact information. End of the month."

Mr. Timberlieve swallows hard and nods. "Done."

Alex

Three months later...

THE CREAM-COLORED ENVELOPE TAPS rhythmically against my desk as I roll it between my fingers like I'm trying to hypnotize myself into caring. It's an invitation to an annual event—one I never miss. But this time, it's different. This time, I'm going alone. I don't give a damn about the press or whatever rumors they'll spin up when they see me solo. "Single" has a nice, blunt ring, and I've had to swallow that reality for nearly three months now.

I stopped calling Marco and Max daily. I'm sure they're grateful for the peace. But there's that gnawing thought every day: she's moved on. Why can't I?

Because you love her.

It's as simple and as complicated as that. I need to apologize, even if it changes nothing. I'm stuck on the last page of our story, unable to close the book until I do. I can't stand the way things ended—the shouting, the accusations, the way I practically threw her out of my penthouse like a damn fool. She had every reason to be furious. Hell, I'd be pissed if I were her. But then she vanished, changed her number, and now my cousin is the gatekeeper to her whereabouts.

The elevator doors slide open, and I step into the hallway leading to the penthouse. I've considered selling the place, especially now that the reality has settled like a weight in my chest—she's not coming back. Every corner of this place holds a memory of her, from the couch where we'd stay up watching movies to the kitchen where she'd devour meals I made only for her. Even her stuff is still here, the things she didn't get a chance to take. What the hell do I do with all of it?

Max offered to pack it up, and yesterday, I finally told him he could. Maybe I'm the one who needs to pack it up and let go. She's moved on, and it's time I do, too.

The door clicks shut behind me, the slam echoing through the empty penthouse. I toss the invitation, keys, and wallet onto the foyer table. I worked late again—it's the only thing keeping me sane. The long hours don't give me time to think, to dwell on everything I did wrong. But I know this game. I can't keep avoiding the pressure forever. Sooner or later, it's going to blow, and it's going to be ugly.

I loosen my tie, dragging myself through the place like it's not mine anymore. This penthouse would look like a disaster zone if it weren't for the maid service twice a week. A grown man wallowing in self-pity is a pathetic sight. My housekeeper started picking up groceries, and my private cook? He's been slipping more meals into the fridge because I'm not eating enough.

It's like even they know I've become a mess without her.

I step down the two marble steps into the living area, and there he is—Marco, sprawled out on my couch like he owns the place. The asshole is in fine form right now.

"What the hell are you doing here?" I snap, striding past the couches to the corner table. I grab the first decanter within reach and pour myself a glass of whiskey. It's one of those nights.

Marco leans back like he's ready for an afternoon nap, a book propped open on his chest, his legs crossed, shoes scuffing up my expensive leather. A pillow is tucked behind him, and he's got that look—like he's found some secret amusement in my misery.

"Cousin, these late nights can't be good for you. Almost eleven. Is that what the legal world requires these days? Working so hard?" His tone is light, but I catch the bite underneath. We both know his hours are much worse—just in a different line of work.

I glare at him, settling into a chair nearby. I yank off my tie, loosen the first two buttons of my shirt, and take a slow sip of whiskey. The burn's comforting and familiar, but I keep it in check—two drinks a night, max. After she left, I went through bottles like water, barely shaved, barely functioning. Not going back down that road.

I nod toward the book he's holding, noticing the cover—a mess of flowers, probably something I'd never touch. "What's with the reading, Marco? Didn't think you knew how."

He smirks, biting his lower lip like he has a secret. "Since I found this little gem. It's good stuff. Hot author, too. Ass that goes for days." He gives me a knowing look, enjoying this way too much. "You should read it, Alex. Think you'd like it."

"I'm good," I mutter, taking another small sip, letting the warmth spread through my chest. I lean back in the chair, kick off my shoes, and put my feet on the coffee table—anything to shut him out.

But Marco isn't done. He stands up and strides over, slamming the book shut dramatically. "No, I think you should read this one." He holds it out, stepping closer.

"I told you, I don't—" My words die as I catch sight of the cover. Right at the bottom, in bold, unmistakable print, is the author's name: *Violet Hart*.

I freeze, staring at the name that sends my heart into overdrive. She wrote and *published* a book.

It was her dream, her life's goal, and she did it. But I wasn't there to see her achieve it. I wasn't the one to read her first draft, as promised. I wasn't the one to celebrate her win, to see the smile on her face when she told her parents she finally did it. And that realization hits harder than the whiskey.

"It's got a nice little following on social media already. I might've had a hand in that, but that's what family is for." Marco's voice oozes with smug satisfaction, and I can't help but bristle.

"She's not your family," I snapped, snatching the book from him. My fingers trace over her name printed at the bottom of the cover. *Violet Hart.* Seeing it in print sends a jolt through me. "She really wrote it..."

Marco swings his legs up, casually kicking my feet off my damn coffee table and dropping down in front of me. He flips open the book, landing on a page near the back. "You should read the acknowledgments. Good stuff." He takes my whiskey glass, draining the last of it.

She finished the book. And I wasn't there. The weight of that realization slams into me. I'd always pictured being the person she ran to when she was excited when she reached this milestone she'd been chasing for years. But I wasn't. I threw that chance away.

"So, she's moved on..." The words taste bitter, and I try to keep my voice steady like it doesn't hurt just saying it.

Marco growls, leaning closer and pointing to the page with a glare. "Read. The. Damn. Page."

I shake my head, still clinging to that tiny thread of hope. "Is she happy?"

He studies me, leaning back against the coffee table like he's weighing his following words carefully. His amber eyes gleam, sharp and unyielding, like he's sizing me up. Finally, he rubs a hand over his jaw and sighs. "No, she's not."

My head snaps from the book resting in my lap, my heartbeat stumbling. "Why not?"

He jerks his chin toward the book—a silent *read it.*

Fine. I take a breath and look down at the page. I've never been one to read acknowledgments, but I remember Violet telling me once that it was her favorite part of any book. To her, it wasn't just names—the author's heart on the page, the people who pushed them forward when the doubts crept in, the driving force behind every word. It's where she found her inspiration.

And now, she's written hers. For everyone to see.

When I started writing, this page—the dedication—was the one that haunted me. I never thought I'd have anything worthy to put here. I imagined I'd skip over it, convinced I'd never have someone to thank for inspiring me to dream bigger. But I was wrong.

I may be single now, which is a bit ironic for a romance author, but that doesn't mean there wasn't a time when I knew what it felt like to be truly loved. Before I could write about love, I had to experience it—its warmth, its light, its ability to turn even the darkest days into something hopeful. And yes, I had to learn what it means to lose it, too.

You can't write love without knowing its joy, ache, and how it changes you. It's not just the moments that make your heart race or bring a smile to your face—it's the ones that leave you breathless, even when they're long gone. The way we met wasn't a perfect meet-cute, but it was ours which made it special. He believed in my wildest dreams, cheered for me even when I doubted myself and taught me what it means to be wanted, cherished, and seen. And for that, I'll always be grateful.

To the man who endured my obsession with romance novels and movies, sat through countless viewings of Pride & Prejudice without complaint, and never stopped believing I could finish this book—thank you. Without you, I would've never known the kind of love that changes your life or the heartbreak that shapes you into someone stronger.

This book wouldn't exist without that love. And I hope, dear reader, that someday you find a love that shifts your world on its axis, even for a little while, because it's worth every moment.

I snap the book shut and toss it onto the couch where Marco lounges before he gets all up in my face. Now he's sitting forward, elbows on his knees, that ever-present smirk tugging at his mouth.

"Riveting stuff, huh?" he says, amusement dripping from every word.

"Go to hell."

Believed in me... The words from her dedication play on repeat in my mind. She believed in me. And the one time she needed it most, I let her down. Yet, she still mentioned me.

Marco lets out a frustrated growl, standing up with a roll of his shoulders. "Look, I owe you that favor, so here it is. She will be in New York for a book signing at the Barnes & Noble on Fifth. Tomorrow. 7 p.m. You can show up and try not to be a total jackass or don't. But it's her first signing, and she's freaking the hell out. I've been dealing with your woman for months now, but even I know it's not me she needs there." He jabs a finger toward the book on the couch, leaning closer until his face is inches from mine. "It's you. The guy she wrote about. You screwed up, so make it right."

I grit my teeth, the reality of his words sinking in. "I can't just show up and say 'I'm sorry.' And I'm not about to ruin her big moment like that."

"Then don't." Marco shrugs like it's the simplest thing in the world. "She's a romance junkie. Do you know how many of those sappy movies she forced me to watch? My eyes are permanently scarred. But there are plenty of cheesy, over-the-top ways to make it right."

"Favor cashed. Oh, and to sweeten the deal, she's staying at one of my places in New York."

I narrow my eyes at him. "Care to be a little more specific? You've got four of them."

Marco's smirk widens into a grin, pure mischief glinting in his eyes. "Where's the fun in that? You'll have to figure it out yourself, cousin."

And with that, he's gone, leaving me with a book in my lap, a racing mind, and a glimmer of hope I don't quite know what to do with.

Violet

"I can't believe it. I know a famous author!" Valeria practically squeals from her spot on Marco's plush sofa. It's one of those designer pieces that looks like they belong more in a magazine than a living room. Marco had handed me the keys to his place, insisting it was mine as long as I needed it—apparently, he had a surplus of apartments scattered around the city. At first, I felt guilty, but Valeria assured me he did have plenty, so I gave in. Why? Because, well, I needed a place to crash.

"I'm not famous, Valeria. It's just a book signing," I mumble, trying to downplay it, but even I can't ignore the tiny flutter of excitement in my chest.

Okay, maybe the book did take off a little faster than I expected. Mr. Timberlieve wasn't kidding when he said the publisher knew how to work social media magic. They turned my book into a hashtag sensation. Reddit threads, Instagram posts, TikToks—my story was everywhere. I never imagined seeing my name in so many posts, and now I'm about to have a book signing—a real one. Sure, I'm nervous that maybe only a handful of people will show up, but it's happening.

I'm officially published. I'm going to a book signing. And... I'm still heartbroken.

Writing the acknowledgment page was like pulling my teeth. It took a week of sobbing, Marcello giving me the side-eye for going through so many tissue boxes and enough cookies to supply a bakery. But once I got the words down, I felt... okay. I confessed my broken heart to the world and admitted that Alex and I were over. But at least I can say that with him, I finally knew what love felt like—the good, the bad, and the punch-you-in-the-gut painful. It all went into the book, so I guess I owe him a thank you.

I even used him as the muse for my main character. Yeah, that might've been a mistake. God, I hope he never reads it.

But channeling him helped me get the emotions right—the passion, the conflict, the longing. I could picture every detail of him: the sharp lines of his jaw, the way his blue eyes seemed to see through me. It made my story come alive. And in the fictional world I created, my version of Alex gets his happily ever after.

Me? I get to be the solo act. And while I'm supposed to be over the moon about this dream coming true, I can't shake the emptiness that lingers.

Even when my parents learned about the book, their first question was about the money: "How much will you make from this?" Hello, I'm a newly published author.

Spoiler alert: it's not much. Not yet, anyway.

Royalties take time, and there are costs to cover. Marco's already taken care of most of those, but I'm still awaiting the big payoff. Mr. Timberlieve—yep, he's officially my agent now—said it's all about the long game, building my name, and keeping the momentum with a second book. The publisher is on board, eager for my next idea.

But the worst part? The one thing that stung more than any rejection letter? Realizing that even this wasn't enough to impress my parents. After all these years of dreaming, hoping, and pushing to have my big moment, finally, their indifference hit me like a sucker punch.

Still, I won't let them ruin this for me. *Not this time.*

So, for the first time, I stood up to my parents.

"So, you're not even making money yet?" My mom's *first* words. Classic.

"It takes time to earn money with a book, Mom. Royalties don't show up overnight. It just published last week! There are payouts from different places—stores, online platforms, and downloadable versions. It all takes time."

"And will you be able to make a living off it?" Not yet, but I wasn't about to give her that satisfaction.

"Of course," I lie, cringing internally.

"I know this is your dream, and you've finally done it. But now it's time to come back to reality. How about you finish school? Or come home, and we can help you get on your feet."

"I have a place to live, and I'm working on my next book."

"But you aren't even making money off the first one, Violet." It's been a *week,* Mom.

"Mom, I will make money. It takes time."

"Just like it takes time to write these books? It took you years to write one, Violet. How are you possibly going to write another and then another?" Her faith in me is inspiring. Not once has she congratulated me. No, she's too busy listing all the ways I'm still failing.

That's my family for you.

"You know what, Mom? Stop calling. I'm fine, and while I appreciate your encouragement over the years," my voice drips with sarcasm, "you can reach out when you're ready to show that you care. Until then, lose my number."

I hung up, ignoring that I called her on an untraceable number. Oops.

"Feel better?" Max asks, lounging on the couch next to Valeria. They've both got wine glasses in hand, trying to salvage our night after my mom's call crashed the vibe. I had *truly* thought she'd be over-the-top excited when I picked up. But nope. That's not how it works—not with them.

"Your mama sounds like a real piece of work," Valeria shoots off the sofa, then freezes. "Oh gosh, sorry."

I snort, swirling my glass. "She is."

There's a knock at the door, and Valeria jumps up. "Oh, finally, the food's here! How long does it take to have DoorDash pick up pasta?"

I don't bother reminding her that she ordered it 45 minutes ago—*during* Manhattan rush hour. Valeria wants something; she expects it *now,* but she refuses to actually pick it up herself.

Muffled voices drift from the door, a low, rumbling tone that sends a shiver down my spine. I head over to check what's taking so long but then freeze. That voice isn't just any delivery guy's. It's *Alex's.*

I don't care if Marco is some mafia kingpin—I'm going to kill him.

When we flew to New York, Marco dropped the bomb: it was time for me to face his cousin. I told him I wasn't ready. We spent hours arguing about it—me going toe-to-toe with a mafia boss over my love life, not caring if I insulted him. His response? "Too fucking bad, Violet."

So, here we are—Marco's way of forcing the conversation.

When our eyes meet, my instinct is to bolt. I know if I told him to leave, he would. Valeria, standing between us like some human barricade, keeps glancing between Alex and me. "I can tell him to go," she says in a low voice.

But I'm stuck, frozen in place. The truth is, I remember every detail of him from when I wrote my book, but seeing him in person is different. I didn't do him justice. He's even more striking—those sharp features, the olive skin, now shadowed under his eyes like he hasn't slept in weeks.

Part of me wants to say, "Leave." But his eyes are locked on mine like he's begging for a chance without actually saying it. He's holding back, fighting the urge to push his way in. He's respecting my space, and I can almost feel how much it's killing him. And, honestly, I don't want him to suffer.

Yeah, he hurt me. Yeah, I felt betrayed. But I get it—he built walls after his trust got shattered once before. A man like him, always in control, had to protect himself. And sure, that stupid, altered tape messed with his head. But my heart, the part of me that still remembers every good thing, every laugh, every quiet moment, can't let go. Meanwhile, my brain's waving a red flag. *He didn't trust you. He might never trust you. If it happens again, then what?* I can't ask Marco to hide me every time things go south.

"Hi," he says, pulling me from my spiral. That voice. I loved it. Okay, I still love it—strong, confident, but now it wavers like he's barely holding it together. "Can we talk? Just five minutes."

I cross my arms, trying to keep my expression neutral. Valeria slips back into the living room with Max, and I know they will listen in. I glance over my shoulder at them before jerking my head toward the hallway behind him. "Outside," I say, pushing past him and stepping into the hallway, closing the door behind us with a click.

Valeria and Max are practically wrestling over who gets to peek through the peephole. They're probably pressing their ears against the door, catching every word, but I hope the wood muffles some of this conversation.

Alex stands across the hallway, looking like he stepped out of a men's fashion magazine—three-piece suit, hair perfectly in place, just the right amount of stubble along his jaw. Meanwhile, I'm over here, arms crossed, leaning against the opposite wall like it's the only thing keeping me from folding into myself. My heart, that traitorous thing, flutters like I'm back in high school, and he's my crush.

"Talk," I say, keeping my voice sharp and letting my brain take the wheel because, deep down, I know what I want to do. I want to run to him, bury myself in his arms, and let the familiar scent of him wrap around me. But no, I won't do that.

"I'm sorry," he says, pushing off the wall and taking a few careful steps toward me. Not close enough to reach, but close enough that I feel the pull. "You didn't do anything wrong, and I didn't believe you. I need you to know how sorry I am. I know you've moved on, and I don't blame you. What I said... all of it... I'm sorry. I should have believed you. I could give you excuses, but they don't matter. I had to see you to apologize. I messed up the one chance I had to prove that I trusted you, and you deserved better than that."

His words wash over me, but I keep my expression cold, ignoring how my skin tingles and how his gaze feels like a punch to the gut. It's been three months. Too long. It's not that he didn't try to reach me—Marco made sure of that—but it's just that the time stretched out, and the pain festered and healed over in a way that makes me wary of reopening old wounds.

"So you just needed to apologize to make yourself feel better?" I snap, letting the bitterness seep into my words.

He took another step, almost close enough for me to reach out if I wanted to. "No. I needed to tell you what you deserve to hear. It doesn't change anything, I know that. But for the last three months, I've only thought about telling you how sorry I am. It's all I've wanted—to apologize, even if it's too late."

"Well, I appreciate that," I say, fighting to keep my tone as icy as possible, even though every word scrapes my throat. I'm trying to stay strong, but a part of me is dangerously close to breaking. I should have faced him months ago, but now, it feels like that window has closed, leaving us stuck in this weird in-between.

"You wrote the book..." His voice softens, and those blue eyes of his search my face, looking for... I don't know what. The first person I wanted to tell when I finished it was him. When I got an agent, I pictured his smile. When it got published, I imagined him being proud. But that version of events doesn't exist anymore.

I nod, keeping my heartache deep where he can't see it.

"I knew you could do it," he says, and the look on his face nearly breaks me. Pain. Regret. It's written all over him and cuts through me like a knife. "Anyway, I just had to see you. I had to tell you how sorry I am and make sure you know I regret it. You do deserve the best."

He takes a step closer, reaching out, and this time, I don't move away. His hand cups my cheek, his thumb brushing softly across my skin. It's warm and steady, and damn it, I've missed this. I've missed how his touch used to calm me, how that simple stroke of his thumb could make me feel seen and understood.

"You don't have to forgive me," he whispers, voice rough. "I don't deserve it."

He looks like he's about to say more, but then his eyes search mine, and something shifts. He drops his hand, clenching and unclenching his fist like he's battling an internal war.

Part of me aches for him to close the distance. Wrap me up in his arms, kiss me like he did that night at the bar—wild, consuming, everything I've craved. But life isn't a romance novel.

Not every story has a neat, perfect ending.

With a resigned nod, he steps back. His smile is small and painful. "I wish you the best, Violet. I do." He turns away, shoulders slumping, and walks down the hallway.

I want to call out to him, to run after him and throw myself into his arms. I want to do all those over-the-top, cheesy things you see in movies—get my happy ending. But it's been too long. Too much has changed, and there's a tension between us that time alone can't erase.

He doesn't look back; he keeps walking toward the stairs, disappearing.

When I finally get back inside, Max and Valeria are still pressed against the door, stumbling when I open it. They're not even trying to hide their nosiness.

"How are you?" Max wraps me up in his long, comforting arms while Valeria rubs circles on my back, her touch gentle.

The tears I've held back come pouring out, and I break down right there, sobbing into Max's chest while Valeria squeezes my hand. It takes twenty minutes before I can catch my breath, or maybe I just cried until I was dehydrated. Either way, we end up in the living room, huddled on the couch with glasses of wine.

"He loves you," Valeria says, all serious, and I roll my eyes. "He does. I know Alex. When he and Natalia broke up, he didn't chase after her. He didn't call or bother family every day. But I've seen him now, and the way he looks when he talks about you? I've never seen that before. My cousin doesn't break, but he's broken."

"You're starting to sound like Marco," I muttered, crossing my arms. Marco's been drilling that same idea into my head for weeks now. "But it's been too long. It's awkward."

Max leans in, wrapping an arm around my shoulders, that knowing look in his eye. "So, are you saying that if he came back right now, professed his love, and promised to show you how much he cares, you'd just say, 'Sorry, it's been too long'? You've truly moved on, and you don't want that?"

I hate how Max can cut right through my defenses.

"I don't know what I'd say," I admit, hating the uncertainty coiling in my chest.

Because the truth is, I'm terrified to hear those three words from Alex. They could break me all over again. If I forgave him and things fell apart again, I'd be left even more shattered than I am now. But if I heard those words, I might fall right back into his arms, forgetting everything I've been through.

Three little words. They have so much power, enough to lift someone or tear them apart. How is that even fair?

Words shouldn't hold that much sway, but those three could unravel me completely. And that thought? It scares me more than anything.

I kept telling myself that his apology was my closure. That I can move on now.

So why do I feel like the storm I've been holding back just broke loose, ripping through me, when I was finally finding peace?

Alex

ALMOST 92 DAYS. 2,100 hours. Over 131,000 minutes.

That's how long it's been, and finally, seeing her took my breath away.

She's always been the most beautiful woman to me, but after waiting so long, she was breathtaking. It was stunning in a way that cracked something deep inside me. I wanted to grab her, press her against the wall, and kiss her like it would fix everything between us.

But I lost that right. I'm unsure if she wants me back—or if she ever will—and that terrifies me more than anything. Her expression was a mystery, not because of the time that's passed, but because in those months apart, she'd learned to shut down, to close herself off.

Considering her relationship with her parents, I wouldn't be surprised if this is the version of her I'm left with now. A woman who's had to put up a shield to protect herself, and I'm the one who made her build it. A shield she may never lower again—for me.

> **Alex:** I saw her. It was the last apartment I checked, and she was there. You could've just told me which one, you bastard.

> **Marco:** And miss out on all the fun? Sad you had to go through every one of them first... but not really sad. Did you say what you needed to?

> **Alex:** Yeah, at least she knows.

> **Marco:** And what did she say?

> **Alex:** Not much. She barely looked at me.

Marco: Can you blame her?

Alex: No, but I guess I hoped that if I said something and apologized, she might at least look at me like she used to.

Marco: You mean before you accused her of lying and leaking info to your competitor?

Alex: I get it. I messed up.

Marco: Then make her remember what she loved about you. She will never forget what you did—women don't let things go, trust me. My mama still brings up crap my papa did 20 years ago. You can't erase it, but you can make up for it.

Alex: Any suggestions?

Marco: Do I look like a relationship guru?

Alex: No, you're probably the last person I should ask.

Marco: Try her best friend. The one Marcello won't shut up about. Maybe we can set those two up when you're done pathetically trying to win Violet back. It's like listening to a lovesick puppy over here.

Alex: Should I go to the book signing?

Marco: Are you planning on stalking her or supporting her?

Alex: What do you think?

Marco: I honestly have no idea. That's why I'm asking.

Alex: Support, obviously.

Marco: You're not her boyfriend right now, even if neither of you has made that public. But, yeah, you should go. Then, text Max and leave me the hell alone. I've got real work to do.

Despite Marco's reputation as a cold-hearted bastard, we've grown closer over the past few months. It's hard not to when I've been blowing up his phone daily, asking for crumbs of information about Violet. It turns out that the man I thought was a more brutal, colder version of Uncle Tony has a heart—one he'll never admit exists.

After talking to Marco, I do what's become a habit since Violet left: I call Max. And even though she's back in the city now, it feels natural to keep checking in with him. It's a strange way to make a friend, but somehow, he's become a solid presence. I'm under no illusions—he'll always choose Violet over me, as he should. Yet, a part of him is rooting for me, like he sees a sliver of hope where I see only mistakes.

"Should I go to her book signing?" I ask, unsure if my presence would be welcome or if it'd just stir things up.

Before Max can answer, Valeria's voice comes through loud and clear. "Don't screw this up for her." Perfect, I'm on speaker with the dynamic duo.

I rub my temples, holding back my frustration. "Care to elaborate on that?"

Max clears his throat, trying to soften her sharp edge. "She means don't... make it a scene."

"Why would I do that?"

"Wasn't saying you would," he replies quickly, but they're concerned.

"Would she be upset if I went?" I don't want to ruin her big moment, but I'm selfish enough to admit I want to see her. It's not like I have any right to want anything from her anymore, but the pull is tightening in my chest.

There's a bit of bickering on the other end before Max finally answers, his voice gentler than I deserve. "No, I don't think she'd be upset. As long as you're there to support her and not to make it about... you two, she'll be okay with it."

Later that night, I lie in bed, staring at the ceiling, my mind circling the same question: Should I even go? My stomach twists, probably paying the price for months of sleepless nights and endless regrets. I know showing up unannounced could backfire. It might irritate her, make her think I'm trying to claim something that's no longer mine. I know better than to bring flowers, too. That's a move for couples, not exes fumbling through apologies.

So, how do I show up for her in a way that doesn't make it about us? How do I be the support she deserves without expecting anything in return?

Violet

I'M NERVOUS.

Like, sweaty-armpits, hands-shaking, might-pass-out nervous.

I'm hiding out in the back room of Barnes & Noble, clutching my coffee like a lifeline and thanking the bookstore gods for their in-store Starbucks. Max sits across from me, his expression between amused and exasperated, like he's watching a slow-motion car crash. Honestly, he kind of is.

Sweat clings to my back, under my arms, and—ugh—between my boobs. Fantastic. Just the vibe I want to give off at my first book signing: damp and frazzled. I dig through my bag, muttering about needing more deodorant.

Max grabs my hands, stopping my frantic search. "I'm pretty sure another layer won't solve this."

"Let me try!" I grab the deodorant he hands me, slathering it on like it's magic armor, even hitting the area between my boobs for good measure.

"Okay, but maybe stop chugging coffee like it's water," he says, tossing my cup into the trash. "You're already jittery enough."

He's not wrong. I barely slept last night, replaying Alex's words and how he looked at me. His voice still lingers, and I can't stop thinking about how much I missed him. His scent, the warmth of his touch, even just the sound of his breathing when he's asleep beside me. God, waking up without him feels like a punch to the chest.

I take a deep breath, forcing myself to ignore how my heart is banging around in my chest like it's trying to escape. Climbing up onto the table—because clearly, the chair isn't dramatic enough—I cross my legs and close my eyes.

"Are you...meditating?" Max's tone is laced with disbelief.

"Yes," I snap back, squeezing my eyes shut tighter. "So if you could stop talking, that'd be great."

He mutters something, but I block it out, trying to focus on breathing. In and out. In and out. Meanwhile, my heart is beating so hard it feels like it might crack a rib. Is that a thing? Could I bruise my sternum from a racing heartbeat?

Breathe, Violet. Just focus on the breathing. Forget about Alex. Forget about the line of strangers waiting to judge my book. Forget about everything except surviving this moment without passing out from anxiety.

Mr. Timberlieve strides into the room, and I swear he's even shorter than I remembered. He was behind a desk when we first met, so I didn't realize how tiny he was. My hands practically dwarf his, and I like to think of myself as dainty, but next to him, I feel like a giant—and not in a good way.

"Quite the line out there," he says with a low whistle, and I immediately feel like I'm about to puke.

"Not helping," Max snaps, giving Mr. Timberlieve a look that could melt steel. Timberlieve mimes an apology before turning to me with a sigh.

"All authors get nervous at their first book signing, my dear. But once you do this, the rest will be a breeze. And hey, at least people showed up. Imagine if they hadn't."

Yeah, thanks for the worst-case scenario, buddy.

Today, I went for a simple outfit. I wanted to look like a woman who writes steamy yet classy romance novels—something sophisticated with a touch of spice. So, I picked a short-sleeved black dress that hits just above my knees, paired with a rose gold belt and black heels. Maybe I do look like a hooker? I sneak a glance at myself, suddenly doubting my choice.

I tug at the hem, smoothing the fabric nervously. "Are you sure this isn't too short? I brought a backup outfit, just in case."

Max groans, probably regretting his life choices that led him here. "You look elegant and sexy—exactly what you need to be if you're a romance author."

Right. Elegant and sexy. That's me—totally my style.

I fumble in my bag, pulling out my glasses. I rarely wear them, but they make me feel like I can see the world beyond ten feet. "Should I wear these?" I shove them on, feeling like a total dork.

Max studies me for a moment, tapping his lips thoughtfully. He glances at Mr. Timberlieve, who nods with him. "Yeah, glasses. Gives you that hot librarian vibe."

Great. Hot librarian it is.

There is a gentle knock at the door, and Mr. Timberlieve's assistant peeks her head in. "We're ready when you are!" she chirps, as bright as a neon sign. Seriously, this woman always smiles, and her enthusiasm is making my eye twitch right now.

I turn to the mirror, ensuring my hair and makeup haven't betrayed me. I've been tugging at my hair so much I'm surprised it still looks half decent. I left it down—long, wavy, and tamed with whatever frizz oil Valeria had in her purse. Max vetoed the librarian bun, claiming it was more "porn star chic" than "author chic." As for makeup, I kept it simple. A little foundation to hide the sleepless nights, a swipe of mascara, and a hint of lip gloss. I wanted to add eyeliner, but Max shut that down, too, suggesting it would only work if I planned on hitting the streets after.

Stepping out of the room, the crowd's buzz hits me like a wave. The bookstore is closed to regular shoppers—tonight, it's all about me. There's a table set up near the front, stacked high with copies of my book for those who didn't bring their own. The store is letting people in a few at a time to keep things under control, and a part of me is glad. It means less chance of me hyperventilating at the sight of the line.

So, I focus straight ahead, plaster on a smile, and make my way to the table, avoiding eye contact with anyone who might see the fear in my eyes. A ridiculous amount of Sharpies waits for me—seriously, they expect me to sign the entire world's library. But then again, I have no clue how many books I'm signing tonight.

All week, I practiced my signature with a Sharpie. And let me tell you; it's more complicated than you think to make an elegant signature with a marker as thick as my thumb. I wanted something classy and refined, with a bit of heart dotting the "I" in my name. It took two days, an entire ream of paper, and one nasty hand cramp to get it right.

Was the heart overkill? Probably. But I'm committed now.

Mr. Timberlieve settles into the chair behind my table, looking like he's about to deliver a literary verdict. Meanwhile, Max looms behind me like some overprotective bouncer, dressed head to toe in black. He's got that serious face on, the one that says, Don't mess with her. I almost laugh, but I'm too busy trying not to lose my mind.

The first reader is ushered in—a woman in her mid-40s, all polished and Manhattan-chic. She's practically excited as she approaches as if she might faint on the carpet.

"I just love your book. Oh my gosh, I came hours early just to be first in line. I can't believe I'm meeting you!" Her hands tremble as she holds out her worn, dog-eared copy. The cover's faded, pages crinkled—like she's read it a million times. My heart swells a bit, and I offer her a big smile.

"Your acknowledgment was beautiful," she says, then leans in like we're swapping secrets. "You are such a lucky woman, living in this world of romance and dating Alexander Bennetti."

Oh, hell.

I force my smile wider, maybe a little too wide, and yank the cap off my Sharpie with more force than necessary—so much so that the cap flies behind me. Max scoops it up without a word and hands it back like this always happens. I sign her book quickly and slide it back to her, smiling like I'm not inwardly screaming. She floats off, still beaming, and I try not to think about how my cheeks are already starting to ache.

Next up is a woman in her 30s, her eyes bright as she talks about how much she loved the book. "The rawness, the story's realness—there's not much of that anymore. Most romance books out there feel so unrealistic. But yours? It felt like it could be me. Like I could be the one in the story."

I smile for real this time. "That's exactly what I was going for," I say, feeling slightly lighter.

That was the dream—to write a romance that felt real. Even though my life had its fairy-tale moments—falling for a billionaire and all—I wanted my book to be about the struggles—of real people finding real love. Not some fantasy where you get swept away into a world of private jets and designer everything—just real, messy, complicated love.

I've lost track of how many books I've signed, but I'm acutely aware of the number of Sharpies I've gone through. How little ink do these things hold? Number six is dead, and I'm fumbling with the cap of number seven when a man places his copy of my book in front of me.

"Just one moment," I mumble, bending over to retrieve the cap that's somehow rolled under the table. Of course, Max picked this exact moment to disappear for a coffee run—because why wouldn't he?

"Take your time."

I freeze mid-reach—that voice. Oh, I know that voice. My fingers wrap around the cap, and I slowly sit back up, willing myself to stay composed. Pushing my hair back, I meet his eyes.

Alex. He's here, standing at my table in a perfectly tailored three-piece black suit with a blue shirt that makes his eyes look even bluer. Is that possible? It is because they're piercing through me in a way that has my stomach doing somersaults.

Behind him, I hear a few women whispering and cooing. Some recognize him. Of course, they do. We've made a few appearances in gossip columns, and those stories make people think they know what we are.

But do I even know? We're not together. He told me to leave his life, then spent weeks trying to track me down. He apologized last night, and now he's here, but that doesn't make us... anything. Right?

Relationships have always felt like a mystery I'm not quite equipped to solve. This whole situation? It is way beyond the scope of any self-help book or advice column. Trust me, I Googled *"Are you broken up if your boyfriend apologizes after breaking your heart?"* this morning. Google just spat out a bunch of articles on how to get over a breakup.

Finishing my book was supposed to help with that, but it didn't.

Do I still have a broken heart? Do I have anything left to mend?

Right now, I genuinely have no idea.

"Violet?"

"Right, sorry." I snap back to reality, meeting his gaze with a forced smile, trying to keep it together. My Sharpie is poised, and I flip the book to the inside front cover. The mechanical rhythm I've fallen into kicks in, ready to scribble my signature and move on. But then, in a low voice, he says, "Can you sign the dedication page?"

I freeze for a moment, then nod, turning to that page. My breath catches when I see what he's written: *I miss you, Violet.*

It feels like swallowing a pile of gravel. My throat tightens as I add my name to those words, trying to ignore the ache in my chest. I snap the book shut and hand it back to him, realizing I've forgotten to breathe.

His blue eyes hold mine, but he doesn't say a word. He takes the book, brushing his lips against the back of my hand before walking out of the store, leaving me standing there, heart racing.

Max strolls back in with his coffee just as Alex disappears.

"Was that Alex?" he asks, and I grab the cup from him, not even caring what he ordered, gulping down a few sips. The line stretches on, and I plaster a smile back. Whoever doesn't get their signature today, well, they'll have another chance tomorrow—I'll be back for one more evening.

Alex

SHE BARELY LOOKED AT me. The only hint of a reaction was how her marker hovered over the words I wrote, hesitating for a moment. Then she signed, returned the book, and moved on like I was just another face in the line.

I hurt her. I deserve it.

If I'd just believed her in the first place, I wouldn't be standing here missing her so damn much. She never would have left. But would anything be different if she hadn't taken Marco's offer to disappear? Would she have stayed, given me another chance? Or would we be in the same mess with fewer miles between us?

Three months is a long time. They say time heals all wounds, but that's bullshit. Mine are still wide open, raw, and bleeding. Seeing her again is like ripping off the scabs with sandpaper, over and over.

Apologizing didn't give me any peace. If anything, it stirred up a storm inside me. A damn tornado of regret and longing, spinning out of control.

But this isn't about me.

I have to remember that. I'm not the one who was betrayed. Sure, she left, but I was the one who pushed her away. I didn't believe her, took the word of a snake over the woman I loved, and told her to get out of my life. She did exactly that, and now I'm lost in the fallout.

My world is cutthroat. There's always some paparazzo or shady business associate looking for a way to take me down, and the quickest target? Loved ones. Significant others. Julian proved that, and I know he won't be the last.

I've been trying to convince myself this is for the best all night. Violet's doing well. Her book is out, and according to the articles I've read—since no one in the family will give me an update—she's working on her second one. Her first launch was a hit. She doesn't need me. Hell, she never did. Soon, she'll move out of Marco's place and maybe even find her own. Who knows? Maybe one day, her family will finally see her for the success she is.

She's got her life together. I saw it in her smile at the signing. The way her green eyes lit up when a fan complimented her work. She's living her dream, and she's moved on.

I've read her acknowledgment a hundred times. And every time, that secret goodbye stands out more. She thanked me for showing her what love could be, but now she's ready to turn the page. And maybe I should be, too. Opening that door again would just hurt her. Hell, it's already killing me. Standing in that line for two hours just to get a few seconds with her was torture. I watched her light up for everyone else but for me? Nothing. Not a smile. Not a flicker of warmth.

Not that I deserved any.

"It's better this way," I mutter, leaning back in my chair and taking a slow sip of scotch. Dante's been here since after the signing, just sitting in silence, waiting for me to crack. Like he thinks I'm one deep breath away from breaking. He didn't realize that dam burst the moment I pushed Violet out of my life, and she did exactly what I told her—she left.

Dante shakes his head, putting his drink on the coffee table. "You can keep telling yourself that. But your mama's been hounding me to get you to talk to her."

I let out a dry laugh. "You're all ridiculous. I did talk to her. Twice. I apologized, showed up at the signing, even wrote 'I miss you' in the damn book, and she signed right over it."

Dante just laughs, as if this whole situation is a joke. Yeah, thanks for the support, asshole.

"It's been three months, Dante. She's moved on. Why does everyone keep pushing me to talk to her when she doesn't want to talk to me?" I growl, frustration seeping into every word.

Dante shakes his head, that same look of exasperation on his face. "Because the rest of us still talk to her. You don't. Valeria said she went through that book signing like a robot. They planned to get drinks afterward, but she bailed and said she wanted to go home. She's not happy, Alex."

"Yeah, because I ripped open old wounds." I grip my glass tighter. "I need to let her move on. She'll get over me."

Dante fixes me with one of his classic I-call-bullshit stares. "Are you over her?"

I sip my drink, and the silence answers for me. "You know I'm not."

"So why do you think she's over you?"

"Because she should be," I mutter. "I'm the one who screwed it all up. It takes longer to get over that kind of betrayal." I put down my glass, trying to ignore the burn of whiskey that's become a little too familiar lately. "And there will be another Julian—someone else who sees her as a way to get to me. And next time, I might fall for it again, hurt her all over. She's better off without this mess. She writes a romance novel, Dante. She's about happy endings and love. Not... this."

My life feels like a barren wasteland—empty, cold, and devoid of joy. The so-called best years of my life are filled with late nights at the office, fighting to repair the damage Julian did to my business, and stumbling through the wreckage of my personal life.

Dante rolls his eyes, pushing up from the sofa to pour another drink. "So now you're the selfless hero, sparing her from your baggage?" He takes a slow sip, then levels me with a hard stare. "That's rich, Alex. Real convenient. But the truth is, you thought an apology would fix it all. You thought she'd hear you out, jump back into your arms, and everything would be perfect again. But that's not how this works. Remember what you did—how you doubted her, kicked her out of your life. You hurt her. Badly. And she won't just forgive you because you say sorry."

He downs his drink in one quick gulp, slamming the glass on the counter. "If you want to sit here, pretending you're doing the noble thing by giving up, go ahead. Tell yourself it's for her sake. But don't kid yourself. It's not about protecting her—it's about you being scared. You know what? Someone might come along and try to mess with your head again. But the question is, will you believe them? Can you trust her enough this time, or will you do it all over again?"

Dante leans in, voice low and fierce. "If you're too cowardly to go through that, fine. Stay here, drowning in your misery. Let her move on. But don't act like you're doing it for her. She's hurting, Alex. And you're the reason. Seeing you probably only makes it worse. So if you're going to give up, do it clean, and don't pretend it's some sacrifice. Because right now, it's just you running away."

I didn't expect her to leap into my arms after one apology. I'm not a complete idiot. I knew I'd hurt her, that she'd be angry. But I guess I expected... something. Anything. Instead, I got those cold, unreadable eyes. She has every right to be upset. But what if I mess it up again? Dante's right—would I fall for another trick? That's the question.

And deep down, I know the answer. *No, I wouldn't.*

Even the first time I listened to that tape, something felt off. My gut twisted, warning me it wasn't right. But I let my emotions take over, let doubt cloud what I knew in my bones—that she would never betray me like that. But knowing it now doesn't change what I did then. I can't erase the damage or unsay the words that tore us apart.

All that matters now is how I act moving forward.

Time slips by unnoticed. It's not until sunlight filters through the windows, casting long streaks across the floor, that I realize I've been sitting here all night. I was still dressed in my suit from the book signing, hands gripping the armrests like they were the only things keeping me grounded.

If I let her go, I have to move on. Leave this penthouse. Start fresh somewhere she won't haunt every room.

But letting her go means never seeing her again, even if that means she stays close to my family. At this point, they'd probably pick her over me, and I wouldn't blame them. She's kind, intelligent, beautiful—everything they've come to love. She's become part of the family she never had, the one that I should have been for her.

And God, I want to be that for her. I want to be the one she leans on. Last night, all I could think about was holding her after the signing, kissing her, and telling her how proud I was. I wanted to be the one who brought her breakfast in bed and celebrated every moment with her.

But I can't do that if I'm on the sidelines.

I push myself out of the chair, a determination settling in my bones. It's time to shower, shave, and change.

Then, it's time to get the woman I love back.

Violet

THE BOOK SIGNING WIPED me out. I signed my name so many times I never wanted to see another marker again. Unfortunately, I've got another signing in two weeks, so my poor hand better recover by then. Right now, it's stuck in this awkward clench like it's still gripping a Sharpie.

But hey, silver lining? I finally perfected my signature—looped a little heart over the "I" like some giddy teenager. I'm a romance author, and I figure a little cheekiness is part of the job description.

This morning, I woke up with a headache that threatened to turn into a full-blown migraine. Fresh air is my go-to remedy, so I pulled on my workout gear, laced up my sneakers, and headed out of Marco's building. It's in a great spot, just a few blocks from Central Park. Marco insists I don't have to pay rent, but I will. Something is unnerving about living rent-free in a mafia boss's apartment. What if the FBI decides to bust in while shampooing my hair? It's not out of the realm of possibility.

So, moving out is definitely on the horizon. Once the royalties start rolling in, I'll pay Marco rent until I find my place. In the meantime, I'm diving into my next book. Writing is my focus now. When I vanished, I lost my job at Hartley & Co., but honestly? I'm okay with it. This is my chance to live my dream. So, I'm grabbing it with both hands... and a slightly sore wrist.

The second I exited the street, I spotted a man in a sharp black suit leaning casually against the building. Impeccably dressed, even though it's barely past seven. And those blue eyes? Yeah, I know them well.

"Good morning," he freaking smiles at me, and all the rage I've buried deep inside explodes like a volcano, lava searing through every bit of self-control I thought I had.

It's like he senses the storm brewing because he slips his hands into his pockets, his earlier confidence fading. "What are you doing here?" My tone is all bite, zero warmth. He doesn't deserve courtesy. Not after the way he threw me out of his life.

"I was waiting for you." His eyes stay locked on mine, but I don't give him the satisfaction of a response. I turn away and start marching toward the park, the sound of his fancy dress shoes trailing behind me. "I thought we could go for breakfast. Maybe just a coffee?" he offers, but I keep my back to him.

Deliberately, I take out my earbuds, pop them in, and blast my music. Let him watch me ignore him. Maybe he'll get the hint.

I focus on my route, making a beeline for the park and its walking trails. Fresh air, exercise—everything I need right now. Florida's humidity might've been good for my skin, but it was suffocating. At least New York's cold snaps remind you you're alive, even if it's freezing. I'll take that over sweating through my clothes any day.

Suddenly, I feel his hand brush my arm. I jerk back, spinning around to face him, yanking my earbuds out. "Do. Not. Touch. Me," I grit out, as I can feel eyes blazing like a fire I want to scorch him with.

Seriously, I don't think he gets just how pissed off I am right now. Why? Because I've spent three months shoving all that anger down, bottling it up like some emotion-hoarding dragon. Not exactly the poster child for healthy coping mechanisms.

I thought I could bury those feelings, move on, and pretend they didn't exist. But now he's here, waiting for me, expecting we'll... grab breakfast together? Like, I'll magically forget the way he shredded my heart?

Yeah, no. Time to unleash the fury.

"Please, Violet. Just coffee," he says, sounding almost desperate.

I spin around, words slicing through the air. "You already apologized. I don't need to hear it again over a cup of overpriced caffeine." I turn on my heel, striding away. "And that means stop following me." But, of course, he's right behind me, a perfectly tailored shadow in a three-piece suit, looking unfairly sexy.

Welcome to New York, where people ignore everything—except when a billionaire is trailing after his ex. I can practically feel the curious stares. Fantastic.

"You know people are watching you," I hiss. "You care about your image, right? Probably not a great look to be caught stalking your ex."

"No one knows you're my ex."

Oh, that stings. Because he's right, he never told anyone we split. Whenever he went out in public, and they asked where I was, he answered smoothly about me being busy with a project. It turned my book launch into the perfect PR cover-up. "Well, maybe it's time you start telling them. It's been three months, and we are not together."

"What if I want us to be?"

Jabbing my finger into his chest, every word like a knife. "I don't give a damn what you want. This isn't about you. The world doesn't revolve around you, Alex. What you want is irrelevant."

He pauses, those blue eyes pinning me in place. "Fair enough. What do you want?"

Yeah, Violet, what do you want?

I ignore his question, mostly because I can't answer it. It's not stubbornness—it's confusion. I genuinely have no idea what I want. Returning to publish my book and do the signing, I knew I'd run into him eventually. But ever since he apologized, I've been stuck in an emotional spiral that's more tangled than my earbuds after a long walk. I love him. I hate him. I want to punch him, kiss him, feel him pressed against me. None of it makes sense, and he's turned me into a walking contradiction.

One minute, I wish he'd disappear forever. The next, I'm crying into a pint of Ben & Jerry's, wondering how to live without him. But he told me to get out of his life, so why is he here, chasing me now?

I spin on my heel, heading back toward my place. I won't find peace with him trailing behind me like a relentless puppy. As I walk, he keeps talking.

"Violet, I said I was sorry, but that's not all. I want to make it up to you. I want to spend the rest of my life apologizing. I missed you so damn much. I haven't been the same without you. When I saw you again, it all came rushing back. I could move on, I thought maybe you had to, but I can't. I just... I can't."

I pause at the door to enter the code, wishing the doorman would show up early so I could breeze in without this heart-wrenching monologue echoing in my ears. But, of course, he's nowhere to be found. And while I should tune Alex out, my ears betray me. My heart, that stupid, traitorous muscle, skips a beat.

"I'm in—"

"Don't you dare say it," I snap, turning to face him, my voice cutting through the morning air. "The only time you said it was when you—"

"I'm in love with you. So in love that not seeing you for 92 days felt like losing pieces of myself. Pieces you took with you. And you can keep them. They're yours. I won't be whole again unless you come back to me."

Damn him and his ridiculously sweet declarations.

I turn the handle as the door opens, facing him one last time. His blue eyes are filled with a raw, aching sincerity. He means every word, but that doesn't erase everything that's happened. "You told me how you felt the day you kicked me out, Alex. So, I will do you a favor and return the sentiment. Get out of my life."

And with that, I step inside, leaving him on the sidewalk.

The second those elevator doors close, I break. Tears spill out, all those emotions I've tried to bury for months coming back with a vengeance. Three months of shoving them down, and here I am, a sobbing mess in a cramped metal box. Great.

"It'll get better," I tell myself, swiping at my face. I told him to leave. Now I have to move on. Easy, right?

Wrong. The rest of the day is a lost cause. I open my laptop, ready to write, but my thoughts keep circling back to Alex. Damn him. He looked good—too good. He's lost some weight, his cheekbones more pronounced, and his hair is a little longer, tousled just enough to make me weak in the knees. But those blue eyes? Still piercing, still glowing, still breaking me apart.

I give up on trying to work from the apartment, figuring a change of scenery might help. Before leaving, I peek outside the door like a spy on a mission, ensuring the coast is clear. No Alex. Thank God. I would've lost it if he'd been loitering out here for three hours.

I head to the café a few blocks down, brainstorming for my next book. I've got a story idea, but the meet-cute is killing me. It's the backbone of any good romance. It needs to be fresh, not the same old "we bumped into each other in a crowded coffee shop" scene. I need something new, something different.

Then again, my whole thing with Alex was straight out of a cliché. Girl meets a hot guy in a bar, they fake date, and—surprise—fall in love. Classic. I roll my eyes just thinking about it.

I'm almost at the café when a sleek black Lexus pulls up beside me. The passenger door opens, and out steps Alex because, of course.

"You've got to be kidding me." I groan, marching toward him, determined not to scream on the streets like a lunatic. I jab a finger at the car. "Get back in, drive away. I was clear."

He shrugs, infuriatingly calm. "I heard you, but don't believe what you said."

"Good for you. It doesn't change a thing. I meant every word." Lies.

"Okay," he says, his smirk in full force. "Well, I will do whatever it takes to make you think otherwise."

"Oh, so you plan to follow me around the city until I cave and beg for you back? Seriously, Alex? You think that highly of yourself?"

He leans in, close enough for me to catch that familiar scent of his cologne, and his smile makes my pulse spike. "Baby, I'm not waiting for you to crawl back. I'm the one doing the crawling. I'll follow you like a love-sick puppy until you agree to go out with me."

"I have zero interest in dating you, Alex." More lies, but I'll stick with them for my sanity. Will I cry about it later? Absolutely. But I'd cry a lot more if I fell for him again, only to end up right here.

"I have zero interest in dating you, too," he says, grinning wider.

What the hell is his game?

My confusion is all over my face because Alex's smile only widens as he leans back against the car. "I'll wait here. When you're done, I can give you a ride to your meeting with the bookstore manager."

How does he know about my appointment? Oh, right. He's Alex. He finds out whatever he wants.

I shake my head and head into the coffee shop. He stands outside, leaning against that fancy car like he's waiting for an Uber. My meeting is in two hours. There's no way Alex Bennetti lasts that long out here in the cold. He'll cave. I'm sure of it.

Settling into a corner booth, I open my laptop and start typing ideas. You never know when a random thought might turn into gold, so I will write anything and everything down. Sometimes, inspiration strikes mid-shampoo.

But my brain keeps replaying his words the whole time: I don't want to date you. Then what does he think he's doing, following me around like a lost puppy?

I try to channel my irritation into another story idea, my fingers drumming the side of my coffee cup as I type. But nothing sticks. I keep glancing out the window, half-expecting to see him give up and drive away. Nope. He's still there, stubborn as ever.

And then it hits me—the meet-cute of all meet-cutes. A guy randomly kisses a girl in a bar to help her save face, and then they fall in love. Oh, Mr. Bennetti, if you're going to be my shadow, I might as well use you as my muse.

I smile, put down my coffee, and let the words flow. But then I glance at the time and curse under my breath—I'm running late. I pack my stuff and head outside, bracing myself for his smug expression.

Of course, he's still there. No wonder he's so successful. Once Alex Bennetti sets his sights on something, he's relentless. He won't back down until he's got what he wants. And, unfortunately for me, I don't know the magic word to get him to stop — and maybe a part of me doesn't want to know the word.

"Good writing session?" Alex leans against the car with a smirk as he nods toward the backseat. I scan the street for a taxi, ignoring him.

"You don't have time to wait for a taxi. Quit being stubborn. I won't even talk. Just get in," he says.

I roll my eyes. Damn it, he's right. I don't have time to flag down a cab and make it to my meeting. With a sigh of resignation, I slide into the backseat while he holds the door open. I scoot as far as I can toward the opposite end, trying to put as much space between us as possible. But it's a losing battle—he's a big guy, and his presence fills the seat next to me.

He gives Antonio the address, and Antonio catches my eye in the rearview mirror, smiling warmly. "So nice to see you again, Miss Hart."

"You too, Antonio." I smile back, genuinely happy to see him. Then I turn my attention back to the window, erasing the smile as soon as I catch Alex watching me like I'm some puzzle he's trying to solve.

I focus on the passing streets, ignoring the urge to ask how he knew about my meeting—no way I'm feeding his ego with even a single question. Instead, I thank Antonio when he pulls up and opens the door for me, slipping out without glancing at Alex.

And honestly, don't ask me what went down in that meeting. Thanks to Alex, my brain's completely scrambled. I'm at a total loss for words and sanity, which drives me mad. He thinks he can show up, trail me like some lovesick puppy, and I'll magically forget everything that happened? That I'll suddenly realize how much I want to be with him and wipe the slate clean?

When I step outside after the meeting, there he is. Again. Same smirk, same car.

"Need a ride home?" he asks as if it's the most natural thing in the world.

Antonio glances out the driver's side window, pretending he's not paying attention but clearly in on the whole charade—wise man, keeping his distance from my impending wrath.

"Some people would call this stalking," I say, keeping a solid foot of space between us.

Alex leans against the car, arms crossed, eyes sparkling with amusement. "And what do you call it?"

"Stalking," I shoot back. "I told you to leave me alone, and here you are, following me around like a lost puppy. I'm pretty sure that's a classic stalker move. Oh, and they're usually obsessed with the person they're stalking, even when she's made it crystal clear she has ZERO interest in him."

His expression shifts, the amusement vanishing, replaced by something serious. "Is that true?"

I swallow hard, avoiding his gaze. "Are you talking?"

He doesn't flinch. "Do you really have zero interest in me?"

"Alex..." I bite my bottom lip, trying to keep my voice steady. I hate this. I hate that admitting how much he hurt me would only drag all those feelings back to the surface. But I can't have him chasing me around the city either. It's just making everything messier. My emotions? He doesn't need to hear them. He doesn't deserve to. "I can't do this. I can't get hurt again. I'm not playing the role of your perfect girlfriend just to get thrown out like trash when you're done with me."

He steps closer, and I see his hand twitch like he wants to reach for me but stops himself. Instead, he inches forward as if I'm a wild animal ready to strike, honestly, not far off, given my mood. "If you truly want me gone, Violet, I'll leave. But I hoped you could believe me when I said I'd never hurt you again. Please."

I narrow my eyes. "What do you mean you don't just want to date me?" It's not the first time he's hinted at it, and now I need to know.

He pulls his hands from his pockets, glancing around as if the bustling streets might lend him the courage he needs. "I don't want to date you. I've already done that. I want more."

"More?" My voice rises, a mix of disbelief and curiosity.

He meets my eyes, unwavering. "I want to marry you."

A bitter laugh escapes me before I can stop it. It bubbles up, raw and harsh. He wants to marry me? After all this? After he told me to get out of his life? We went from fake dating to real dating to a messy breakup, and now he's leaping straight to forever?

His jaw tightens. "I take it that's not what you expected."

"Do you honestly think I'd just go along with that? After everything we've been through? You think I'd be like, '*Sure, great idea, let's get married,*' when we haven't even been together for three months?"

"95 days," he grits out, voice rough.

He's counting? A flutter stirs in my stomach, even though I try to shut it down. He's been keeping track of our days apart, just like I have. I counted them to remind myself I was inching closer to being over him—to feeling relief. But ever since he reappeared, all determined and intense, that relief has turned into a sinking feeling I can't shake.

"I have to go. I have a meeting." My head shakes slightly because I don't know what else he expects me to say. Before I could step in, he moved quickly, opened the car door, and gestured for me to get in.

"I can walk," I snap.

"I know. I'm offering you a ride."

This is getting strange. He's showing up out of nowhere, trying to talk, playing chauffeur like he doesn't have a billion-dollar empire to run, and now he's babbling about marriage. "What do you want from me, Alex?"

"I thought I made that clear the past few days."

I step closer, challenging him with my glare. "No, really. What's the game here? You told me to leave, so I did. You chased down my friends and reached out to your own family just to get an apology off your chest. And now what? You're driving me around until I cave and agree to marry you?"

His eyes dart from me to the ground, his jaw clenching. "No, it's more than that. I miss you. The penthouse feels empty without you. If you don't return, I will sell it, because it's different. It's filled with too many memories. I feel... incomplete. I think I always have. But when you were there, I finally knew what it felt like to be whole. Now that you're gone, that emptiness is back, gnawing at me."

He pauses, like he's choosing his words carefully, then meets my gaze. "I could apologize for years, but that won't erase what I did. All I can do is prove that I love you and wouldn't repeat that mistake. Sure, I'll probably hurt you, but not like that. I want to fight with you, make up with you, and be with you. I want you to challenge me. Come to family dinners with me. Hell, my own family has already adopted you and practically written me off." He glances down the street, the frustration in his voice barely concealed. "I want you back. And I will follow you around New York and prove it daily."

I watch him momentarily, my chest tight with emotions I can't untangle. I know what he's talking about—that sense of completion when you find the missing piece of yourself. But I also see the risk. I can't go through that again. I can't let my heart shatter just for a chance at happiness that might only last a few months or years. I deserve better.

"You should sell the penthouse," I say, my voice flat, before turning away and walking down the street.

Violet

"You told him to do it," Max says, peering over my shoulder at the listing. Alex put his penthouse up for sale, and it's already under contract.

I'd told him to sell it out of anger. He'd said the place held too many memories of me, that he couldn't live there without me. I didn't want to live there either, but when I told him to sell, it was supposed to be my way of telling him to move on. To let go.

Yet here we are. Despite not showing up outside my appointments or lurking near my building, he somehow found my number. Now, he calls and texts daily.

I send every call to voicemail. Ignore every text. But he keeps reaching out like he's determined to stay in my orbit, even if I'm doing everything to push him away.

Maybe selling the penthouse will be good for him. A clean slate. No more ghosts of us lingering in every room. Maybe without those memories, he'll realize he never really wanted me.

I shut my laptop, taking a deep breath. "He told me he doesn't want to date me. He wants to marry me."

Max's eyebrows shoot up. "He proposed?"

I shake my head. "No, not like that. It was more about him stating his intentions. Like, if we got back together, it wouldn't be to just date."

Max leans against the kitchen island, fingers drumming a steady rhythm on the marble. "And how do you feel about that?"

"He kicked me out, Max. He didn't believe me. Told me to leave, so I did. He wants to make things right, but what does that even mean for us? Jumping from being apart to married feels like skipping a few hundred steps."

"Yes and no."

I take a sip of my coffee, glancing down at my phone. It had pinged an hour ago with another message from Alex. And here I am, still not knowing what to do with it.

Alex: I just wanted to tell you good morning. I miss you. It's been over 100 days since we were together, and I haven't stopped thinking about you for a second.

His message pings, pulling me from my thoughts, and I stare at the screen. It's been 101 days. That's a long time. Too long, right? A third of a year gone. A third of a year apart. "You fly out tonight?" Max's voice breaks through my haze.

I nod, still staring at the thread. "Yeah, in about an hour." My thumb hovers over the keyboard; then, I finally type out a reply.

Violet: I'm going out of town for a few days. So, if you plan on stalking me, I won't be around.

I sighed, setting down my coffee and trying to focus on the kitchen around me. I'm still staying at Marco's, but the book money is finally rolling in. When I get back from Los Angeles, I'll pay him rent. I've got a book promotion there—thanks to Mr. Timberlieve's hustle.

I glance back down at my phone. The dots start bouncing, and my heart does a little flip. He's typing again. Why am I excited? I'm supposed to be pushing away, not giving into the pull.

Alex: Where are you going?

Violet: Los Angeles. A book promotion.

Alex: Can I see you when you get back?

Violet: I don't think that's a good idea. This is better.

Alex: Do you really think that?

I freeze, my fingers hovering over the screen. What do I even say to that? Max leans over my shoulder, reading the conversation, then wraps an arm around me, pulling me close. "Do you really think that?" he asks, his voice gentle.

No. But I can't admit that.

"It's for the best," I say with a casual shrug, trying to sound like I believe it.

Max spins me around on the barstool, almost making me spill my coffee. "For someone who writes romance novels, you are being ridiculous, Violet." His words hit hard, but he doesn't let up. "He messed up. He apologized. He even followed you around when he didn't have to and texts you daily now that you finally stopped blocking him. And he called me when you were gone—every day, multiple times. He never gave up. It wasn't some creepy obsession; he was desperate to fix things, to show you how much you mean to him."

I try to keep my face neutral, but he's not wrong, and we both know it. "I don't know how I feel, Max."

"Sure you do." He wraps an arm around my shoulders, pulling me into a comforting hug. "You're scared he'll hurt you again, which means you still love him."

"Love isn't enough," I counter, which is rich coming from someone who makes a living writing about love.

"I never said it was," he agrees, rubbing my back. "But you left, and I'm not saying you were wrong. You had every right. But maybe if you hadn't cut him off completely, things might've turned out differently. The time apart gave you both space, but it also gave you room to build walls."

He's right; the "what-ifs" have haunted me for months. What if I hadn't gone to Florida? What if he found me sooner and apologized then? Would I still be this angry, this confused? Instead, I had three months to stew, letting the hurt fester and grow.

I pick up my phone, intending to reply to Alex's last message, but a new one pops up before I can type.

> Alex: I'm going to leave you alone, Violet. Having me around isn't easy—it's a constant reminder. I'm not giving up, but I'll give you space. Even if it means I have to wait 101 more days.

Max reads the message over my shoulder and sighs. "See, that just kills me, Vi. He's trying."

Alex

I GLANCE AT MY phone again—still, no reply from Violet since I said I'd give her space.

I'm a fucking idiot.

Why the hell did I say that? Shouldn't I be fighting for her instead?

"What's up with you?" Dante's eyes narrow as he catches my frustration. I shove my phone back into my jacket, scanning the space around us. We're touring a brownstone on the Upper West Side, near Central Park. It's close to my favorite restaurants and near the office. It's perfect.

The real estate agent leads us through, pointing out every feature like she's giving a guided tour, even though I've been here several times. "Four bedrooms upstairs, a guest suite on the first floor, and a nanny's suite in the basement. The previous owner did some extensive remodeling but kept the charm."

I take it all in, noting the classic finishes, updated just enough to keep that old-world character without feeling dated. It's nothing like the sleek, modern lines of my penthouse. This place feels warmer—more like a home than just a space to sleep in.

"It's a lot of space," Dante mutters, glancing out the bay window at the tree-lined street. "But good views."

"Perfect for a family," the agent chimes in, giving me a knowing look. Like everyone else, she assumes I'm still with Violet. When I don't respond, she sets a key on the counter. "Take your time. Just put the key back in the lockbox when you're done. But it'll go fast—so if you want it, let's get an offer today."

After she leaves, the front door shuts, and silence fills the space. I stand in the middle of the living room, staring up at a chandelier that perfectly matches the colonial-style fireplace. I can already picture it—big, cozy sofas, blankets tossed over the armrests. Violet curled up on one, her laptop balanced on her knees, typing away.

Dante breaks the silence, stepping up beside me. "And what if she doesn't come back? You gonna live here alone in a place big enough for half the family?"

I shrug, trying to hide how badly that thought stings. "Guess I'll have a lot of guest rooms then. You and the rest of the family better get used to visiting."

Just then, my phone vibrates in my suit pocket. I pull it out, and seeing Violet's name on the screen, my heart kicks into overdrive. I have to take a few deep breaths before I work up the nerve to unlock it.

> **Violet: I will be back on Monday.**

> **Alex: That's three days from now. I can wait.**

> **Violet: You sold the penthouse.**

> **Alex: I did. Time to move on and start fresh.**

> **Violet: I agree. It's for the best.**

I stare at the screen, reading her last message over and over. She agrees. But is she agreeing that starting fresh is the right move? Or is moving on from each other what we need?

I hate this. I hate not being able to read her like I used to. I hate that I'm dissecting every word, analyzing every message, hoping for some hidden meaning that says she still cares.

After signing the papers to put in an offer on a house that feels like it could swallow me whole with its emptiness, I head to the office. Rico and Dom had reached out, insisting I come in, and Dante is right behind me—because apparently, even I need a babysitter now.

When I enter the conference room, Dom is seated at the table with a younger guy I've never seen before. A lanyard around the kid's neck tells me he works here, but with over a hundred employees spread across multiple floors, I can't know them all.

"What's going on?" I ask, stepping in. The kid doesn't look up, eyes glued to the stack of papers before him. I catch the word "IT" on his badge. *Great.*

"Our spy?" I don't need to ask; I already know.

Rico gives a curt nod from his spot in the corner. He's a man of few words—partly by nature, partly by choice. His eyes shift to Dom, who seems to be running the show.

Dom sighs as he meets my gaze. "Turns out Mr. Parker here has been accessing the acquisition team's files. He's in IT support, so it took a while to find him." In other words, he was too low on the totem pole for us to suspect initially.

I fold my arms, staying on my feet. "Okay, so what did Stone pay you to do this?" I don't plan to sit down. He'll be escorted out once I get the answer, and we'll decide whether to press charges.

The kid's eyes widen, genuine confusion written across his face. "Who is Stone?" His voice wavers and I can tell he's not lying.

Dom gets up, gesturing for me to follow him out of the room. Rico stays behind, watching the kid who can't be more than twenty-one.

"Stone didn't pay him?" I ask once the door closes behind us.

Dom shakes his head. "I'm sure Stone is behind this, but Parker's been dating a very attractive, tall Italian woman."

It's like a bomb goes off in my mind. Natalia. She had shared my company secrets before, spreading them like wildfire while she bedded half my competitors. And she'd shown up that night with Stone at the charity event—something I had dismissed at the time. After all, she'd already gone through Julian, just one name on her long list. I figured she picked Stone to get under my skin, to flaunt in front of me.

"She's in your office," Dom cuts through my thoughts. "I told her you wanted to talk and maybe reconcile." He winks, and I know that was enough to bring her running.

I nod once. "Handle the kid. Rico must dig through his computers and see what else he has. Then have him taken to the police station." I turn on my heel, not bothering to mask the tension in my stride. No, I'm on a warpath.

Natalia is lounging on the sofa in my office, her legs crossed, her tight skirt riding up just enough to reveal smooth, olive-toned skin—no doubt a calculated move. She greets me with a smile, the kind she used to reserve for when she thought I'd play the fool again. But today, she's about to learn I'm no knight in shining armor.

"I like to think I'm a gentleman, but even the best man's patience runs thin," I say, leaning against the edge of my desk, my gaze fixed on her. She moves to stand, but I raise a hand, stopping her cold. "Sit. Down. Now."

She pauses, uncertainty flickering in her eyes. "What's going on? I thought you wanted to talk about us?" Her voice carries that same old syrupy sweetness, but her eyes dart around the room, avoiding mine.

"I did." I allow a hint of a smile to touch my lips. She has no idea what's coming.

"I wanted to discuss how you'll be named in a lawsuit and how you'll manage your lawyer's fees when facing criminal charges." Her face drains of color, the smile slipping away as she shifts uncomfortably in her seat, tugging down her skirt in a rare display of modesty. Gone is the act; for once, she's not playing the temptress.

I lean forward, my voice low and cold. "I have one question before you're escorted out of here. Why did you do it? Was it to get back at me for dating Violet?"

She lets out a bitter laugh. "Julian was always asking about your business. I'd feed him what I knew, we'd sleep together, and then I'd come back to you. After we broke up, he had no use for me anymore. He cut me off. You cut me off."

"So, you kept screwing with my business? What could you possibly gain from that?" My patience hangs by a thread, my fingers digging into the desk behind me.

She shrugs as if the answer is obvious. "I thought maybe we could reconcile. I knew I messed up. But when you brought Violet to family dinner, I thought I could use Julian to get her out of the way. He was on board, of course. He loves games."

Of course, he does. The man's a twisted bastard, but Natalia? She's just as ruthless.

"You thought I'd take you back after you slept with half my competitors, leaked my company's secrets, and then what—got rid of your competition? Violet had nothing to do with it, and I made the mistake of thinking she was like you. That's on me."

My jaw tightens, my molars grinding until I'm sure I'll crack one. "Natalia, whatever you think we had, you were nothing to me. And you never will be. You're just a mistake from my past."

I signal to the officers waiting outside my assistant's desk, and they escort her out. She doesn't protest; she stares at me, realizing this is the end of her game. After she's gone, Dom joins me, a grim look on his face.

"Parker went with them, too. But we might not be able to touch Julian. He didn't pay Parker directly—it was Natalia, and she passed everything along to Julian. He's covered his tracks well."

I nod. Julian's always been a snake, but he knows how to stay inside the lines, never enough to end up in cuffs. God, how I fucking hate that guy.

"Feel any better?" Dom asks, thinking this might be some form of closure.

But it's not. If anything, it's like a fissure has split wide open in my chest. "Not even a little." My voice comes out rough. I thought Natalia had ruined my life before, but the truth is, she ruined something far more precious—and I let her. I let the past dictate my future, and now, I deserve the emptiness I'm left with.

Alex

I REREAD MAX'S TEXT as Antonio pulls up outside the Velvet Clover. It's a few minutes past eight—traffic from the office wasn't in my favor tonight. As I step out of the car, I can't help but wonder why Max insisted on meeting here, of all places. The last thing I need is to drown myself in memories, and this place? It's practically soaked in them.

> Max: What are you doing?

> Alex: Looking at boxes in my new home.

> Max: Wait, you bought a home?

> Alex: I really don't want to get into it right now.

> Max: I need you to come to the Velvet Clover tonight.

> Alex: Why the hell would I go there? I just sold my penthouse to avoid memories. I'm not taking a stroll down memory lane.

> Max: Can you trust me and do it?

> Alex: Fine.

> Max: Be there at 8.

The last message gnaws at me—*Can you trust me?* Max doesn't usually make cryptic requests, so either he's up to something or thinks I need a distraction. And if it's the latter, he couldn't have picked a worse place. The Velvet Clover is a cocktail of my past—some good, a lot of bad, and more than enough regrets.

I push open the door, the familiar hum of conversation and the soft clink of glasses washing over me. Part of me wants to turn around, but I can't shake the nagging curiosity of why Max insisted on this place tonight.

Monday came and went, and I heard nothing from Violet. I sent a message wishing her a safe flight home and another on Wednesday, checking in and hoping things were going well.

Silence. Total radio silence.

As I step into the bar, my stomach twists into knots. The air feels heavier here as if the walls are closing in with memories of the nights we spent together. I don't want to be here. Hell, I shouldn't be here. It almost feels like a betrayal, like I'm treading on ground that should belong to both of us.

I spot Max across the room and give him a quick nod, intending to join him, but he shakes his head and jerks his chin toward the back hallway. Confusion ripples through me—*until I see her.*

Violet.

She's standing at the bar, her back to me, wearing an old NYU sweatshirt that's seen better days and a pair of jeans that hug her just right. Max leans in, saying something to her, and I catch the flicker of annoyance in her expression. But she doesn't look my way and keeps staring straight ahead, nursing that same green apple martini she ordered the last time we were together. My chest tightens. How often does she come here without me?

Before I know it, I slip into the hallway, trying to grasp the storm brewing inside me. Moments later, Max joins me, looking smug. "Okay, I did my part. It's on you now."

I blink at him, incredulous. "Excuse me?"

He rolls his eyes like I'm missing something obvious, glancing over his shoulder to ensure we're out of earshot. "You two are ridiculous. She's in love with you. You're in love with her. So here we are. I recreated the scene of your first date—romantic, cozy, all that crap she loves."

I stare at him, stunned. "Are you out of your mind?" I hiss, keeping my voice low. "I'm not just going to go over there and kiss her after everything that's happened. I'm not eager to get slapped—or worse, she might knee me in the balls. You know that's her style."

Max shrugs, a smirk playing on his lips. "She won't."

"Easy to say when it's not your balls on the line or your pride." I let out a breath, running a hand through my hair. "She hasn't said a word to me since she got back. We were supposed to talk, and she ghosted me."

Max sighs, his expression softening. "Look, she got back from L.A. after a meeting with her folks—remember them? Yeah. Well, if you recall, she tends to spiral after seeing them. She went out there to promote her book, feeling good about herself, and agreed to dinner with them last night. And, as usual, they tore her down. She came back here practically a zombie. Honestly, it's a miracle I got her to shower, get dressed, and come here tonight. She's wearing her NYU sweatshirt, which might as well be her minky because when she's down, that is glued to her skin."

"And you think me just marching over there and assaulting her mouth is going to fix that?"

"Yes!" Max's eyes gleam with determination. "Because she needs to know you're not giving up on her. That she's worth fighting for."

I shake my head, rubbing the back of my neck. "This is insane," I mutter, but even as I say it, I feel that flicker of hope—the one I've been trying to ignore since the second I saw her tonight. Maybe Max is right. Maybe it's time to stop holding back.

Or maybe this entire idea is fucking nuts.

"I appreciate the effort, Max. You care about her, and she's lucky to have a friend like you. But I'm not doing this. Not to her."

I turn to leave, but Max's hand clamps down on my arm, stopping me in my tracks. His grip is firm, but the look in his eyes gives me pause—pure, unfiltered determination and possibly a little rage.

"Yes, you are," he insists. "You both need something crazy and bold. That's how this whole thing started, and it's the only way it will start again."

I pinch the bridge of my nose. What's the worst that could happen? She slaps me? Pulls away? All those scenarios would gut me, but what would hurt more is the gnawing question of what if. If I walk out of here now, I'll always wonder what would have happened if I'd had the guts to leap.

"Fine," I mutter, letting out a resigned sigh. "But when she kicks me in the nuts, I'm fully paying you back."

Max grins. That infuriating, knowing smile tells me he thinks he's already won.

I turn toward the bar, edging down the hallway like I expect some monster to leap out and drag me back. My heart pounds like a war drum; each beat echoes louder than the music in the bar. Yeah, I'm scared—no shame in admitting it. This whole thing is reckless and impulsive, with disaster written all over it.

But what do I have to lose? *Oh, right. I already lost it all.*

I force my feet forward, my gaze locking on her. She's staring at the books on the shelves behind the bar, lost in some faraway thought. It's like the noise and chatter around her don't even register. I hadn't noticed it before, but she's got that same haunted, empty look she always wears after seeing her parents. If they were standing here right now, I'd give them a piece of my mind.

I weave through the crowd, slipping past patrons too busy nursing their drinks to notice me. I'm only a few feet behind her when she shifts slightly, turning her head as Max slides in next to her. She still doesn't see me, and her attention stays fixed on the line of bottles like they hold the answers to all her problems. The bar is packed—every stool was taken, the after-work crowd buzzing with mid-week relief—more witnesses to my potential humiliation.

Fantastic.

I take one last deep breath, steadying the chaos in my chest, and then I move.

Violet

I CAN'T BELIEVE MAX dragged me here. Here, of all places. I know his game—he thinks I'll sit here, sip my drink, and wallow over Alex. But nope, it's not happening. I'm already mentally fried from my parents' latest performance. Spoiler alert: I'm still nothing impressive to them. I mean, I'm published, I'm making money, and yet somehow, they find new ways to be disappointed.

Shocking, right?

Okay, not really, but still. It stings.

The emptiness settles in, heavier than before, now that I've seen them again, and the whole "never quite enough" reality hits like a sucker punch to the gut. I signaled the bartender that I was ready to order another martini because I had practically inhaled the first one. But just as I'm about to raise my hand, the barstool whips around, and suddenly, strong hands are on me.

One grips my face, and the other presses against my back, pulling me into a fierce kiss that knocks the air out of my lungs. His hand trails up my spine, tangling in my hair, and just like that, I'm breathing again—because his mouth gives me the oxygen I didn't realize I was starved for.

The kiss isn't gentle. It's urgent, hungry, like we're both trying to make up for lost time. His tongue doesn't need to ask before I'm there, meeting him, pulling him closer by his jacket. It's like a match striking dry kindling—fire, sparks, everything reigniting inside me. My body wakes up with a heat that's been dormant for months, every nerve alive as his teeth graze my lips, his fingers tightening in my hair, and—holy hell—this is hands-down the best kiss of my life.

When he finally slows, he doesn't pull away. He shifts, pressing softer kisses to my lips like he's savoring every second, every taste. His hands are steady—one cradling my face, the other still buried in my hair, keeping me anchored. And I melt into that hold, into how he guides my head just right, giving him access to explore and claim. It's always been like this with him—like he knows how to hold me, body and soul.

When he finally pulls away, he slows the kiss first, saying more with his lips than words ever could. My mouth tingles, left hungry for more. He brushes a gentle kiss against my forehead, his scent wrapping around me, making me feel dizzy in the best way. Our foreheads rest together, his breath mingling with mine. One hand stays tangled in my hair, the other arm holding me tight like he's afraid I might disappear if he lets go.

The moment his lips touched mine, I knew it was him. And sure, I told myself I'd push him away if he tried to kiss me during all this wooing of his. But when his mouth found mine, everything clicked into place. It felt right. I felt whole like I'd been missing a piece of myself all this time, and I wasn't about to waste a second of it.

"I want to tell you a story," he murmurs against my lips. His voice is low and intimate as if it's just for me. I'm sure people are watching us, but it's like the world has faded, leaving just the two of us in this crowded bar right now.

"Okay..." I draw out the word, unsure where he's going with this, but his grip on me doesn't loosen. If anything, it tightens, anchoring me closer.

"There was this woman in a bar," he begins, his tone serious yet soft. "She caught my attention the second I saw her. A woman I fell for at first sight. Yeah, I know it sounds cliché, but I don't care. The moment I laid eyes on her, I knew. I knew she was meant for me. It was like this electric current was in the air, pulling me straight to her, even though I didn't know anything about her."

His forehead presses a little harder against mine like he's now grounding himself. "The first time I kissed her, those lips—sweet, perfect, and just a little swollen. She kissed me back like we weren't strangers like we'd known each other forever, and it blew my mind. That was the best kiss of my life. It melted me and made me realize she wasn't just a woman in a bar—she was *the* woman. Maybe soul mates aren't real, but this woman? She completes me. She makes me whole. And ever since that kiss, I knew I couldn't live without her. Every day I've spent apart from her has only made me miss her more, made me want to savor every second—even if she tells me to fuck off."

I can't help but laugh, the sound bubbling out of me despite the knot of emotions in my chest.

"I sold my penthouse because she told me to," he says, his voice low and rough, "but it wasn't so I could move on—or so she could, either. I bought a house, hoping she'd move in with me. Walking through it, I pictured her sprawled on the couch, working on her next book. I imagined her coming down the stairs in the morning with that messy bun and sleepy scowl she wears until she gets her coffee. I saw her sitting in the kitchen, watching me cook and making love on every surface we could find. It's a big house, but we'd cover it all quickly. It's not about starting over—it's about restarting and hitting the gas."

His words hang between us, and we're both breathing hard like we've run a marathon. I'm half expecting him to kiss me again, to close the distance between us. Instead, he whispers, "Marry me, Violet."

I pull back a little, just enough to search his eyes. He lets me, but his grip stays firm, his gaze locked on mine. "I want to see you working on your next book in our living room, enjoy your coffee on the back deck, and come home to you every day. I told you before—I don't want to date you, and I meant it. I'm not on one knee. I know—shame on me for all the romance readers out there. But I can't let go of your face or how you feel against me right now. But if you say yes... could you do me a favor?"

For a moment, I think about stepping back, about taking a breath of space. But then his arm tightens around me, and I melt into him. The way I fit against him, his familiar scent—it's intoxicating. I can't stand losing that warmth, even for a second. "What?"

"My jacket pocket left side—my left," he says, his voice rough with anticipation.

I glance down, my brows furrowing. I release my hold on his jacket and slip my hand into the pocket. My fingers brush against something smooth and small, and when I pull it out, I find myself staring at a little black velvet box. My breath catches, and I look back up at him, heart pounding.

He leans in, pressing a soft kiss to my lips. "If you say yes, I've got a ring. So maybe I'm not on one knee yet, but I've been carrying this around for a while."

"How long?" My voice barely comes out, a shaky whisper.

He smiles, that lopsided grin that always makes my knees weak. "Longer than is appropriate." And then, without letting go of me, he lowers himself onto one knee on the bar floor in his very expensive suit. "I bought it before everything before you left. Before Julian. I knew back then that I wanted to marry you."

Hearing he bought the ring before everything makes me want to say yes even more. It's not some grand gesture to win me back—he'd planned on asking me all along. I shove aside the little voice whispering that if he'd wanted to marry me, he would have believed me back then. Nope, not today.

That's the past, and I'm not letting it ruin this moment.

"What if I want to date you first?" I ask, quirking a brow, but I catch the flash of disappointment in his eyes.

"I'll take what I can get," he says, then pops the black velvet box open. Inside, there's a thin platinum band with a single diamond—large but simple. Elegant. It's perfect.

Honestly, nothing about us has ever been conventional. This is the guy who kissed me in a bar so I wouldn't look pathetic in front of my ex. The guy I pretended to date so we could both dodge the messiness of real dating... and then ended up falling for him anyway. And now, he's kissing me in the same bar where it all began, proposing where we had our not-so-meet-cute. It might not be traditional, but damn if it isn't perfect.

"Yes," I breathe, and his mouth crashes onto mine before I can say another word. He claims my lips, kissing me like he's making up for a lost time, like he's afraid I'll change my mind if he stops.

And I'd be lying if I said it wasn't great inspiration for my next book—because honestly, I couldn't have dreamed up a better proposal if I tried.

Epilogue

ALEX

I DIDN'T WASTE ANY time, but I didn't have to. I knew Violet's dream wedding inside out, every little detail she'd ever mentioned—her ideal venue, the colors, the flowers. I hired the best wedding planner in town, Bella Rose, and she brought it all to life with Violet's input. I might've booked the venue with a few dates I knew she'd pick from, letting her romantic side guide every decision.

The day was perfect, just like she'd imagined, which made me love her even more. I still see her walking down the aisle, my father beside her. She'd invited her parents and told them they were welcome to attend but to sit in the back while her real family, our family, was there to support her. That moment is burned into my memory—her strength, her grace, and that look in her eyes when she reached me.

For the first time since college, I took a real vacation. Technically, it was a honeymoon, but we made a deal: absolutely no work. So here I am, lying on a beach in Greece, soaking up the sun and the sounds of the ocean. I glance at my wife, lounging in our private cabana, looking like she belongs here in this paradise. She's got her sunglasses on, a lazy smile playing on her lips, and I can't tell if her eyes are closed or hidden beneath the tint.

I shift closer to our shared chaise lounge, kissing her neck. The scent of jasmine fills my lungs—somehow, it feels like it's her, through and through. I may have had my way with her from the private jet ride to the hotel room, and even here in this cabana. After a year together, my need for her only grows stronger.

Her first book took off all on its own. I swore I wouldn't interfere, and I kept my word. When it became a hit, publishers lined up with offers. Now, she's got three bestsellers under her belt and is working on her fourth.

"You're happy, aren't you?" I ask, my lips brushing against her skin as I nuzzle closer.

She tilts her head, a teasing smile on her lips. "Even more so now," she replies, her fingers tracing a slow, tingling path up my arm.

"And why is that, Mrs. Bennetti?" I ask, letting my voice drop low, loving how her name sounds.

Before she can answer, our private server approaches the cabana. Our suite includes a private beach—my choice since I had every intention of enjoying my wife with nothing but the sound of the waves behind us. And I already had. Twice. This interruption isn't exactly welcome.

"Can I get you anything to drink? We have a fine selection of cocktails," he says, handing over the menu. I glance at it, smirking, knowing precisely what she'll want. Pulling her sunglasses down, she squints at the list before spotting their signature vanilla cream piña colada.

I point to it. "Two, please," I say, but before he can leave, Violet speaks up. "Can you make mine a virgin?"

The word does things to me, and I lean down, pressing kisses into the curve of her neck, sucking gently at her skin, my mind racing. She hasn't touched a drop of alcohol since we've been here. She opted for sparkling cider over champagne, claiming she didn't want a headache to ruin the honeymoon. She barely sipped the wine, and her drink choices have all been alcohol-free.

It's like she's been waiting for me to catch on, and suddenly, it clicks. I pull back, my mind scrambling to make sense of it. Her lips curl into a smirk. "You know, for such a smart, successful man, you can be slow, Mr. Bennetti," she teases, kissing my mouth.

My eyes scan her face, then slowly drift down, my hand trailing over her body, wanting to unhook that bikini top but stopping at her stomach instead. My breath catches, the realization hitting me like a wave. "You are..."

She nods, a coy smile tugging at her lips. "Very."

"What does very mean?" I arch a brow, trying to keep my cool, but my mind is racing.

A month before the wedding, we agreed she'd stop taking birth control. We figured getting pregnant might take a few months, but we were okay with letting it happen naturally. We weren't trying, but we weren't not trying either. The wedding was only a week ago, though.

She bites down on her lower lip, looking like she's fighting back a grin. "I quit the pill, Alex, but I guess if you have as much sex as we do... well, it happens. And I'm pregnant. I waited until I was sure, then I waited for the right moment to tell you. It's been killing me, but... call it my wedding gift. I'm nine weeks."

She sucks in her bottom lip, and all I want to do is kiss the nerves right out of her. But I'm trying to keep my excitement under wraps, barely. "Are you mad?" she asks softly.

"Sooo... a baby?" My brain is still trying to catch up.

She nods again, and I can see the anticipation flickering in her eyes.

"Is now a good time to mention that twins run on my mom's side? She's a twin, my aunts are twins, my brothers..."

She shoots up, her eyes wide with something close to panic. "Please tell me you're joking."

"Nope," I murmur, nipping at her jaw, gripping her face, and kissing her gently. The moment stretches between us, her smile turning wickedly, my heart pounding with something I can't quite name. I roll her on top of me, fingers slowly unhooking her bikini top. "I suppose you'll have to get used to being on top because if you think being pregnant is going to stop me from having my way with you every night... and day... think again."

She lets out a breathy laugh, but it cuts off when she kisses me, her mouth hot and desperate against mine as she tugs down my swim trunks.

Maybe it's the sight of her—bare skin against mine, her hair wild and loose, the waves crashing behind us on our private beach. Or maybe it's the knowledge that this fiery, beautiful woman—is mine, now and forever. Whatever it is, I don't last long, and neither does she. My hands grip her hips, guiding her rhythm, pushing deeper until I feel her tighten around me, her body trembling as I spill over the edge, following her into that perfect, dizzying oblivion.

After that, she collapses on top of me, both of us breathless and tangled together in the heat. I trace lazy circles on her back as the sound of the waves fills the silence. Her head rests against my chest, her breaths slow and warm against my skin.

Yeah, I could stay like this forever.

**

Seven-ish months later...

"Mr. Bennetti, meet your sons." Yeah, so that whole twin thing? It turned into triplets. Violet nearly fainted at the ultrasound while I grinned like an idiot. Let's say the pregnancy was a wild ride: morning sickness, unpredictable cravings, and those hormones.

Apparently, the more babies, the more hormones, and I had no clue what I was signing up for. But I wasn't much better—turns out, I became an overprotective grizzly bear, practically growling at anyone who so much as glanced at my pregnant wife.

Karma, according to my mama, I took it all with a grin. Midnight craving runs, dealing with her swinging from laughter to frustration over a single dirty dish—it was all part of the package. And my personal favorite? The hormones turned her insatiable. I used to think my married friends were crazy when they raved about pregnancy sex. Turns out, they were onto something. And now? I'm already wondering if it's too soon to ask the doctor when I can knock her up again.

When the family arrives to meet the boys, Violet is out cold, and I don't blame her. After a 23-hour labor that ended in an emergency C-section, she's beyond exhausted. Despite my objections, she insisted on naming one of them, Marco. Sure, my cousin helped her during a rough patch, but you can bet he'll let it go straight to his head. So now we've got Marco, Ricardo after my father, and Dominic after my mother's deceased twin brother and not my actual brother.

The Bennetti clan takes turns holding the boys, each relative squabbling over who gets to cuddle which one. But I slip onto the hospital bed beside my wife, careful not to jostle her. She snuggles into my side, her breath warm against my neck, her voice groggy as she whispers, "How are they?"

"Perfect, just like their mother," I murmur, kissing her forehead.

She smiles sleepily, tugging on my shirt. "Don't get any ideas, Mr. Bennetti," she smirks, her voice barely above a whisper.

"Did I mention how sexy you are, Mrs. Bennetti?" I tease, my hand slipping around her waist.

"I think three babies is more than enough," she mumbles, yawning before drifting back into sleep.

She can think that all she wants, but I've got my sights set on more like eight. We'll chat about that later...

***

Thank you for spending time with Alex and Violet. I hope they made you laugh, cry with joy, and maybe even fall a little in love...

Ready for more Bennetti charm?

Meet Dominic in **Playing House.**

He's a single dad. She's the quirky young neighbor across the hall. They couldn't be more opposite, and yet...

Go ahead, turn the page and get a sneak peek at Dom's book. I double doggy dare you...

A Sneak Peek at "Playing House"

(Dom & Sienna's Story) A single dad, opposites attract romance with all the LOLs and feels...

Prologue

Sienna

The universe, I've concluded, has it out for me, and I'm not sure why.

It's possible I pilfered candy from a baby in a past life or cut in line at the pearly gates, but whatever I did, karma's been dumping its cosmic trash all over me, and today it backed up the entire truck and let it loose while I sat there, pitiful and bawling.

My sobs? They've graduated.

We're talking full-on ugly crying. Snot streaming, shoulders convulsing, all with sounds that could double as a dying animal coupled with the honk of a seal. *Not pretty.*

Naturally, this is the moment my neighbor—the one who looks like he moonlights as a demigod sculpted by Michelangelo himself—shows up. I swear, he's so jaw-droppingly capital "H" hot, he could single-handedly melt the polar ice caps.

I was mid-wail, mid-questioning-my-life-choices, when there's a knock on my door. I assumed it was Kiera, my best friend and emotional support human, here to save the day with emergency donuts and vodka (or both, if she was feeling heroic).

Why was I in need of saving?

Jason, the walking cautionary tale I somehow convinced myself was relationship material, didn't just break up with me this time. Oh, no. That would've been too merciful. He disposed of me like week-old, fridge-dwelling biohazard takeout. You know the kind—green fuzz, smells like death, and gets yeeted into the trash from a safe distance.

I should've seen it coming, honestly. Not a new situation for me. Ghosted, bread crumbed, benched—you name it, I've got the badge for it.

Only this was now the third time that human jiggerwad has dumped me. Yes, I know what you're thinking: Fool me once, shame on him. Fool me twice, shame on me. Fool me three times? I might need a therapist and a self-help book.

It wasn't even a "we need to talk" breakup. Oh, no. This was a full-on ghosted me while I was planning our future vacations and then posted a selfie with *her* situation.

So here I am, curled up on my couch, wearing the ultimate post-breakup uniform. Oversized sweats, a paint-splattered T-shirt that I stole from my college ex, because irony is my brand, and let's not forget the pièce de résistance: fluffy bunny slippers. Yes, I'm a grown flipping woman wearing bunny slippers. These gems were a gift from Kiera, and they're like walking on tiny clouds of happiness. They stay.

So yeah, there I was, wallowing in my self-pity, when fate—or just cruel irony—knocks on my door. I shuffle over, expecting Kiera as I check the peephole, but nope, the universe is a petty, vindictive wench.

There he stood in all his sculpted, chiseled, probably-makes-angels-weep glory. My squeak of panic echoed in my apartment—*he definitely heard that*—and I whipped around to check the mirror by the door. What stared back? A tragic goblin. No amount of dry shampoo, concealer, or witchcraft could fix this mess.

For a split second, I consider not answering. Pretend I'm not home. Or, better yet, climb out the window and shimmy down the fire escape. Except, I live on the twenty-fifth floor, and my cardio game is weak at best.

Resigned to my fate, I opened the door to greet the man candy of all man candies, rocking a perfectly tailored three-piece suit. His mouth opened like he was about to say something—until his gaze traveled down, stopping on my bunny slippers.

Of course.

"Good evening…"

Oh. My. Lanta. His voice is pure silk, the kind you want to roll around in — preferably with him.

He's tall but somehow makes all six-plus feet of him appear as if they belong on a GQ cover. His suit isn't just tailored; it's painted on. Broad shoulders? Check. Sculpted jawline? Double check. A face that could make any woman swoon? Just toss out the list because this man checked all the boxes—and invented some for fun.

I've seen him before, of course. Just not at *my* door.

We do the Manhattan neighborly thing—you know, the polite nod of acknowledgement that says, *I know you exist, but let's not pretend we'll ever have a conversation because this is New York, and we don't do that here.* Our building has two penthouses—his on one end, mine on the other—and we're the only two people with access to the private elevator that dumps us directly into our shared hallway. So, yeah, we cross paths.

The first time I saw him, I chirped, "Hi there!" because I'm me and can't resist being friendly. I got a nod.

Another time in the elevator, I tried, "Happy Monday!" Another nod. Wow, sir, don't overwhelm me with all that personality.

Then there was the time I upped the ante with a cheery "Howdy there!" hoping he'd possibly crack a smile or—dare I dream—say something. Nope. This gal got another nod.

His son? Adorable and way more neighborly. Did I mention he's a single dad? Don't ask me why that cranks his attractiveness to level 10,000, but it does. Something about a hot guy who loves his kid? Ovaries flipping like pancakes at a diner is what that does to a woman.

His son came skipping down the hall one day holding a stuffed dinosaur and his dad's hand. "Hi, my name is Luca!" he chirped, looking up at me with a grin that could cure seasonal depression. His dad? Nothing. Nada. Just nodded and kept walking, all disapproving frowns and silent brooding, and yet, I still found it knee-buckling, gosh darny darn sexy. It was as if his unsociable nature made him seem alluring, something you longed to experience, or even get a whiff of.

But now? Mr. Gloriously Handsome is at my door. I'm half convinced I've cried myself into dehydration, and I'm hallucinating. Isn't this how people see mirages in the desert? Except instead of water, my delusional brain serves me up a walking thirst trap in a suit.

The air practically shifted the moment I opened the door, like the universe turned up the drama dial. This man doesn't just step into a room—he claims it. Dominates it. Owns it. His chocolate-brown hair is styled with glorious precision, and those glowing amber eyes...? Dissecting me like I was a frog in ninth-grade biology.

Good luck figuring me out, buddy. That list is long and starts somewhere between questionable life choices and a mild addiction to pastries.

"Uh..." His eyes raked over me, and I swear my body couldn't decide whether to overheat or shiver itself into a coma. "Is this a bad time?"

Yes. No. It's the perfect time. Why wouldn't I want to look like the poster child for post-breakup meltdowns when the hottest man alive shows up at my door? "Just a bad day."

He didn't even pretend to be subtle. His gaze landed on my bunny slippers—fluffy ears and all—and his jaw tightened ever so slightly. Of course, this is when interacts with me. Not when I'm dressed like a semi-functional adult. I'm just thanking my lucky stars that I did indeed shower and put on deodorant today, so I'm not a hot mess ogre with an ick trail swirling behind me.

"I can see that..." he mutters, his voice sinful, sultry, and *dear gawd.*

He cleared his throat, straightened his suit jacket (as if perfection needed adjusting), and said, "My name is Dominic." Of course, it is. No man looking like that is named Bob, but he could name himself Bob and make it the hottest name.

"I live across the hall," he adds, as if I didn't already know where this glorious creature lived. "I know this isn't the best time for introductions, but I'm in a bind."

Because, as we've established, karma has it out for me, I tried to sniffle my watery nose gracefully, but out came a snort instead. Yup. Queue up the paper shredder and toss my last sheet of dignity right on in it, please-and-thank-you.

"I'm Sienna." Offering the most awkward of waves with a tissue that was less "pristine white" and more "wet mess" in my hand. Shaking hands felt unnecessary—and probably unhygienic given the whole holding a soggy tissue situation.

He shifted uncomfortably, clearly recalibrating his comfort level for crying women in bunny slippers.

"Listen, I hate to ask, especially since you're..." He trailed off, gesturing vaguely at the disaster that was me taking my self-confidence down to its last notch. "Having a rough day. But I'm between nannies. My housekeeper had to run out, and I just got called into work for an emergency. She'll be back in thirty minutes, tops. Any chance you could sit with Luca until she gets back?"

"Oh." I glance down at myself. Clearly, freshening up wasn't an option. This man was already running late, and my track record with him was... well, this. Why impress him now?

"Sure," I mumbled, sagging in defeat. "Why not?"

His shoulders visibly relaxed, and he seemed genuinely grateful. "Thank you so much. I appreciate it, Sienna."

The way he said my name? Like molten velvet.

My stomach hit the floor, and I had to physically stop myself from blurting out, *Could you say my name again? Perhaps slower this time? Three times in a row would be great, thanks.*

"Sure, no problem," I say, grabbing my phone e and shoving it into the pocket of my oversized pants. Sweatpants I now wish would poof-be-gone. Then I trail behind Dominic, crossing the hall.

And, oh boy, the view of what that man has from behind. That suit? It hugs him in all the ways that make my brain fire off synapses faster than 4th of July fireworks, especially around what looks to be a gloriously sculpted rear. Then there's the smell. Cedar, sea salt, and pure, unfiltered man. Walking behind him is like being hit by a sexy cologne freight train.

He opens his door, and I'm greeted by my apartment's high-end twin. Not surprising, given these are the only two penthouses on this floor. The layout's nearly identical, but his is much bigger, complete with a second floor.

The space screams rich people live here. Floor-to-ceiling windows and boasting an open floor plan. But where my apartment says "cozy and lived-in," his says "featured in Architectural Digest." Cream-colored sofas, a dining table with a marble top and—wait for it—a massive wooden table in the entryway topped with a fresh floral arrangement. Who is this man?

I take it all in, marveling at the perfection. Not that my place is a dump—I mean, I am on the penthouse level. But standing here, looking like a stressed-out Muppet, I can't help but think Dominic is calculating how I even afford to live here.

Not a conversation we're having today. *Or ever.*

But let's talk about the genuine mystery: doesn't a kid live here? Because I don't see a single toy, shoe, or even a rogue crayon. Everything is pristine. And that cream sofa? A bold choice for someone with a small child. Or, you know, anyone who eats Cheetos.

"Luca!" Dominic's rich voice rumbles through the space, bouncing off the vaulted ceilings. It's like he has a built-in sound system. Meanwhile, I can't stop wondering if my sobs were echoing like that from mine. Did he hear my wailing from his side of the hall and choose to ignore it? Probably.

The pitter-patter of little feet breaks my stroll down Humiliation Lane as Luca comes barreling down a curved staircase, leaps off the last step with a solid thud, and races straight toward me. He's clutching that orange dinosaur he always has with him, his eyes locking on my bunny slippers with pure joy. "Those are so cool!" At least he's impressed.

Dominic crouches down, all business, his hands gripping little Luca's shoulders, so he stops looking at my bunny slippers and directs his focus on him. "Luca, I have to run to work, and Rosa will be back any minute. Sienna will stay with you until she gets here, okay?"

Luca is a pint-sized carbon copy of his dad—it's like Dominic hit "Ctrl+C, Ctrl+V" on his genetics.

Dominic straightens, turning to me. "There's a sheet on the refrigerator with my cell, office line, and main office number. Call if there's anything—*anything* at all." His gaze sweeps over me again, and I can see it. That flicker of doubt. Like he's wondering if asking his emotionally unstable neighbor of six months, who he just met, to babysit his kid was a terrible decision. I can't vouch for myself right now, considering my appearance.

I stuff my crumpled tissue into my pocket, suddenly aware I've been clutching it like a security blanket. "We'll be fine." I give a forced smile I'm 98% sure screams hot mess express, but it's the best I've got.

He nods stiffly, clearly unconvinced. "Okay. But call if anything happens. Rosa should be here in thirty minutes."

I nod, keeping my eyes fixed anywhere but on his. Those amber pools are a hazard. One prolonged look, and I'll be wobbling like a baby deer learning to walk. "Yup, we're fine," I say, sounding (hopefully) more confident than I feel. It's a kid. A five-year-old. No diapers, no bottles, no mysterious baby cries to decode. It's only thirty minutes, but this man is acting like he's leaving me here for the weekend.

Dominic checks his watch, sighing like this is going to be the most stressful thirty minutes of his life. "Okay. Okay." He kneels to address his mini-me once more. "Be good. You can watch a show, but only because this is an emergency. Got it, buddy?"

Luca's face lights up. "Yes! Dino Pals!" he fist bumps the air before sprinting toward the living room and launching himself onto the pristine sofa.

Dominic turns to leave, but brakes mid-stride and spins back. "I should get your number." He pulls his phone out, taps the screen, and hands it to me with a blank contact card open. Our hands brush during the exchange, and I swear a jolt of electricity zips straight through me.

Did he feel that? Probably not. He's too busy being perfect.

I fill in my info and hand the phone back, hoping he doesn't see the shake to my hands and assume I'm now the soggy mess next door with a nervous tick.

"Let me just send you a message." He's already typing on his phone, and a second later, my phone pings. "Now you have my number. Call me if anything happens. I mean it."

Okay, I get it. My current "crying, fluffy-slipper wreck" look isn't inspiring confidence, but really? It's thirty minutes. I'm not going to lose your child in thirty minutes. Unless he runs faster than I can, which might be a concern.

Dominic hesitates again, glancing back at me. "Thanks, I owe you one."

A hug would be a nice way to show his appreciation, but I doubt that's in the cards. "No big deal," I say.

His eyes flick down to my bunny slippers—again—and I make a mental note to burn them as soon as I'm back in my apartment. "Okay. Thanks again."

The door clicks shut, and I let out a long, shaky exhale, only for Luca's voice to pipe up from the couch. "Come on, Sienna! You gotta see this!"

I wander over and plop down next to him. "This is Louie," he says, waving the orange stuffed dinosaur in my face.

"Well, hello, Louie," I reply, smiling despite myself. Something about this kid is contagious, and not in the germy kindergarten way. The ache in my chest from earlier feels... lighter.

"You look weird. Why's your face all red? Are you sick?" Luca asks, his face scrunched up in confusion.

Well, that moment of feeling better was just a blink I see. Leave it to a kid to call out all your insecurities in one go. "Nope, just... allergies." Though I'm pretty sure my allergy is to his father's hotness.

Luca seems satisfied with that answer, turning back to the TV, while I sit here enjoying my new reality. The way Dominic saw me today—an absolute disaster wrapped in heartbreak and bad fashion choices—is now cemented in his brain forever. So much for first impressions.

Not that it matters. He's older. Gorgeous. Refined. Basically, a real-life Disney prince without the singing animals. And I'm, well, me.

I settle in to watch the show with Luca, only to see adults in rubber suits, roaring like they're auditioning for a prehistoric soap opera. Honestly, it's like someone tossed Sesame Street and Teletubbies into a blender, hit the "chaotic nightmare" setting, and called it a day.

But then I glance down at my bunny slippers and paint-stained sweatshirt. *Right*. Not in a position to judge.

Ten minutes into this crime against children's television, my phone pings. I assume it's Kiera wondering where I am. I wasn't expecting her for another hour, but she's unpredictable when donuts (and hope-to-god booze) are involved.

Nope. It's *him*.

Because, of course, he texted. He asked for my number, after all. You're watching his kid, you absolute dork.

> Dominic: Is everything okay? Rosa let me know she's headed back, but traffic is bad at this hour.

He's been gone ten minutes. Is this kid made of porcelain? How much trouble can a five-year-old and I get into in ten minutes?

> Sienna: Everything is fine. We're watching his show. No worries about Rosa. I don't have anywhere to be.

Nothing screams "pathetic single woman" like admitting you have no Friday night plans. Just me, this kid, and my oversized sweatpants of shame, and a lot more soggy tissues on the agenda.

> Dominic: Okay, thank you again.

I set my phone down on the marble white coffee table. Yet another bold choice for a house with a kid, then turn back to the disaster on the screen. Louie the dinosaur looks like he's ready to start a union for better costume rights, if you ask me.

Ten more minutes. Another ping.

> Dominic: How is Luca doing?

Heavens to Betsy, is this man serious? It's been twenty minutes. I must've looked like a Category 5 disaster if he's checking in like I'm babysitting the crown jewels and not qualified to watch them.

> Sienna: Everything is fine. He's still on the same episode.

> Dominic: Okay, please let me know when Rosa gets there.

> Sienna: Sure thing.

Another ten minutes? You guessed it. *Ping.*

> Dominic: Is Rosa still not there yet?

I'm convinced he thinks I'll sell his child to a traveling circus. I turn to Luca, curating my words.

"Is your dad always so..." How do I phrase this delicately? For all I know, the little guy is a snitch, and I have to be careful what I say. "Worrisome?"

"Oh, yeah, Daddy doesn't like anyone watching me except my nonnas or uncles. Or my Aunt Violet."

Ah, so I'm on a brief list of non-approved babysitters or a last-minute last-resort—the world is ending option. Perfect.

> Sienna: Not yet, but we're fine. Really. I know traffic is bad.

The reply comes instantly, like he's hovering over his phone, ready to leap into action. For a man at work, he's spending more time helicopter texting than working, but what do I know.

> Dominic: Okay. Rosa should be there soon.

> Sienna: Sounds good.

At this rate, there's no point in putting my phone down. In five minutes, I'll likely need my phone again to reassure him the apartment isn't on fire and Luca hasn't joined a gang of misfits.

Instead of my phone interrupting a show that I can never erase from memory, it's the sound of the front door's locking system clicking. A small woman bustles in, throwing herself through the doorway. "I'm here! I'm here!" she shouts, waving one hand like she's surrendering while balancing a giant paper sack in the other. Her rich Italian accent makes me want a cannoli. I have a pastry obsession—there are worse things in life.

A younger man follows her in, juggling two more bags. They both head straight for the entryway table, where they unload their apparent grocery heist.

I get up from the couch, leaving Luca glued to the show. As I approach, the older woman sighs dramatically, setting the bag down and dusting her hands. She's petite—shorter than my 5'3" self—with her dark hair twisted into a perfect knot and not looking like the shambles I'm stewing in.

"Hi," I say, offering a little wave. "I'm Sienna. I live across the hall."

She gives me a once-over, and yep, it's another moment to reflect on the tragic disaster that is my outfit. She huffs out, "Rosa," introducing herself with all the authority of a headmistress, then gestures to the young guy hauling bags toward the kitchen. Not going to lie, he's quite the looker. Not the refined, aged sexy look of Dominic, but worth a second, okay third, glance. "That's Elias, Mr. Bennetti's driver."

Bennetti?

I freeze, my brain doing a hard reboot. "Mr. Bennetti?" I repeat, because, that's all my vocabulary can muster.

I'm positive she's questioning my intelligence. "Yes," dragging the word out like it's a chore. "Mr. Dominic is Mr. Bennetti."

I need a minute to remember how to breathe.

See, I don't fangirl. Except when I do, like right now. Because there's only one Bennetti I know of—the same Bennetti who's married to *the* Violet Hart. You know, the queen of romance novels. Savior of single women everywhere. The woman whose books have not only kept me warm at night but have nearly scorched my fingertips flipping through her steamy, swoon-worthy pages.

I feel a sudden, overwhelming urge to ask for an autograph. On one of the well-loved, dog-eared books sitting proudly on my bookshelf. Then I realize how horrifyingly awkward it would be to let Dominic know I've read—and possibly memorized—his sister-in-law's novels. My dignity can't take that kind of hit. Right now, I'm in the negative as it is with that man.

I straighten up, attempting to play it cool. "Well, it was nice to meet you," I say, my squeaky voice betraying me. My phone buzzed in my hand, but I ignored it, turning to Luca instead, who remained glued to the TV show as if it were the best entertainment possible. I have a feeling I will need to introduce him to something from the Pixar family so he knows a good show when he sees it. "Thanks for the hangout, little guy!"

Luca bolts off the couch and rushes over, throwing his tiny arms around me in a hug that's adorable in theory but lands him at butt level.

"Come back soon?" he asks, looking up at me with those big, pleading eyes and pouty lips that probably win him everything he wants. Heck, he could ask for my social security number, and I'd write it down for him while handing over my credit card for good measure.

"Sure," I say, because how can you say no to that face or the fluttering eyelashes he's putting to good use?

I wave goodbye to Rosa and Elias and scurry out to the hall before humiliation takes over.

Once I'm in neutral territory, I check my phone and send Dominic a quick text.

> Sienna: Rosa's here, and I'm headed back home.

He replies almost immediately.

> Dominic: Thank you so much for watching him. It won't happen again. I have a new nanny starting Monday.

Spoiler alert: it *does* happen again. And again. And again.

Before you go!

Loved what you just read? Don't ghost me now — there's more heat, heart, and Bennetti boyswaiting for you.

More from the *Ben netti Boys* Series:

- **Dom & Sienna's story** is ready for your one-click pleasure. Available in paperback and free on Kindle Unlimited.

- **Rico & Allie's story** is grumpy, broody, and not safe for your emotional stability. Also in paperback and KU.

Coming Soon from Everly Summers:

- **Marco's Story** – The TBD stands for *Totally. Bloody. Delicious.* He's worth the wait.

- **The Kiss List Series** – Launching Fall 2025. Think enemies-to-lovers, fake dating, slow burns, and morally gray charmers who get absolutely wrecked by the right kiss.

Let's Stay Book Besties:

- **Join me on Patreon** for daily posts, sneak peeks, unhinged ramblings, and all the behind-the-scenes drama (free memberships available!).

- **Join my newsletter** where I attempt to keep up with emailing once a week, but also share teasers and updates about upcoming releases, giveaways, and more.

- **Follow on social** for giveaways, teasers, and the occasional thirst trap disguised as a quote graphic:

  - Instagram: @everlysummersbooks

  - TikTok: @everlysummers

Leave a Little Love?

If Alex and Violet stole your heart (or your sanity), a quick review helps other readers find them too. It's the indie author version of a standing ovation—and I'd be so grateful.

Acknowledgements

I've been dreaming of this moment since I was 13—writing and publishing a book, with me, my typewriter (yes, really), and all the melodrama of a teenager on a mission. Fast forward a few *cough* years, and here I am, actually holding this book, the one I knew had to be my debut, even after every twist, turn, and *"maybe this is a terrible idea"* thought along the way.

Spoiler alert: there were a lot of those.

Writing a book and then handing it over to the world? Not for the faint of heart. So here's a massive, heart-bursting THANK YOU to everyone who made it possible. To my incredible family and friends who cheered me on, were my sounding boards, and endured my impassioned rants about characters who aren't real. And to my beta readers who braved every plot twist, version, and mind-change I threw at them—you guys are the real MVPs.

To my cover designer, who patiently worked with me as I obsessively searched for the "perfect" cover (and didn't flinch at my constant edits and late-night emails—thank you).

To my amazing kiddos, who sacrificed mom-time while I was holed up in my "writing cave" knowing that I was embarking on a journey not only to do what I have always wanted to do, but to provide for you all. I love you guys for letting me chase this dream. And to my kids, who won't get to read this book until, oh, maybe never (or until you're older, I swear!), thanks for the endless hugs and support.

Finally, to YOU, the reader holding this book right now—thank you for being here, for reading, for every bit of feedback, and for giving this story a place in your world. I can't wait to take you on another wild, wordy journey soon!

About the Author

Everly Summers is a new member of romance writing, weaving stories that tug at your heartstrings, make you laugh out loud, and leave you believing in love's magic. From fun and flirty to intense and angsty, Everly brings every kind of romance to life, exploring all the emotions in between. Every book dives deep, making you so engrossed in the characters' lives that you want to learn more, and you root for the good and loathe the bad. She's a true sucker for all the tropes—be it second chances, enemies to lovers, or the slow burn that keeps you up all night. But no matter the story, she always guarantees one thing: a happily ever after that will make you swoon.

It's worth the wait...

When she's not dreaming up her next love story, Everly can be found with her nose in a romance novel, a cup of coffee in hand, and plotting her next fictional happily ever after. She lives in Utah with her four children, husband, and a herd of Siberian Huskies.

Whether you're new to romance or a long-time fan, Everly's stories will remind you why we all crave a little love in our lives.